PEAR-SHAP

Stella Newman studied English at Sussex University. She lives in London and is a freelance copywriter and keen amateur cook. She is currently writing her second novel and her first screenplay. She blogs about restaurants, food and writing at www.stellanewmansblog.blogspot.com.

STELLA NEWMAN

PEAR–SHAPED

AVON

This novel is entirely a work of fiction.
The names, characters and incidents portrayed in it are
the work of the author's imagination. Any resemblance to
actual persons, living or dead, events or localities is
entirely coincidental.

AVON

A division of HarperCollins*Publishers*
77–85 Fulham Palace Road,
London W6 8JB

www.harpercollins.co.uk

A Paperback Original 2011

1

Copyright © Stella Newman 2011

Stella Newman asserts the moral right to
be identified as the author of this work

A catalogue record for this book is
available from the British Library

ISBN-13: 978-1-84756-270-8

Set in Bembo MT Pro by Palimpsest Book Production Limited,
Falkirk, Stirlingshire

Printed and bound in Great Britain by
Clays Ltd, St Ives plc

MIX
Paper from
responsible sources
FSC
www.fsc.org
FSC C007454

To my parents, and in loving memory of
my grandparents.

Oh, the tiger will love you. There is no sincerer love than the love of food.

George Bernard Shaw

If I can't have too many truffles, I'll do without truffles.

Colette

Parfait

1. *noun* – a rich frozen dessert, made with eggs, cream and sugar
2. *noun* [from French] perfect

Two girls walk into a bar. There is no punchline.

I'm the girl on the left in the wildly inappropriate black and white spotty summer dress. It is the snowiest February in thirty-eight years but I flew back from a month in Buenos Aires three days ago and this tan ain't going to waste.

A month in Buenos Aires: sounds glamorous? Ok: a month in a £6 a night hostel in the Boedo barrio – think Kilburn with 98% humidity. No air con, no overhead lighting, shared showers. I'm thirty-three. I earn okay money. I don't like sharing showers, not least with 18-year-old Austrians proclaiming *Wiener Blut* the greatest Falco album ever released. Wieners aside, Laura and I have the time of our lives.

Laura is the girl on the right in the bar. Best friend, tough crowd, northerner. She's wearing a polo neck and a woolly hat. Together we look ridiculous; we don't care.

It is one of those evenings. Whether it's the outfits, the tans or the sociability that a snowy Friday night in London brings, we end up being the epicentre of it all. One guy, Rob, has been trying to impress me for the last twenty minutes. He's too pretty for my taste and he's spouting off about knowing Martin Scorsese's casting director.

'I can see you playing a gangster's moll in that dress,' he says. 'Those big green eyes. Real curves.'

I laugh. I'm a size 10, with tits and an arse, and the girl he's abandoned at the bar talking to his mate is one of those girls you can count the vertebrae of through her silk shirt.

'Are your eyes real?' he says.

'No, they're mint imperials, I paint the irises on every morning to match my shoes,' I say.

'I like your brushwork,' he says, smirking.

'Your girlfriend's getting pissed off,' says Laura.

'She's with my mate,' says Rob, fiddling with his watch. 'Actually, do you girls want a drink? Two more margaritas?' He heads to the bar. Before he's even back there, his mate, who is less pretty and far more my type, heads towards us.

'He doesn't waste his time . . .' says Laura.

I say nothing. I look at Rob's friend and a rare but familiar feeling grabs me: something big is about to happen.

'Why are you talking to Rob?' he says to me, grinning. 'You don't fancy him.'

'What business is it of yours?' I say. 'Do you fancy me?'

He looks at me for a heartbeat. 'Yeah.'

'Well, then you talk to me instead. What's your name?'

'James.'

'James what?'

'James Stephens.'

'Like the poet.'

'Ooh, a clever girl.'

'I'm not,' I say. 'My granny has a poem of his she likes to quote.'

'A love poem?'

'Yeah, it's about a man who throttles his over-attentive wife to death.' He laughs.

'I can tell you're smart,' he says. 'And warm. It's in your eyes. Don't waste your time with Rob, waste it with me.'

So I did. I talked to him, danced a tango round the bar with him, sank three margaritas with him and at the end of the night gave him my number.

He calls when he says he will – the next day. Why do I feel so grateful for this? Because the world of dating has deigned this sort of behaviour too keen.

'I want to see you again,' he says.

'Good.'

'But I'm going away for a fortnight tomorrow.'

'Oh.'

'It's work. I travel quite a bit.'

'Where are you going?'

'China.'

'What do you actually do?' I'd imagined he was a high-end builder or something to do with running a warehouse.

He's very masculine, hefty, a bit rough round the edges, and his shirt last night didn't quite fit.

'You'll laugh,' he says.

'Are you an international clown?'

'No. I sell socks.'

'What, like in a shop?'

'Sort of.'

'Everybody needs socks,' I say.

'At least two pairs,' he says. 'I'm back in a fortnight, I'd like to take you for dinner.'

'Great. I like dinner.'

'But do you like to eat?'

'Are you joking? It's what I do.'

'You're not one of those girls who orders salad and just pushes it round the plate? You're pretty skinny.'

'You've got the wrong number.' I have slender arms and a small waist. You can fool most of the people most of the time with this combo.

'Good. I know the perfect place. I'll call you in two weeks.'

I work in a twelve-storey shiny building in Soho. Up until six months ago, I had one of the greatest jobs in the world and one of the greatest bosses. I am a Pudding Developer for Fletchers, one of the biggest supermarkets in the country. I worked for a genius called Maggie Bainbridge. She never compromised on quality and had bigger balls than any of the men here.

Six months ago she quit after management fired a bunch of our top talent and brought in a grunt of accountants, intent on putting the bottom line above everything else. Even our loo roll has been downgraded to that tracing paper crap from the 80s that you have to fish out of a cardboard slit.

Maggie's started up a one-woman brownie business, 'Happy Tuesday'. Even though we speak often, I miss her, and daydream about running off to work with her again.

So, I still have a great job, but I no longer have a great boss. No. I have Devron.

Devron used to work for a supermarket that was chewed up and spat out by a large American supermarket. He was regional manager for London South East, which is a Big Deal in Retail. Apparently he was very good at driving up and down motorways in his BMW.

His sole qualification for being head of my department seems to be that he is fat, ergo he 'knows food'. Devron would be happy eating every meal from a service station on the M4. He thinks he's an alpha male, he's actually an aggressive little gamma.

The first thing Devron did when he joined was to make us all switch desks. Wanting to make his mark, and attempting to convey his profound creativity he decided to arrange us alphabetically. I used to sit with 'Hot Puddings', 'Family Treats' and 'Patisserie'. Makes sense – we share the same buyers, technical advisers and packaging team. We liaise constantly about pastries, sugar prices, trends in the Treat market – all elements that are pudding specific.

But now, because I do Cold Desserts, I sit between Lisa, who does 'Cocina' – our fake-a Mexicana range of variety nachos, and Eddie: Curry. Devron says 'we can learn a lot from talking to our colleagues'. True. I have learnt that Lisa, Eddie and I all agree: Devron is a nob.

The only thing more moronic than splitting us up from the people we need constant contact with, is Devron's introduction of 'cross-discipline platform solutions'. He has dumped a marketing wang on our bank of desks: Ton of Fun Tom.

Tom always wants to show me some great viral on YouTube featuring a gorilla or a dancing mouse. Tom's knowledge of marketing is like my knowledge of Chechen history: he knows three random facts and feels guilty about not knowing more. However, I do not try to bullshit my livelihood as a Chechen historian.

Laura has come for lunch at the Fletchers' canteen en route to do a voice-over for a car insurance website who want her husky Yorkshire accent to add 'honest northern values' to their shonky brand. Laura only has to do two voice-over sessions a month to pay her mortgage, and spends the rest of her time helping her boyfriend Dave run his eBay business selling vintage magazines.

This week's canteen theme is 'Pre-Valentine's Value' and we have the choice of heart-shaped pork bites or asparagus pasties. Sounds better than the falafel Eddie ordered last month, within which lurked a dog's tooth.

'James sounds keen,' says Laura.

'D'you think?' If he was that keen, he wouldn't wait two weeks to call me.

'He wouldn't let go of you the other night. You were dancing for ages.'

I love dancing. My ex, Nick, an introvert, danced with me once in five years: quarter-heartedly, for thirty-eight seconds, at his best friend's wedding, and only after I'd threatened to embarrass him by dancing on my own if he didn't.

'Bet his friend wasn't pleased,' says Laura.

'Rob's an arse,' I say. 'That girl with them was Rob's fiancée!'

'She's stood there while he chats you up?' I nod. 'You're going to have some fun double dating . . .' says Laura.

'Early days, love. He might meet some sock model in China and never call again.'

My mother phones from California. She lives in an apartment in Newport Beach, OC heartland, with her second husband Lenny, a retired orthodontist and professional doormat.

'Have you spoken to your brother?' she asks, saving the pleasantries for another time.

'Why?'

'It's Shellii.' Or 'the-scrawny-tramp-who-is-bleeding-your-brother-dry-with-her-spirituality-crystals-and-Lee-Strasberg-acting-classes'.

'What now?'

'She's bloody pregnant.'

'That's good news, isn't it?' It means you won't harangue me to have children for at least another two years.

A heavy silence on the other end.

'Mum, she's not that bad.' Shellii's so much worse than 'that bad', but I never agree with my mother on point of principle.

'Huh. What's news with you? How's the flat?'

'The flat's fine. I'm fine.'

'Job going well?'

'I'm heading up cold puddings.'

'Good, well eat some. Your grandmother said you're looking very thin.' My mother speaks to her ex-mother-in-law twice a year and it seems their sole remaining common ground is my weight.

I am currently slim and mostly toned but by no means 'thin'. I will never be 'thin' – the Kleins are big boned. But since I split up with Nick last summer, I have lost a stone and a half through exercise and taking proper care of myself. For the first time since I was twelve, I'm almost happy with my body, save for a few inches around my bottom.

My mother takes my weight loss as a personal slight. A rejection of body fat is a direct rejection of what unites our family and everything she stands for. Food equals love, too much food equals Jewish love. At weddings, my genetically freakish thin cousin is the subject of whispered snipes about anorexia and suspect parentage. My mother feeds Lenny three large meals and half a cake every day. She will feed that man to an early grave and then overfeed everyone at the shiva (think full on Irish wake, but with egg-mayo sandwiches instead of whiskies).

'Lenny's just walked in, I've got to start lunch.'

Two weeks later James calls from Beijing airport. 'Remember me?'

'Clown school's out for summer?'

'You should see what I can do with three chopsticks and a scorpion.'

'Sounds painful. Anyway, how can I help you?'

'Tell me when you're free for some spaghetti.'

My favourite. 'A week on Wednesday.'

'Too far away. I want to see you before then.'

Then you should have called me before now. 'Sorry.'

'Seriously, what are you doing between now and then?'

'All sorts. Wednesday week, then?'

'Okay. I'll call you nearer the time with a plan. Got to go, they're calling my flight.'

Is an average brownie better than none at all?

This is not the same as asking if a taste of honey is worse than none at all. When Smokey Robinson sang that, we can assume the 'honey' in question was just fine.

No, this question goes to the heart of what separates people like my old boss Maggie Bainbridge from most people on the planet who simply like cake.

When I went for the interview at Fletchers two years ago, I received an email from Maggie a week in advance:

Please bring:

1) A cake you've baked from a recipe book
2) A supermarket pudding you rate highly

It was like being asked to cook for Michel Roux Jr. on *Masterchef*. After agonising for days, I decided to keep it simple and make a Claudia Roden orange and almond cake that my mother makes at Passover. The texture is fantastic

– totally squidgy yet light. The flesh and zest of the orange offset the sweetness and give the cake a fragrance that makes you think you're in a Moroccan souk, rather than a fluorescent lit office block round the corner from the most toxic kebab shop on Oxford Street.

Maggie took a bite and her brow furrowed. My first thought: Christ, I hope she doesn't have a nut allergy. But then she went over to her immense bookshelf, picked up a volume and slowly nodded.

'It's based on the Roden,' she said. 'But the depth of flavour you've got is superior to the original . . . there's a pinch of cinnamon in there, you've put in slightly less sugar than ground almonds, and you've used blood orange, which is quite clever.'

I realise later that 'quite clever', from Maggie Bainbridge is like winning a Michelin star.

'And what did you buy on the high street?'

Maggie Bainbridge famously invented the molten middle caramel pudding. Many chefs claim to have invented this pudding, but Maggie actually did. So, even though it is my favourite shop-bought pudding, there's no way I could bring it in – far too creepy. Instead, I found a pudding in Marks and Spencer involving cream cheese, mascarpone, raspberries and dark chocolate that I thought was amazing, and took that in.

She gives me a strange look when I take it out of my bag. Shit. Of course, I should have brought in a Fletchers pudding, utterly stupid of me.

'Why did you pick this?' she says, with surprise verging on irritation.

'You said bring something that you really like . . . it's four of my favourite ingredients, the texture is amazing, the sharpness and the creaminess work perfectly together, and the chocolate they've used is at least 70% cocoa solids. . . .'

'Do you know anyone in new product development at M&S?' she asks, looking concerned.

No, I shake my head. I wish – I'd be going for a job there if I did!

'Have you tried it?' I ask. I feel I have upset her but I'm not sure why.

'Yes.'

'Do you like it?' I ask.

'Yes. It's good. One last question.'

One last question! She hasn't asked me any proper questions, and now she's about to get rid of me. What a bitch. . . .

'Do you think that an average brownie is better than none at all?'

What? What sort of a question is that for an interview? Clearly this must be a trick. Is she just finding out if I'm greedy? Or if I genuinely love pudding, or what? I don't know what she wants me to say, but all I can tell her is the truth. Well, not quite the truth – my honest answer would be 'if you are stoned, absolutely'. But then if you are stoned, an average brownie is transformed into a superior brownie anyway.

13

My truth is this: I would rather not eat a brownie than eat an average brownie.

Not because of the calories.

Not because I'm a snob.

But because for me, brownies are sacred; where they're concerned I don't do half measures. In the same way that I couldn't marry a man I didn't love, or be in a relationship with someone I didn't respect, or sleep with a man who wasn't funny.

'I'd rather have nothing,' I say.

She looks at me with the merest hint of approval in her eyes.

'That M&S pudding you brought in,' she says. Oh no, what is it? I knew there was something wrong. 'I created that. Freelance. Entirely against the terms of my contract here, but M&S are the best and I couldn't stop myself. I tried to push through a similar one here last summer and couldn't get it signed off. The reason I'm telling you this is because I know I can trust you, because I only ever employ people I can trust.'

And that is how I got my job and came to work for Maggie Bainbridge, the best boss in the world.

Now that Maggie is no longer my boss, I only get to see her every few months. She is busy with her new brownie empire and has a wide circle of friends. She's a 51-year-old single woman, but it's harder to get a date in her diary than a table at Rao's.

She has invited me for dinner the night before my planned first date with James. I would really like to stay at home, eat light and sleep properly so I can look my best for tomorrow. But he still hasn't called, so I don't know if we're on or not. Besides, if I don't see Maggie tonight I won't get in her diary for ages, so after work I walk over to her flat in Marylebone.

She opens the door in a well-worn apron and the smell of freshly baked bread and roast chicken wafts through to me like a Bisto ad.

'My God! You're practically anorexic!' she says, holding on to my shoulders and examining me up and down before squeezing me close for a hug. Her grey hair smells of fried onions – it's wonderful.

'As if! Look at the size of my arse,' I say, turning around and offering her a feel.

She pinches my bottom. 'There's nothing of you, crazy girl. Come and let me fatten you up.'

We sit down in her kitchen and start drinking. If I don't drink I'll be thinking about my phone not ringing all night. Even if I do drink I'll still be on edge, but it'll dull the focus a bit.

'How's that odious little rat doing?' she asks, holding out a wooden spoon with a dark golden sauce on it. 'Honey, soy, tamari, toasted sesame . . .'

'Devron's Devron,' I say. 'He's talking about 20% cuts across the board but he's just upgraded his car to a convertible, and he's hanging his new suit jacket the wrong way round on his chair so we can all see it's Prada.'

'Is he still dating that poor cow?'

'Mands, yes. It was her nineteenth birthday last weekend, he took her to The Grove, showed us all the picture of the freestanding bath in their suite. With her in it, wearing only bubbles . . .'

She shakes her head in disbelief. 'And Eddie, Lisa?'

'Eddie's good, Lisa's angry. The usual.'

Over dinner we talk about her business. She's just signed a distribution deal with a chain of luxury boutique hotels – each night at turndown guests will find a box of her mini brownies, beautifully wrapped, left on their pillow.

'How's the man situation?' she asks, handing me a bowl of warm 'blondies' – her new vanilla brownies that she's trialling for the hotels. 'Macadamia on the left, Vermont maple on the right.'

'Actually, I'm so sorry but do you mind?' I say, popping to the hall and fishing my phone from my bag. It's been on silent and I'm convinced that my removal of it from eyeline and earshot will have elicited a call. I vowed I wouldn't check till I was on the bus home, but lying to yourself is fine, right?

A flashing light!

Fuck. A text from Laura asking if he's rung yet.

'What's wrong?' says Maggie.

'Nothing,' I say, despondently. 'Just waiting for a call.' I

16

explain the scenario, and call upon her greater wisdom of life and men: 'When is he going to call?'

I still believe James will ring. But I fully object to him not having called by now. I am someone who books up my diary weeks in advance to the time and place of meeting. I often check the menu online in advance, as I like to have something very specific to look forward to. I'm not a control freak, I can do spontaneous as well as the best free spirit (sometimes), but I am uncomfortable with uncertainty, and this man is an unknown unknown.

She refills my wine glass. 'He said definitely this Wednesday?'

'Yes.'

'And he called you from China to fix the date?'

I nod.

'He'll call. Some men don't like nattering on the phone. If he doesn't call, he's an idiot.'

'I want him to call tonight.'

'Out of your control,' she says, opening a second bottle of wine.

I still believe that willing something to happen can make it happen. I also believe that particular idea is insane. Isn't that a sign of intelligence, holding two opposing thoughts at the same time, or is that just a sign of schizophrenia?

I wake at three in the morning to a blue light on my phone. A text message. Is James out, drunk? Is he cancelling?

It's my friend Lee, on a business trip to New York, wanting to know the name of that Vietnamese sandwich bar near Washington Square I was raving about. I text back, turn off my phone and wake again at 5.30am, dehydrated and in a bad mood.

★

It's 2.15pm. I'm sitting in a meeting with Ton of Fun Tom, talking about marketing my new products for spring. My phone is on the desk in front of me and I am increasingly anxious, irritable and pissy. To be fair, every meeting I have with Tom makes me feel like this, but today is worse than usual. If James can call me from China, why can't he call me now that he's back in town?

'Sophie, these raspberry and cream trifles – what are they?'

'They're trifles, Tom. Clue's in the name.'

'Right, yeah, but how does it work?'

'How does what work?'

'The cream and stuff?'

'Here's the picture. Those small pink things on top are called 'raspberries', that creamy coloured layer is 'cream', and underneath is the raspberry and cream trifle.'

'Oh, so like a fruit trifle but with raspberries.'

My phone starts ringing. My heart pauses. It's him. 'Sorry, I have to get this.'

I leap up and leave the meeting – rude, but Tom always

fiddles with his apps when I'm talking, so now we're quits.

'It's James. Are you still free for dinner?'

'Sure.' I can pretend to be cool for at least one phone call.

'Great. It's a little Italian place at the top of Archway Road, I've booked a table at 8pm. Do you mind if we meet there? I've got something in town beforehand.'

'See you there at 8pm.'

I breathe a sigh of relief. He's just one of those guys who doesn't like nattering. I walk back into the meeting. 'Cup of tea, Tom?'

'You look happy,' says Lisa, Lady of the Nachos, when I return to my desk. I daren't tell Lisa the smile on my face is because of some guy. Lisa's turning forty and in a 'bad place' right now. She hates her husband, ever since he ran off with their two-doors-down neighbour. She hates her new boyfriend, because he's not her husband. She hates her estate agent after he inquired if she was a teacher because she wore flat shoes and no make-up when she viewed the one-bedroom flats in her area. And she hates Devron, because he's asked her to look at making her nachos range 'bigger, cheaper and lower in fat'. That's a tough order with a cuisine based on sour cream, cheap ground mince, cheese and tortilla chips.

'I've been thinking about your nacho problem,' I say. 'Tell Devron that if he cuts out the cheese, sour cream and

mince he'll save loads of cash and the fat barometer will
go from 9.7 to below a 5.'

She grunts a laugh. 'He's already brainstormed names
with Tom and come up with Nach-Lows, Nosh-os and
Skinny Bandito,' she says, grimacing. 'I spent a year in South
America researching chillies and look at me now. I'm going
to kill myself,' she says. She looks like she means it.

'Cheer up, Lisa,' says Eddie, who is our desk's resident
optimist. 'At least he hasn't asked you to rethink your entire
range based on what his girlfriend likes.'

'No way.'

'Apparently Mandy thinks our Chicken Korma's not a
patch on Asda's, and says our Madras tastes a bit spicy . . .'

Lisa rolls her eyes, grabs her fag packet and marches off.

★

If I'm meeting James at 8pm, I need two hours prep time
which means ducking out of work early – doable if Devron
is in one of his endless meetings or on the phone to his
barely-legal girlfriend, and if Janelle is walking the floors.
Janelle is Devron's rottweiler PA. Devron's swollen self-impor-
tance comes from the fact that he is Head of Food Development
at the UK's seventh largest supermarket. La-di-da. Janelle's
comes from the fact that she is 'PA to the Head of Food
Development at the UK's seventh largest supermarket'. If you
printed that on a t-shirt, she'd wear it at the weekends.

Janelle and I have had an uncomfortable relationship since my first week here, when I saved a status report in a more logical place on the shared drive than:

S:/a4/janellestott/general/dayfiles/2010/js/Qzgg67/4/ac/dc/Y-me

By creating: S:/status reports, I have created a nemesis for life.

Janelle thinks I am disobedient. I think 'I don't care what you think,' and we chafe against each other like an extra-small belt on a woman who likes custard *and* cream with her apple crumble. (No prizes for guessing who is who in that metaphor.)

I'm in luck – neither of them is visible and I bolt out the door and jump in a cab home.

Home is a mansion block in Little Venice: misleading. When I hear mansion, I think Krystle Carrington's sweeping staircase, not a one-bedroom, fifth floor flat with no lift. And Little Venice is pushing it – more like Little A40, within a Tango can's throw of the Westway. Still, Little's accurate. And if I walk out of my flat and turn left I can be at Regent's Canal in two minutes, and at Baker and Spice eating a blueberry muffin in three and a half.

I take the stairs two at a time – work to do! I dump my bag on top of my mail on the doormat and head straight for the bathroom, disrobing en route. I'm the lowest maintenance girlfriend on the planet after six months, but a first date is a first date and I have waited three weeks to see this man; I am going to look my absolute best.

My long brown hair is naturally curly. No one but Laura and my immediate family have seen me with curly hair since I was fourteen and no one ever will and live to write about it. When I blow-dry it carefully it takes an hour. Today: seventy minutes. Make up is light and for once I don't cut myself shaving my legs.

To the bedroom: it takes me seven minutes just to find tights that don't have a ladder below the knee. I find one of the holy un-holey pairs, and ferret out my best four-inch black heels from the bottom of my wardrobe. One day I'm going to be the type of woman with Polaroids on the front of her shoeboxes. Probably the same day I win the Nobel for Services to Custard.

My dress is fantastic – clingy and low on top, flirty and loose from the waist, in a deep purple that makes my eyes look very green. £40 from Topshop and it passes for Roland Mouret. I'd never normally think it, let alone say it, but I leave the flat looking great. Well, I look great, the flat looks like I've been burgled – twelve pairs of tights decorating the bedroom floor and my work clothes strewn down the hallway. Ben, the caretaker in my block, double takes and wolf whistles as he helps me into my minicab.

I'm insanely nervous and hopeful and excited. I haven't been this excited about a man since I met Nick five years ago. I try not to think about Nick and instead pick up the phone to call Laura, my dating guru, the happiest person I know. She and Dave have been together a decade and yet they look at each other like they're on a fourth date.

'I'm on my way,' I say.

'Relax. Be happy, keep it light, don't talk about Nick. Just remember, you are exceptional and smart and gorgeous and funny and any man would be lucky to have you.' I nod. I believe at least half this sentence.

'What if I don't fancy him? It's been so long I can't remember what he looks like.' Other than that he's manly and his eyes have a deviant twinkle.

'If nothing else it's a free dinner.'

No such thing, as even the biggest fool knows.

My cab pulls up outside the restaurant a perfect ten minutes late. I see James through the glass looking slightly panicked that he's going to be stood up, but when I walk in, his eyes open wide and his whole face lights up.

'Remember me?' I say.

'You're even better than I remember,' he grins.

So is he. Thick brown hair with just a smattering of grey, blue eyes, a large Roman nose. Tall and broad, with a stomach that he wears well. I love big men; I love big noses. He must drink a lot of water, his skin is amazing – he looks late thirties, tops. Not a hint of hair product or jewellery or any of the metrosexual accoutrements that adorn modern girly-boys. As he stands to kiss me, he rests

23

a firm hand on my back. There is such confidence in his gesture – a mix of strength and gentleness – that I feel myself start to blush.

'I've never noticed this place before,' I say, taking a seat and trying to stay cool as he pours me a glass of red wine. From the outside it looks like nothing special but inside it's cosy and romantic: dark oak tables, simple silver cutlery, half-burned candles, warm grey walls. Every table is full.

'An Italian friend introduced me to it.' I wonder fleetingly if the friend was female.

'So how's your friend Rob?' I say.

'Sends his love! He got an earful from Lena that night.'

'He shouldn't flirt with other women in front of her,' I say.

'Rob's a dog. A feisty girl like you wouldn't put up with that, would you?'

'Don't try finding out.'

'Not my style – I'm too forgetful to be a love-rat. Always better to be honest.'

'So if your memory was better you'd be Tiger Woods?'

He shakes his head. 'I'm a one-woman man. I never lie.'

My mother's voice pops into my head telling my anxious 7-year-old self, 'An axe murderer doesn't have axe murderer written on his forehead'.

'How was your day?' I ask, taking a sip of wine.

'Good,' he says.

'What did you do?'

'Had a few meetings about a new project, then had a set-to with Camden Council . . .'

'Been dodging your council tax?' I say.

He laughs. 'No. I'm advising them on a clothing recycling website for schools.'

'Sounds interesting.' And quite worthy. I hadn't pegged him as a leftie.

'They're using a panel of industry advisors – I'm helping on the digital architecture side.'

'And how come they picked you, are you really Green?'

He laughs. 'No. I live in Camden, my background's in clothing and online. And I don't mean to sound arrogant, but I'm good at what I do . . .'

He doesn't sound arrogant, just extremely confident. 'And what was the row, are you arguing about your fee?'

'Fee?' he sounds surprised. 'They're not paying. No, I think they should take a more aggressive approach, be more ambitious: sell space on the site to other green brands. It all feeds back into the budget and that means lower taxes.'

'Ah, so you are trying to get out of paying your council tax!'

'Good point! Smart woman.' He grins and hands me the menu. 'What are we eating?'

'It all sounds delicious . . . pappardelle with lamb ragu and rosemary, or steak – I do love rosemary . . .'

'I was thinking tortellini or steak. The pasta here is great . . .'

25

'I'll have pasta,' I say. He looks at me intently and smiles.

'Me too. And something healthy on the side . . . let's see . . .'

Call me shallow but I think I fell for James Stephens when he ordered the steak as our side dish.

★

We are a game of snap.

We both love chips with 2 parts ketchup: 1 part mayo, and think brown sauce is the devil's own condiment.

We both hated our fifth-year maths teachers, and were the second naughtiest in class.

We both only recycle what's easy to recycle, and think the idea of compost in your kitchen is a bridge too far.

We both have one parent who selfishly died on us before we hit puberty, and one parent who remarried and moved abroad (Victor Stephens, Switzerland/Ruth Klein, California.)

We both suspect Ricky Gervais will never do anything as funny as *The Office* ever again, and that he's probably just like David Brent in real life.

We both have a 39-year-old brother (Edward/Josh) who was/is our mother's favourite, who we see once a year, and who is a reformed playboy, lives in a hot country (Singapore/America) and drives a Porsche (red/navy). Snap x 6.

We both believe that drink drivers who kill should get life, and never be allowed behind the wheel again.

We both feel that getting married in one's twenties usually doesn't work out, and that we both know ourselves pretty well by now.

We both think the greatest pleasure in life is to eat and drink slightly too much and then have a little lie down.

We are both narcissists and agree that our evening has been exciting, and that the person sitting opposite us is deeply alluring and fun and we would like to see them again, very soon.

My friend Pete and I are at his local cinema, sitting in overpriced armchairs waiting for a Norwegian vampire movie to start. Having checked the coast is clear, I remove the family pack of Revels I've smuggled in under my jacket. I've paid £14 for this seat, if they think I'm paying another £6 for their Valrhona chocolate buttons they can think again.

Pete is a serial commitment-phobe. When we were fifteen, Pete and I had a heated dry-hump on the floor of David Marks's parents' guest bathroom. Pete has never gotten over the fact that I wouldn't let him touch me up when I'd allowed David Marks a brief foray the previous summer, and in a tiny part of Pete's still-teenage mind I am The One That Got Away. If this were a rom-com movie, I'd be played by Kate Hudson and Pete would be played by someone appropriately dreamy and thick-looking – Ryan Reynolds, perhaps – and we'd end up together. That is not how this story ends.

'Did you kiss him?' Pete always wants full details of my scant sex life, which is nowhere near as prolific, athletic or incessant as his. Pete's phone is full of picture-messages from various twenty-something actresses and stylists gazing over their own naked shoulders at their bottoms reflected in Venetian mirrors. These photos make me feel depressed and prudish and make Pete feel moderately aroused and then bored.

'Briefly, as he put me in a taxi.'

'Old fashioned!'

'Old full stop. Did I tell you he's forty-five? He doesn't look it or act it. He has way more energy than me.' I have never dated anyone this much older. One of my few memories of my father was blowing out the candles with him on his forty-fifth birthday cake, when I was six. Forty-five is properly grown up. It is dad aged. Yet James radiates vitality – he is a man in the prime of his life. His expression seems to say 'I am going where the good times are.' I want to go with him.

'You'd like him, Pete. You should meet him.' If he sticks around. 'How's your love life?'

Pete shrugs. 'I'm seeing one of the PR girls at work, I'm not sure about her . . .'

'What is it this time?'

'Don't know. She's gorgeous but she's a bit . . . she's never heard of *Bladerunner*.'

'How old is she?'

'Twenty-two.'

'Try dating someone your own age. Or IQ.'

'Why would I want to do either of those things?' he says, smiling as he shoves a handful of contraband Revels into his mouth as the trailers start.

James and I are three lightning hours in to our second date, stretching out our meal, the last ones in the restaurant. We are in Curry Paradise, my local, my treat. The manager is hovering, the waiter is hoovering. I wish we'd met earlier; I don't want to go home. I want to keep talking, and keep looking at the way this man smiles at me when I do, with pure delight in his eyes.

'So, how on earth is a girl like you single, Sophie Klein?'

I've made bad choices. I've been unlucky. Because it's really hard out there.

'I don't know.' I say. 'Why are you single, James Stephens?'

Tall. Charismatic. Good at your job. Such a thick head of hair. Manly: strong features – strong nose, strong jaw. That look in his eye that says 'take it or leave it, but you'd be better off taking it'. Why has no one snapped this man up in the last twenty years?

He shrugs quickly. 'Just haven't met the right person yet.'

'You're not secretly married, are you?'

He chuckles and his hand comes up and rubs his cheek. 'No.'

In poker that would be a tell. 'Are you sure?'

'Quite sure,' he laughs, but his fingers pause briefly near his mouth.

'Ever been engaged?'

He picks up his beer and takes a long sip, then nods slowly.

'Who to?'

'A girl called Lacey Macbride.'

Ironic. 'How long ago was that?'

'I was nineteen. She grew up round the corner from me in Wanstead. My first true love. Broke my heart, the Jezebel,' he laughs.

'What happened?'

He shrugs and picks up his glass again. I imagine classic childhood sweetheart territory.

'Any other ex-fiancées knocking about?'

A tiny flicker of discomfort passes through his expression. He nods very slowly. 'Celine.'

'Engaged to her as well? How many ex-fiancées do you have?'

'Just the pair, don't need a hat-trick,' he says.

Better than two ex-wives, I suppose.

'Long relationship?'

'Three years. Can you pass the spinach?' He smiles softly, trying to change the subject.

32

'How long ago did you split up?'

'Four years.'

Okay. Definitely beyond statute of limitations for a rebound.

'Are you on good terms?' Are you still in love with her?

He pours us both more beer, filling his glass almost to the rim. 'She went back to Paris, married an Argie. She's a Wolford model. . . .' He turns to the waiter, 'Could we get two more beers, please?'

'Wolford tights?'

'And stockings . . .'

The news that his long-term ex is a French hosiery model has put me right off my chicken balti. I put my fork down.

'Why do girls always have a problem with that?' he says, his face crinkling in confusion. I don't like that word 'always'.

'I don't. It's just . . . a man who dates models is . . . a certain type.' The type who likes women with abnormally tall, slim bodies. Not my type. Mind you, he's the type taking me out to dinner.

'Celine was lovely but totally insecure. Anyway, I'm over beautiful women, they're all mad.' He grins, but I do not like those sentences at all. 'I'm looking for a soul mate. A woman I can talk to.' That's a bit better. 'A wife,' he says, fixing me with an intense look. His pale blue shirt is making his eyes a deeper blue than usual tonight. I catch myself staring.

33

'Tell me something else,' I say, picking up my fork.

'What do you want to know?'

Why you'd mention that your ex is a leg model? Was that information strictly necessary?

And how a sock-seller procures that type of trophy girlfriend anyway?

Maybe her legs were perfect but she had a face like a monkfish. I make a note to google her.

'His ex is a leg model,' I say to Laura. I'm treating her to an Ottolenghi brunch near her flat in Islington to celebrate my forthcoming end-of-fiscal £100 bonus. When I say treating *her*, I mean I have already eaten my egg and bacon pie, and have started on her blueberry ricotta pancakes before she's even halfway through.

'So?'

'Well . . . her figure must be perfect.'

She tuts. 'You are one of the best women I have ever met, and I don't give a flying fuck who's got a perfect body and who hasn't. It's not like he's perfect looking . . .'

I know Laura didn't warm to him the night we met him – she thought he was overly confident and slightly shifty. She has some random psychological theory that this actually masks some deep fear within himself.

I do trust her instincts, she is invariably on the nail; however, in this instance, she is being overly protective of me. She spoke to James for all of ten minutes. I know if she spent any time with him, she'd like him.

'I suppose models are usually quite vain, aren't they . . .' I say, pondering whether to order the pecan praline Danish, then imagining Celine's thighs, and ordering a sparkling water instead.

'Are you kidding? Do you not remember Washington Avenue, New Year's Eve, 1993? Ladies and gentleman, we bring you Ericc and Thor . . .'

I throw my head back with laughter. How could I ever forget? Laura and I had spent the night with two male models we'd met in a bar Mickey Rourke used to own. We were so overexcitable, having been introduced to Mickey Rourke by some ageing gallery owner who was lusting after our 18-year-old flesh, that we'd been swept like a wave into The Miami Beach Fashion Awards.

'Ericc with two 'c's. God, he was so ridiculously chiselled. That was the most boring eight minutes of my life,' I say, remembering his pillow talk, detailing his awesome nutritional supplements: chromium picolinate – super-awesome, apparently.

'I rest my case,' says Laura.

At the end of our last date James said 'I'll be in touch.'

That was six days ago: no call, no text. I'm scared it's because I kissed him for a full twenty minutes outside the curry house, and maybe he thought that was tacky or overly eager. Or perhaps it's because I made that silly comment about him dating models, which made me look insecure and jealous.

Hmm, time to make myself feel more insecure and jealous. Excellent idea.

I google image search for 'Celine' 'Wolford' 'model' 'French' 'leg' and immediately come up with over 700 photos of her. In none of them does she remotely resemble a monkfish.

I know I should stop myself right now. She's married. What difference if she's beautiful or not anyway? He is dating me.

Okay, I click on the first image. Relief. Dark blond hair, brown eyes, generic Disney features, looks like she eats a lot of yoghurt and apples. Swiss looking. Maybe she's from the Alps. Second photo, a close up. Even though she's smiling, she looks fearful, like she's just found out her currency's in free fall. Third photo, taken last year at the Cannes Film Festival. That must be the Argie husband. He's corpulent. Mid-fifties. Oligarch-y. She is Botoxed to the hilt, skeletal, clutching his arm with a jewelled hand.

It's not until the fourth photo that I see her in suspenders and a thong and start to feel in any way envious.

Her legs are perfect, long, shapely, amazing. Of course they are. She owns two Wolford legs. That's her job. I decide it's high time I get back to *my* job.

I go to the C-drive and click on the kitchen sample report for my latest trifles.

Besides. She's married now. And not to James.

Ah, good: thicker, more even deposit of custards with 38% stabilised whipping cream . . .

And just because her legs are amazing doesn't mean she's smart or kind or funny.

Let's see . . . uneven almond spread rectified, shelf life now at seven days . . . Devron will like that . . .

Just because her legs are amazing doesn't mean she isn't also *smart and kind and funny.*

Get a grip – he'll call. And if he doesn't? So be it. They are not together; she is irrelevant. He is dating you. Or is he . . .?

I'm going to call him because if he likes me it won't matter, and if he doesn't, it'll expedite the ending of the relationship. I don't want this loop of crap in my head; I have a big Phase 4 meeting in two days that I need to prepare for. Call him: then it's done, either way.

I dial his number before the sensible voice can stop me. It's a foreign ring tone. I hang up immediately.

He hadn't mentioned he'd be going away. Why not? He's flown to Paris! The Alps!

Enough. I delete James's number from my phone and from my dialled list. I am not going to do this to myself. Nick called me at least once a day from the first day we met. He loved me and he could show it. He never made

38

me feel insecure, not once. Bored, enraged, despairing, sure. But insecure? Never.

If James Stephens wants me, he's going to have to make a lot more effort.

The average human touches their nose dozens of times a day. In this sole regard, Devron is a well-above-average human. He touches his nose at least three times a minute. Sometimes he gives it little tugs and pinches. Sometimes he fiddles with the end and you can tell he's trying to fish something out surreptitiously. Sometimes he holds, squeezes, sniffs loudly and wipes his hands on his trousers. Eddie and I always play 'Devron Nose Bingo' – whoever is the first to observe twenty nose manoeuvres in any given meeting and whisper 'wanker', wins a luxury hot chocolate from the canteen.

The worst ever time that Devron touches his nose though, is in a Phase 4 meeting.

A Phase 4 meeting is the final stage in taking a new range to market. Phases 1 to 3 involve briefing suppliers, tasting initial product ideas, doing shelf life, transport and safety tests, and evolving the products accordingly.

Phase 4 meetings are the reason why I will never leave

this job voluntarily – you'll have to cart me away in a straitjacket.

At a Phase 4, you basically sit around like a bunch of Roman emperors dressed in Next suits instead of togas, and eat the entire range – whether that's 12 fools and 8 trifles, like my meeting today, or Eddie's meeting last week where I sampled 23 different curries in an hour. Of course, you don't eat the whole dish – you just take a bite, and the majority of people 'spit in the cup'. Yup, they gob out their food in a paper cup, like a Bulimics Anonymous Christmas party.

I never ever 'spit in the cup'. It's not about etiquette. Many women, and even some men, manage to spit quite discreetly, so you barely notice the person next to you opening their mouth to eject a half-chewed lump of naan bread. No, I refuse to 'spit in the cup' because I think it's cheating. Any food that goes in my mouth goes in my stomach. Admittedly, I also see it as a badge of honour – there were six men and four women at Eddie's Phase 4, and I was the only one to make it through all 23 curries without spitting. It's just as well I only go to the Phase 4s that are mine, Lisa's or Eddie's, and that I walk in to work every day.

The official rules of a Phase 4 are as follows:

- you change forks with every dish you taste
- you don't double-dip your fork in a communal dish

41

- you pretend you're only eating as a duty, not getting
  real pleasure from the food, for fear you'll be taxed
  on it as a perk

Devron ignores all three rules and invariably digs in to the food with the hand that has just been inside his nasal cavity.

Whenever I'm arranging a Phase 4, I make sure to order two of everything – one for Devron and one for everyone else. However, this rarely stops Devron sitting in front of two identical cherry pies, flitting between the two with his sucked fingers. Fingers/nose/fingers/nose. Once Devron has touched a pudding I can't eat that pudding, even if I try eating it from the other side. I just can't. I'm pretty sure one day I'll flip and pie Devron in the face, or ram a churro up his nose and kill him.

Today I pop down to the fridge to fetch the samples my supplier, Appletree, has sent in. I love working with my contact there, Will Slater, not least because he always sends me down a box of custard-filled éclairs he's had the head chef make specially.

Zoe, our fridge manager, tells me I'm looking a bit skinny, she prefers me with curves. If I ever decide to date a woman it will be Zoe. She has Pantene hair, great Patti Smith t-shirts and a super-fast wit, and above all else, she has an even better job than I do: FRIDGE MANAGER.

This is not just any fridge. This is a fridge the size of a WHSmiths at a major railway station. If it wasn't quite so cold I would seriously think about living in this fridge. Rows upon rows of shelves, floor to ceiling, stacked with samples of everything we sell and everything we're thinking about selling, and everything our competitors sell. Zoe calls it 'Paradise Frost'. I can never think of anything funny that rhymes with fridge in response.

And then there's the freezer! While I daydream about moving in to the work fridge, I have nightmares about being locked in the work freezer. Our fifteen ice cream variants would only keep me diverted for the first hour or so, and then the thought of a slow icy death with nothing to eat but Coated Protein (that's fish fingers to you) – death, there is thy sting.

'Zoe, I can see the fools, but where are the trifles? Zoe?' I walk through the fridge and back out, and find Zoe deep in the freezer, headphones on, sorting through a stack of giant frozen turkeys.

'Huh?'

'Didn't Appletree send in the trifles and fools on the same courier?'

'New system . . . Div-ron's making us file by packaging colour . . .'

'What?'

'Ridiculous, worse than organising your books by colour . . .'

43

'No, that is *really* bloody ridiculous. They're all in different colours according to the fruit.'

'Don't worry, babe, I've got you covered. Aisle G, shelf 3 on the left – your éclairs are there too. He's checking in on me this week, but as soon as he gets bored I'll switch back . . . man, he is one giant fucking dickhead . . .'

I load two of every pudding into a giant orange crate and schlep it round to Tasting Room 12.

There's only three of us attending today – Devron, Ton of Fun Tom and me. I lay sixty spoons, a stack of paper plates, and three glasses of water, then arrange the fools and trifles in the most ramshackle, non-colour co-ordinated order I can think of.

I wait for Devron and Tom to arrive. It's quarter past, they're late . . . Neither of them answers their phone. At half past, I head back up to my desk and find Devron and Janelle laughing at a website that features a selection of goats wearing jumpers.

'Are you coming to the Phase 4, Devron?' I say.

Janelle intercepts. 'I had to move it to next month, I just sent you an email a minute ago.'

'There's twenty products that need sign off today, launch date is May,' I say.

'Sophie, I'm sure you can push back on suppliers, we give them enough business,' says Devron impatiently.

'Fine.' I go back to the fridge and call up my friends from various departments and tell them to come to Room

44

12, immediately. Zoe puts the kettle on and six of us eat fruit trifles, chocolate trifles and eight types of fool and take it in turns to do impressions of Devron at the point of orgasm with a frozen turkey.

Afterwards, I return to my desk and a flashing light on my phone. A text message. From James!

'What are you doing tomorrow?' Ah, the relief.

I know I should be cooler – he's left it till Thursday afternoon to ask me out for a Friday night – but I believe in momentum and if I don't see him soon, I fear I'm going to lose it.

We agree to meet at the Dean Street Townhouse at 9pm. It occurs to me that I have no idea what country he's texting from.

I wonder if he'd have contacted me if I hadn't called him.

What does that matter now?

On Friday, I run out of the door at 5.54pm. I'm sure I see Janelle make a note of this in her Book of Snitch. I consider waiting for the bus. I have only three hours' turnaround time before I'm due back in Soho and an über-emergency-face-and-body-makeover to perform. On Tottenham Court Road I hail a cab, even though I really can't afford it.

Last night I did as much of the home makeover as I could bear to. I washed my sheets, hoovered for the first time in a fortnight, dried the sheets, and attempted to tidy the piles of recipes, post-it notes and newspapers that adorn any horizontal space in my flat.

I then tried to re-arrange my bathroom products to convey the fact that I am a natural beauty who doesn't sweat or have body hair: hide all make-up, my razor and deodorant, bring out the cheapest, simplest £3 Superdrug moisturiser (it's very good, actually).

I am not a total sloven, just messy. My bathroom is always clean, and my kitchen is spotless. I love to cook, and this kitchen brings me more joy than any other room in the flat. Although it's only Ikea, it's fairly gorgeous. White units, a grey worktop, a pale yellow glass splashback. The only thing I did in the kitchen last night was pop the bottle of beautiful white wine that Maggie Bainbridge gave me for Christmas into the fridge, just in case.

It's 6.24pm. Two hours and twenty before I have to leave the house to meet him. I perform all ablutions as carefully as possible but I'm in such a panic that I cut my leg shaving. This happens to me about once every three shaves. I'm clumsy and impatient, but I have the added bonus of having Factor XI deficiency, a harmless but irritating disorder I inherited from my dad that means when I bleed, I take a while to stop bleeding. I once cut myself shaving before I had to get on the Eurostar to Paris for a choux pastry seminar and by the time I got to the Champs Elysees, I had a shoe full of blood. Pas très chic.

It will bleed for at least twenty minutes now, but I don't have time to sit with my leg up and wait for it to stop, so I end up Sellotaping a wodge of toilet paper to my ankle while I go about drying my hair, flossing, and moisturising.

7.59pm, I remove my makeshift tourniquet and my ankle proceeds to drip blood like a slow-leaking tap. I was planning on wearing tights anyway – it's freezing out – but I can't just put them over the wound. I settle for two giant plasters and take a spare pair of tights in my handbag – I'll have to pop to the loo in the restaurant as soon as I get there and change these, and clean up the blood stains from my foot . . . sexy stuff.

I put on my soft, slinky Topshop black dress and notice with a hiccup of delight that it has never been this loose on me. Final touches of make-up, perfume, a spritz of fig room spray in the hall, and I'm off.

★

James is sitting nursing a gin and tonic, chatting to the barman, when I walk in. He grins when he sees me and the barman gives me the once-over too. I have made an effort – high heels, earrings, the hair is behaving well. Or maybe the barman checks me out because there aren't that many younger women in here – the clientele seems to be 60% gay men, and the rest are middle-aged fashion and media types sporting faux spectacles, frowns and unseasonal tans.

'Have a drink,' says James, handing me the cocktail list.

'I don't need that, I'll have an Old Fashioned please, Maker's Mark,' I say to the barman, who winks his approval.

James immediately rests his hand on my knee. 'A girl who knows what she wants.'

'Well, it took me years of research in the field, but I finally found a drink that I love.'

'And you never drink other cocktails?'

'Sometimes. But an Old Fashioned has all the qualities I look for in my booze. Not too sweet, the right size, pretty hard for a barman to mess up. . . .'

'And what about men, what qualities do you look for in a man?'

I stop myself saying 'not too sweet, the right size, pretty hard . . .'-it'll sound cheap. Instead I run through the essential criteria that twenty years of dating has reduced me to:

Kind

Funny

Clean

Not mentally ill

Tall, big nosed, and a thick head of hair is a bonus. James appears to tick most of these boxes so far (you can't judge mentally ill after just two dates). If I say anything on this list, I'll look too keen.

'I'm looking for a grown-up,' I say.

He makes to get up from the bar and leave.

'And someone thoughtful. What about you?' I say.

'I'm looking for someone warm and smart. Feisty. Reasonably attractive . . .' he grins.

I wonder if his definition of 'reasonably attractive' can encompass a woman with a few stretch marks and a light smattering of cellulite.

'Would you go out with Nigella?' I say. Such a good test of a man's shallowness – can he appreciate a gorgeous woman with a real body.

'Far too old for me!' he says.

'She's near enough your age, you cheeky git!'

He shrugs.

'Don't you think she's beautiful?' I say.

'She's nice looking. Anyway, looks aren't everything.'

The maître d' beckons us over, and as we stand, James reaches under his bar stool and presents me with a bag.

'I got you something,' he says.

'Really?' I say, shocked. Inside the bag is a large bottle of Aromatherapy Associates Rosemary Bath Oil that he must have bought me in Duty Free, wherever he has been.

'I know you like rosemary,' he says. I do? 'The pasta you ordered at the Italian . . .'

Bless him, I love the taste of rosemary but I don't want to smell like a roast lamb. Still, extremely thoughtful and sweet of him.

'That's lovely of you, James Stephens. Thank you.' I kiss him briefly on the mouth and feel his eyes on the back of me as I walk to the ladies' room to check whether my ankle has stopped bleeding.

The ankle is fine, but I change tights anyway as I have to take off the old ones to dab a slight blood stain on my foot.

When I return five minutes later, there is a bottle of decent red on the table.

'One of the chefs at work was telling me that this place is famous for its mince and potatoes,' I say, looking at the menu.

'I knew you'd be a good woman to go out with,' he says, 'I can't stand girls who don't eat.' Men always say this. It is often bullshit and means 'I can't stand girls who don't eat but neither can I stand girls who show signs of having eaten'. It is invariably the same men who say 'I like girls who look natural', but actually mean girls who only wear foundation, cover up, pressed powder, blush, a bit of eye pencil and a lot of mascara.

'Oh, and save room for The Queen of Puddings, it's meant to be amazing.'

'Queen of Puddings, isn't that your job?' he says, smiling.

'I wish, I'm only a junior developer,' I say.

'Still, it sounds great. I think it's brilliant what you do for a living . . . Queen of Puddings. So you just sit around stuffing your face with cake all day, do you?'

'There's a little more to it than that. You have to think

50

of new concepts, follow market trends, brief suppliers, work out if a product's manageable in budget, there's all the microbiotics, health and safety, shelf life, packaging, travel testing . . .'

'So you do, you basically get paid to eat cake,' he clinks his glass against mine in congratulation.

'Sometimes I bake cakes all day . . .'

'You cook at work?'

'Great job, huh?' I say.

'Is that why you don't paint your nails?' He makes it sound like I have half a finger missing that he's been too polite to ask about, but has been dying to know the story behind – did a squirrel bite it off?

'No,' I say, tucking my hands away on to my lap. 'I'm just not always a full hair and make-up kind of girl. I don't have the time. Why, do you like painted fingernails?'

'A little red nail polish never goes amiss . . .' he says.

'You really did have your teenage sexual awakening in the 80s,' I say, shaking my head.

He laughs and fills my glass, then rests his hands on the table. My hands spontaneously float up from my lap to be beside his.

'God, you don't see many women out like that anymore,' says James, as a six-foot, heavily made-up twenty-something in a full-length fur walks in, flanked by a tubby man of around fifty.

'Bimbos with sugar daddies? London's full of them!'

'No, I mean the coat. That's Russian sable!' he says admiringly.

'– I think it's a bit tacky,' I say.

'The coat?'

'No, them – he looks like he's paying her by the hour. – How do you know it's a Russian sable?'

'The bluish tinge. Do you know that the mating ritual of the Russian sable can last up to eight hours?' he says, leaning forward, a huge smile breaking across his face.

'Sounds like Sting . . . anyway, how do you know all this?'

'My grandfather was a furrier – Stephanikov Furs, in the East End. Do you like fur?'

'I don't like the thought of animals being hurt just for my benefit, but then I eat meat, so . . . No, I don't have a problem with fur, not vintage anyway. Sorry, does that make me mean, horrible and heartless?'

'No, just asking.'

'Well, if there are any mink jackets lying round your garage that you need a good home for . . .'

He laughs and orders a couple of vodka shots.

'Are you trying to get me drunk, Mr Stephens?' I say.

He raises an eyebrow and grins. 'So, what's the best pudding in the world?' he says.

'Hot pudding, cold pudding, cake, tart, fool, mousse, flan, trifle – define your terms, please.'

'Cake,' he says.

'Number one: a Jean Clement praline millefeuille, you can only get them in Paris. Number two: my mother's chocolate and raspberry cream cheesecake – only available in California, and when my mother is in a good mood. And three: Ottolenghi's apple and sultana cake – Upper Street, any day of the week.'

He beams back at me. 'You're not like anyone else I've ever dated,' he says.

'Why?' I say.

He shrugs.

'In a good way?' I say.

He nods. I feel a little flutter in my chest.

'What do you actually do, anyway? I mean, I know you sell socks, but very specifically what do you do?'

'Okay, where do you buy your socks?'

'M&S.'

'Why?'

'Good quality.'

'Why else?'

'The right amount of stretch.'

'Why else?'

'No other reason. I'm not that into socks. Sorry.'

'Never apologise. What about tights?'

'M&S, same reasons. Do you sell tights too?' I hope so. I could do with a man who could keep me in tights, the rate I'm going through them tonight . . .

'Just socks for now but I'm starting something new in

legwear this summer. Another bottle of red?' He smiles at me and I can't help but beam back.

The main course arrives. I realise he still hasn't told me exactly what he does. This man could be a drug dealer or a pimp for all I know – he has the hustle to be either – but I don't care because whatever he is, I am bewitched.

★

We stumble out onto Dean Street to hail a cab. It is freezing and he tucks me inside his coat with him. 'Come here, you tiny thing.'

On the corner of an alley is a tramp of about sixty. A pink tiara rests on her patchy orange hair. She is wearing a sheepskin coat, a velvet sailor suit that stops mid-calf, and house slippers. When she sees James she points at him and shouts 'Jackie Boy, you're a useless cont,' in a thick Ulster accent.

'Another one of your ex-fiancées?' I say, giggling.

He tries not to smile. 'I told you all beautiful women are mad.'

'Yeah, well, maybe guys like you make them mad.'

'Nah, it's just the way you're built. Speaking of which, come here.'

I'm already inside his coat with him but he puts both arms around me and kisses me. We stay like this until the tramp lurches towards us and asks James for some change.

I expect him to fob her off like the Tory-boy I suspect he really is, but instead he reaches into his wallet and hands her a £20 note. 'Buy yourself something to eat, please?' he says.

I'm more amazed than she is.

'What?' he says.

'Nothing. Generous, that's all.'

He shrugs. 'Always been a sucker for a well-turned ankle.' He laughs and grabs my hand and we walk up to Oxford Street to find a taxi.

'So, how was the morning after?' says Laura, when I call her back the following afternoon.

'Great! We had a fry-up in bed, read the papers, then he left to go to White Hart Lane with Rob,' I say, surveying the mess of pans, wine glasses and crumbs in my kitchen.

'And the night before?'

I blush remembering it. We had sex. We had quite a lot of sex, all of it good.

I once dated a gorgeous Italian Jewish lawyer who was tall, funny, kind and spoke five languages. The first (and last) time we slept together, it came to light that he had a rare psychosomatic sexual disorder that meant he had a fit at the point of orgasm.

As Eskimos with 'snow', Jews have multiple words for 'disappointment'. None of these came close to covering off that scenario.

Still, since then, whenever I sleep with someone for the

first time and they don't nearly swallow their own tongue and go blue, I'm profoundly grateful.

'It was good, really natural. I like his body, it's big – it makes me feel small.'

'How did you leave it with him?' says Laura.

'He rang just after he left to say goodbye, he's off again tomorrow for five days, to Portugal.'

'Is he going to call you?'

'Well, he said "you're not going to forget about me are you?" and I said why don't you call me from Portugal, and he sort of evaded the question.'

'Hmm.'

'Weird, isn't it?'

'Do you think there's another girl?'

'No.' That thought hadn't actually occurred to me. 'He's visiting some financiers, definitely. But I feel like he's project managing me, putting me on ice for a week.' And I don't like it.

'Ah well, it's early days, isn't it. Let's see what happens when he gets back.'

After I put the phone down, I ignore the washing up and go back to lie on my bed. The pillow still smells strongly of James. I should wash this pillowcase today, and these sheets, or I'll lie here later and miss him.

I'll miss his body, his strong arms, his broad shoulders. The weight of him. I'll miss his mouth. Those confident hands. His head coming to rest in the curve of my neck. His heartbeat finally slowing under my palm. . . .

Who am I kidding – Persil Bio on a 60 isn't going to wash away those memories. I force myself to get up and make a cup of tea and wash up the pans. The sheets can wait.

It's nearly 4pm now, so I pop round to the florist in Maida Vale to buy my grandma a bunch of orange tulips, then drive round to her flat in Highgate. I park in the courtyard next to the communal garden. My grandma lived here with my grandpa for thirty-eight of their fifty-five years together. There's a beautiful teak bench at the back of the garden under an apple tree, bought for them on their ruby wedding anniversary by the residents in the block. The inscription is from The Bible, The Song of Songs: 'I am my beloved's and my beloved is mine'. My grandparents would sit together on this bench on balmy summer nights, one or both of them dozing off against each other's shoulder.

I do love coming to my grandma's flat. It reminds me of Saturday afternoons spent with my brother, riding up and down in the lift with its old-fashioned sliding cage door. Of being chased along the red-carpeted corridors by my dad till my grandma would poke her head out of her door, and announce in a deeply serious tone that if we wanted any of her world famous spaghetti with tomato sauce and meatballs, we'd better come quick before my grandpa ate the last mouthful.

58

I ring the bell and Evie, my grandma's part-time carer, buzzes me in. 'She didn't sleep well,' she says, opening the door and greeting me with a kiss. Evie is the longest-serving carer my granny has had. My grandma has despatched various Eastern European carers over the last decade for looking miserable or talking too much or too little ('the stumers'). Evie is perpetually cheery, talks just the right amount and paints my granny's impressive finger-nails purple and jangly like a west London rude-girl.

My grandma is ninety-seven. Her legs don't work and her boredom has morphed into depression, but her brain and her tongue are razor sharp.

She is sitting in her pale blue wing back chair, staring out of the window towards the Heath, but her face lights up when I walk in.

'For you,' I say, handing her the tulips.

'My favourite!' she says. 'Evie! A vase please? Now sit. Have a biscuit,' she says, pointing at a dozen star-shaped, sugar-dusted biscuits arranged neatly on a red and white Delft plate. I nibble a lemon shortbread even though I hate lemon with sweet things. 'What's new then, Sophola? How was that pistachio lamb?'

We'd discussed that dish more than a month ago.

'Needed longer on a lower heat,' I say.

'Always the lowest heat,' she says, shaking her head.

My foodie genes come from my grandma, who is my dad's mother, and my mum. My grandma was an excellent cook before she tired of food in her dotage. Now all she eats is boiling hot soup, stale lemon biscuits and coffee ice cream, washed down with a small whisky of an evening. I inherited her habit of always trying something new, and my mother's habit of always ordering three times too much of it.

'So your brother's making me feel old – a great-grandmother indeed!'

'It's so exciting, I can't wait!'

'I'm not sure I'll still be here when the baby arrives.'

'Oh, stop it. Of course you will.'

'This is my last winter, I can feel it,' she shakes her head.

'Nonsense, you say that every year!'

'I'm ready to go,' she says, her shoulders rising and falling slowly. 'And you? When are you going to stop flitting about?'

'I'm not ready for all that baby stuff yet.'

'Of course not, you need to find a decent man first. Is there no one nice at work?'

Raymond Cowell-Trousers in accounts? 'Not at work, no. But I have met someone who I think you might approve of.'

'Tell me more.'

'He's . . . he's very bright. And handsome. Nice and tall.' I won't mention his age; I don't think she'd approve of that.

'What does he do?'

'He runs his own company, he sells socks.'

'Jewish?' she says, a faint trace of hope in her voice.

'I think his grandfather was.' We both know this doesn't count. 'East End, furrier.'

'Your grandfather knew some people in the schmutter trade. What's this creature's name?'

'Stephens. James Stephens, in fact!'

'Oh dear!' she raises her hands to her face in mock horror. 'Don't be too nice to him! You know how that poem ends . . .'

Chance would be a fine thing. He's now been in Portugal for four days and hasn't even texted me. Still, he's busy working. And he's forty-five. Do 45-year-olds really text? Isn't that a bit teenage? I hate texts anyway, so avoidant, I'd much rather talk. He's due back tomorrow. I'm sure he'll call then.

Three days later he phones from Lisbon airport.

'I was starting to think I'd imagined you,' I say. And I'm starting to think Laura's right and there is another woman.

'Is that a dig?' he says, with good humour.

'Have you been terribly busy with work?'

'It's not been too bad, actually. A bit of work, a bit of fun.'

'Are you just one of those people who compartmentalises their life?'

'No, not really.'

'So you stayed a few days longer than planned?'

'Yeah, the Bonders own a place down the coast, they invited me for some golf.'

'The Bonders?'

'The venture capital guys.'

'Are they Portuguese?'

'Swiss, but they've got houses all over the place.'

I daren't go for a sixth question, the only one I want the answer to, which is: why didn't you call? Because he is calling.

And I know I'd sound needy and weird. Besides, he's forty-five. He's been on a business trip. It's very early days. We've only had three dates. Three great dates and some good sex. Still, you aren't allowed to expect too much attention at this stage, so Pete tells me, and I should stop being paranoid.

'So, when are you free to see me, woman?'

I pause. I am genuinely busy this week, plus I want to spend more than just an evening and a morning with him. 'At the weekend?'

'What are you doing in the week?'

'I'm busy.'

'Friday night?'

'Busy . . . I wasn't sure when you'd be back, so I made other plans.' And if you'd called me sooner then I wouldn't have had to . . .

'I'm not surprised you're so popular, a girl with your qualities. Okay, Sunday afternoon, let's see a movie – all these dinners with you are making me fat!' Nonsense, he had a gut when I met him!

'I might be free Saturday night . . .' I say.

'Seeing Rob and the boys,' he says quickly.

'Fine, no, Sunday then . . .'

'I'll pick you up at 3pm, I'll choose the film.'

I like a man who takes control.

'I'm outside your flat, come on down,' he says at 3pm on the dot.

'What car are you in?'

'The little blue one that makes a funny noise.'

For some reason I imagined he'd drive a BMW or a Golf GTi – something mainstream and fast and solid and a little bit flash.

But no. No, no, no. He is, in fact, behind the wheel of a very shiny, fancy sports car.

What make is it? There is a little crown insignia at the front, but I can't tell. I know the difference between a Porsche, a Ferrari and a Lamborghini. James does not have a small penis and clearly doesn't feel the need to drive any of these.

But nowadays Jaguars, Aston Martins, even that Ford with the old Steve McQueen ad – all meld into one.

'Listen to this,' he says, and revs the engine, 'it has the best purr of any car. And it's shaped like a woman's body . . .'

'Sometimes you sound like such an 80s dickhead,' I say, smiling as he leans over to open the door for me.

As I step in, I see a large Maserati logo in silver on the floor. Handy. In case you forget which of your cars you're driving.

I am surprised and pleased to see what a tip it is inside, as bad as my Honda Accord. Boots, fleeces, mud, sweet wrappers, even an empty white mug in the drinks holder, that's surely meant to accommodate a goblet of Krug.

I do so like this about James. He is not precious about things, he's carefree, careless even. I had a boyfriend at college who had a three-day tantrum after I knocked his

Raybans onto the floor as I handed him an orange juice at a Happy Chef on the M6. I hate people who treat generic branded goods like they're family heirlooms; it's just stuff.

'So, what's with this car?' I say, trying not to sound impressed.

'A little toy I bought myself when the Bonders bought 25% equity in JSA. I do like the occasional toy.'

'How much did they pay you?' Blunt, but I'm trying to work out just how fancy this car is.

'Three.'

'£300,000?' If that's 25%, that's a £1.2 million pound business. Not bad for selling socks.

And a whole house in Camden must be worth a million at least.

He laughs. 'You're so sweet, Soph. Add an 0.'

'Oh.' Oh, oh, oh.

★

We're driving to the Curzon in Soho. I am still in shock about his wealth.

My immediate reaction had been: my God. I've found a prince, the last handsome, tall, not-bald multimillionaire in London. That's lottery ticket win money. That doesn't happen. Well, the odds are 1 in 12 million.

But a nanosecond later the discovery has started to bother me. It has set off various small alarms that I'm trying to put on snooze:

That sort of money rockets him in to a different universe.

That sort of money lets him do whatever he wants, whenever he wants, without consequence.

That sort of money goes to a man's head. It is power.

No one makes that much money without being ruthless and hard as nails along the way.

People want to be close to a man like that. Men, yes, but the women. The type of women who would not look at him twice if he was a regular guy. That explains the Wolford model.

I'm bloody glad I didn't know he was rich when I first met him. I wish I didn't know now.

Maybe he doesn't own the whole company; maybe his dad and brother own half . . .

'Play some music, would you?' I say, stroking his thick dark hair and thinking how good his genes are, and hoping if we have kids they'll inherit his straight, shiny locks rather than my curls.

James fiddles with his CD player and on comes the sound-track to the inner circle of hell: Dido, Flo Rida, some vocoder crap, the sort of banging dance music they play in gyms.

'Have you not got the Crazy Frog tune?' I say.

He presses the forward button and on comes Sam Cook.

'Well recovered,' I say.

There is a queue of cars in front of us, and James suddenly pulls to the left and speeds down the bus lane.

'Bus lane,' I say.

'It's fine.'

'It says "At any time".'

'It's fine.'

'You'll get a ticket.'

'Doesn't matter.'

'Just because you've got a crown on your steering wheel doesn't mean you can act like royalty.'

'It's a trident, love.'

'What about the people on buses? There are bus lanes for a reason.'

'They'll still get there,' he says.

'If I was on that bus, I'd think you were a dick,' I say.

'But you're not. You're in my car.'

★

He has booked tickets to see *Antichrist*, because he thought I'd like an art house film. The cinema is very warm, and half an hour into the film, he falls asleep. Occasionally I nudge him but he looks extremely content, and quite frankly I wish I could sleep through it too.

As the end credits roll I wake him up. 'You missed the bit where she drills through his leg, and the bit where she wanks him off and blood spurts out of his cock,' I say.

He shudders. 'Thank God.'

'What now,' I say, 'Chinatown for some duck pancakes?'

'I thought you might like to have dinner at mine.'

67

'You're going to cook for me?'

'I was thinking more like a takeaway,' he says.

'Why don't we cook?'

'You'll see why.'

'Are you sure your wife's not at home tonight?'

'She's on holiday with the kids and my three mistresses,' he says.

★

He pulls up outside a house in Fitzroy Road. That's Primrose Hill, not Camden. It has the loveliest front door of all the houses on the street – a deep, inky blue, with a semi-circular glass window at the top, like the sun rising.

This is all too good to be true. He's too sexy, too rich, too tall, too much fun, too interesting, too smart, that door is too perfect. You don't get to have all this in one person. Maybe you get three of the above but the guy turns out to be a cokehead or a depressive. James is the golden ticket. Something must be wrong.

Inside, everything is homely and unpretentious. On a low wooden sideboard sits a beautiful old-fashioned globe, the countries in faded pinks and yellows and greens and blues.

'Who are these guys?' I say, looking at the framed photos next to the globe.

'That's me and Rob in Mexico.'

'You look happy,' I say.

68

'We'd just been skydiving,' he says. 'I think I was still high.'

'And in this one? That must be your grandfather . . . father's side?' I say, looking at a faded photo of a stern looking man with James's nose and dark eyebrows, his hand on the shoulder of a young boy who's trying not to giggle. 'Your hair was so blonde!'

'My grandad was, what, early seventies? Still smoking thirty a day and drinking a large whisky before lunch. He made me go and find ten different types of leaves in Epping Forest while he sat on that bench with a hip flask, smoking and reading the *Essex Chronicle*.'

'And this one! Look at your hair! How old are you here?'

'Ten. June 3rd, 1975, Woodford Under 11s Junior Chess Champion.'

'Such a nerd!' I say. 'Do you still play?'

'Not really. But I'll give you a game if you don't mind losing,' he says.

'I love losing. So, why can't we cook?' I say, as we head downstairs to his kitchen.

'You'll see.' And I do. His kitchen is like a student dig. He has a double electric hob, a microwave and a tiny, none-too-clean oven. I open one cupboard and see three Pot Noodles and two tins of tuna. In the next cupboard is some Tesco own brand pasta. 'I need a wife,' he says. 'A wife who can cook!'

'What's in here?' I say, spying a waist-high fridge in the corner.

69

'Don't look!' he says, but it's too late. I open the door and see that his fridge has no shelves at all. The few things in it are all stacked on top of each other at the bottom.

'What's that all about?'

'I broke the shelves a while back, I keep meaning to replace them, but I never get round to it . . .' he says.

'How do you even break a fridge shelf?'

'Ask Jack Daniels,' he says.

'I have never seen anything like that,' I say. 'How come the rest of your house is so lovely and your kitchen's so shit?'

He laughs. 'I've been travelling so much in the last year, it's not been a priority. I'll get round to it soon.'

'Takeaway it is,' I say.

'There's a great Japanese on Parkway, I'll pop out and get some,' he says, 'No, it's Sunday . . . pizza?'

'Pizza's good,' I say. 'Or I see you're harbouring a lovely selection of Pot Noodles in your cupboard.'

'Don't say you like Pot Noodle or I'll think I've dreamt you,' he says.

'I don't mind it, if I'm drunk,' I say. 'Let's get pizza. A bit more sociable, isn't it?'

★

We lie on his sofa and eat a spicy meat pizza from his local takeaway. I'd never normally eat meatballs from a delivery place – I work at Fletchers, I know how bad a bad meatball can be. But James fancies meatballs, and I fancy James, and they taste delicious.

'My friend in New York's just had a baby and called him "Domino",' I say.

'That's a terrible name,' he says.

'Isn't it?'

'If I had a boy I'd call him Genghis,' he says.

'Gengis Stephens, nice ring. What about girls' names?'

'What do you think's nice?'

'Don't know. Lauren's pretty. Olivia, maybe too posh. Martha?'

'Martha's a fat girl's name,' he says.

'No, it's not!'

'How about Yasmine Jayde, and Anoushka Rose.'

'You're not calling our daughters after Bratz dolls and air fresheners.'

'I'm the husband, you will obey,' he says, beating his chest.

'Don't hold your breath,' I say. '– By the way, do you normally date women a lot younger than you?' I know Celine is now forty-two, but presumably if he wants children, he'll want a wife under forty.

'You're a few years older than what I'd normally go for,' he says.

'Outrageous! You're pushing fifty!' I say.

'Shhhh,' he puts his finger to my lips.

Truth is we both know his age doesn't matter. You can knock a year off his real age for every million in his bank

71

account: Forty-five, thirty-five, thirty-three . . . now he's my age. Knock another year off for each inch over five foot seven. Twenty-six. A full head of hair buys at least five. Excellent personal hygiene, another couple. Good in bed, another five. He's officially fourteen.

Yep, I am dating a teenage boy.

He has two very different faces. When he frowns, concentrates or looks anxious – 40% of the time – he looks Sicilian and cruel and sexy; when he smiles he looks like a warm, happy, child. His face glazes with delight. Later, when we are together, I take photos of him, and when people ask to see them, they think they're looking at two different people. He is a chameleon. There is something about him that makes me want to hold on to him forever.

'He is really, really rich,' I say to Laura the following day.

'Good for him.'

'I wish he didn't have that much money.'

'What would you prefer, three million?'

'I could even go to four . . .'

'Whatever, Soph. It's a number, isn't it? Doesn't make anyone truly happy.'

Insert the cliché of your choice, but she is, I promise you, correct.

It is almost April and I have finally pinned Devron down and made him taste the trifles and fools he should've eaten weeks ago. I hate waiting for anything and anyone, but I particularly hate waiting for product sign-off from a man who won't go to a restaurant that doesn't serve a well-done steak and wedges.

'What's the life like on this one?' he says, sliding his finger along the top of a chocolate trifle I was planning on taking round to Laura and Dave's at the weekend.

'Seven. This is life minus three,' I say – we're three days off the 'eat by' date, so four days into the pudding's life.

'And how does the consistency of that hold up on minus one?' He points to a raspberry trifle. Devron will always ask one question that makes him sound knowledgeable, but blindfold him and he doesn't know the difference between a blackberry and a blackcurrant.

'Flavour's good, texture and mouthfeel maintained till end of life.'

He nods. 'Custard's good on that lot,' he says. 'Approved.'

I feel like the proud mother of twenty kids, all of whom have just won the egg-and-spoon race.

'Appletree are great with custard,' I say. 'Brûlées, tarts, crème anglaise . . .'

'Brûlées . . . can you look at a microwaveable brûlée for autumn?'

'The custard part?'

'Whole lot.'

'You won't get crispy, browned sugar from a microwave, you need direct overhead heat for caramelisation.'

'Orangy custards? Mands loves tangerines.'

'Not ideal – citric acid interferes with the protein network, the fat globules separate at heat.'

'Huh . . . what's our margin on those trifles?'

'38%'

'And the cost of custard as percentage of total?'

'Low. Bulk of cost is fruit and labour.'

'Right, work up a dozen or so new custard-based puddings for launch next summer, margin of 40% plus. Yeah?'

I do like a challenge when there's custard involved.

*

James has gone to Paris. When I left his house on Monday morning, he'd said, 'I'll call you on Friday.'

And he does. He always calls when he says he will, and

very rarely at any other time. Although I've been busy all week with Devron's new brief and out every night with friends, I've been distracted, hoping he'll call just for the hell of it, just to say hi, but that doesn't seem to be his style.

'I'm on the Eurostar, so it might cut out. What are you doing tomorrow?' he says.

I have kept my Saturday free in the hope that I'll see him, but I'm bothered by his presumption that I'll have done this.

'Why?'

'Meet me at the Tate Modern at 5pm.'

'I'm not sure if I'm free.'

'I've got something for you, it won't keep.'

'What sort of something?'

'Trust me, you'll like it. The man in the shop said it'll be okay till 6pm Paris time, so don't be late.'

'We could meet earlier?' I'd like to spend a bit of the day together.

'I've got some errands. Meet me at the top of the slope?'

I wear a white cotton sundress that I bought in a New York flea market for five dollars. When I bought it two summers ago it was too tight, but I fell in love with the idea of one day fitting into it, and the fact that it cost less than the Thomas Keller chicken sandwich I'd just eaten. My wardrobe has a smattering of random, very cheap clothes like this, most of which will never fit, but when I try the dress on today it's perfect. I put on a pair of beautiful pale pink silk French knickers. And at the last minute, I grab the large brimmed floppy straw hat that I've never dared wear outside of my flat. I feel French. I feel pretty and delicate and like someone in a Vanessa Bruno advert, rather than someone who spends most of her life with perpetual underarm stubble.

Today is the first proper day of spring. As I walk along the embankment from Waterloo I feel like the person I always wanted to be: happy, confident, cool. God, I wish I could make myself feel like this every day. Men stare. Fashiony girls surreptitiously look with a mix of envy and admiration. I should wear this hat more often.

There's so much I want to do around here with James. Late night cocktails at the Festival Hall overlooking the Thames. A Sunday tea-dance at the Savoy with champagne and scones! Ice-skating, come winter, over at Somerset House. Afternoon Billy Wilder double-bills at the NFT. I browse the second-hand book stalls along the river and find a near-perfect copy of *Rapture* by Carol Ann Duffy. I'd love to buy it for James, but I suspect he'd be more comfortable with the John le Carré on the next table, or last year's *Top Gear* annual.

I have spent too long pottering. I'm fifteen minutes late and as I approach the Tate, I see James from a distance looking at his watch with an anxious frown. God, I love the size of him. He's so man-shaped, so masculine, so male. He's wearing

76

a navy coat and his dark blue Levis. This is a man who would never countenance wearing a pair of jeans with Lycra in them. He turns his head in my direction, then does a double take. I have to order myself not to break into a run towards him.

'Good hat,' he says, and kisses me for a full five minutes.

'For you.' He holds out a box wrapped in pistachio coloured paper with a big pink ribbon. 'I hope this kitten's got big lungs or you'll have one guilty conscience, Miss Klein.'

'If there's a dead cat in here it's your fault for kissing me so long,' I say.

'You shouldn't be such a temptress,' he says. 'Come on, open up before the RSPCA nick us.'

Inside the box is a Jean Clement praline millefeuille: a mythical dessert. The cakes in Jean Clement are displayed like diamonds on velvet casings. They cost more than diamonds, and the praline millefeuille is the Great Star of Africa. I once had a migraine that lasted three days, and a Jean Clement millefeuille cured it. They only make ten a day and if you're not in the queue when the store opens, you'll just have to take my word for it that you'll never put anything better in your mouth.

'I had to wrestle a very determined Japanese lady with a dead fox round her neck to get you this.'

'Oh my God. You're a very good boyfriend.' I kiss him and he smiles. 'Open wide,' I say, and attempt to feed him the cake.

77

He shakes his head. 'I bought it for you, Queen of Puddings.'

'I want you to have the first bite,' I say. He takes a small nibble then looks at me in wonder. 'Jesus, is that even legal?' He takes a bigger bite and pretends he's going to eat the whole thing. I wouldn't even begrudge him if he did, that is how much I fancy this man.

He grabs my hand and I follow him into the gallery. 'I read about this guy in the paper. I know how cultured you are,' he says. I don't know where he gets this idea from. Oh, yes – it was the fact that I mentioned a poet on the first night we met. I'm entirely not cultured, really. I like art and books and films but I can't explain Martin Kippenberger. The thought of seeing Ewan McGregor play Shakespeare leaves me cold, and I'd rather watch *Trading Places* than a Bergman film. However, I get the impression that his previous girlfriends spend a lot of time down the gym and consider Paolo Coelho the best writer in the world, so I guess in the kingdom of the blind. . . .

We kiss on all the escalators up to the fifth floor. If I was behind us on the escalators I'd hate us, we are so goddamned happy.

Tucked away in one of the smaller galleries is the entrance to a tiny exhibit with a grumpy security guard standing outside. A placard on the wall reads, 'The Beauty of the World, the Paragon of Animals.'

When the guard sees my dress he shakes his head. 'Put the boots on. And don't spend more than a couple of minutes in there, it's bad for your lungs,' he says ushering us through a door into a narrow corridor, lined with wellies. He closes the door behind us and we're in darkness, stumbling and giggling as we feel our way along the walls in ill-fitting boots, taking a sharp left, then a right. And then all of a sudden the tunnel ends and our eyes automatically shut and then slowly open against the light, and we're standing in a room full of sparkling silver glitter. Piles and piles of shimmering dots like a disco moonscape, dazzling and beautiful, shifting softly under our feet.

James dances me to the centre of the room and my dress does a perfect 50s prom twirl, and he laughs in delight. He grabs a handful of the dust and throws it up into the air, and it falls like rainbows of light down on us and suddenly he lifts me up and we kiss passionately and before I know it he has pulled my knickers to one side and he is inside me and I am thinking this hat is going to fall off and laughing and panicking and I don't want him to stop but I'm scared the guard is going to come in and wondering if there is CCTV in this room and thinking well if this footage ends up on YouTube at least the hat will hide my face and wondering if anyone else has done this in here and then I don't even care if the guard comes in and finally I am not thinking anything at all.

'I can't believe you shagged him in public just because he bought you a cake, you are such a cheap date,' says Pete, placing a third double gin and tonic and a packet of Tyrell's in front of me.

'Trust me, that cake was not cheap,' I say, ripping open the bag of crisps. I have told Pete about the incident in the gallery because I am very drunk.

The reason I am very drunk is because I feel insecure, because I have not spoken to James since Monday morning when he left my flat, and it is now Thursday night. So I have dragged Pete to my local, the Prince Alfred, and have banged my head twice in the last hour en route to the bar, on the low wooden partitions that carve up the pub into snug little areas.

I have not told Pete about how James and I spent all of Sunday walking in Regent's Park, holding hands and talking about our shared family values, because he will find this nauseating, and like any right-thinking person he is only interested in hearing about the sex.

I have also not told Pete about the way James looks at me – like he's amazed and surprised that he found me. He smiles all the time. Because I have no context for him, no mutual friends, I have no idea if this means he's specifically happy to be with me, or is generally a very happy man. Either way, it is contagious, and I find myself smiling too. Except for now, when I am not smiling at all.

'He sent me a text on Monday,' I say.

'So what's your problem?' says Pete, who it's fair to say, is neither the paranoid nor the romantic type.

'It said "I had a wonderful time with you".'

'And?'

'Something's not right.' Laura says he must be hiding something.

'Women are so neurotic. He's saying he had a great time, what more do you want?'

'I want to know when I'm seeing him again. We've been seeing each other for nearly two months, this isn't normal.'

'Look, Soph, this guy is not Nick. Nick didn't have a job.'

'Nick's a musician.'

'Which is basically the same as being unemployed, so he had loads of time to sit around writing you faggy romantic emails. This guy runs a business, plus he's older. He's busy. I hate it when girls text me all the time.'

I'm not texting James 'all the time'. At all, in fact. I am being very careful not to treat him like I treated Nick. I'd text Nick to tell him the filling of my sandwich because I was fundamentally bored in my old job, and because Nick was also bored pottering around our flat. Eventually we bored each other and then we split up.

I can be guarded and I can be cool and I can hold back, but at the same time today I saw a man on the bus with a moustache that was so long it curled round his ears and I would like to tell James about this moustache because it would make him laugh, and yet I feel I can't. And that is why I'm not happy.

'He'll call. Now tell me about the bit with the glitter again.'

I wake early the next day, hung-over. Outside the sky is already bright and from my bedroom window I can just see a patch of daffodils pushing through, down by the banks of the canal. I consider going for a walk to clear my head – past the colourful boats and vast white stucco houses – then think better of it and climb back under my duvet to replay last night's conversation.

According to Pete, there's nothing untoward about James's behaviour. My instinct tells me something is strange, but I can't put my finger on it.

When James is with me, he's highly attentive.

He notices everything. If I apply lip balm when he's popped to the loo, he'll notice as soon as he walks back in. Not gloss. Clear lip balm. Nick wouldn't have noticed if I'd grown a Salvador Dali moustache and started speaking Aramaic, as long as I was still padding around the flat.

If I leave the room, James asks where I'm going.

When I'm cooking a meal, he'll watch me, try to impress me, touch me.

When we're in bed he is generous and energetic and passionate. He has the libido of a man half his age.

Afterwards we lie for hours having iPod shuffle conversations, flicking from time travel to Bernie Winters to why mosquitoes don't get AIDS. We should be sleeping. Our combined age is seventy-eight, we both have work in the morning. It's 3.47, 2.48, 4.15am. Neither of us ever wants to stop the conversation. Eventually we fall asleep, my hand curled around his fingers.

But when he's not with me, I feel like 'we' don't exist. The randomness of meeting someone in a bar, of having no mutual friends, of having entirely separate lives, is brought home. He could disappear and I would never cross paths with him again. Sometimes I wake up and wonder if he's even real.

On days when we don't speak, I feel laden down with the things I didn't get to share with him. He won't call for two, three days. Then, it's like he has a CCTV on my psyche, and at the precise mid-point between when I've done a deal with the devil so that he'll call, and the point at which I think fuck you, James Stephens, this is not acceptable, he'll ring. My anxiety will be punctured, he'll come round and we'll carry on mid-conversation where we left off, and I'll realise I am a paranoid, silly woman.

Come on, paranoid, silly woman – get out of bed. Go to work.

It's four in the morning on Good Friday. James and I are at his house, lying in bed, facing each other. My head is resting on his arm. Everything feels so entirely natural and comfortable and right. I think we are falling in love. He looks at me intently. 'What's wrong with you, Sophie Klein? There must be something.'

'Plenty.'

He shakes his head.

'I'm impatient,' I say. 'I'm not very thoughtful. I never remember birthdays. I forget to send my godchildren cards at Christmas. I'm greedy. I'm sarcastic. Sometimes I get a bit depressed and can't shrug it off.'

He shakes his head again. 'No, you don't. You're generous. You're a good woman.' Why does that sound so church-y?

'What's wrong with you, James Stephens?'

He pauses and shrugs. He doesn't answer. He will never show a weakness. He is a master at evading questions.

84

'Say something.' I mean say something nice. I feel like I'm trying to force a compliment out of him and I know this is bad but he's looking at me like he adores me, but nothing is coming out of his mouth.

'Who was the last person you went out with before me?' I ask.

'Svetlana.'

Beautiful Russians are two a penny in this city. James has a lot of pennies. I see these women slicing down Bond Street, hard bodies, steely eyes, spiky boots; russet-faced older men in bad jackets dragging behind in their wake.

'How long did that last?'

'Two years.'

'Why did it end?'

'It wasn't going anywhere.'

'Why not?'

'I couldn't talk to her the way I can talk to you.'

'What did you do for two years?'

He raises his eyebrows and gives me a look that instantly makes me regret having asked the question. I turn to face the window and James's arm wraps itself around my waist.

'Sophie Klein. I haven't felt this way about anyone in twenty years.' I turn back to look at him. 'I am truly myself with you.'

He is telling me the truth.

*

85

I love him, I love him, I love him.

I love the way he moves his fingers when he explains something. I love the way he loses his temper with an obnoxious waiter at exactly the same point that I would. I love the fact that I can flick a spoonful of spaghetti with meatballs at him and he doesn't have a hissy fit that I've stained his shirt. I love talking to him and I love looking at him and I love thinking about him.

★

It is a rainy Saturday night in April and I'm teaching James the secret of a foolproof Yorkshire pudding, when my mother rings.

'Have you spoken to your brother?' she says.

'What's wrong?'

'You're not going to believe what that lunatic girlfriend of his is up to . . .'

'Go on . . .'

'She's booked a Caesarean for the third week in August.'

'Isn't the baby due at the start of September?' I say.

'Exactly!'

'So how does . . .'

'She's *having it* two weeks *early* so that *it's the same star sign as her*!' No amount of italics can convey the utter disdain in my mother's voice.

'Jesus, what is wrong with her?' I say. 'Is that even safe?'

'Apparently. Sheer lunacy. And your bloody brother's saying he can't see what all the fuss is about. I said to him . . .'

'Mum, my Yorkshire puddings have just pinged . . . I can't talk . . .'

'I haven't even told you what dreadful names they're thinking of calling my first grandchild . . .'

'It'll have to wait.'

I hang up and explain Shellii to James.

'All women are mad,' he says, again. This time I can't really disagree.

After dinner, James asks what's for pudding.

'An experiment,' I say. 'Step into my office.'

He follows me to the fridge. Inside are two large pots of custard sent by Will at Appletree, as Phase 1 of the new custard project Devron's briefed me on.

'Take your tie off and sit down. . . .' I wrap it round his eyes in a blindfold and he screams 'Help!'

'Just be quiet and focus on your mouth,' I say.

'Can't we focus a bit lower down?'

'Mouth first.' I take the custards out and put a spoon in each. 'First one – what does this taste of?' I say.

'Custard. I could do your job, Soph!'

'Ha, funny. What else?'

'Vanilla?'

'And?'

'Something with alcohol?'

87

'Good. Bourbon! Now have a sip of water.' I carefully pass over a glass, and he deliberately misses his mouth and pours half of it down his shirt, and then takes it off and drops it on the floor.

'Would sir like a bib?' I say.

'Can't we do this naked?'

'Health and Safety 101! Ok, second custard – what does this one taste of?'

'Custard,' he says.

'Very clever. What else?'

'Maple syrup?'

'Bingo. And does it make you want to eat anything else?'

'You!' he says.

'Engage your brain.'

'. . . maybe something crunchy?'

'Ten out of ten! Your brain's making a connection between the maple syrup and granola. So I might take this custard and create a dessert that has a layer of almond granola, then the custard, and then something lighter on top, three different textures. With this flavour profile I'd want something less sweet, that complements the custard . . .'

'How about my cock?'

'Great idea! Not sure it can feed 40,000 Fletchers shoppers each week . . .'

'We'll start with just the one, shall we?' he says, taking his blindfold off, unzipping his fly and taking his pants down.

'James, do not put your penis in my custard samples. I have to feed those to Devron on Monday. James! Stop it!'

'You told me you don't like Devron anyway,' he says.

'True, but I do like this custard!'

Too late.

My boyfriend is a custard-covered dick, and I adore him.

*

'Devron, I'm sorry but the custard samples aren't ready for tasting,' I say on Monday morning.

'Fine, what are you doing on May 3rd?'

Two weeks' time – no idea. James is rubbish at forward planning, but as he invariably ends up asking to see me at the weekends, I'm now avoiding making plans with other people.

'Why, Devron?'

'I need you to do a quick New York inspiration trip. If I don't complete last year's number of trips within a month of year-end financials, I won't get like for like in this year's allowance.'

Cool. So, because you have to tick a box on a sheet, I get a free trip to New York! Devron, I'm warming to you.

'Is there actually anything you need me to do out there?'

'Yeah, go for a night, have a look at a few cakes and whatnot, take some photos.'

'For one night?'

'Budget's only going to pay for one night in a hotel.'

I love New York too much for a one-night stand.

'I'll stay at a friend's, then can I go for a bit longer? If I stay a Saturday night, the airfare's always cheaper.'

'Fine, go for a long weekend, just come back with an idea I can take to the board. I want to show them what success looks like.'

★

New York! New York! I email my old friend Pauly asking if I can stay at his place for a few nights, and a minute later he mails back a yes.

It's Saturday night and I'm off to meet James at the pub. As I leave my block of flats I see someone waving at me as they're getting out of a black cab.

It's my neighbour, Amber: part-time sarong designer and full-time halfwit.

Amber has seen James and me get in to his car several times. Each time she has stared, looking confused.

Now she rushes over to me with her miniature schnauzer, Annalex, in tow, and grabs my arm. 'Sophie, long time . . . who is that guy you're always with? Is that your brother, is he back from the States?'

'No. That's my boyfriend.'

'Really?! I never think of you as someone who goes out with a Porsche driver.'

Welcome to Amber-World.

'It's not a Porsche, it's a Maserati 3200GT.' I have not told anybody about James's car because I am mildly embarrassed by his money, but I take pleasure in telling Amber. 'Anyway, what do you mean by that?'

'You know, you go out with struggling artist types. Does your boyfriend have any single mates?'

I think about Rob. Rob would love Amber – she is a size 4, has no body fat and sports a permanent Ibiza tan. Tonight she is dressed in cowboy boots, tiny denim shorts and a cutaway silver vest.

'Yes, his friend Rob. He's really handsome, thirty-six, *he* drives a Porsche, works for Goldman Sachs . . .'

Her eyes couldn't be any wider if she'd necked a fistful of Es.

'Oh. Sorry, Amber, I forgot – he's engaged . . . Oh well. Anyway, aren't you still seeing Ritchie?'

She shrugs. This shrug means 'I am thirty-one, very soon I will have to stop dating sexy rock 'n' roll wannabe music-producer cokeheads, and bag myself a pudgy older Notting Hill banker. He'll give me shitloads of cash to do up a huge three-storey second home with a pool in Oxfordshire and then I can ride horses and shag the local talent while the au pair looks after the kids and Rory bankrolls my Moroccan scented candle business.'

'By the way, remember that £100 I lent you . . .' I say, as she hands the cabbie a £50 note.

This always works like a charm whenever I want to get rid of Amber and sure enough, as she takes the £30 change from the cabbie, she says, 'Babe, I'm totally skint at the

moment but I'll pop round soon,' and hurries into our
block.

★

James and I are three months into our relationship and I
haven't met any of his friends yet, apart from Rob. Laura
thinks this is sinister, but I don't – he hasn't met any of
mine, apart from her. Most of his friends have kids. James
says he doesn't want to share me with anyone. We keep
each other endlessly entertained.

But now Laura has made me feel paranoid. So at the
pub on Saturday I invited James round for dinner with Pete
tonight. Perhaps if I introduce James to more of my friends
he'll follow suit. Besides, he'll get on well with Pete – they're
both juvenile, charming, fun. Maybe James might register
that Pete has a residual crush on me – perhaps it'll make
him more vocal in his affections.

When James left my flat this morning I said 'Pete's coming
at 7pm.' He nodded. I haven't heard from him since. Although
I reason I'll see him later, when he hasn't rung by 7.40pm,
I have a low ache in my stomach, and it isn't hunger.

The chicken will be ready any minute. Pete's asking if
we should invite my sexy blonde neighbour instead.

James must be working late.

At 7.50pm I take the chicken out, put it under foil and
call James.

'Hello you,' he says.

'Where are you?' I say.

'At home.'

'Are you coming for dinner or what?'

'Sure, see you soon.'

'That was weird,' I say to Pete.

'What? He's coming, isn't he?'

'He is now.'

James arrives looking slightly nervous. The two shake hands and from their posture I sense a mild rivalry in the air.

'So, are you a North Londoner too?' says Pete. I've already told him all the facts about James, but I've forced these two together and Pete's having to make small talk.

'East,' says James. 'Woodford, born and bred.'

'My cousins grew up there. What school did you go to?'

'Forest.'

'Do you know Alex and Adam Foster, twins?'

'One of them amazing at football?' says James.

'Alex.'

'Rings a bell.'

I am delighted that there is now a common link as it brings me closer to James.

With a glass of wine they relax and turn their

conversation to cars and girls, as though I'm not here. James says Pete's Saab is a weird choice for a bloke in his thirties, and Pete says Maseratis are for hairdressers and they both laugh. Pete says his ideal woman would be half Danish, half Brazilian, while apparently my boyfriend's would be eastern European, definitely.

My grandfather was Polish. Does that count?

I ask Pete to help carve the chicken, and in the kitchen he whispers to me, 'I was expecting some hunk. He's just a normal looking bloke.'

'Don't you think he looks young for his age?'

'No, he looks like a 45-year-old who eats a lot of cheese.'

'You're just jealous,' I say.

'Seriously, Soph, he's punching above his weight.'

Because of James's utter self-belief, the confidence that emanates from every pore of him, I always think of it as the other way round. Like I'm punching above mine.

'Anyway, what do you think Pete?'

'Seems alright.'

'And?'

'What do you want me to say?'

'. . . Don't you find him fascinating?'

'He's just a man who sells socks.'

'Shut up, he's coming.'

★

95

'Eat some more chicken, Soph, you're looking too skinny,' says Pete.

'Do you think?' says James, raising an eyebrow.

'You need to put a bit of weight back on,' says Pete, looking at my arms.

'Don't tell her that!' says James.

Pete only thinks I'm too skinny because he likes big boobs. It's true my boobs are smaller than they used to be, but that's always the way when you lose weight. If only I could transplant the small handful of flab left on my bottom to my tits, I'd be laughing, but if I do lose any more weight, I'll have no bust left, so I'm happy enough where I am.

I head back to the kitchen to take the ice cream out of the freezer and make coffee. When I return, Pete's already putting on his jacket.

'You're leaving?' I say, 'we haven't even had dessert . . .'

'I'm really sorry, hon, I have an early meeting. We'll catch up properly when you're back from New York.'

He sends me a text on his way home: 'Thanks for dinner. You seem very happy. I'm glad x.'

In bed later, I turn to James. 'You're a bugger to make plans with, you know that?'

'What do you mean?'

'It's infuriating, I mean I didn't know if you were coming tonight or not.'

'I said I was, didn't I?'

'You were actually quite non-committal. I feel like if I hadn't phoned you, you wouldn't have turned up at all.'

He shrugs.

'And I never know when I'm going to see you next. What's all that about?' I say.

He looks back at me as if he's keeping a secret.

'What is it? Are you scared?' It's scary for me too, being vulnerable.

'I'm not scared,' he says.

I say nothing but he's better at this silent tactic than I am.

'What is it?' I blurt, after what feels like a full minute.

'I'm just getting to know you, slowly.'

Wouldn't it be nice if we could just get on with this? I think. You're heading to fifty, I'm thirty-four this year – we're not teenagers anymore. Does he not realise that?

I feel like I'm so far down the road of saying something that I might as well follow through, though I have to take a deep breath before I do.

'Slowly, quickly . . . you're either in it or you're not,' I say.

He nods, looks at me and smiles. His smile: beautiful.

On Friday morning James drops me at Paddington for the Heathrow Express. I could walk, it's only ten minutes from my front door, but he insists.

'You want to make sure I'm leaving town!' I say. 'You're not out with Rob tonight by any chance?'

'No, quiet weekend, honest, Guv.' He holds three fingers up in a boy scout salute. '– Behave yourself with this Paul person . . .' he says, frowning.

'I didn't know you were the jealous type,' I say, taking his hand and running my finger along one of his knuckles. He has the tiniest scar, like a white eyelash, just to the right of the bone.

'I'm not,' he says. 'I just know what men are like.'

'You mean you know what you're like,' I say, raising an eyebrow.

'Hurry up, you'll miss your train,' he says, grabbing my face in both hands and kissing me.

I hate goodbyes.

★

New York is great; New York always is.

I stay at Pauly's apartment in Tribeca. I met Pauly seven years ago, queuing for a table outside Corner Bistro in the West Village. It was midnight. I'd hopped in a cab straight from JFK to West 4th Street. Pauly had staggered over from the White Horse Tavern, having just split from another poor girl who was at the tiresome stage of demanding a smidgen of emotional intimacy from him. We bonded standing in line with beers, then sitting with cheeseburgers. We carried on after at a dive bar in Chinatown where Pauly explained how the CIA *and* Sinatra *and* Castro killed Kennedy. I kissed him just to shut him up, then made out with him on the rooftop until 8am. (Pauly has some insane conspiracy theories, but he's so hot and so good-natured, you can forgive him most things.)

Over French toast with strawberry butter the following morning, he explained how he'd never gotten over being dumped by Carissa, his volatile high-school girlfriend, the week before prom night, and how his whole twenties had been spent working through a series of beautiful women, trying to find crazy Carissa 2.0.

I realised quickly that Pauly would be a terrible love interest but a great friend. Like me he'll happily eat a bowl of $4 hand-pulled noodles down an alley off Mott Street, then trek north twenty-five blocks to queue for an hour at the Gramercy Tavern for their $12 warm chocolate bread pudding with cocoa nib ice cream.

Pauly seems to have finally met his match in Giovanna who sounds like the perfect lunatic for him: she thinks George Bush engineered 9/11 and that there were no planes, only holograms. She designs erotic underwear, and is currently in Milan on a buying trip. Even though she's only been dating Pauly a month, she's currently got him living in her Nolita apartment over on Elizabeth Street, babysitting her Schnoodles, Basquiat and Warhol. This is a total result – not only do I not have to hang around with an insane woman who owns a pair of Schnoodles, but it means I have Pauly's place all to myself.

Pauly works in the music business and his place is small but supremely cool, with a giant projector screen instead of a TV, and one sleek silver remote control that seems to govern everything from his state of the art espresso machine to the bathtub. Best of all, the apartment has one wall made entirely of glass with the most amazing views of Brooklyn Bridge.

I wish James was here with me, he'd love it, I think, as I hurriedly unpack the handful of clothes I've brought. Still, if there's one city I know how to have fun in regardless, it's this one. I head out the door and walk north on Broadway towards Soho.

It's the first week of May, and the weather's a perfect 75 degrees with cloudless blue skies. I'm so unbelievably lucky that this is my day job, I think, as I pull open the door of Dean and Deluca and feel the air-con start to cool me down.

I'm meeting Pauly in a few hours up by the Lincoln Centre, so I grab a tuna sandwich for now. I dream about these sandwiches: the perfect softness of the white bread, the fineness of the red onions, the saltiness of the capers, the ratio of mayo to tuna, the little fronds of almost sweet fresh dill – I've tried to recreate these at home but they're never quite the same.

I spend the next twenty minutes in the store admiring the packaging of the spices, another twenty in the fruit and veg section marvelling at the price tags. I then head west along Bleeker Street to Rocco's for a chocolate chip cannoli, up to Chelsea Farmer's Market to pick up some Fat Witch caramel brownies for Maggie, then hop on the subway uptown for a night out, Pauly-style.

We go to three tequila-soaked Cinco de Mayo parties, and end up wearing purple sombreros, eating guacamole and drinking pomegranate margaritas at Rosa Mexicana, where they make the best guacamole north of Mexico. I think I could live solely on Mexican food for the rest of my life: they put chocolate in their chicken casseroles, they eat avocados every day, and limes, chillies and burritos (my three favourite food groups) are the founding pillars of their national cuisine. Around midnight, we swing by the roof party of a rapper with diamond teeth – James will never, ever believe me – and after a final Old Fashioned at a Lower East Side dive bar, I call it a night.

I spend the following days mostly hung-over, visiting

farmers' markets and bakeries, restaurants dedicated just to puddings, and mobile Bolivian food-carts in Queens. I eat desserts from 3 boroughs, 4 continents, 26 countries, without ever leaving the city. In the evenings, Pauly and I go to gallery openings in Chelsea, secret late-night speak-easies in the East Village and one cocktail bar staffed entirely by Stevie Nicks lookalikes.

I am having an exhausting but amazing time, and yet I can't wait to fly back and see James. I text him to tell him I've just seen a man feeding a giant Hyacinth Macaw an Arnold Palmer in Madison Square Gardens. He texts me back saying, 'I'll feed you my Arnold Palmer when you get home,' and I snigger like Sid James. When I roll in drunk at 2am I send him a photo of the Brooklyn Bridge at night, its strings of light reflected in the East River. He sends me back a photo of his feet resting on the coffee table in his living room – Sainsbury's ready meal in the foreground, Spurs on the telly in the background.

On my final night I take Pauly back to Corner Bistro for dinner to thank him for letting me stay. I want to take him somewhere fancier but he's adamant he wants a burger. I don't push it – I know there isn't a burger in London that comes close.

I tell Pauly briefly about how things are going with James, how he's so vague and non-committal with arrangements.

'How old did you say this guy was? He's older, right?'

102

'Oh, old, forty-five,' I say. 'So what, you think it's just a generation thing?' I say, hopefully.

Pauly looks at me with pity. 'No, sweetheart, I don't think that's it.'

'Well what?' I say, putting down my burger, feeling suddenly nervous.

'He's late forties, attractive and rich?'

'Yeah, so?'

'And you haven't met his friends?'

'He's met a couple of mine.'

'Not the same thing. You say he travels a lot?'

'He does business all over the place, the Far East, Europe. All over. Factories, investors . . . what?'

'But he's away regularly?'

I count the number of times James has gone away for business since I met him. Maybe six.

'What, Pauly? Just say it, you're worrying me.'

'I hate to break it to you, but I think your dude's married.'

I laugh, relieved. 'He's not married. Definitely not. He stayed over last Saturday and Sunday. And Monday. There's no way his wife wouldn't twig.'

'Maybe he tells *her* he's away on business.'

'His phone's always on, she'd call.' Now I think about it, I'm not sure I've ever heard it ring. Maybe it's on silent . . .

'He has two cell phones, cheaters always do,' says Pauly, grabbing some fries from my plate. 'There's a wife.'

103

'No, definitely not. I've been to his house, no trace of one.'

'Okay, maybe not a wife but it sounds like there's another woman, maybe several.'

You know what? I have a lot of time for Pauly but I'm not going to take advice from a guy whose longest relationship was three and a half months, and who expresses doubts that man ever landed on the moon.

'Look, he's just a commitment-phobe, plain and simple.'

'No. Something's up. If you're okay to keep going, just taking these crumbs he's giving you, that's cool – but that doesn't sound like your style.'

'Let's change the subject. Where are we going for pudding?'

*

On my way to the airport the following evening, I replay what Pauly was saying about James offering me 'crumbs', and how little I'm demanding from him. Maybe I should say something the next time I see him . . .

Then, as I board my flight, I get a text from James saying, 'I'll pick you up tomorrow at 7pm, you choose the restaurant.' Now that's more like it.

I open my front door to him and his eyes widen and he breaks into a grin.

'Nice top,' he says, kissing me.

'You like? $20 from Loehmanns.'

'I like. Where are we eating? Claridges? The Ivy?'

'God, no,' I say. 'Head west, my treat.'

We are halfway through dinner at my favourite, favourite restaurant, Number One Thai, off Ladbroke Grove. Under the table our legs are touching and when I tell him about all the places I went to in New York, he says, 'Next time I'm coming with you.' (He doesn't believe me about the diamond teeth.)

I pop to the toilet and as I come back to the table he grabs my waist, pulls me toward him and kisses me, holding the back of my head with both hands. I love you, James Stephens. I do, I do.

'So your friend, Paul . . .' he says.

'Pauly, yes?'

'Did he try it on then? I bet he did . . .'

'Of course not, he's got some crazy sexy Italian girlfriend.'

'But you used to have a thing with him.'

'Not at all, just a snog, years ago. It was nothing, we didn't have sex or anything.'

'I don't believe you,' he says.

'We didn't! We just fooled around, it was all very innocent.'

'I still don't think it's right that you stayed at his apartment.'

'Why ever not? He wasn't even there!'

'It's just . . . I don't know.'

'There's nothing whatsoever to be jealous about,' I say.

'I'm not jealous. I just think it's odd. One of you must fancy the other one . . .'

'Just because you can't be friends with a woman you don't want to shag doesn't mean other men can't . . . now please could you pour me some wine?'

He fills my glass up.

'It's not right,' he says.

'James, I've told you all about Pauly. I'm being totally honest with you because I'm trying to be a grown-up. Because I like you.'

I lift my glass to my mouth and smile, but James looks like he's been slapped.

'What? What's wrong?' I say.

He takes a long breath.

'What is it, are you okay?' I say. He suddenly looks queasy with nerves.

He nods slowly.

'Ever since I met you, since that first night, I've felt there was something very special about you . . .'

Oh my God. He's going to propose.

'And I've tried to keep my distance but when I'm not with you I miss you . . .'

He's going to propose!

'And when I don't speak to you, I just want to call you . . .'

HE IS GOING TO PROPOSE!

'But there's a problem.'

He's not going to propose.

'What is it?' I say. 'Are you okay?' Jesus, he's terminally ill.

He's looking at me with a helplessness in his eyes. I reach out my hand and put it over his and he looks up at me with pain.

'What is it James? It's okay. You can tell me. You can tell me. It's okay, whatever it is.'

He looks like he's struggling with a dreadful secret. He's married. Fucking hell. Pauly was right and he fucking *is* married. Or he has HIV. At this point in the relationship, I don't know which would be worse. If he's married, I can't see him again, really, but maybe he's separated. It would

107

make sense of all the disappearing, the not calling. HIV – well, you can live a long and happy life nowadays. We'd have to work out whether we adopted, or tried to have kids, but it's manageable, it really is . . .

'James, it's okay. Please, tell me.'

'. . . I'm worried . . . you're not my normal type . . . physically . . .'

I. Am. Dumbstruck.

'The other night . . . when I fell asleep . . .'

I can't really remember. Oh yes, we had loads of pasta and red wine, and he passed out around midnight . . .

'Yes?' I say.

'Normally I'd still want to make love even if I was tired, but I didn't . . .'

Oh my good God.

'But I do tonight,' he says.

Why thank you. How excessively charitable of you.

'Look, Soph, I know I'm no Adonis, but . . .'

BUT WHAT? You're rich and male so it doesn't matter?

'Let's get the bill,' I say. I feel like I am about to vomit. I want to go home.

I urgently wave the waitress over and the bill comes. £38.70.

'Let me, please,' he says, reaching for it.

'Oh no, I said I'd pay,' I say. Do you really think £38.70 gets you off the hook, you utter, utter dickhead?

★

I am in severe shock. After he has dropped me home, I puke.

And it is only after vomiting that the fury kicks in: what he said, and just as importantly, where he said it.

I will never, ever be able to go back to Number One Thai again, and for this, as much as everything else, I think I hate him.

I wake up at 3.30am from the flashing blue light of my phone. Suddenly the man's a teenage text-a-holic.

'I'm not saying this to make you feel better but I had the best time ever with you. Always.'

Splendid. This serves to make me feel three times more hurt and twice as angry.

Because to me what that means is this: your looks are too great an obstacle for me to overcome, in spite of the fact that I have spent months willing myself to fall in love with you.

Therefore he also means: every time I slept with you it was an ordeal which I endured because I wanted to hang out with you so much in the non-horizontal time in our relationship.

And I think – no one put a gun to your head, James. Or your penis.

I turn my phone off and drift back to sleep.

I dream of James sitting alone in a vast warehouse filled with boy's toys – a pinball machine, a table tennis table, a floor-standing Pacman console. He is smiling bravely but he looks like he's faking it.

My subconscious is not really pushing the boat out on this one, I have to say. I was hoping for some giant spiders, or at the very least James to morph into my dead dad halfway through. Disappointed.

★

When I turn on my phone the following morning I have two missed calls. I assume now that he's lost me as an option he suddenly wants me back, but the calls are from my grandma's number. Two calls, too early in the morning.

I call straight back and Evie says come round. My grandma's had a bad night.

I find my grandma under the impression that the flat is full of Stasi.

I sit with her for an hour, stroking her brow, and she calms down and then perks up momentarily. 'Have you ever met my best friend Cecily?' she says, her left hand resting almost weightlessly on my knee.

I shake my head, even though I took my grandma to Cecily's funeral six years ago.

'What a creature!' she sighs. 'We used to have such fun together. When your father and I got married, he asked her to be his best man. We used to call ourselves "the horse stealers".'

'Why?'

'We were fearless.' Her grip on my arm tightens. 'We knew we could take on the world.'

He has called every day for five days but left no messages.

Here's the thing: it makes no sense. 'I didn't want to make love to you six days ago, but I do today.' Six days ago I had the same face and the same body. In fact, six days ago I was younger, and, pre-New York, thinner.

I don't believe it's actually anything to do with me not being his type. It's either his ego's need for a trophy, or his fear of commitment. Whatever the problem is, I reckon it's about his head, not my body.

And while I'm furious and crushed, I still yearn for him. I feel it in my ribcage, this desperate desire to get in my car, drive to his house and join my body with his, my heart, my mouth.

I'm scared he'll give up and stop calling me.

Some of my best friends are black and white.

Pete and Laura come round with bags of food from Ottolenghi. I'd told them not to, that I've lost my appetite,

111

but they know me better than that and they've chosen everything I love most: the aubergine salad, the chargrilled broccoli, the apple and sultana cake.

'I'm going to call him back,' I say.

'No way,' says Laura.

'No,' says Pete. 'You're not.'

'I have to,' I say.

'Turn your back on him,' says Laura. 'He's not good enough for you.'

'What he said was not okay,' says Pete.

'That's rich, coming from you!' I say to Pete, 'What about Marcella?' The girl he dumped for saying 'Ciao' all the time.

'I never told her it was because she had an annoying verbal tick,' he says,

'She was Italian!' I say.

'Don't compare me to James,' says Pete.

'You don't understand,' I say. 'He's just tactless, he blurts out exactly what he thinks. . . .' Normally I find this trait endearing; normally I'm not on the receiving end of it.

'He's forty-five, I think he should have learnt to censor his more unpalatable thoughts,' says Laura. 'You're not on this planet to teach a middle-aged man how to be a grown-up.'

'Look, I know it sounds bad but you weren't there so you don't understand the context,' I say.

'He only beats me 'cause he loves me? Come on, Sophie, get a grip,' says Laura.

I feel my face flush with shame. 'You wouldn't say that if you'd seen him.' Laura flashes Pete a look of incredulity. 'Laura. He looked incredibly uncomfortable when he said it. I think it was very hard for him.'

'Oooh, poor him,' says Pete.

'Yeah, poor him,' says Laura, 'shall we send him a card, Pete? Some flowers?'

'Stop it. I know you are trying to protect me, but I need to hear what he has to say. And I want to tell him what I have to say. So I'm going to call him tomorrow.'

'It's a bad idea,' says Laura.

'Very bad,' says Pete.

'I have to see this thing through. Everyone deserves a second chance.' And besides, I'm too far gone.

I look at my body in the mirror and here's what I see:

Relatively recent clavicles and collarbones that please me.

Breasts that are losing buoyancy and looked better a year ago when I was a size 14.

Good arms. Toned, no bingo wings.

A small, curvy waist.

Hip bones – three months ago they started to stick out. I love this; it makes me feel I could be a backing dancer in a Christina Aguilera video.

Legs – not my best feature. Too chunky, too short, the knees and ankles nowhere near birdlike. But generally toned

113

and muscular apart from the bit at the bottom of my bottom, which is still flabby. I figure if I ran twenty minutes every day for six weeks, it'd be gone. I know I will never be bothered enough to do this.

Dimples on my thighs – a smattering, which, like my freckles, only come out in the sun. Skinny women have cellulite too . . .

I take out the tape measure. Waist – 22 inches. Hips – 40 inches (that was 44 this time last year.) Bust – 32D. I'll never be on the cover of Sports Illustrated. Such is life.

I try to look at my body through James's eyes:

Legs – too short. Distance between knee and hip – should be at least one inch longer, preferably three.

Area between knee and mid-calf – not indented sufficiently.

Hips – too wide.

Stretch marks on hips.

Bottom – very large. Flabby.

Cellulite – on thighs. Unacceptable.

Bones – generally – too wide.

Arms – good? Hadn't really noticed.

Breasts – breasts of a 33-year-old woman. Not ideal.

And then through the only lens that's actually worth looking through:

Knees, ankles – same as my father's. Inherited along with the ability to see the funny side of things, trusting people who shouldn't be trusted, a love of the world.

Waist – from my mother's side. Inherited along with a quickness to judge, a fear of abandonment, a generosity that is inconsistent but magnificent when it comes.

Hands, feet – from my father's mother. Inherited along with a passion for food, a fighting spirit, an utter inability to cope with boredom.

Hips – from my mother's mother. Inherited along with a warmth that meant her seven grandchildren called her every day without being nagged to do so by their parents.

Cellulite – all my own work. From a lifetime of putting a love of food and pleasure above exercise. That'll be the way the cookie crumbles.

On the basis of the above, I'm doing just fine.

James picks up on the sixth ring. I imagine he's wondering whether to give me a taste of my own medicine by not answering, but he's itching to see what I'm going to say. I know exactly what I'm going to say – I've rehearsed it all morning.

'Hello,' he says.

'Hi,' I say. 'Are you well?'

'I'm okay. You?'

'Yup,' I say. Does he want me to be devastated or not

115

give a damn? I have no idea. 'Why have you been calling me?' I say.

There is a long pause. 'I think I might have made a mistake,' he says.

My heart leaps.

'You think?' I say.

'I'm confused,' he says.

'I'm not,' I say. 'I'm thirty-three and I know who I am, and I know what I want. You should too, at your age. You said you were ready for a commitment.'

'I am . . . just not necessarily with you.'

'For God's sake, listen to yourself – you're an idiot. If you don't fancy me, why have you been having sex with me for the last three months?'

'I do fancy you, I'm just not sure I fancy you enough to sustain a long-term relationship.'

I take a deep breath. 'Listen: you are forty-five and single and you say you want to get married. Whatever your "type" is, that "type" clearly hasn't been working out for you so well. Some men have a turning point in their lives where they realise what long-term relationships are all about. Love isn't all about crazy hot sex in a glass lift. It's about finding someone you fancy and like and respect and who you can be yourself with. Find that and you're very, very lucky. The reason I'm calling you back is because I don't think you're a total idiot; I think you might be smart enough to grow up and realise that.'

116

There is a long silence at the other end of the line.

'I want to see you tomorrow,' he says.

'You can't, I'm visiting a factory.'

'I'll come and pick you up.'

'No, you won't, it's in Sheffield,' I say.

'What time do you finish?'

'What difference?'

'What's the address?'

'I'm not telling you.'

'I'll call your boss and offer him a grand to tell me.'

'Suit yourself,' I say.

'Seriously, I want to see you.'

'Why?'

'Because.'

'Because what?'

'Because,' he says.

'Well, I finish at 5pm, so I'll see you if I see you,' I say.

'Give me the address.'

I hang up. This is a man who always gets what he wants. If he wants the address, let him get it.

Favourite part of my job: Phase 4 meetings.

Second favourite part of my job: factory visits.

Appletree is my favourite supplier. Will, my contact there, is a total sweetheart, the most kind, forgiving man in the world. His wife ran off with her second cousin a few years ago, and all he's ever said about it is that 'things happen for a reason'; yeah, the reason being his ex-wife's a weird, cousin-shagging slapper.

I'm here today to see the next stage of development on custard desserts, as per Devron's instructions. Appletree have been working on the triple layer granola, custard and cream pudding, some flavoured custards (raspberry, ultra-vanilla and butterscotch) – and a flummery – a traditional old English pudding based on oats. Oats are cheap; margins should be high.

'You're looking very gorgeous,' says Will, kissing me hello.

I'm wearing a strappy red sundress, wedge heels, and

good make-up – just in case. 'I might be meeting a friend later,' I say.

'A friend! Oh . . .' says Will. 'I have something for you.' Will always picks me up from the train station with a little treat for the ten-minute drive to the factory. It's hot today and he's brought a mini icebox, inside of which is a rhubarb and custard flavoured ice cream. 'What do you think?'

I'm determined not to obsess about my weight after the James debacle, but as the ice cream passes my lips, the thought crosses my mind: fat arse.

'Delicious!' I say, 'Can you bring it in under 80p per 500ml?'

'For you? Anything.'

I catch myself staring at his mouth and wondering why I've never noticed how perfect his smile is.

Before we go into the production area we have to get washed and dressed. The handwashing procedure is as thorough as any surgeon's – I'm an expert at turning a tap on and off with my knees. Then it's wardrobe time – clompy dark rubber soled shoes, a calf-length white apron, earplugs and a vast blue paper hairnet. I can't imagine anyone who works in this factory ever has sex with anyone else who works here.

One final dousing of anti-bacterial gel, and then Will opens the double doors and we're on. The first room we walk through is for dried fruit and glacé cherries, and smells like a Christmas pudding, which is not the worst thing a room can smell of, but it's the next room that's my favourite. The size of a football pitch, it's where the main sponge cakes are baked, and it's like walking off an aeroplane into warm air that smells of vanilla and sugar. The room is full of people bent over the line, sticking dozens of buttons on to triple chocolate birthday gateaux, or waiting for the hopper to dispense a perfect dollop of buttercream that they can then palette-knife between two halves of a Victoria sponge.

I want to stay in this room, always, but we go to another vast room where the chilled products are made, and over to a corner where a mini-line has been set up to trial the flavoured custards. I want to see if we can do something original with the packaging, so that the product stands out on-shelf. Will and I have discussed squeezy tubes, spherical packs with a small flat bottom, and triangular pots. I want the product to be fun but not too childlike – the flavours are relatively sophisticated.

'We're still having a few problems with the plastics,' says Will. I watch as a long metal arm drops a tablespoon of crunchy nut granola into a pale pink translucent pot, then another robot arm deposits a teacup's worth of raspberry custard on top, a third arm squirts a light layer of Madagascan vanilla cream and then the final arm seals plastic over it and the pot whizzes along to the end of the line and drops neatly into a tray. God, I love dessert factories.

Will buys me lunch in the canteen, and then we go to his office and talk through all the costs, macrobiotics and life tests on every product. The meeting is over-running. It is now 5.09pm. I have been checking my watch every ten minutes since 3.30pm. I'm desperate to know if James is outside, and if he is, how long will he wait? I can barely swallow my throat is so dry. My nerves can't take it any longer and I apologise to Will and say I have to pop out for a minute. I dash to the loo and with trembling hands wipe the slightly smudged mascara from under my eyes, and powder the shine from my nose and when I finally do step outside, my heart racing, I see James, leaning against his car, arms folded. He holds up a little white flag and I can't help but laugh.

'Two minutes,' I say, trying not to skip back into the factory and up to Will's office.

'Will? My friend's here, sorry, but I have to go,' I say, as I feel my heart doing cartwheels.

'Already?' he says. 'Oh . . . okay . . .' Maybe I imagine it but he seems a little peeved. I guess it is bad form to walk out mid-meeting.

'I'll call you about everything tomorrow,' I say. He escorts me to the front door, and as I turn to wave goodbye I see him checking out James's car with a slightly raised brow.

'Nice dress,' says James. Ah, the dress! I think. Not me, the dress. Will said I looked gorgeous, James instead comments on the packaging.

He holds the car door open and I get in. He sits looking at me, grinning, for a full minute.

'Drive, please,' I say. 'It's hot in here.'

He turns the CD player on and I press stop. 'I've had enough Dido for one lifetime thank you. I'll plug my iPod in.'

'Feisty today, aren't you,' he says, smiling.

I put on my playlist that I've been listening to for the last week. First song, The Beatles, 'And Your Bird Can Sing.'

'I like this,' he says.

'You would – it's about you,' I say.

'Huh?'

'Listen to the lyrics,' I say. He does, then says, 'but you're my bird, and you can sing.'

'I'm not *your bird* anymore. And you're entirely missing the point.'

Next up comes Willy Nelson, 'Always on My Mind.' He listens for ten seconds, then tries to flick forward.

'That's a beautiful song!' I say.

'No,' he shakes his head. 'It's sad. What a waste, spending all that time thinking about someone.'

'That's why it's beautiful, dummy,' I say. 'Not as beautiful as Flo Rida I know . . .'

He laughs. 'I watched a DVD the other night, *Being John Malkovich*, have you seen it? It's your sort of mad, artsy thing,' he says.

'Brilliant film,' I say. That and *Eternal Sunshine* . . .'

'Is that where they're trying to turn the sun out?'

'No, that's *Sunshine*. *Eternal Sunshine* is about love and memory – if you could, would you zap away all your painful memories. You should watch it, even Jim Carrey is great in it.'

'Doesn't sound as good as *Dumb and Dumber*,' he says, laughing.

'I love John Malkovich,' I say. 'He can do *Con Air* and *Dangerous Liaisons* and be entirely seductive in both.'

'*Dangerous Liaisons*! I love that film. He destroys her, even though he loves her.'

'I can barely watch it,' I say. 'Such cruelty . . .'

For the rest of the drive home we discuss music and film and TV and we sing the theme tune to The Muppets, and talk about how much we love that scene in *Airplane!* where the girl is on the drip, and before I know it, we are pulling up outside my block of flats.

'Thanks for the ride,' I say, raising my eyebrows.

'I'm coming in,' he says.

'Coming in where?' I say.

'To your flat.'

'Are you?'

'Yes.'

'That's my flat. Where I live.'

'Yes,' he nods. 'I know that.'

'Why are you coming in?'

'Because.'

'Because what?'

'Because I want to.'

'You want to.'

He nods.

'What, just for a cup of tea, to pass the time?'

'No, not just for a cup of tea, to pass the time,' he says.

'Because if you really just want something simple – like a cup of tea – to pass the time, you could just go to the tea shop round the corner. You know that, right?'

'I don't just want a cup of tea, Sophie,' he says, and opens the car door and gets out.

And we both fully understand the significance of this conversation, even though the words remain unspoken.

★

That night we have a lot of sex, and at first I feel a self-loathing that makes me weak.

'What is it, what's wrong?' says James.

'I feel like I'm on death row,' I say.

'Why?'

124

'What if you turn around in five minutes or five months and say exactly the same thing . . .'

'So what if I do? People break up for a million reasons.'

'If I take you back and you pull this shit again, I'll blame myself, as well as you. Fool me once . . .'

'Soph, you have got to let your guard down. This is never going to work if you're going to be all defensive.'

'No, you should be the one trying to prove that you're good enough for me,' I say.

He shrugs: take it or leave it.

If I could zap away all my painful memories, I'd probably do so at exactly this point, in this conversation. That, or head straight for the lobotomy.

'You've got to take a risk,' he says.

Yes, I agree. But all the risk is on my side.

And then I think of being a horse stealer and how I can take on the world and I think: I know I am more than good enough for this man. I can win this.

A week after the 'outburst', as he has coyly named it, James asks me, nervously, if I'd like to come for a drink with his friend Mallard.

'Mallard?'

'Gary. He's one of my oldest friends from uni.'

'Why Mallard?'

'A particularly drunken incident at the Nottingham Fresher's Fair, 1982 . . .'

'Is he married?'

'Divorced. Twice.'

'What happened?'

'Mal's got a rather different definition of fidelity than either of the women he married.'

'Nice.'

'You know how it is. He's a bond trader, those guys work hard, play hard . . .'

'Kids?'

'Five.'

'By the wives?'

'Two, one, and two by his secretary. You'll like him, he's fun.'

What's that line about judging someone by the company they keep? Still, wouldn't be too much fun if all his friends were of the cloth . . .

The following Saturday night we are in the bar at the Soho Hotel, eating the 'free' spicy peanuts that accompany £11 glasses of wine, waiting for Mal and his new girlfriend to join us.

James has eaten handfuls of nuts and pushes the bowl in my direction. I carry on eating them.

'Don't ruin your appetite, gannet,' says James.

I feel myself turn scarlet, but Mal and his girlfriend arrive arm in arm, giggling, before I can pick him up on it.

I've imagined the girlfriend would be some young bimbo but she is nothing of the sort. She has intelligent eyes, bobbed brown hair, glasses. She's at least forty, very natural, looks like an optician. She is wearing a simple black dress, flat shoes, discreet silver earrings.

'I'm Julia,' she says, extending a hand to James, who looks at her with surprise and a touch of disappointment.

'You must be Sophie,' says Mal. From the little James has told me about him, I'm convinced I'm going to hate Mal.

He is five foot ten with a huge gut, red hair, crap teeth. He's wearing a stripy polo shirt and jeans, and unlike James, he really does look like a 45-year-old. That'll be five kids and two sets of alimony.

But there is something about him that is entirely charming. He's very bright, very quick-witted, very funny. He buys a bottle of champagne, and promptly tells us an obscene anecdote about his colleague, a lap dancer and a bathtub filled with Chablis. I wonder if he is actually the 'colleague' in question. His arm rests round Julia's shoulder; she holds his hand. We are all laughing.

Another bottle down and Julia excuses herself for the loo.

'What do you think, mate?' says Mal, leaning in towards James the moment she's out of earshot.

'What's going on there?' says James.

'I knew you'd be surprised. I'm telling you, I think she's the one.'

'Really?' says James, doubt in his voice.

'Mate, all those years chasing beautiful dumb women. But this one, God! I never had a woman who makes me laugh like she does.'

I am pondering how tragic this statement is as James now leans forward, interested. 'But how do you know you're not going to get, you know, bored with the plain, funny one . . ?'

The plain, funny one? I can't believe these two are having this conversation within my earshot. I get up to go to the bar.

'Where are you off to?' demands James.

'To get some water.' To get away from you two.

'Sit. Mal, get Soph some water.' Mal goes off to the bar and gives my shoulder a friendly squeeze.

'Did I tell you Mal's got another kid on the way?' says James.

'Number six!' I'm surprised, given Julia's age.

'He's got super-spunk – he could hit you from here,' says James, looking behind him at Mal who is standing at the bar.

'I could hit *you* from here,' I say, thinking back to the gannet comment.

He gives me a look of incomprehension as Julia comes back to the table and sits down.

'Sophie, I hear you're a pudding maker!' she smiles warmly.

'She's the Queen of Puddings,' says James proudly.

'That sounds like the best job in the world,' says Julia, 'what do you actually do?'

'Oooh, it's very tough. I spend about six hours a day eating custard,' I say.

'I love custard,' says Julia, patting her tiny belly.

'Me too,' says James. 'She keeps stuffing me with it, trying to kill me off with an early heart attack.'

'Yeah, I'm a feeder, like one of those freaky Arizona perverts,' I say.

'So, when's it due?' says James, pointing at Julia's stomach.

'Sorry?' She looks confused. Maybe she's less than three months and Mal shouldn't have told James.

129

I realise a split second before James does what's happened. A look of panic passes over his face. How the fuck's he going to get out of this one? Why is he friends with such a shitbag?

'When are we due? At the restaurant . . . tummies . . . need filling.' I jump in, cack-handed, red-faced.

'Er, Mal booked the table,' she says, taking a swig of her champagne, and giving James a look of slow understanding. 'Excuse me a minute,' she says, putting her half-drunk glass on the table, pushing herself up from the chair, and heading to the bar.

James looks at me, crestfallen.

I shake my head. Behind him, I can see Julia and Mal talking. He looks as though he's been slapped in the face, though Julia's hands remain by her sides. A moment later she walks out calmly, ten seconds later he chases after.

'Looks like it's a table for two,' I say, the least shocked of the four of us, but still shocked.

'Jesus,' he says. 'That's something, even for Mal.'

'Your friend is an utter imbecile. How has a man who looks like that got the audacity to shit on a woman like Julia, what, just 'cause he's got money? And who's he got pregnant this time? His secretary again? What a pig.'

'Don't judge him so harshly, Soph.'

'Why ever not?'

'There are two sides to every story.'

'There are at least three sides to this one and none of them reflect well on your idiot friend.'

He looks troubled. Is he bothered that he blurted his friend's secret? That his gaffe has cost Mal a shag? Or that I am slagging off one of his best mates? It seems like the latter.

'Let's go to the restaurant, babe.'

Mal must have really been trying to impress Julia as he's booked a table at a supremely poncey Michelin starred restaurant in Covent Garden. When James and I walk in, squabbling about who would win in an underwater back-gammon championship – him, because he can hold his breath longer, or me, because I play quicker and I'm better at backgammon – we seem to be the only ones in even vaguely ebullient mood.

It's like walking into synagogue on Yom Kippur, except with a bit more food – but not much. On people's plates, tiny offerings sit surrounded in spittles of froth and dots of jus. Faces turn to look at us, slightly angry and confused. How has it come to this? Why am I paying £85 before wine for two bites of a duck with a rhubarb foam on the side?

'Should have eaten more of those peanuts at the bar,' I say, raising an eyebrow at James. He nods grudgingly and we give Mal's name to the maître d'.

'This is a table for four, yes? We cannot seat you till the other guests arrive.'

'It's just us,' says James, politely.

'But sir, the booking has been made for four. No one has telephoned to let us know.'

'Ok, fair enough, it was a last minute change.'

'But our policy is that we must be notified by telephone in advance if the numbers change.'

James looks at the room, which has five empty tables. 'Do you want me to phone you now and tell you?' he takes out his mobile and looks the guy in the eye with a fraction of a smile.

The maître d' sighs. 'Follow me please, sir.'

We sit down and I ask for a glass of tap water. I've had a bit too much wine on too empty a stomach.

'Sparkling or still, Madame?'

'Tap. Please,' I say, blushing.

Ten minutes later the waiter brings over a couple of menus. 'Please could I have some tap water?' I ask, and the waiter nods and disappears again.

I can feel myself on the verge of impatience and open the menu.

'I'm starving,' I say, then read on the menu a list of expensive and overly complex combinations, none of which appeal. 'Shot glass of samphire and pike soup; Pork and cannellini bean risotto with vanilla pod and heirloom tomatoes; Sour cherry mousse with Crottin de Chavignol goat's cheese from La Maison de Fromage . . .' What I really fancy is a Big Mac, with plastique cheese from La Maison de McDonalds.

James is twitching. His fourth finger niggles at his right eyebrow, a sign I have come to learn means he's slightly angry.

The waiter is suddenly upon us with a basket of five amazing looking breads. 'Bread?' he says impatiently.

'Wow. What are they?' I say.

'Walnut-and-raisin-brioche-sourdough-potato-and-rosemary-sunblushed-tomato,' he recites, as if I'm a total dolt for not knowing.

He dumps a piece of brioche on my plate with shiny tongs.

'Could we please have some butter, and a glass of tap water?' I say, but the waiter has already walked away. I raise my eyebrows at James, and he rubs his face with his hand, covering his mouth.

'Good bread . . . Right! Tell me more about your new business,' I say.

'Yeah, so the Bonders are financing 40%, and we'll raise the equity through investment funds. We should launch this side of the year.'

'That soon? You'll be busy. I'm drunk, I need more bread, do you need more bread?'

He nods firmly.

'Excuse me!' I say as the waiter steams past us, refusing to make eye contact. 'Excuse me?'

He emits an audible huff, makes a pointed turn and then stands to attention at our table. And then puts on his smile. 'Yes?'

'Could we please have some more bread?' I say.

'You do know there is a surcharge for extra bread,' he says with a tiny smile. He is 'joking' and James and I both 'understand' that he is 'joking'.

'I'll tell you what,' says James, with an even tinier smile. 'Why don't you practise your stand-up routine while you're getting our coats?'

The waiter pulls a face I can only describe as ultra-French, and goes to fetch our coats. I high-five James, and tell him I couldn't agree with him more.

Outside it's pouring with rain. We're standing on the junction of Shaftesbury Avenue and Tottenham Court Road. There's no chance of a taxi.

On the night bus home there is only one seat, halfway down, behind the doors, next to a grey-haired woman whose eyes are closed and who rocks gently back and forth looking like she has moderate toothache.

James sits and grabs me on to his lap and we whisper about all the things we're going to eat when we get home: fish finger sandwich on white bread with loads of ketchup, leftover cold roast beef with a pickle, buttered toast and Marmite, Hula Hoops while we're waiting for the toast to pop . . .

Behind James sits a sallow pipsqueak in an oversized black hoody playing whiny crap out of shitty phone speakers. He nods his head and stares sullenly at us, sucking loudly on a McDonalds straw jammed into a large plastic cup. The music speeds up and the lyrics 'we balling, we jumping, we hit it from the side,' screech out. This must be his favourite, as he decides to amp up the sound to maximum irritation. The old lady shakes her head in despair.

James turns round and looks at the guy; James can give good menace face when called for. The guy kisses his teeth, flicking a bit of spit on James, and says, 'Yeah, maaate?'

I'm immediately sober. I whisper to James to come stand near the front, but he says no, the guy is out of line.

Christ, these are not times in which to be a hero.

'Could you please turn down your music, there are other people on the bus,' says James. Everyone behind us is staring silently. The old lady next to us has opened her eyes and given James a gentle tap of thanks on his arm.

'James, please, he might have a knife,' I whisper, resolutely ignoring the guy as I stand up and try to take James's arm.

'Yeah, cunt?' says the guy in a high voice. 'You fucking fat white cunt.' He rips his straw out of his drink and flicks the end of it towards James's face. A creamy streak of vanilla milkshake flecks James's shoulder.

He must be high as a kite, or have a knife, or both, to take on someone 50% bigger than him with a McDonalds' straw.

The audience is transfixed, waiting for my boyfriend to get sliced up on the N24.

We are now at the top of Tottenham Court Road, and

135

the driver has stopped the bus and opened the doors, waiting for this mess to sort itself out.

Two lone females get off the bus quickly, but the other rubberneckers have paid their entry price – they're staying for the show.

'Come on, James, this is where we get the 168,' I say, hoping I'm not emasculating him, but desperately trying to remove him from the situation.

James looks at me with an expression that says don't worry, then looks back at the guy and moves to stand up.

'Yeah, cunt, do what your bitch tells you, YOU FUCKING PUSSY CUNT.'

'James, please,' I am now dragging him by his jacket, trying not to panic. The man I am falling in love with is about to get stabbed, and in two days' time my tear-swollen photo will appear on page five of the *Evening Standard*, with a statement from Ken Livingstone saying that if he was still Mayor instead of Boris this tragedy would never have happened.

The spectators lean back. No doubt they've fast-forwarded in their minds and fear the arterial blood spray might spatter their Saturday night best 'up-west' outfits. . . .

James stands to his full height and the guy stands up too, but before James can throw a punch the guy has thrown the milkshake directly in James's face and run off the bus. James tries to grab his hoody as he pushes past but the guy has gone before the first thick drop of beige gloop has even fallen from James's chin.

There is a collective sigh of relief and a bloke who has had ringside seats says, 'Nice one, mate.'

James turns to me and smiles. 'No good deed goes unpunished . . .'

I laugh and lick him from the bottom of his chin to his top lip. James puts his hands on my cheeks and kisses me deeply. Someone behind us wolf-whistles. I can feel cold milkshake all over my nose from his nose, and we smile into each others' open mouths.

'If only he'd thrown a quarter pounder . . . a few McNuggets,' I say. And James kisses me again: a kiss that says I have never met a woman who makes me laugh like you do.

'You've cast a spell on me, witch,' he says as we're lying later side by side on his living room floor, bodies pressed together like palms in prayer.

I know what he means. I keep expecting this bubble we float around in to burst. Any day now he's going to see me for who I really am: a jealous, selfish, scared, normal human being and not this fantasy.

I wonder, when this bubble bursts, who he'll turn out to be.

'What shall we do today?' he says, as he's lying in the bath the following morning and I'm washing the last traces of milkshake out of his hair.

'How long have I got you for?' I ask. One of the things that's still infuriating me is his lack of letting me know where I stand with regard to our time together. I figure as we get closer this will change and is part of his general commitment-phobia. I've already said my piece about him being hard to make arrangements with, I don't want to sound like a moaning cow.

'I've got to meet Rob and the boys at 7pm in Covent Garden,' he says, as if he's checking in with his mum whether he's allowed to go out. 'But let's do something cultural.'

'There's the Sophie Calle on at The Whitechapel?'

'Paintings?'

'No, I don't even know how to describe her stuff – conceptual? She did this brilliant thing I saw in New York, she'd been dumped by this guy and he wrote her a 'Dear John'

138

e-mail, and she got, like, a hundred different people to deconstruct it – a graphologist, a psychiatrist . . . She even filmed a parrot reading parts of it out.'

He wrinkles his nose. 'Sounds mad. Same name as you, not surprised . . .'

'Shut up, she's brilliant. All these different perspectives just from this one letter.'

'Why dwell on it like that?' he says. 'She should just shag a barman and get over it.'

★

We decide to go to the British Museum. I love that building and I want to pick something up at the gift shop for my grandma. James wants to pop into his office first. He's working on his new project, 'a move into women's tights' as he likes to put it. I haven't been to his office, and as we head towards Piccadilly I realise that I still feel at arm's length from large chunks of his life. His dad and brother live abroad, I've met his best friend, but our lives feel very parallel. I still talk to Nick's parents and grandparents often, and I used to know exactly what colour pants Nick was wearing every day and that was before we lived together.

I think about it and I rationalise that this is the reason Nick and I split up. Too close = not enough distance: desire needs distance. Knowing every domestic detail breeds unsexiness; you become like brother and sister. Intimacy can turn into taking someone for granted. Distance is fine, I think. Yep, distance = longing = wanting someone. Yay, distance!

James pulls in to a disabled parking space in St James's Square.

'Here we are,' he says.

'Did you get them to rename this square in your honour?' I say.

'Nah, it'd be King–Lord–Emperor–God James's Square if I had my way,' he says.

'Still, a beautiful old-fashioned square . . . makes sense, with your taste in music,' I say.

'Ouch,' he says. 'Wait here, I'll be two minutes.'

'You're not parking in the disabled bay are you?' I say.

'Soph, I'll be two minutes.'

'What if a warden comes, you'll get done . . .'

'You worry too much.'

'God, you just skate along the surface of things, don't you,' I say.

'What do you mean?'

'Nothing, hurry up.' What I mean is this: you do exactly what you want and the consequences don't really matter because you have loads of money to throw at stuff. *That* is why you look young for your age. Your money buys you freedom from responsibility. It protects you from having to grow up.

And then I think, Christ, I'm a sanctimonious idiot,

probably because subconsciously I'm pissed off that he's seeing his friends tonight instead of me – what difference does it really make where he parks? The chance of someone needing this space in the next few minutes is 0.1%. It's not like he's strangling grannies.

He's back a few minutes later with some files marked 'L'Esteeme'.

'What's all that?' I ask.

'Oh, research,' he says.

'Can I look?'

'If you like.' I flick through a file and see the Executive Summary: the qualitative research shows that certain female demographics will be willing to pay between £120 and £160 for a pair of cashmere silk mix tights with built in anti-cellulite enablers.

'£160 for a pair of tights, you're having a laugh, aren't you?' I can't imagine ever paying that for a pair of tights.

'Ah, it's all dollies, isn't it,' he says, 'husband's money.'

'But that's just insane.'

'What, 'cause there are kids starving in Africa?' he says.

'Basically, yes.'

'There's a big enough market for it, the BRIC countries, the Middle East . . .'

'That sort of clientele must be liposuctioned to within an inch of their lives anyway. What do they even need anti-cellulite enablers for?'

'There's always someone younger and thinner,' he says. Yeah, married to someone older and fatter.

'You're so smart, James, why don't you put your talents to good use? You don't even need the money, do you?'

'I just want to see if I can do it,' he says.

'I'm sure you can. But wouldn't it give you more satisfaction to do something for other people? You're great with kids, why don't you set up some sort of project . . . charity . . .'

'Yeah, I probably will,' he smiles, 'that would be nice.'

I put my hand on his cheek and he purrs like a cat.

'I love doing stuff like this with you,' he says as we stroll the museum, arm in arm, making up stories about all the exhibits.

'Here's one for you,' I say. 'A coin of King James III, the 'Old Pretender', made by the engraver Norbert Roettier. Oh look, Norbert's brother and Norbert's son are also called James! How is dear Norbert these days?'

'Norby's good. He's shacked up with a 34DD Latvian stripper in a loft in Chelsea Harbour,' he says.

'I trust she's called James too,' I say. 'And another one . . . Saint James, James the Greater, no less . . . beheaded, oh dear . . . son of Zebedee! I thought you said your dad's name was Victor.'

'Zebedee Victor but people take the piss 'cause of The Magic Roundabout . . .' he says.

In the Ancient Cyprus room we come across a terracotta fertility figure from around 1300 BC.

She has a head like a pretzel and is carrying a strange little baby in her arms.

'Don't fancy her much,' says James.

'What, just because she's got four eyes?'

'No, four eyes is fine, she's dumpy,' he says, 'needs to lay off the mezze.'

'Cock,' I say. 'She's beautiful. Well, apart from her head. She's a sign of new life, birth, wide hips.'

'Yuk,' he says. 'Get her on the treadmill.'

Ha-ha-ha-ha-ha, I think. I might find that funny if I wasn't on death row.

But I am.

So I don't.

He texts me ten minutes after he's dropped me off: Your company, as always, was amazing.

These 'compliments' are like olives when you're craving a steak: even the plumpest Gordal olives stuffed with orange and oregano are still just olives. Actually, some of these compliments are more like stones. Not olive stones – larger, and shaped like sugared almonds but made out of rock. You're a 'good woman', a 'clever girl', 'great company'. Who wants to be 'great company'? I'm not a hostess service, I'm his girlfriend.

When I get into bed that night, it feels like this particular stone is wedged at the base of my throat.

I am in a meeting with Devron to discuss potential new products from my New York trip.

This meeting was meant to take place two days after I got back, the morning after James's 'outburst'.

Luckily, Devron cancelled and then booked himself on a week long 'Total Leader Journey' course at Ashridge, costing Fletchers just short of £10k, followed by two weeks in the Maldives with Mandy, so we're now in June.

'How was your holiday, Devron?'

'Killer. Me and Mands had an amazing time. Beautiful hotel, steak every night, caught up on my Dan Browns.'

'You look very tanned.' Apart from your eye area, where it appears you have fallen asleep on the beach on your last day with your Oakleys on at a strange angle.

'85 degrees every day, Mands's already booked us in for a month at New Year's. How was your trip then?'

'Very good,' I say, taking out the document I've prepared for him. I've kept it short but it has all the key market and product info, margin breakdowns and potential launch plans.

'Nah, nah, nah, just topline, I'm big picture, E-S-F-P.' D-I-C-K.

'Okay. There are three things I want to look at for launch next autumn . . .'

'Whoa, whoa, hold on. We only need one.'

'I know that. I just want to be thorough – and we'll need stuff for Christmas . . .'

'Alright, alright.' He nods rapidly.

'Okay. So . . .'

He holds his hand up. 'Sophie. Is this going to take long? Just Mands's having a minor procedure, needs me to pick her up from Harley Street at 3pm so you've got ten minutes.'

This meeting was meant to be an hour. Still, less is more, where spending time with Devron's concerned.

'Fine. Number 1 – Cannoli, 2 – Frozen Custards, 3 – Compost Cookies. Cannoli are Sicilian . . .'

'Yeah, I've had cannoli, Mands makes it. Pasta tubes, cheese, tomato.'

'Cannelloni, right, same principle as cannoli, a tube shape with a filling . . .'

'That's cannoli. Mands is half-Italian, I think she'd know.'

'The pasta's cannelloni. Cannoli's the pastry, same Latin root, "canna", for "reed" . . .'

He looks at me like I'm talking bollocks.

'Anyway, Devron, they're amazing little pastries, filled with

145

ricotta and chocolate chips or pistachios. Rocco's on Bleeker Street does a classic one, but there's a new artisan maker on the Lower East Side, doing loads of innovative contemporary flavours: peanut butter and jam, apple pie, lychee . . .'

He wrinkles his nose. 'Number 2?'

'Ah, the custards. So, Shake Shack, burger joint famous for milkshakes, they do a "frozen custard" selection, like a . . .'

'I don't think you need to explain what custard is to me at this stage in my career . . . I get it.'

'No. It's not like our custard, but I do think we could ask Appletree to make it. It's like a soft ice cream . . .'

'Yeah, yeah, yeah, sounds fine, and 3?'

'Compost Cookies . . .'

'I thought that's what you said. Explain.'

'Right, David Chang, chef, opened Momofuku restaurant, now has loads of places, has a bakery/milk bar, and they sell Compost Cookies, which I admit sound weird but they're the best things ever. This genius chef, Christina Tosi, invented the recipe, and now they're famous for them. I brought you some back but then you went on that course . . .'

'They're made of compost? What have you been smoking, Sophie?'

'No, not compost. Pretzels and crisps and chocolate chips . . .'

He does a fake retching, like a cat with furballs.

'Honestly, Devron, I've got the recipe, I'll bake you some this week.'

146

'No, thanks.'

'The salt/sweet thing is key, and the texture . . .'

He shakes his head. 'Not sure about any of those, let's catch up next week, gotta go.'

And he's out the door before I can even show him the photos of what success looks like.

★

'Of course they sound weird and gross. That's why they're interesting.'

James and I are baking Compost Cookies. In spite of Devron's protestations, I am determined I can convince him if he just tries one.

James wrinkles his nose and sticks his tongue out.

'Stop being such a baby and tell me how much brown to white sugar.'

'One cup white, three quarters of a cup brown,' he says, 'what's a stick of butter?'

'Half a cup, I think, check the magnet on the fridge. Right, here's the fun bit – your favourite baking ingredients and your favourite snacks . . .'

'Are you serious? Crisps and pretzels? Trust Americans to take a cookie and make it more fattening.'

'When have I ever let you down on the food front?'

'That Japanese thing you made . . .'

'That was Korean. Okay. I reckon Hula Hoops,

chocolate chips and maybe Ritz crackers . . . and there was coffee in it too, the bitterness was tempering the butter-scotch chips . . . give me that paper . . . coffee grounds . . . huh.'

'Like old crap at the bottom of the cafetière? If you think I'm eating that . . .'

'Hang on . . . what are coffee grounds? Surely not the used, wet bits. Maybe it's American for granules . . . google it, would you?'

He pads back in a minute later carrying my laptop and looking jubilant. 'There you go, Soph, third one down.'

He shows me a page on Wikipedia which reads 'Coffee ground vomitus'.

'Told you so,' he says, 'do you want to read the bit about blackened stools?'

'Shut up, nincompoop. Can you make yourself useful and sift the flour.'

He giggles to himself and gets to work. He keeps looking over at me as I break the eggs and measure out the rest of the dry ingredients.

'This is nice, isn't it,' he says, smiling.

'Isn't it,' I say.

'I'm happy,' he says.

'Good! Now in that drawer on the left is a rolling pin . . .'

I've put the crisps and crackers in a Ziploc bag. He hands me the rolling pin and I give the bag a few thumps, smashing the contents to tiny pieces.

148

'I'd better behave myself!' he says. 'You've got a fierce swing going on there.'

'Years of repressed rage,' I say. 'You haven't met my mother.'

'Don't worry, I'll do whatever you want, Boss.'

'Are they ready yet? They smell good,' says James, peering through the oven door.

'One more minute . . . do they look light brown in the middle to you?'

'I definitely think they're ready.'

'You can't eat them till they're cool, they're too buttery to lift, they break.'

'I'm taking them out.'

I make him walk round the block with me ten times, in order to stop him eating the cookies while they're too warm. On lap eight he breaks into a run and together we jog round the block breathlessly joking about what we'll put in them next time: pork scratchings, teabags, James's Tikka Masala Pot Noodles.

Finally he hoicks me into a piggyback and we return home.

I pop to my room and by the time I return to the kitchen James is on his third cookie.

'Oy, save some for Devron!'

'Not bad!' he says, with a mouth full. 'Not bad at all.'

'What did you expect? It's basically a chocolate chip cookie with built-in pub snacks. How could the British public not fall in love with that idea?'

'Such a clever girl, you,' he says, sticking a biscuit in my mouth. 'Very clever.'

★

'Your company as ever was truly wonderful,' he says as he kisses me goodbye later.

My company. Not me. My company. As if they were detachable.

My grandma has left a message on my voice mail:

'Hello? Hello? Are you there, who is this? Evie, there's no one there. I heard a voice but it's gone . . . Hello? Sophie? . . . Sophie? It's Grandma.'

Then Evie's voice comes on: 'Sophie, it is Evie and your grandmother calling on Monday at one o'clock. Your grandmother would like you to visit one night this week please, thank you, Sophie.'

The guilt. I have not been round for three weeks. Every weekend I have seen James and in the week I'm with him or friends.

Three weeks is a heartbeat when you're in love, but a very long time when you're lonely.

I bake a lemon drizzle cake, but am in such a rush taking it out of the oven to pour the syrup on immediately, that I burn myself halfway up my inner forearm, just where the oven gloves stop and my flesh starts. Careless. It is only two centimetres long but it hurts like hell. I hold it under the cold tap as long as I can bear, then hurry down and out to her flat while the cake is still warm.

Evie opens the door dressed in one of my grandma's cloche hats and a tailored suit from the 40s. The skirt is too long, but the jacket looks great.

'Sorry, Sophie, your grandmother is making me try on all her old clothes. She wants them to go to a good home . . .' She raises her hands and shrugs her shoulders in a typical Jewish gesture that she's picked up since she moved in.

'It's a little bit long for me, Mrs Klein,' she says, heading back into the living room, where my granny looks like she's fallen into a nap, slumped over in her chair, her legs at an awkward Kerplunk angle.

'Grandma?' I rush over to her in a panic and grab her arm.

She's dead.

'Teddy? Not the good china!' she says, rolling her head to the other side and opening one eye.

Not so dead.

'Is that you, Sophola?' Her hand reaches out to touch my face. You can see every vein, bone, sinew on this aged hand; it's like an anatomical drawing. Yet her nails, as ever, look immaculate.

'Yes, Grandma. It's me. I brought you a lemon cake.'

'Bless you, darling. Evie! Three plates please! And that hat doesn't go with that suit. Sit, Sophola, let me look at you.'

I sit on the velvet footstool by her feet. Her ankles are swollen but her legs are so fragile and knobbly now, they look like twiglets in sheepskin slippers.

'What news?' she says.

'Work's very busy. I'm in charge of my own new product development, I saw some delicious cannolis in New York . . .'

'New York, New York, it's a wonderful town!' she croons. 'Your father was in New York during the war. He'd only been back a few months when we met: June. So hot that year. I used to sit in the back of Papa's shop, help serve the ices . . .'

I nod. I have heard this story so many times, but apart from her confusing my father with my grandfather, the details are always perfect.

'And one day Papa bumped into Reuben Meyers who told him of a young man, newly returned, of good family, living in Bloomsbury. Papa invited him for lemon tea after threatening to throw me out of the house if I made a bad impression by foolish talk.'

My great-grandfather had managed to offload his three younger, more docile daughters already.

'In Papa's eyes, at twenty-five I was an "alte meid", a disgrace!'

Evie hands over a plate of lemon cake and my grand-mother curls her hand round the spoon.

'Papa always said "if anyone better looking than a monkey

asks you to marry him, go down on your knees and thank God".' Sound advice. 'He said "don't order more than a Bath bun – he'll think you extravagant and unsuitable for a wife" . . . ooh, this cake!'

'Your recipe.'

'I know.' There are crumbs stuck to her lipstick. She looks so very, very old now. 'How's your new chap?'

I wonder if she would actually like James. He's very charming, always, but she'd see beyond that veneer. If I had to pinpoint his greatest appeal it would be his combination of manliness and boyishness. He is assertive and confident and tough, and yet has a boundless energy and silliness. Would she find him endearing or just immature? I'd really like her to meet him; her instincts are sound. 'I'll bring him round soon, shall I?'

'I'd like that. How is Nicholas doing? Such a handsome boy.'

Nick was always so sweet with my grandma. When she was more mobile, he'd take her round to the local Austrian pastry shop and buy her strudel and coffees in the afternoon, and listen to her recite poetry or moan about the state of the nation. I can't quite imagine James doing that.

'Nick's good. He's in Paris making a record with a band. They're very popular, nice melodies.'

'Tell him I wish him all the best. Now if you'll excuse me. Evie?' She yawns for what seems like half a minute.

She has gone from being sparky to drained in the space of

thirty seconds. There is so little energy left in her body, yet her mind is still operating on almost all cylinders. But I know that she's so desperately bored, if she could she'd take a pill and be gone tomorrow.

I kiss her goodbye and watch as Evie leads her down the corridor.

'What happened here?' says James, taking my wrist gently and holding my arm.

I'd forgotten about the burn, though my skin is still angry and red.

'Oh. Yeah . . . oven gloves.'

'When?'

'Erm . . . last week.'

'Did you put cream on?'

'No, I put it under water . . . it's fine. I always scar for ages. Look, see?'

I hold out my other arm to show him the long thin scratches on the inside of my elbow that look like a feral cat has attacked.

'I wondered where those had come from . . .' He's giving me a suspicious look.

'James? Do I look like someone who self-harms?' I do all my self-harming internally, thank you.

'No! That's not what I thought . . .'

156

'So what? Oh! You thought I might be an IV drug user! Cool. Yep, I keep my smack habit pretty well hidden, it's true.'

'I don't know, they're just – they've been there ever since we met.'

'I fell down a rather large rock in Mendoza in January, I was just wearing a vest. I scraped my arm on some stupid bracken shit. Shouldn't have had that extra glass of Merlot before the hike.'

'You've still got the scar though.'

'Yes! Idiot. I'm telling you, it takes ages for stuff to fade. I think it's to do with the Factor XI. I bruise really easily.'

'Do you want to see my scars?' he says.

'You've already talked me through them . . . remember?' He sometimes forgets what he has and hasn't told me. Must be his age.

'I have?'

'Yes. Right elbow – sixth form rugby match, Forest vs. Chigwell, all Terry Watson's fault. Second knuckle, right hand – unidentified drinking injury. Left knee – rafting, Canada, 1984 with Mallard. Right eyebrow – bumper cars, South Woodford Fairground, 1969. Remind me, was everything still in black and white then?'

'Your memory is scary. Anyway, what's for dinner, Wench?'

'I was thinking maybe some nice, fresh Scottish heroin, or would sir perhaps prefer a crack omelette?'

He pretends to throttle me, and I fall on the floor and pretend to die.

At work the following day my phone rings – Maggie Bainbridge.

'I have a question for you and you have ten seconds to answer. Ready?'

Please say your business is now big enough to employ me. Please ask me to work for you again!

'Would you like to go to El Bulli on August 1st?' Popes, woods, bears, Catholics . . .

'You got a table! I can't believe you're inviting me as your guest! I would LOVE to!' My high-pitched yelping has caused Lisa to frown and Eddie to smile.

'I'm not inviting you,' she says.

Oh shit, that's embarrassing.

'I finally got a table in my fifth year of trying and now I've got a bleeding trade show all weekend in Harrogate, with fourteen clients to wine and dine at Harry Ramsden's.'

'You want me to help with the trade show? I can do the stand with you if you like . . .'

'No, silly girl, listen: I want you to take my table for two at El Bulli and put it to bloody good use with whoever you think deserves it . . .'

Since I told Maggie about the whole 'not my normal type' conversation, she's formed the opinion that James is an obnoxious arsehole.

158

'Maggie, I owe you big time. THANK YOU!'

I hang up and immediately order her a £50 bunch of peonies – her favourite.

El Bulli! The best restaurant in the world, ever. Two million applications for a table each year, chance of getting one – thin as carpaccio.

I should take Laura. I know she'll be my best friend till the day I die. She is my fellow horse-stealer. She is the platonic love of my life.

Besides, maybe Maggie's right – I'm not sure James deserves such a treat.

I pick up my mobile before I can change my mind. 'It's me, are you free on August 1st?'

'Why?'

'Yes or no?'

'. . .Yes?'

'I have a table at El Bulli with our name on it, I'll call you later about flights.' And before he has a chance to ask what El Bulli is, or flights to where, I hang up, overexcited and ever so slightly disappointed with myself.

*

A week later, James and I are sitting on my living room floor with my computer on my lap.

'So El Bulli is in Rosas,' I say, pointing to a map on the screen, 'and we fly to Barcelona . . .'

'It's near France; you could fly to Perpignan couldn't you?' asks James, taking the computer from me. 'Bonder Junior has a little place there, we could go down to the Languedoc for a few days, drink good wine, eat cheese. . . .' he says, patting his belly.

'Good plan,' I say, standing up and leaning over to kiss him upside down.

'Mmmm, where are you going?' he says, trying to pull me back.

'Water, you want?' He nods. While I'm in the kitchen, the doorbell rings.

My neighbour, Amber.

What's she doing here? She must have heard us come in – probably wants to see if she can get in there with James and date one of his friends.

She is wearing tiny shorts rolled down from the waist to an inch above the top of her bikini line, and a fuchsia sports bra – not bra top – BRA. Her long, wavy blond hair is artfully scooped up to give the impression that she is just about to jump off a yacht in to the Aegean, and she seems to have lightly spritzed herself with oil that smells like a Primrose Hill boutique.

I can hear James knocking around in the bathroom and I pray he won't come out and see her, because although she is inane, and I have meanly christened her Zoolamber due to the fact that she thinks Pakistan is the capital of India, she has a terrific body, and James might fancy her.

'Babe, my kitchen tap's not working, is yours?' she says.

'I just used it.'

'Oh.'

'Call the caretaker.'

'He's not answering. Have you got a friend here?'

'Yes.'

'Could I fill my Evian bottle? I can't drink sparkling water when I'm doing Pilates, too bloating . . . oh, hi there . . .' Too late.

'Hi, I'm James. You must be the famous Zoolamber.'

I turn round and give him a look of pure horror.

'It's Amber,' she says, looking confused. 'Who's Zoolamber?'

'Oh, Zolanda, no, that's my friend, er, from work . . . James, Amber is my neighbour. Her water's broken, tap's not working, would you mind filling this in the kitchen?'

'I'll come too,' she says, bouncing along behind him in true gym bunny style. 'I've been doing the Bolshoi Pilates DVD, God, it's amay-zing. Works your core soo hard, my core is soo tight now . . .'

I can tell he's trying not to react but his eyebrows raise, and as he turns to give her the full bottle he can't help but check out her body. I feel it like a short hard punch, but then realise I'm being over-sensitive – any man would stare.

'Sophie, shall I show you the basics? It would really help your shape.'

What would help my shape is showing your shape my front door. 'No, thanks.'

'It won't take a sec, I'll just do some simple floor work.' Before I can shoo her out she has lain down on my hall carpet, knees bent, groin thrust into the air, her skinny arms pulsing at her sides. 'You count to 100, it's all about the breath.' She exhales hard little puffs while James stares at her clenching, thrusting small buttocks. She has the body of a young boy – a young boy with Harley Street breast implants.

'James, can you put on the water for the pasta, please?' I push him with both hands back into the kitchen and shut the door. 'Amber, another time.' I stand over her with my arm outstretched. She pouts and very slowly rolls on to her side. She pauses there and I can almost see the machinations in her head. *Can I get back into the kitchen? How can I get in with this guy's friends? How come she's got a boyfriend with a nicer car than mine when I'm thinner than her?* She lifts herself delicately off the floor as if she's made of blown sugar.

'You guys should come round for food,' she calls out. 'I've got this wicked recipe for Mystical Braised Tofu from my facial analyst. She's put me on a strictly no wheat, no dairy regime. My energy is amazing.'

'Presumably you have to cut booze and drugs too?'

Amber looks confused. 'Those are natural toxins, I'm just not allowed manmade chemicals. Do you even *know* what they put in milk?'

'Listen, I don't mean to be rude, but I have to speak to James about our trip so we'd best get on.' I hold open the front door.

Instead she opens the kitchen door, sticks her head round it and says 'Great to finally meet you James, Soph talks about you all the time. You guys are coming for food at mine soon. Next weekend?'

He murmurs some response, and she turns, gives me a sharp smile and finally leaves.

'Nice one, calling her Zoolamber to her face,' I say, grabbing a stick of celery and whacking him on the arm.

'I didn't realise till after I'd said it. Anyway, you covered up alright. She seems sweet.'

Sweet. He means toned.

'She's not sweet. Did I not tell you about the birthday present?'

He takes the celery and starts chopping it.

'She gave me some stupidly expensive Diptyque candle, then the next day came round and said it was actually meant for her masseuse and took it back, gave me one from Superdrug instead.'

He laughs.

'Oh, you like that, do you? Well, when my plumbing broke she wouldn't let me use her bath – said she couldn't risk someone who uses non-organic skincare "infiltrating her biosystem". She makes Geri Halliwell look like Einstein.'

'Ah, my little Green Eyed Monster . . .'

'I am not jealous! I don't like her, that's all. She accused

163

me of being tight after I refused to lend her £50 for her dealer, after she'd already borrowed £100 and never paid me back. She's an idiot.'

'Well, you shouldn't have people like that in your life who take advantage of you. Why do you put up with it?'

Because I'm a masochist? 'She's my neighbour, what am I meant to do?'

'Cut her off.'

On the Ryanair flight over to France, James and I are separated, having mucked about too long choosing our in-flight snacks at Prêt. There is one seat at the back of the plane, next to the loo and two middle-aged women wearing *High School Musical* jackets, or a seat with a couple and their screaming five-year-old boy.

I choose the back seat and watch as James, seven rows in front, not only manages to stop this child's tantrum, but plays games with him the entire journey. The pair of them giggle and plot like twins.

At the Hertz desk, we rent an ironically named Sprint and head towards Narbonne. We are so busy warbling along to Supertramp on Nostalgie FM that we miss the exit for the toll road and end up driving the scenic route.

'Fitou,' James says. 'Let's stop there,' he says, pointing to a building under a tree at the side of the road.

In the wine shop, a man who looks as old as the stones

offers us samples of amazing rosés and reds and Muscats de Rivesaltes.

'Four of each,' says James.

'We're here for two nights . . . we won't get through 12 bottles.'

'They're so cheap it'd be wrong not to,' he says.

We load the car up with booze and head north, then west to a tiny village by the river Aude.

It is perfect. No tourists, two bakeries, beautiful buildings surrounded by fields, flat and green and yellow. I have never been to France on holiday. I go to Paris for work often, but I had no conception of how unbelievably awesome the south is.

James has told me nothing about where we are staying, other than that it belongs to Lucien Bonder, who uses it as an occasional weekend pad with his wife and daughter, and that it used to be a warehouse of some sort. I fear it will be dank and smell of cat's piss.

In a narrow backstreet we come to a high iron gate behind which is a courtyard with a fountain and a large two-storey stone building, part covered in ivy.

'It must have been a stable,' I say, looking up at a small terracotta horse's head pinned high above the large wooden front door.

James opens the door and starts to laugh.

'What? Is there a horse still in there?' I say.

He grabs my hand and we step in to a World of Interiors dream.

It is a vast, bright space – concrete floors, exposed white stone walls, high ceilings with wooden beams. A floating staircase on the right leads up to a mezzanine kitchen with a pale blue Smeg fridge, and then out onto the pool area. Our own pool!

In the main living space on the ground floor is a blue table tennis table, and its colour is echoed by an illuminated square of aquamarine at the far end of the room, a cut-through window looking into the swimming pool. I stare through the window and up to the surface of the water and watch pine needles floating on the ceiling. It is so calm and still, I want to lie down on the bottom on the smooth white tiles.

When I look back into the main room my eyes are still mesmerised by the pale blue – everything looks peachy.

We race up the stairs from the mezzanine to find four bedrooms and four bathrooms, each more beautiful than the last. Floor tiles in pale grey and sage patterns, white wooden cupboards, blue linen sheets, freestanding baths, skylights . . . everything is simple and elegant and under-stated. Even the little girl's room is stylish, *Tintin* posters on the walls and Barbie dolls arranged in a white wicker basket covered in tiny lavender hearts.

We finish in the master bedroom that looks down onto

the pool and has an en suite rain shower with four extra taps on the wall that spray sideways and tickle you ever so gently.

It is the nicest place I have ever seen, and for this brief, glorious moment it is our home.

★

We have 48 hours till we need to drive to El Bulli and James insists on spending around 44 of them butt naked.

'If you must,' I say, 'but I haven't even met the Bonders, I don't feel right sitting at their dining table nude.' I wear a bikini and shorts that cover my cellulite. I should have bought a new bikini. Swimsuit shopping used to be such an arduous experience. I've brought old ones, and with my reduced bust, I feel mildly unsupported.

Day one is spent eating bread and cheese and cheese and bread, and drinking four bottles of wine. At 2am we play table tennis and James thrashes me 21-0.

'Play nice,' I say. 'Can't we rally?'

In the next game, he sits on his competitiveness for all of three points, but by point four he is adding slice so that the ball bounces and swerves irritatingly out of reach. I think I have it and then it's gone the other way completely.

'Oi, no spin!' I say.

'Drunkard, the ball was straight.'

I serve hard and the ball thwacks him in the stomach and he looks impressed and mildly aroused.

'Hustler!' he says.

'Wanna bet?'

'If you lose, you have to run round the courtyard naked,' he says.

'No. I'll do the washing up and if you lose, you can run to the recycling bins with those bottles.'

'Boring. You lose, once round the courtyard or I won't play with you anymore.'

'Are you five years old?'

He pretends to have a tantrum and then we argue for seventeen minutes about the terms of the bet; because it's so dark outside that I don't mind running naked round the courtyard, and because James's favourite thing in the world is winning, I agree to his terms, and he promptly thrashes me 21-2, then nods and smiles while I dance in as dignified a manner as possible round the fountain.

'Good woman,' he says, as I put my bikini back on and grab the wine.

It is so hot in the night we sleep on the sheets, and when James climbs on top of me in the morning I think about how rough I must look, how red my face, how frizzy my hair.

I feel ropey and dehydrated and by the time I've showered and made tea, James is splashing about in the pool. Where does he get his energy from?

I wave and go down to the window onto the pool. He swims towards me and presses his arse against the glass. I shake my head and laugh as he performs a pirouette, then jumps up and down, pointing at his willy.

'You are five,' I mouth, and he sticks his thumbs up and nods.

I study his long, strong legs, as the hairs all drift up, drift down. He pushes himself off the glass and I watch as he moves quickly to the other side of the pool. He is a strong swimmer and within seconds he is just a shape and then he has disappeared entirely. Come back, I think. I want to look at you. And then he's there, ploughing towards me, face forward, eyes open, like a shark.

He vanishes again and I hear him clattering around upstairs. 'James?'

A few minutes later, I'm staring back through the glass into the now calm pool and a green bean comes into view, top right, and bounces along the top of the screen like it's going for a stroll. From the top left, a courgette comes into view and rushes towards the bean, and the two do a dance.

The bean disappears and a bottle of Sauza tequila replaces it. Seeing the liquor, the courgette takes fright and disappears upwards, to be replaced by a pair of long, slim, unnaturally perfect legs.

Plastic ones.

Barbie has arrived. James makes Barbie drink the

tequila, then whips away the bottle and Ken drops into the game, taking Barbie roughly from behind, then rubbing his smooth crotch in her face. Ken is then ejected from the pool and James brings Barbie down to his own crotch.

I race up the stairs. 'Stop it,' I say, laughing. 'You'd better buy that poor little girl a new Barbie.'

He chuckles. 'Get in and I'll dump Barbie for you. She's hot but boring as hell . . .' he says.

'Go to the window and watch me, it's so cool,' I say.

He climbs out of the pool and hugs me and I think how much I love his size. He is so broad and big, he feels so strong.

'Come on then,' he says and pads through the kitchen and down the stairs.

I jump in the pool, swim to the window and do a somersault. By the time I resurface, he is shouting something at me.

'What?' I say.

'Top off!' he says.

Fine. I take my bikini top off and go back under the surface.

He bounds back up the stairs. 'My God, I love the way your tits move in the water.'

'Wow, finally, the "L" word,' I say. 'What a romantic . . .'

He runs away into the kitchen.

I climb out of the pool, grab a towel and join him.

'Coffee?' he says, eyeing up a shiny black and silver machine on the counter.

'I tried earlier, I couldn't find the manual. It's very hi-tech, I wouldn't . . .'

He ignores me.

'You're still drunk,' I say.

He is happy fiddling away with the machine, and as I open the fridge to get some water I hear a loud snap and then the sound of glass breaking.

'Oops,' he says, giggling.

'Oh for fuck's sake, you idiot. Put some shoes on!' I kiss him, and step into my flip flops and hunt for a dustpan and brush.

He patters off to lie on the sofa, still sopping wet.

'Right, off that sofa; come to the farm shop with me. We're going to eat some fruit. We need a day off the cheese. You might consider putting on some clothes . . .'

The day is hot and humid and hung-over. We have no map and walk aimlessly in the direction we think the farm shop is in. Eventually we pass a barn with a chalk sign that reads 'Abricots'. A woman is standing in front of dozens of wooden crates piled with fruit that look like amber eggs, speckled with pink and red, like kissing rashes.

She holds an apricot in her hand and twists, cleanly

172

separating it, and offers James and me half each. It tastes of honey, and like any good dealer she offers us each one more half: hooked.

We buy 30 apricots and a jar of apricot jam and stumble back home to lie together on one sun lounger in the shade.

'Feel how perfect this apricot is,' I say, weighing the fruit in my hand, its skin cool and smooth.

'Nice,' he says, his eyes shut against the light. I brush the apricot on my cheek and then brush it gently against his.

'Look,' I say, 'when you stroke it with your thumb it's almost like marble, but when you do it against your cheek you can feel the fur.'

'Feel the fur and do it anyway . . .' mumbles James, his face lighting up with a smile as it does every time he makes a bad pun.

'And smell it,' I say. 'It smells like an apricot should smell.'

He buries his nose in my neck. 'You smell like an apricot should smell,' he says. God, I love his nose.

I look behind me at the white china dish, 14 apricots piled up, and I breathe deeply and feel tears start to well up. James senses something and opens one eye.

How can I explain that lying here next to him in the shade, with these apricots, has made me happier than I've ever been. I'm scared this won't last, and I'm overwhelmed with joy, and I suspect he'll take the piss and call me a weirdo if I try to explain myself.

'It's just so perfect,' I say, laughing, and he beams and nods and says, 'You're mad, Soph. You know that?'

*

We have dinner reservations at 9pm in the neighbouring village and have been drinking and dozing consistently all day and yet at 7pm James pokes me in the thigh and says, 'Time for a run – too much cheese.'

I prop myself up on one elbow. 'Don't be ridiculous . . . I'm resting.'

'No, big dinner tonight, need to work off those calories. You've been eating Fi-tou.'

'Ha bloody ha. I'm not running anywhere. You go.'

'Lazy. Slothie.'

'Fuck off,' I say, sitting up. 'I'm relaxing. You're pissed. It's still baking out there.'

He puts on his shorts and a t-shirt and I grudgingly do the same. 'I'll ride the bike next to you,' I say.

'That's not exercise, that's just sitting down,' he says.

'Whatever. I'm fitter than you,' I say. And I am.

'Don't be ridiculous.'

We head across the main road and round the back of the village to a wide path that leads through the fields. James is charging along, making me sing the soundtrack to *Rocky*, and then he sprints ahead and tells me to move my giant arse.

174

I whizz past him, flipping him the finger, and as I pedal past the vines I'm thinking that actually this was a bloody great idea. While the sun is still fierce, the breeze on the bike is cool, and the wind rushes loudly in my ears. The saddle is digging in so I stand on the pedals and think about ET and how much I love that film. Then I think how lucky we are to be in this amazing countryside, the yellow grass, the deep green vines, these amazing black and white butterflies . . . And tiny purple flowers, I wish I knew the names of more flowers. The crickets are chirruping, and I'm thinking I'll create an amazing pudding for next summer, using French apricots, maybe with dark chocolate and toasted almonds and . . . where's James?

I turn the bike around and see him in the distance, bent double, and I race back.

He is deep red, sweat pouring off him, gulping for breath.

'Are you okay?' I rest my hand on his back as panic grips me. We have been boozing for two days solid and eating too much. Because he behaves like a teenager I forget that he's actually middle-aged and averagely fit, and maybe his body can't take this abuse.

'I'm fine, I'm fine, I'll catch you up,' he says, waving me away.

I touch his neck and feel his pulse racing.

'Come on. Home,' I say. 'Cold shower, drink some water. It's boiling out here.'

'I'm fine, Soph.'

'Well, I'm not. I'm too hot. And I can't do the front door on my own.' We both know this is a lie. 'Besides, this saddle has given me bruises all over the inside of my thighs.'

'I'll kiss them better . . .' he says, grinning. 'See, Dr Klein, I'm in rude health.'

'I think you need emergency surgery,' I say, 'remove the "bad pun" generator in your brain.' I put one arm around his waist and wheel my bike along with the other.

Back home I force him to drink a litre of water and sit calmly, and he says, 'Thank you, thank you, you're so sweet,' and I think: I'm not particularly sweet but this is what anyone would do for a friend, let alone a lover.

He looks a much better colour now, and as we dress for dinner I can feel him watching me. My mind briefly flits to 'the outburst' and I force myself to stop – things are great, and I am not alone in this bubble of happiness. He is here with me. We are in this together.

We drive to the restaurant in the next village and he is once again ebullient. It is the annual summer fête in the town square and before we sit down to eat, James insists on a little dance, under strings of red, green, yellow and blue light bulbs. There are a handful of old ladies in housedresses and comfy sandals, and James takes them each for a twirl on the dance floor, to Aretha Franklin and a random French song about Carcassonne, and then to Neil Diamond. I sit on a low stone wall and think how charming he is, how sincere and comfortable around people, how comfortable in his own skin. I wish again that he didn't have so much money, because it feels like a vast inequality that separates us, and I would sign a pre-nup tomorrow and stay with him if he lost every penny, because I see who he truly is and I love that person. Then I think about his age and that in an ideal world I'd have kids with someone under forty, but what does it matter when he's such a vital, enthusiastic, exuberant man.

We eat in a tiny little place by the river, and James orders a bottle of cheap but fantastic local red the minute we sit down.

'Yum yum, fois gras, and then lamb,' he says, taking a chunk of crusty white bread.

'Is that a good idea, before tomorrow?' And after today . . .

'Stop worrying!'

'I'm going to have the fig salad, then the duck millefeuille sounds amazing.' I think back to the millefeuille and glitter date at the Tate and blush.

'I'll have that too, the millefeuille thing,' he says.

'You can't have the same as me, that's out of order,' I say, my bad self rising to the surface.

'Don't worry, there's different sauces . . . pepper, Roquefort, honey . . .'

'Honey!'

'I'll do Roquefort. See? Done. And let's get another bottle of Minervois.'

He is about to eat foie gras, followed by duck, layered with crispy goose-fat-fried potatoes, smothered in blue cheese sauce, and he is going to be ill off the back of it. But what can I say, he's forty-five, he's a grown-up . . .

Two hours later we are back in bathroom four in our luxury stable and James is hugging the toilet bowl and shivering.

I am forcing him to drink water and mopping his brow with a wet flannel. 'Now you know how those poor foie gras geese feel . . .' I say, smoothing back the damp hair from his forehead.

He rests his head on my knee. 'Will you always be this patient with me, Soph?'

'Of course. We don't have to go tomorrow, if you don't feel better,' I say, and I absolutely mean it.

He looks at me with profound gratitude and amazement. 'I'll be better, I promise.'

*

I think anyone on the planet would enjoy themselves at El Bulli.

You can sense it in the air, along with the smell of pine and eucalyptus; a swell of excitement, the feeling that you are on hallowed ground, the lucky few.

James and I sit on the stone terrace overlooking the beach, and as the sun sets and the ocean turns from indigo to black we are served 36 courses, each more miraculous than the last.

A plate of almonds arrives around course 20, and they're like the Saddam-Hussein-lookalikes of almonds. Some are dead-ringers for almonds but are made from sesame. Some are white and taste intensely of cherry. Some are actually almonds, and taste like the best almonds you've ever eaten. And some of them are transparent, and seem to be made of magic.

Then, at course 33, a giant white egg appears, as if freshly laid by a small dinosaur, alongside a tiny shaker full of curry powder, and the waitress cracks the egg open and it's made of frozen iced coconut, and you can't help but laugh with delight.

The box of chocolates at the end is worth the price of the meal alone. It's like the jewellery box your 8-year-old self imagines a princess would have, rammed with the most extraordinary confections. The waitress tries to wrestle the box away from us after five minutes – I suspect we're the only customers tonight who are going to insist on trying one of everything.

While the whole experience is truly spectacular

and an astounding feat of imagination and technical expertise, throughout the meal I am slightly anxious that James is going to have a heart attack, and I wish we were still sitting, just the two of us in the shade, eating apricots.

The next day at Perpignan airport, I am pulled over to have my bag searched.

The x-ray woman digs around and finds my jar of apricot jam, then wags her finger at me.

'It's not liquid! It's food . . .' I say. 'On mange . . .'

'Non, 300 ml, not allowed,' she says.

'. . . I thought it was only liquid . . .'

'Non,' she says. 'Bin. There.'

I haven't even tasted it, and it's such a bloody waste. 'Vous voulez?' I say, offering it to her.

She shakes her head as if I've offered her a tube of out-of-date Primula.

Now she's just being arsey for the sake of it. 'Next time I fly Ryanair, I'm going to make a peanut butter, jam and semtex sandwich, that'll learn them . . .' I say to James under my breath.

I'm wondering whether to try and escalate – my French isn't anywhere near good enough, and it's only a four euro pot of jam, but it's a principle, isn't it? You can't drink this through a straw: it isn't liquid. Besides, it's local bloody jam; I'm supporting their economy, the ingrates.

James observes me trying to figure out an angle and he intercepts and touches the lady gently on the elbow. He looks over his shoulder at me, then turns to her and in a low voice has a conversation during which she nods, raises her eyebrows, nods again and looks embarrassed. Eventually she holds her hands up, laughs at whatever he's said and apologises to me.

My boyfriend is really great at reading a situation. He always judges perfectly whether to attack or whether to schmooze, and he's excellent at both. Lord only knows what he's said to her but she points to the jam, then points us through the door to the departure gate.

'Well?' I say, once we're out of her eyeline.

'What?'

'What did you say to her?'

He shrugs.

'Stop with the evasiveness! Did you pretend I was up the duff?'

He looks up and to the left.

'Diabetic? James! How did you do that?'

'Pass me the jam.' He unscrews the lid and sticks his tongue in. 'Not bad,' he says, holding it out to me.

'Tell me . . .'

'Done is done, what does it matter?'

That's another thing my boyfriend's really great at. Avoiding a question. Or rather, avoiding a straight answer.

Two weeks after we're back from holiday and six months into the relationship, I finally drag James round to meet my granny.

She has put on her best navy crêpe dress, a diamante brooch in the shape of a Fleur de Lys, and her nails are painted Thunderbird red.

Apart from calling James 'Nicholas' all afternoon, tea goes well. She talks about her childhood in Leytonstone. She and James both played in Epping Forest when they were kids.

My granny tells her favourite story, about how the Rabbi caught her in synagogue chanting 'Jesus, I love you, Jesus, I love you'.

'I was the only Jew in a Roman Catholic School, and Sister Eugenia had told me every "Jesus, I love you" would earn me another flowerbed in heaven.' Her father had given her an almighty clip round the ear that not even the good Lord could save her from.

She tells James the story of how she ate all the toffee creams in her father's sweetshop, replaced them with stones, and how her father's best customer broke a tooth on one. And she tells of how when I was four, I'd crawled under the sideboard and found a diamond earring she'd lost six years earlier – and since that day she'd known I was the one in the family to inherit her brains.

James talks about China, and my grandma is fascinated. 'So many bicycles,' she says.

'And when my suppliers take me for dinner,' says James, 'they'll order a £200 bottle of wine and add Coca Cola to it – they don't actually like the taste of wine!'

'Daft vain buggers,' says my grandma.

'Your grandma's great fun,' says James, as we're driving home.

I can't work out how much she warmed to him. She was hospitable and welcoming as always, but I saw her examining him with a look she used to save for when she was about to accuse one of her carers of deliberately over-salting her soup. To be fair, my grandma does not impress easily. I remember when my friend Gerry 'The Magician' Katzman was visiting from New York. I'd brought him round to cheer her up after a nasty bout of flu. He'd performed various tricks, culminating in one where he'd asked her to think of a card. He'd then coughed once and plucked a folded card from the back of his throat, which happened to be the card she'd been thinking of.

Her response: 'That can't be terribly hygienic.'

★

It is mid-August, a week before Shellii's due date, and I am round at my grandmother's, speaking to her upstairs neighbour, Jack, about borrowing his access code to tap into his WiFi. My grandmother is just a bit too old to get into the internet – I think she'd love it. Having said that, my grandmother holds her cordless home phone out in front of her like a walkie-talkie when she speaks into it, and can't really understand that a voice on an answering machine is pre-recorded.

Jack is an architect, extremely attractive, forty, single and definitely flirting with me. I always thought it was strange that he was unmarried at forty, but being with James, I've forgotten how unusual it is for an attractive man to get past his mid-thirties without biting the bullet. If I wasn't dating James, I might fancy Jack. I'd have dismissed him as being too old for me a year ago, but forty seems positively youthful now. Besides, I never think of James as nearly fifty – he doesn't look it, he rarely acts it.

'How's your grandma doing?' says Jack. 'I haven't seen her in the garden all summer.'

'She's okay,' I say. 'Ninety-seven takes its toll. I sometimes think she's holding out just to see this baby, and then she'll turn out the lights . . .'

'She's unbelievable for her age though — always quoting poetry. Amazing memory. So, when's this baby due then?'

'8pm next Saturday, which is midday Pacific Standard Time.'

'Are you psychic or is that a Caesarean?'

'It's a Leo . . .' I mutter. I'm too ashamed to explain that my brother is having a child with a woman who is being unzipped two weeks early to determine her unborn child's star sign. 'Anyway, thanks for the code, I promise I won't download a wealth of German porn between now and then.'

'Take my number . . .' he says, taking his phone from his jeans pocket. 'Or better still, give me yours, I'll call you, then you'll have mine.'

'Really?'

'In case you have any problems with the WEP code,' he says, smiling as I blush.

'Thank you for helping, it's very kind,' I say.

'Swing by after the call next week and I'll open a bottle of something fizzy. Not every day you become an auntie . . .'

'Thanks, but . . . I'm not sure when we'll be done.'

'No worries.' He kisses me goodbye. 'Another time perhaps . . .'

'Another time.'

★

185

James is out for drinks with the Bonders to talk about the launch of his new business on the Saturday evening when the baby's due, so I drive round to my grandma's on my own with my laptop.

She's been so excited about today, she's barely slept. She looks so fragile I'm scared to hug her and Evie says she hasn't been eating much recently.

I hook up to the internet and click on my Skype account. I'm trying to explain the concept of Skype to my grandma, without success, when my brother phones.

His face appears on screen and my grandma looks at me with wide eyes and starts shaking her head. 'Incredible,' she says.

'Hey! How ya doing?' Nowadays my brother sounds like he's auditioning for *Entourage*. He was the biggest nerd in his year at St Paul's and these days he wears jeans that cost £300 and ponces around drinking spirulina health-shots and eating sushi without the rice. I blame Shellii.

He looks ecstatically happy, and waves to my grandma, who turns to me and says 'Can he see us?'

'Yes, and hear us. Say hello.'

My grandma clears her throat and shouts at the screen, 'Hello, Josh. It's your grandmother! Remember me?'

'Do you want to see your great-granddaughter?' he says.

She turns to me and asks what he's just said.

'Show us the baby, what's her name?' I say.

He holds up a tiny, perfect little girl, wrapped in a pale

pink blanket, and my grandma looks at me again. 'Whose baby is that?'

'What's her name, Josh?' I say.

'Say hello to Elektra Dylan Klein,' he says.

'Did he say the little boy's name is Dylan?' says my grandmother.

'That's your great-granddaughter,' I say. 'Elektra.'

She reaches out her hand and her fingers tremble as she touches the screen and strokes the baby's face. 'My God,' she says, 'Sophie, is this real or am I asleep?'

The start of autumn is a golden dream. James and I spend our weekends walking through leaves, drinking whisky and ginger in pubs and cooking bread and butter puddings. When it rains, we have marathon DVD box set nights, play backgammon and look at the weirdos on Chatroulette.com.

One night in early October, we are lying in his bed, legs entwined, drifting into sleep. I can feel James staring at me. I open my eyes and he is smiling.

'What?' I say.

'How would you feel about helping me out with the kitchen?'

'It's two in the morning!' I say into his chest. 'I'm not cleaning your bloody oven, James, even your cleaner won't touch it.'

'No, dummy, I mean helping me choose a new kitchen.'

I raise myself up on one elbow. 'You're actually going to do something about that pit?'

'You're a good influence on me, Soph. Besides, I can't have a girlfriend with a nicer kitchen than me.'

'Wow, alpha male competitive kitchen war . . . how can I say no.' I lie back down and bury my face into his chest.

'So how about I give you the budget, and you just . . . choose the perfect kitchen. You've got great taste, you know kitchens . . .'

'But . . . it's your kitchen . . . I'm totally happy to help you, but . . . why don't you just go to Wigmore Street and find a designer.'

'See, Wigmore Street, you know all the places.' he says.

'I'll help but . . . it should be your taste, it's your kitchen.'

'That's the thing. I was thinking one day maybe it might be our kitchen . . .'

'I think he's asked me to move in,' I say.

'What do you mean, you think?' says Laura.

'You know how non-committal he is with the words – everything's always . . . *maybe* . . . *it might* . . . *one day* . . .'

'What did he say specifically?'

'I was half asleep. But I think he wants me to choose a new kitchen for his house. He's giving me a budget, and when the kitchen's done, he wants me to move in.'

'Fucking hell. That's . . . great, I'm really happy for you. He makes you happy. What did you say?'

'Well, then we sort of had a row the following morning about the budget . . .'

'God, Soph, can't you just keep your mouth shut? He'll give you as much as you need, he's not tight.'

'No, that's the point. He wants me to spend like a hundred grand on it, and I won't. It's a ridiculous waste of money.'

'Bloody hell. You are playing this all so wrong!'

'Laura, it's not a game. I just don't feel comfortable wasting anyone's money. You can get an amazing kitchen for half that. Look, I don't have a problem buying beautiful things, but I'm not buying a Swarovski-encrusted bloody extractor fan just for the sake of it, it's bullshit. All I've ever wanted is a fridge with an ice machine in the door. If I can have that I'll be happy.'

James is busy working on the launch of L'Esteeme, and my new range of desserts is progressing well. Will and I have developed 12 products that are at Stage 3: testing the production lines, macrobiotics and nutritionals.

My weekends and lunch breaks are spent sorting out our-'our!'-new kitchen. I've been up and down Wigmore Street and found a lovely independent showroom, 'LSW Kitchens,' run by a man called Luke.

I've decided on a modern, simple design that isn't too obnoxiously priced. James is so not bothered about the money, but I am; so unnecessary to spend fifty grand on a kitchen, let alone more. The things that matter to me are a decent double oven, a double sink and a gas hob. Everything else is a bonus. Three days into the process and I wonder how I have managed to live, let alone cook, without a £4,000 steam oven with a plate-warming drawer.

James wants the kitchen fitted by December, and by

the end of September Luke and I have costed out a perfect kitchen for forty five grand. I drive James to the show-room on a Saturday afternoon to talk him through the plans.

'We've looked at grey oak for the breakfast island,' I say, 'with the counter tops in pure white composite.'

'That's 94% quartz, 6% resin,' chimes in Luke.

'Then high gloss white units, keep the look clean. And here's the oven!'

'Anthracite on the outside . . .' says Luke.

'But look at the inside!' I say, overlapping Luke as he smiles at me. 'Isn't it beautiful! The pyrolytic finish is the most gorgeous royal blue contrast to the grey exterior. 'And! It cleans itself! Tell Rosie she'll never have to worry about cleaning your oven again. And the dial is digital! Digital! How cool is that?'

James grins his approval.

'And the hob is flush-fitted – it's one single piece of metal, just like your Maserati,' I say.

'Sold,' says James.

'And finally the fridge, look, it has an ice maker in the door!'

'What's that fridge over there?' says James, pointing at a mammoth double-doored stainless steel beast in the corner.

'That's the Sub-Zero,' says Luke. 'State of the Art, NASA technology, comes with a GPS tracking system so that central control know what's wrong with the fridge before they send an engineer out. Not that anything ever goes wrong with these fridges.'

I shake my head. 'James, it's ridiculous. It's too big, we don't need a fridge that big. And it costs more than seven grand.'

'But it has two compressors, one for the fridge, one for the freezer,' says Luke. 'Your vanilla ice cream will never taste of foie gras . . .'

'It'd be a result if it did taste of foie gras!' I say. 'Water into wine and all that . . .'

'And the food stays fresher much longer.' Luke opens the door to the fridge. On the bottom shelf are lined up nine bottles of Bollinger.

'Yep, that's the one,' says James.

Luke goes into the back office and James grabs me, lifts me on to the kitchen counter and positions himself between my legs.

'Stop it! He'll be back in a minute,' I say, as his hands reach under my top to undo my bra.

'Won't take more than forty seconds, love . . .' he says.

'I can't believe it! You're turned on by that bloody fridge, aren't you?' I say, pushing him away and laughing.

'Nice, new, shiny toy,' he says.

'I am not getting the Sub-Zero fridge, James. It's a ridiculous waste of money. I'll look at that fridge and always see in its place a big pile of cash that could have paid for an amazing holiday or school fees or . . .'

'Soph, it's not either/or. I've got the money. I want that fridge.'

'But what are you paying for, beyond keeping lettuce cold? It doesn't even have an ice machine in the door.'

'It has perma-ice in the freezer drawer. You're paying for state-of-the-art technology. I just like knowing it's there.'

'You lived for the last ten years with a mini booze fridge without shelves! Suddenly you can't live without the NASA engineering?'

'You're the only girl I've ever been out with who wanted me to spend less of my money on them.'

Why doesn't that tell him something about those other girls?

'Soph. Does the ice-machine mean that much to you?'

'Well . . . kind of. It's just the crushed ice part really . . . margaritas, daiquiris . . .?'

'Okay, we'll get the Sub-Zero and I will buy you the world's best ice-crusher, and if the Sub-Zero ice cubes are not to my lady's liking, I will personally crush them smaller for you whenever you click your fingers. How does that sound? Me, James Stephens – your own personal ice crusher. Call Debrett's and tell them I'm moving up in the world.'

194

We drive out to Colchester the following Saturday to eat fresh, cheap shellfish at The Company Shed. We sit chatting to the couple squashed next to us who are in their seventies, and who hold hands across the table while they drink a bottle of Cava. They talk about how much joy they get from being grandparents, but how they're happiest of all when it's just the two of them, playing cards and listening to the radio.

After they've left I say to James, 'Do you ever think you'll have what those two have?'

'Absolutely,' he says, 'but I'm not going to marry just anyone.'

I have drunk two-thirds of the bottle of wine we've brought, and so although my instant reaction is to take this comment personally, I realise he must be referring to the fact that *that's why* he's never been married before.

I pop to the loo and stand by the sink looking in the mirror. I haven't weighed myself for ages but my face is looking a little gaunt. Don't they say that as you get older your face looks better if you're not too skinny? Typical – I've lived my life back to front, spent my youth a dress size over, and now that I'm an ancient thirty-three, I'm finally a dress size under.

My face is quite flushed from the booze and I splash it with cold water. By the time I come out, James is chatting to a new couple seated next to us. They're already laughing and so even if I wanted to ask James what he actually meant by that comment, I've missed my chance.

★

On the drive home we stop off in Stratford to see my friends Debbie and Dan. Debbie is beautiful but is carrying an extra two stone that she hasn't lost after giving birth to their second child a year ago. Debbie has mild post-natal depression and Debbie and Dan are having counselling to get them through the bumpy patch. I warn James of this so that he can avoid the subject and not stick his foot in it like he often does.

He is abnormally quiet, probably too scared to say the wrong thing. He watches Debbie closely as she eats a third slice of Victoria Sponge, her finger erasing the last stripe of jam from the plate. In the car on the way home I say I'm a bit worried about their relationship.

'She should take better care of herself,' he says.

'I told you she's depressed.'

'She'll be more depressed when he leaves her for someone thin.'

'Oi, that's my friend you're talking about.'

'Why are you taking it personally?'

'Because sometimes people are vulnerable. And they need love and support, not criticism. She put on that weight giving birth to his children.'

'He's supposed to be eternally grateful that she's a lard arse? A wife should make an effort for her husband. She should get down the gym, get on the high heels and suspenders, that'll sort out their marriage better than some stupid therapy.'

'You are such a dick sometimes,' I say, poking his stomach. 'We shouldn't have to dress like prostitutes to win your affection. God, you really are an 80s cheeseball throwback, aren't you?'

He laughs. I laugh, but only for the soundtrack.

*

James has signed a contract on the kitchen, and LSW are ripping out his old kitchen and starting to fit the new one next week. It'll take eight weeks if all goes according to plan, and I'm moving in the first week of January. I am so over-excited about co-habiting that I have pushed the flecks of doubt I have about this relationship well beneath the surface.

Occasionally they rise up and I am forced to examine them:

Four months ago he said you weren't his normal type. Why would that ever change?

Think of Celine's legs compared to yours.

Think of why he isn't married at forty-five. That's not normal.

And then I think:

We have fallen in love.

He has asked me to move in.

He is truly himself when he's with me.

We never stop laughing and talking and that's what makes a relationship last.

Remember the way he looks at you when he thinks you're not watching: that is real, that is real, that is real.

L'Esteeme is launching in mid-November. James is away a couple of times in October, and it is on a Friday morning, while he is in Cape Town for a week shooting the press campaign, that Evie calls to tell me my grandmother has died.

I have been at my grandma's every night this week; she's been on morphine to manage the increasing pain that's been creeping up in the last few months, and if she's been awake when I've been there, she's been barely lucid. I baked her a lemon cake on Monday, but she hasn't eaten anything solid since Saturday, and it's a struggle even to make her drink water.

Wednesday was the last time we spoke. I took round a bunch of her favourite orange tulips and sat on her bed, scared that the weight of me next to her might disturb her. She smiled softly and stroked my hand with one finger.

'Your nails look beautiful, Grandma,' I said.

She nodded slowly and in a voice weakened by utter exhaustion said 'goodnight, Sophola.'

On Thursday night she'd been unconscious, and on Friday, just before dawn, the phone rang.

I rush over to find Evie, teary-eyed and looking like she hasn't slept for days. I make her a coffee, and we call the doctor and the synagogue.

'Did she say anything before she died?' I say, curious to know if she'd mentioned my grandfather, or my dad. Maybe a final word of advice for me?

'Sophie, she did, but I don't think I heard her properly,' says Evie.

'Was it "horse stealer"?'

'No, nothing about a horse. I think . . . I think she said "Jesus, I love you".'

★

My mother can't fly over for the funeral, because Shellii has hired a maternity nurse for three months, and my mother doesn't trust the maternity nurse, or Shellii, not to kill the baby, so she's shadowing them 24/7. Meanwhile, Shellii seems to be spending all her time at The Beverly Hills Hotel, pitching her new Spiritual Slimming video blog to producers, so just as well my niece has two surrogate mummies, given that her real one's not doing the job.

My grandma died on the Friday, and by Monday she's in the ground. She chose 'Fly Me to the Moon' as the final piece of music at the funeral, and it was *so* my grandma, stealing the show, as always, not a dry eye in the house.

She lived such a long and mostly-blessed life that I suppose

I thought she'd always be around. I can't quite compute that she's not on the other end of the phone to moan about how bored she is, or ask about what I'm cooking for supper tonight. I cried at the funeral and at the prayers, but I don't feel a huge sense of grief. Nonetheless, I really wish James was here to help – not with the admin, but it would just be nice to have someone to come home to, just to be there.

On Wednesday night I go round to help Evie sort through my grandma's stuff. My grandma wanted most of her possessions to go to charity. She's left me the diamond earrings I found under the sideboard, her photos, papers and cookery books. The only other things I take from the flat are her pink fluffy dressing gown – it smells so much of her – and a stash of diazepam. I do like the occasional sleeping pill on an aeroplane. I consider whether I should pocket the bottle of liquid morphine the doctor prescribed for her, but figure with my semi-addictive personality that's probably not the smartest idea I ever had. I make Evie take any and all the clothes that fit her, and after four hours of boxing and bagging, the job is mostly done.

I call James when I get home at midnight but his phone goes straight to voicemail. Are they one hour ahead in Cape Town? Something like that. He'll have been on the shoot all day, he must be tired. Besides, all I wanted to say was hello. He's back in two days anyway, and I spoke to him a couple of days ago.

It doesn't matter, does it?

But as I get in to bed, I think that actually yes – it does matter, a bit, to me.

When James comes back the following week, we're in the final stages of the kitchen being fitted. I am at work in a meeting with Will from Appletree discussing vanilla pods when my phone rings: James. I ignore it.

'I really want to use the Madagascan again if we can,' I say to Will, sliding a knife along the slit-open pod and marvelling at the tiny black specks that make all the difference between good custard and great.

'So much better than the essence, I know. But have you thought about Tahitian? It's more floral, it should work well on the ultra-vanilla,' he says, taking out what looks like a cigar tube from his bag, popping open the lid and passing it to me.

My phone rings: James again. 'Sorry Will, I'll just get rid of this . . . James? Can I call you back, I'm in a meeting.'

'It's very important,' he says.

'What's wrong?'

'Nothing. Be outside your office in twenty minutes, I need to show you something.'

I check my watch – 4.30pm. We're practically done but I was considering taking Will across to the Japanese cream bun specialist on Dean Street as I wanted his technical opinion on how they make their custard so thick and yet light.

'Is it really important?' I ask, thinking I could always take Will there another time – he's down in London quite a lot at the moment.

'Yes. Very,' says James, 'see you soon.'

'Sorry, Will. Right, so the Tahitian . . . for the ultra-vanilla. And maybe for the raspberry custard? Would that work?'

'Yep, it works with cherry too, and almond.'

'Almond . . . interesting. Okay, could you do comparative costs with the Madagascan? Then I can get Devron to choose between the two, and hopefully he'll forget that essence is even an option.'

'Done. Are you heading off somewhere now? I was going to say we should check out Shake Away for a milkshake up in Islington at some point.'

'Oh! I want to go there! But now's not good . . .'

'Don't worry, it's just my train's not till 7pm – I just thought if you were free . . . Another time.'

'Deal,' I say, and he reaches for my hand to shake on it.

★

Twenty minutes later James pulls up outside my office.

'Hop in, Wench. With any luck we'll beat the rush hour,'

he says through his car window, pushing my door open from the inside.

'Alright, what's the hurry and where are we going?'

'St. James's Palace!' he says, flashing me a smile.

'You've dragged me out of work why exactly?'

'I'm taking you down to the basement!'

'The units are in, I've already seen them.'

'Aha, but there's more! I called Luke from Cape Town and told him I'd give him a bonus if he got all the kit in while I was away. Nothing like a bit of cash in hand to get things done.'

'You did that? Why didn't one of you let me know? I thought I was project managing?'

'Oh, well, what difference? Anyway, you wouldn't have wanted to think about that stuff, what with your grandma . . .'

I guess.

'What's wrong?' he says. 'You look pissed off.'

'No, you're right. I was busy,' I say, remembering how shitty it felt when I tried to call you and you weren't there.

'Don't look, don't look,' he says, his hand clasping mine as he guides me slowly down the stairs. He pulls me to the centre of the room, then stands close behind me, placing both hands firmly on my shoulders. 'Now look.'

The kitchen is amazing. Nothing actually works yet but it all looks terrific. Bright and light and shiny, full of the potential of a thousand perfect unbaked cakes.

'What do you think?' he says, looking at me nervously. I walk over to the Gaggenau oven and open and close the door a dozen times. That beautiful purplish blue – I wonder if it's okay to keep the oven door open all the time?

'Come on, Rain Man, it's not just about the oven, what about the Sub-Zero?' he says, standing hands on hips admiring his baby.

I am strongly of the opinion that it looks too big, but he is so overjoyed with it I just give him a hug and tell him it's all wonderful.

He picks up a big glossy brochure from the counter top. 'And did you know, the guys who make Sub-Zeros also do an oven range, Soph? And it's called Wolf. Wolf! Next time we do up a kitchen everything has to be Wolf!'

I shake my head in wonder. How have I managed to end up with James, the most alpha male on the planet?

My ex, Nick, was shy. He used to write me the most tender, heartfelt love songs and sing them to me while I was in the bath. I'd sometimes call him Bluebird: his eyes were bright blue, he was supremely gentle, and his voice was beautiful, but that wasn't why. It was after a poem by Charles Bukowski, Nick's favourite poem, my favourite poem.

I have flown from a bluebird to a wolf.

★

Two weeks later, the kitchen is still not quite finished. James is working all hours in the run-up to his launch, now just a week away. I'm at his house meeting with Luke to discuss when the various valves that are stuck on an autobahn outside Munich will arrive, so that our shiny new hob and oven will actually work.

By the time we've finished it's nearly ten, and James calls to say he's on his way home and can't bear the thought of another takeaway.

We can't cook at mine. My fridge is crammed with pre-Phase 4 samples of my puddings at various life-stages. I'm presenting final products to Devron when he's back from the Maldives next February, but I'm trying to finish all my work before Christmas. I'd love to spend my first Christmas with James doing absolutely nothing but eating, drinking, going for the occasional whisky-fuelled walk and watching old films.

I ask Luke to drop me round at the Sainsbury's in Chalk Farm and then can't work out what I feel like eating that doesn't involve cooking. I opt for my favourite student fallback plan and head home, laden with jars. I swing by the posh offie round the corner from James and buy a lovely bottle of Fitou.

'Where have you been, woman?' says James, coming to the door in just his trousers. 'I thought you were shagging Luke round the back, I know he's got a thing for you.'

'Don't be ridiculous,' I say. 'I was fetching your supper.'

'Good wifelet,' he says, tapping me on the head. 'What's in the bag?'

'Well. Currently in your kitchen the only heat sources are matches and a toaster. I don't much fancy holding a marshmallow over your Swan Vestas, so I propose a night of toast and Philadelphia, inspired by our little trip to El Bulli . . .'

'Toast?'

'Yes. What?'

'If we just need the toaster, let's do it in the bedroom . . .'

He takes wine glasses, cutlery and the toaster up to his room and puts the blanket from his bed on the floor.

'Naked picnic,' he says, taking his trousers off.

I don't ever, ever eat or drink anything hot when I'm naked, after I spilt boiling coffee down my torso while in my underwear three years ago. Nick had to sit with me in A&E for four hours with a wet towel wrapped around my middle. I couldn't put on clothes as the burn went from under my bra to the top of my pants, and the incident scarred me more psychologically than physically.

'Lend me a t-shirt. Okay, you're going to have to trust me,' I say.

'Never trust anyone,' says James.

'Shhh . . . pour the wine. Okay, wholegrain toast. First round, butter under the Philadelphia.'

While we're waiting for the toast to pop we fool around and James tries to shag me. 'Even you can't do it in less

207

than two minutes,' I say, as I push him off and take a sip of wine. 'Right, try this.'

'Mmmm, really good with the butter. Why have I never tried that?'

'Next – a taste of France . . .' I say.

I put another slice in and James attempts to maul me and I don't put up much of a struggle. 'Okay, stop – toast . . .'

'Apricot jam on cream cheese? Yuk.'

'Trust me.'

'Fuck, that's good.'

'Same basis as a cheesecake. Next . . .'

We indulge in considerable heavy petting, and seven variants of cream cheese on toast (pickled cucumber: excellent; black olives: also excellent; avocado: surprisingly excellent).

After I have made James check the toaster is unplugged, twice, we snuggle under the rug, and by the time I've popped to the bathroom to clean my teeth and returned, he is snoring.

I stroke his hair, fetch another pillow to lodge under his head and curl up beside him.

Tonight's the big night – November 17th – the launch of L'Esteeme. James seems anxious – normally he's so confident, I rarely see him like this. He almost looks scared, though I can't imagine why. He's bloody good at selling; I know whatever he applies himself to he'll do well.

The launch event is at a bar off Mount Street in Mayfair. I'm wearing my best black silk dress from Zara. It's very 1950s Gina Lollobrigida, with a nipped-in waist and a full skirt. Normally I feel great in this dress, but tonight James's nervousness seems contagious.

He introduces me to his business associates with a reticence that makes me paranoid. When he says 'this is my girlfriend, Sophie', the word 'girlfriend' sits heavily on his tongue like an ulcer.

On the table next to us sit the financiers, four men straight out of *Rosemary's Baby*, but with George Hamilton tans. Nothing but their eyes move, darting to the podium or to the champagne waiter to beckon him to fill up the long, thin flutes that their wives' collagen-mouths are suckered to like plastic frogs in a bath.

The wives, the wives. Trophies growing tarnished. The average age of the men I'd put at sixty-five, the women fifty, but with the foreheads and wardrobes of 28-year-olds. Full beauty queen make-up cannot hide their strained expressions.

Their heads swivel, glancing at their neighbours' earrings, necklaces, brooches. Heads left, right, down. Fingers stretch and clasp, stretch and clasp, like they're warming up for a concerto. Rubies and emeralds and Christmas-cracker diamonds glare off each other. Between them they must be wearing £10 million in rocks.

None of them speaks. I have never seen four more miserable looking women in my life.

Up on the screen the new face of L'Esteeme is projected.

Noushka. Russian, 5' 11". Discovered in a Moscow shopping mall: long dark chestnut hair, too-wide pale blue eyes. Her face is all angles as if drawn with a set square by a German engineering student. Cheek bones to jaw – jaw to chin. A nose so sharp you could pop a balloon on it. Pow!

It is a striking face. Hard. Determined. It is not a face I envy. It is, in fact, a weird face but it shoots well on film. But the point of Noushka is not the face. It is the body. Known as 'Legs', she has, of course, the most perfect legs. Genetically blessed, shapely, endless, not a trace of fat but not too musclar, ending in perfect ankles at one end, a perfect bottom at the other. The bottom you see on the anti-cellulite ads that you convince yourself must belong to an 8-year-old boy or else life is too unfair.

The picture has probably been retouched, these things always are nowadays. James is staring at the screen as the letters spelling 'L'Esteeme' curl out from between Noushka's knees, snake between her thighs and crawl to rest across her bottom.

'Oh Lordy, who did the graphic design?' I say. 'It looks like the 't' is going right up her arse.'

He looks plagued with irritation.

'What?' he says.

'Great legs,' I say smiling. He continues to look as if he needs a Rennie.

The photographer Seyon comes out on stage and wanks on for five minutes about what a privilege it has been to work on the job. Yes, a $20,000 a day privilege, to be sure. Then he introduces Noushka herself, who comes out to a standing ovation made up entirely of the men in the audience.

In real life she is thinner – they always are. And the angles of her face that work so well in print are over-exaggerated in the flesh. She looks as if she's harbouring a bread stick in her lower jaw. Unlikely.

She waves to the audience, proper, practised Miss World wave, and her elbow slices back and forth through the air like the apex of a wishbone.

James is staring at her in a way that I have never, ever seen him look at me. It is the way he sometimes looks when he is driving his car too fast.

Up on stage Seyon is introducing the behind-the-scenes footage. There are sound bites of Seyon shot on the beach in Cape Town, talking about the challenges of shooting 70 dernier stockings in 80 degree heat. God, Afghan mine-sweepers have got nothing on you, love.

Then there is Noushka, sitting on a yacht, her long, frizz-free hair blowing in the humid breeze. She is cradling some sort of ratty handbag dog, waving the dog's paws to the camera. 'Say hi to everybody, Mona-Coco,' she says to the dog, before kissing it on the mouth.

I look over at James and roll my eyes. 'Mona-Coco?'

'Monaco, Coco Chanel. Be quiet,' he snaps.

'How would I describe my personality?' she asks herself, in a surprised voice. 'I love jewels. High heels. And of course stockings. I am sensuous Russian woman.' The 's's of 'sensuous' hiss out of her mouth like poisoned gas. 'When I was little girl, I have dream that one day I will be Russian Cinder Cror-ford.'

'Wow, it's like Martin Luther King all over again . . .' I say, wishing Laura was here with me to witness this nonsense.

James turns to me, exasperated. 'Why do you have to be so bitchy?'

'Oh come on! I love jewels and high heels? That's not a personality, that's a shopping list.'

212

'She's a sweet girl. You're just jealous.'

A kind boyfriend would laugh at my joke, or tell me I'm way more gorgeous than Noushka, even though we'd both know he was lying. Actually, one time in New York, Nick and I had sat in McNally's on the next table to Cindy Crawford. He had looked at her only once, in passing, and only because she was sitting next to the bass player in one of his favourite bands. Even when I'd commented on how much more beautiful she looked in real life than in magazines, he'd just shrugged: 'too skinny'.

I miss Nick.

'Noushka's actually very bright, very driven. She's launching her own brand of toenail polish in Eastern Europe,' says James.

'Toenail polish? Just toes, not fingers?'

He nods. 'Toenails need a thicker consistency than finger nails . . . I don't know.'

'What bollocks, nails are nails,' I say.

'Give it a rest, Soph. Why are you attacking her?'

Why are you defending her? I take a deep breath, force a smile. 'I'm going to the bar, do you want anything?'

'Actually, I'm going to pop backstage and speak to the guys.'

'Which guys?'

'Those guys,' he motions at the stage, as Noushka kisses both her palms and shakes them goodbye at the crowd.

'Shall I come?'

'I'll be two minutes,' and he's off, weaving his way through the crowd.

'I thought IWCs never broke?'

'What?'

'That was a long two minutes.' I am alone at the bar, three gin and tonics and a large bowl of Japanese crackers down.

He shrugs. This man has never apologised for anything. Ever. 'You've not been too slow with the drinks, Soph. And what was in that bowl? Not shy with the snacks tonight either, are you?'

'Sorry?'

'We're going to Cecconi's for drinks and dinner with the Bonders. You know that.'

'And how has me eating 32 Japanese peanuts got anything to do with that fact? Or with you?'

He pulls his head back as if I've belched.

'Are you going to be this aggressive all night?' he says.

'No. No, I'm not.' I snatch my bag and step down from my bar stool, clutching the seat tight. My heels are high but my legs aren't quite long enough. – Okay, landed okay.

'Where are you going?' he asks, suddenly conciliatory, almost forlorn.

'Away from here,' I say, exhaustion and rage making me sound like I'm in a South American soap opera.

'What is wrong with you?' He looks genuinely confused.

What indeed.

214

You have spent seventy minutes backstage with Noushka when you said you'd be two.

Yes, I can and have fended for myself, talking to various dullards about joint ventures/venture capital/capital gains tax/why taxing the rich at 50% is sooooo unfair.

But I would rather not have to.

And more than anything I think you want that perfectly thin young Russian model to be by your side instead of me.

'I'm just tired,' I say. 'Sorry.' It's his big night. I'm ruining it, I'm being a brat. It isn't about me. I'm paranoid, over-sensitive, insecure.

Maybe. But it doesn't mean I'm wrong.

Be the bigger person. Be gracious. 'Look, why don't you take Noushka to Cecconi's with the Bonders instead, it's business after all . . .' His face lights up like it's Christmas. I know I am making a giant tactical error.

'If you're sure, I'll text you when I get in, I'll give you some money for a cab . . .' He's frantically looking for his wallet, desperate to rush backstage and grab her before she heads back to her hotel.

'I'll pay for my own cab. Have a good time.' He nods, and I leave him there with his £20 in his hand.

I'm lying in bed. It's 2.44am. He hasn't texted. Cecconi's will have shut by midnight, I figure. Even with a late night drink with the Bonders he should be home by now.

There's no possible way I can text him to say 'goodnight' without looking like an insecure freak.

He's probably on his last drink of the evening; they'll have gone to Soho House or some other club . . .

You have to trust people. How else can you be in a relationship? I do trust him.

I turn my phone off. The lack of the flashing blue light is bugging me more than a flashing blue light. If I turn it off, he'll text five minutes later. That's often happened with him.

When I wake up at 5.30am, I immediately turn my phone on.

No messages.

I have a weird tingling feeling in my arms. My instinct is entirely telling me something is wrong, but I don't trust my instinct any more because I think I'm paranoid.

I get out of bed and go for a run round the block to try and clear my head. I manage ten minutes, then come home, shower, and lie back on the bed.

I am going to have to wait for him to call me this morning, and when he does, I'm not going to be able to have a go at him, because if I do I'll sound like a fishwife.

I make it through to midday without hearing from him, feeling increasingly sick with anxiety. This is so entirely,

entirely ridiculous, I think. We're moving in together. He is with me. He is with me. Why am I scared to text him after nearly a year together? That in itself is weird, and the problem must be me. Think positive.

I text him: 'Sore head?'

A minute later he calls me, and I pretend everything is hunky dory, and he is at his desk and very perky and says he had quite a fun evening, and what am I doing tonight, he'd like to see me.

My stomach drops. He's going to dump me. I can feel it, I know it, I absolutely know it.

'Why do you want to see me?' I say.

'I want to take you somewhere nice for dinner,' he says. His voice sounds slightly guilty.

He's not going to dump me in public, surely.

'I can't do tonight,' I say.

'Okay then, tomorrow?'

'No,' I say.

'. . . Okay.'

'Well, sorry, yes, tomorrow's Thursday, sorry, got my days confused . . .'

'Okay.'

The following day he picks me up at 8pm. I am so wracked with paranoia that I feel sick.

'Hungry?' he says.

'Where are we going?'

'It's a surprise.' That doesn't sound like I'm en route to a dumping.

We head into town and I stare out of the window as we drive through Regent's Park, thinking: I have to learn to say when things bother me. I've bitten my tongue too often in this relationship.

'I'm really sorry but I need to ask you something,' I say.

He looks panicked.

'Why didn't you text me when you got in the other night?'

'I was tired . . . it was late . . . I forgot . . .'

'Okay,' I say. 'Actually, not okay. It can't be all of those three. Which was it?'

'It was late . . .' He is rubbing his thumb against his middle finger, and it's setting off another alarm in my brain.

'Your body language is weird,' I say. 'Look at your fingers . . .'

'You're reading far too much into this.' People always say that when you're on to something.

'– So you had a good time with the Bonders, that's good, I'm glad,' I say.

I swallow it, but it sticks in my throat, another stone.

He parks off Berwick Street and takes my arm in his. He stops outside a Spanish restaurant that I've been desperate to try for months. 'I hope you haven't been here already, you mentioned it the other day . . .'

'Good choice,' I say, as we're seated at a small corner table looking out onto Soho. It's so cosy we're practically sitting on each other's laps, and James puts his arm around me.

'Isn't this nice,' he says, smiling and taking my hand.

Ridiculous. There is nothing wrong, and I'm basically mad, and I need to learn to not be paranoid anymore.

We have such a great night, it's like our first date. It's so weird, but almost every date has been like that first date, apart from the unfortunate night of the outburst. If we weathered that storm and can still sit here blissfully, we're going to be just fine, I think.

When we get home, I have a bath, and by the time I get out, James is asleep in my bed. But when I get in, I feel his arm snake around me, and a moment later we are kissing and then he is on top of me in the semi-darkness and I am thinking 'this is how love is, natural and close and intimate and beautiful'.

My legs are bent, my knees up towards my shoulders, and after a while James looks down at me, and then moves my right leg down. For some reason his action sticks in my mind over the following days. It reminds me of those 'How to Sunbathe and Look Your Best' articles they used to run in *Just 17*: Put your arms over your head to lift your breasts. Stomach in. Chin down. Legs just so.

There I go, reading too much into things . . .

'Happy birthday, Soph,' says James, handing me a Harrods bag with a box inside it. 'Don't shake it, just open it!'

'Shouldn't I read the card first?'

'Nah, present. More exciting.'

I rip off the paper.

'I knew you wouldn't buy it for the kitchen 'cause you think it's too extravagant, but you said they were the best . . .'

'A Bamix! I love it.' Bamix are the best, best handheld blenders in the business. They're expensive but they're worth it.

'And it comes with a 30-year guarantee.'

If only *you* did too, I think. 'Let's keep it at yours, save it till the kitchen's done. I'll use it the night I move in.'

'Good idea,' he says.

He starts picking up my other birthday cards from the side.

'Who's Will and why is he making you a cake?'

'Just a supplier,' I say, grabbing the card off him. 'His chef's making me one, not him.'

'And who's this? From, 'Z', 'I know one day you'll change your mind!'

I laugh. 'My secret lover, Zoltan . . .'

'Who is it?'

'My friend Zoe who works in the fridge, I think she has a crush on me.'

'Really?'

'Some people do find me attractive you know, James!'

'No, I just . . . lesbians . . .' Every other boyfriend I've had would immediately say 'Can I watch?' But instead James proceeds to outline his theory about why all lesbians are predators.

'Women crave attention more than men, and they'll take it from any source . . .'

'Excuse me?'

'Seriously. Lesbians take advantage of that . . .'

'I think you're confusing lesbians with heterosexual men,' I say.

He looks mildly irked that I am treating his argument with such disdain, when actually I am restraining myself from calling him a halfwit. He's not a halfwit at all, he's unbelievably shrewd, but maybe just a reactionary chauvinist. Either way, he looks hot when he's angry.

I open his card. It has a black and white picture of an

old granny, sitting on a sofa with a teapot on her lap. Inside he has written:

'To my favourite Sofa. I'm never more comfortable than when I'm with you.'

I have moved from 'Queen of Puddings' to 'Green-eyed monster' via 'Slothie' and have ended up as a 'Sofa'. I'm not sure I'm moving in the right direction.

*

We go for dinner at Locatelli's, and eat the entire bread basket, then pasta, then lamb, then pudding. We drink two bottles of amazing red wine, then eat the truffle, the amaretto and the little jelly cube that comes with the coffee. We have the most fun of anyone in the restaurant, trying to work out which women are hookers and which are just eastern European. There's a B-list celeb here with a guy I grew up with, and the four of us have more cocktails, and while the B-list is off in the toilet doing coke, my friend gives James and me the low-down on who's really shagging who in the world of nonentity celebrity.

We hail a cab around midnight and at home collapse on top of his bed. I unbutton my skirt so I can breathe, and untuck his shirt and loosen his belt for the sake of his gut.

'So. Thirty-four!' he says. 'I think you're now officially a spinster.'

'Piss off.'

'Seriously, I might have to call Svetlana, she's still in her twenties, wrinkle free . . .'

'Grim. You're old enough to be her dad.'

'First sign of senility: jealousy of beautiful young girls . . .'

Happy birthday to you, too.

'James, if we have kids in a few years you'll hit sixty before they're even teenagers. At Yasmine Jayde's eighteenth birthday party, you'll be the sad randy 70-year-old everyone assumes is the granddad. I'll probably find you trying to grope her school friends from the confines of your Maserati wheelchair, so don't give me any grief about my age, you mean old bastard.'

'Touched a nerve . . . you never used to be this irritable back when you were young . . .'

I grab his chin in my hand. 'Shut up and kiss me you fool, while you still have your own teeth.'

We kiss and smile and kiss. I don't want to have sex – I'm full of food and booze, but I roll on top of him just to look at how handsome he is.

'Get off me, you big lump,' he says.

And while I try in the following days to re-remember his tone as playful or affectionate or the result of me squashing his over-full stomach, the truth is it was none of those.

'3rd December, what are you doing?' says James.

'. . . next Saturday, seeing you?'

'Rob and Lena have invited us to a Vicars and Tarts party at The Electric. What are you going to wear?'

'Christ, I have no idea.'

I think about Rob and Lena. The handful of times we've been for drinks with them, the guys have spent the night talking about football and money, while Lena talks about how often she and Rob go to The Four Seasons for mini-breaks, and how once she saw Danielle Lloyd there, wearing the same Cavalli as her.

I imagine their friends will be a bunch of arrogant bankers and underweight girls with fake tits who all aspire to live in Chelsea but actually live in Fulham.

'I'm going as a raspberry tart. And I think you should come as a pudding so I don't look like a total idiot on my own,' I say.

'What pudding would I be?' he says.

'Hmm. A fool's too obvious. I'd actually say a millefeuille. You have many layers, James. On top, you're all smooth and quite sweet, then underneath there's a really soft bit, and then under that you're hard. And then there's another bit deeper down that's soft again. But I think at the bottom, it's a bit flaky, and at the very base, you're hard.'

'I'll be hard if you go as a proper tart . . . Go on, Soph – suspenders, rubber dress, no knickers, thigh-high boots. Just once . . .'

'Not my style.'

On Saturday night I'm sitting in front of the mirror, putting on my make-up. I can feel James staring at me.

'One of your eyes is bigger than the other,' he says.

I have noticed this only recently myself when looking at photos of Laura and me in Argentina. It is truly a micro-scopic difference, but he has spotted it and seen fit to comment on it. Not in a 'your flaws make you unique/beautiful to me' way. Just in a 'you are not perfect' way.

'Cheers for that. Can you pass me my costume?'

He pulls a face and hands over my outfit. I am wearing fantastically sexy black lacy underwear, but I feel like an utter dork in this get-up of cardboard, red polyboard and string.

I can see James looks uncomfortable, and even though I don't want to cave in and dress like a slapper, I take the outfit off, and put on the tightest, shortest dress I own. I dig out a vile shiny blue handbag I had when I was fifteen, put some scarlet lipstick on, and my highest, most uncomfortable pointy heels.

'You look nice,' he says.

'I'm still wearing the raspberry,' I say, putting on the hat that Will at Appletree has sent down for me. It's a giant raspberry, made of sugar icing baked at a high temperature, so it's totally solid. Will, bless him, got the chief wedding cake designer to fix it to a little round brown biscuit-looking base made of soft plastic, which has two ribbon holes drilled through, so I can tie the hat on to my head, with a little bow under my chin.

'The hat's cute,' says James. 'Come on, let's go.'

★

The party is awful. It is the only night I have spent with James, other than the night of The Outburst and the night L'Esteeme launched, that I do not enjoy myself.

James is talking to Rob for ages, and I'm stuck with Lena, who makes Amber look like Susan Sontag. All the girlfriends of Rob's mates are heavily made-up ex-regional beauty queens, and it's really hard to see where the girl ends and the tart begins. All they talk about is handbags, the gym, and which luxury spas in Asia their boyfriends are taking them to for Christmas.

I notice James staring at one girl who's standing at the

bar, who reminds me a bit of Noushka. She is tall, long brown hair, very leggy. He points her out to Rob and they smile and Rob punches him in the arm. James catches me staring, and I feel shame burning my face, and head downstairs to the ladies' room to check my make-up.

When I come back up, James has disappeared, and I can't see the brunette girl anywhere. I look around the room, then pop down to the bar below and scan for them, feeling my heart begin to race. I check the loo in the restaurant area – she's not there either. By the time I go back up to the party James is back, whispering to Rob, and a moment later the girl comes back in and I see James looking at her again and quietly smiling. I feel sick.

A floodgate opens in my mind of all the things I've been ignoring since we broke up in May: that comment he made about not marrying just anyone. The time on my birthday he called me a big lump. The way he looked at Noushka on the launch night, the way his fingers moved in the car. The way he looked at this girl just now. I am paranoid, I am paranoid, I am paranoid, but I know I'm right.

I go over to him and tell him I don't feel well and that I'm going home.

I rush down the two flights of stairs, grab my coat from the cloakroom, then stand outside on Portobello Road, trying to find a cab.

A moment later James is standing next to me, grabbing my arm.

'Are you okay?'

'No,' I say.

'What's wrong?' he says, panic in his voice.

I want this man.

I have so much desire for him I don't know where to put it.

But I can no longer live like this. I can hardly breathe.

'I don't think I can do this anymore. I can't be your girlfriend, James, I just can't do it.'

He looks lost. Scared. Not in control. He opens his mouth to say something, then stops himself.

'I don't understand you, James. You ask me to move in, and then you say these things that make me feel like shit. And I don't have to be in this relationship, you know, I can leave.'

'What do you mean?' he says, shocked.

'I mean Nick made me feel special and you make me feel totally insecure. I don't understand. Do you even want me to be your girlfriend?'

He stares at me for what seems like an age. Oh, my life to know what is going on inside that messed up, crazy head of his.

'No,' he says finally. I swallow hard and nod. I was right. And I've lost. There's nothing more I can do. He grabs my hand and I try to snatch it back. 'Sophie . . .'

'Don't patronise me by saying how fond you are of me, or how I deserve better . . .'

228

'Shhh, please,' he says.

'. . . or how great my company is . . .'

'Shut up, Sophie Klein. I don't want you to be my girlfriend.'

'Yeah I know, you don't need to say it twice.'

'SHUT UP, WOMAN! I don't want you to be my girlfriend. I want you to be my wife.'

I can safely say it was a strange proposal.

There's something funny about all this, and it has nothing to do with the giant raspberry on my head.

We have been dating almost a year, I am about to move in to this man's house, he has asked me to be his wife.

The funny thing? He has never once said he loves me.

★

Nick used to say 'I love you' ten times a day. I learnt to understand that this was his shorthand for 'I'm happy', 'Goodnight', 'I'm lonely', 'I feel weird and I can't put my finger on why,' 'Thanks for making spag bol,' and 'Please don't be angry with me'.

You overuse it and you wear it out.

But isn't there a happy medium?

★

That night, I dream that James and I are at a party in Bangkok, in the Bonders' hotel suite. James is deep in conversation with Roger Federer and Shania Twain, and I'm trying to tell him that the train for Las Vegas leaves in five minutes and we're going to miss our own wedding, but he just nods and smiles, nods and smiles. Still no giant spiders.

James wants to wait till January before thinking about a ring or a party. The kitchen is days from being finished, my custards are keeping me busy, and he has to fly to Moscow three times between December 4th and the 14th to finalise distribution deals with one of his biggest clients. I've barely seen him since he proposed. I went to three Christmas parties without him last week – it almost feels like I'm single again.

There is no one I want to be with more than him. This is it. I have found the person I will grow old with. We are to be married. I am finally safe. So why do I feel like I'm on red alert? I'm waking up at 4am every morning, adrenalin coursing through me. It must be excitement. Must be.

It is now the 15th of December and James and I haven't worked out our New Year's Eve plans. I've mentioned it twice in the last fortnight and twice James says we'll discuss it nearer the time. Maybe when you get to his age it ceases

231

to be a big deal. I don't like New Year's Eve at the best of times so I don't care what we do – see some friends, drink too much, have a laugh somewhere locally.

We're in his car on the way to his friends Ed and Rachel for dinner.

'So, New Year's Eve – shall we go to Laura's party or do you want to do something else?' I say, thinking he won't be able to escape the conversation now, he's in the car.

'Oh. I've been meaning to talk to you about that.' He looks straight ahead and I can see him swallow.

Then why haven't you? 'And?'

'Yeah . . . Rob's going to Vegas with the boys for Oliver Newman's stag do. Or the Bonders have invited me to join them at their villa in the Cayman Islands. What do you think?' He turns to look at me briefly.

'What do you mean, "invited you"? Just you?'

'I haven't told them we're engaged yet. So . . . what do you think?'

I can feel the blood has drained from my face. 'Er. I think I'd like to see my fiancé on New Year's Eve?'

'I didn't think you could get time off work, all the custard stuff . . .'

'You never asked.'

'I could see how busy you were.'

'Hang on, Rob's going to Vegas without Lena?'

'It's a stag, Soph.'

'And the lovely Mal's going, presumably . . .'

232

He nods.

'So whoring and boozing in Vegas. Or you go to some tropical paradise with a married couple but without me?'

He looks at me helplessly.

'Can I come *with* you to the Cayman Islands?' I'm thinking that if the bank holidays fall on the right days, I could just about get five days off, it's a long flight, sure, but I could just about justify it . . .

'If we're going away together, I'd like us to go to our own private place. We can go away for Valentine's Day. I'll only be gone a week, it's no big deal.'

'Hang on. When did the Bonders invite you?'

He shrugs.

'More than a few weeks ago, presumably.'

He nods.

'At dinner after the launch party?' When he went out all night with Noushka.

He nods.

'And Oliver Newman's stag must have been planned for a while, 'cause Vegas is busy at Christmas and flights get booked up, people going home for the holidays . . . at least six weeks, I'd say.'

He nods. Christ, I'm getting really good at this game.

'So, you've known about both trips for over a month.'

'Come on, it's been a crazy month, the launch, the kitchen, the engagement . . .'

'And when you said "I've been meaning to talk to you

233

about New Year's Eve", what you actually meant was "you're going to have to interrogate me with twenty questions before I'll admit to a grain of the truth", so in essence you've lied to me.'

Suddenly he pulls the car over and puts it in neutral. His face has switched from sheepish grin to righteous indignation. 'I have not lied!'

'No, you just haven't told the truth.'

He is on the verge of being enraged.

'I didn't tell you, Soph, because I *knew* you'd be like this.'

'I AM LIKE THIS *BECAUSE* YOU DIDN'T TELL ME.'

He turns the engine back on and pulls out. 'Look, we'll be late for Ed and Rachel. I don't want to have a row about this in front of them. Can we talk about it later?'

'I can almost understand if you go to Vegas – it's a stag. You might have told me before now . . . but to go to a beach with a couple, it's too weird . . .'

'Please. I don't want tonight ruined, it's their anniversary.'

'I'm not going to ruin their bloody anniversary. We'll talk about it in the car and then it's done. Vegas, I can just about accept, but the Cayman Islands . . .'

'Okay, okay, I get it, Sophie, Vegas. Enough. We'll go away in February.'

★

Since James revealed he's going off to Vegas, my mind has been on paranoia overdrive. When he popped out of my flat on Sunday morning to buy the papers I convinced myself he was never coming back. The sense of relief I felt when I heard my front door open made me sick with shame. I have become obsessed with the way he moves his fingers and thumb on his right hand whenever he talks about his trips to Moscow.

Of course I cannot live like this and so I have tried to explain to my brain that thoughts of abandonment will become a self-fulfilling prophecy. Focus on the negative and bad things will happen. I tell myself 'everything's better than fine' a dozen times a day. But as much as I may have pulled the wool over my mind, it seems I cannot trick my body. The collection of anxiety stones that I carry inside me has grown into a Japanese rock garden in my chest.

It is now a week later and we're having a pizza at The Lansdowne, James's local pub.

'Have you even looked up flight availability for Vegas?' James is such a last-minute person at times. Plus he's rich – he can afford to book flights late.

'There's loads of space, it's fine.'

'Is it still hot at this time of year?'

'It'll be mild, mid-60s?'

'Why don't you book it?'

'It'll be fine. Let's just enjoy tonight.'

★

Two days later, on the 23rd, we're in Selfridges buying last minute presents. The sale has started early and the store is rammed with bargain hunters demonstrating a marked lack of Christmas spirit. Earlier, I saw two grown women literally come to blows over the last Eve Lom travel set. The handbag hall is like a zoo; leopard print totes, pony-skin satchels and python clutches expose the fact that the human is the scariest animal of all. Up on second, women's shoes must be carnage.

We've retreated down to the basement. I'm scanning the bookshelves trying to remember which football autobiography Laura told me to buy for Dave. James is flicking through an oversized coffee table book with black and white photos of models in various states of undress.

'I don't even know what day you're leaving,' I say, turning to James who is slowly turning the pages – too slowly for my liking. 'When did you say the flight to Vegas was?'

He freezes. 'Oh. Yeah. There's a flight to Vegas out of Heathrow at 10am on the 25th.'

'The 25th.'

He nods, then quickly closes the book and moves behind a pillar, towards a table of bestsellers.

'The 25th of December,' I say, hurrying to catch him up.

He looks guilty and grabs the nearest book to hand – the

latest Katie Price – and starts studiously reading the blurb on the back.

'You're unbelievable,' I say, dumping my shopping bags on the floor and waiting for him to put the book down. Ten long seconds later he is still hiding behind the pink and white cover, pretending to read, and I'm forced to snatch it out of his hands.

He sighs. 'If I'm going to Vegas I really want to be there with the boys. They're going on the 25th . . .'

'You can say it, you know, you can say 'I AM FLYING ON **CHRISTMAS DAY** AND I WILL BE AWAY **FOR CHRISTMAS DAY AND NEW YEAR'S EVE.**'

'What? You said you don't even like New Year's Eve,' he says.

'I don't like New Year's Eve, that's not the point. You didn't tell me you were flying so soon. I thought I'd see you on Boxing Day, or on Christmas Day in the evening.'

'You're going to Laura's.'

'For lunch. But I'll be home later. It's Christmas Day.'

'You're Jewish, Soph,' he says,

'I still do Christmas,' I say. 'You said you were going away for *New Year's.*'

'I am,' he says, 'it's only a few days difference. We'll go away in February, somewhere nice and sunny.' He picks up my shopping and gestures for us to head towards the escalator.

Oh, fuck it. He's going to do what he wants. You might as well be gracious. You'll have another forty Christmases together.

'Fine. Fine,' I say, shaking my head and following him out through the crowds.

It's not that big a deal.

It's only a few days difference.

We'll go away in February. Somewhere nice and sunny.

On Christmas Eve, just before midnight, James tells me he's flying to the Cayman Islands the following morning, without me.

For the second time in this relationship I feel like he's punched me full on in the guts.

He's decided against Vegas. Though there is indeed a 10am flight to Vegas on the 25th. And the weather is indeed mild – mid-60s. But he'd been booked on the 2pm flight to the Cayman Islands a week before we'd even had that conversation.

Oh, he wasn't lying; apparently I was asking the wrong question.

He wants some quiet time away.

I point out that he's staying with a married couple and their three screaming kids.

Turns out he wants some quiet time away from me.

★

I am silent for five minutes, during which time I start to piece together what has actually been going on in this relationship. James stares at me with scared eyes. I can't work out if he'd rather I was devastated or furious.

'Is this still about that ridiculous thing from before?'

He nods.

'This is about my weight?'

He doesn't react.

'I'm not fucking fat, James.'

'It's something to do with your weight . . .'

He's confused.

He 'doesn't know if he loves me enough' to marry me.

Here's a little clue: he doesn't.

Merry Christmas.

Crumble

1. *noun* – a baked pudding consisting of a crumbly mixture over stewed fruit
2. *verb* – to fall into tiny fragments, disintegrate

Boxing Day.

My alarm goes off at 5am. 5am?

For a brief moment, I'm so confused with tiredness I forget I'm 'in a bad place'.

Then I spy the untouched Christmas dinner on my bedside table that Laura insisted on bringing round yesterday, while I lay here in shock.

With instant despair I remember everything, including the fact that I'm due in a *really* bad place within the hour: Fletchers, Kilburn High Road.

*

Today is 'Patronise The Shopfloor Workers Day'; those of us from Head Office who couldn't think of an excuse quickly enough spend eight whole hours 'mucking in' at our local store, pretending to be at one with the shelf stackers. Outside it is snowing, but the automatic doors stay open due to the flurry of customers coming to take advantage of our exciting Boxing Day bargains: selected turkey pâtés are now half-price.

I end up in Wet Fish. No one told me to bring gloves, so my fingers are like frozen crab sticks, hoisting leaky pouches of protein from a stack of crates. I feel sorry for myself. I feel sorry for these mackerel too – bet their Christmas wasn't great either.

Five hours into my shift and I'm finally starting to enjoy myself. My hands no longer reek of fish residue. I've finished stacking, and am now price checking with a cool gun that picks up barcodes from 20 feet. Joyce on Ambient is telling me about her ex who left her when she was eight months pregnant, for a girl with a tattoo of Robbie Williams on her breast.

'So, why did you split up with this nob-head then?'

I pause my gun over the Sugar-Free Santa Lollipops. 'I'm not sure we've actually split up . . .' Her eyebrows rise.

A woman with too many layers in her hair and a Regional Manager badge reading 'K Dobbs', swoops on us from the Bakery section. 'What are you doing?' she says to me.

'Price checking.'

'You are who?' she says, so close now I can smell last night's sherry binge.

'Sophie Klein. Head Office.'

'I didn't ask where you work. You're doing that all wrong. Chilled first, then Frozen.'

'Denise in the office said start here . . .'

Her gaze drifts over my shoulder towards biscuits. 'Chilled, Frozen.'

The 'normal' me would never let a K Dobbs bother me. But today I'm very far from normal. I go to the loo thinking I'll splash my face and come back in a moment. Forty minutes later, I'm still sitting on the cubicle floor trying to stop sobbing. My eye make-up tracks down my cheeks. There's no loo roll so I've been forced to blow my nose on my own t-shirt: classy.

And now I have acute pains in my lower gut which, if last night's bathroom performance is anything to go by means I have a Very Big Problem. And a dilemma. What to use as makeshift toilet paper: my yellow Fletchers fleece or my t-shirt? I'm screwed either way. There's no bin in here. How am I going to dispose of either without attracting attention and then sudden death by humiliation?

If I run really, really fast can I make it the mile back home in the next three minutes?

Stick around. It gets a lot worse.

I need to leave town.

Don't worry, not because I shat myself at work. I didn't, though I might as well have. In the end K Dobbs came to hunt me down and found me on the loo, knickers round my ankles, sobbing. I begged her to fetch Joyce. Joyce came in, bless her, and went back to the shop floor to buy me some bog roll (they only had the Jumbo 12 pack with Rudolphs on, I must remember to pop in and give her the cash back).

Turns out K Dobbs is no stranger to heartache either. She, Joyce and I had a cup of tea and some whisky in the staff room, then my two new best friends put me in a double fare minicab and sent me on my way, 11 rolls of Rudolph toilet tissue under my arm.

No, I need to leave town because I have the keys to my new home, a dream kitchen, and the future I dreamed of, but for one thing.

Where do broken hearts go? Whitney?

Probably best not to turn to Whitney Houston for relationship advice.

I have five days off work. I need to do something exhilarating, lift my spirits.

I should climb a mountain, learn to kitesurf, swim with sharks. I should go Ayurvedic in India, meditate, get perspective, get food poisoning and get properly thin.

Or the really scary option.

I love my mother, I truly do. When I'm in London, I miss her and I worry about her. She sends me funny very-safe-for-work jokes on email, and recipes, and photos of her and Lenny looking downtrodden.

But I think I have perhaps made a poor choice of holiday destination.

On New Year's Eve I took two of my grandma's diazepam, swallowed down with a cup of tea, and got into bed at 9pm. No point ruining any one else's night.

On New Year's Day I got in a cab, got on a plane, took another two mazzies and eleven hours later landed in California, where dreams can come true. Let's hope not. Last night I dreamt James was living in a gold castle with a Bulgarian hooker who looked like Mel Gibson's latest paramour. When I tried to talk to James he said he could remember my face, but couldn't quite place me.

I have been here for four days, and fly home tomorrow

evening. Stupid, to come for such a short time, but I'd needed to move; I didn't think it through properly.

When I split up with Nick, I got the feeling that my mother would have rather kept Nick in the family and seen the back of me.

'What did you do to that poor boy?' she'd asked. I'd tried to explain, but she was sure I'd made a huge error of judgement, and driven away the best thing that ever happened to me.

So I have not told her about James. I will not even say his name. I fear she will either tell me that he was too old and what was I thinking of going out with a paedophile in the first place; or that he was right, and I am looking a bit large round the hips.

*

I had thought my brother and Shellii would be in town, that I'd meet my niece, but Shellii has dragged them to some insanely expensive post-natal raw foods spa in Arizona, so it is Mum, Lenny and me.

Every day I wake up at 7am, then go back to sleep till around midday. I emerge from my room for lunch – usually picking at half a bagel from their breakfast. Then I sit by the pool for an hour or two and read the *LA Times*, including all the money-off coupons. My favourite headline so far: 'Guinea Pigs – not from Guinea, and not Pigs!'

I then go for a run down to the boat club, passing power-walkers with power-walking dogs, admiring all the Christmas decorations that the Balboa residents adorn their houses with. Elves and Elvises. Six-foot-tall fairies and penguins and angels. Illuminated giant gingerbread men, bigger than James. Damn. Bigger than a tall man.

After my run I will pop in to Ralphs, my favourite American supermarket. I love the smell of American super-markets like I love the smell of fresh coffee.

Then I will come home to find my mother watching the 70-inch TV while Lenny rests. We'll then argue for twenty minutes about what to have for dinner. I keep telling her I'm not hungry, but she insists I eat something. And then when I say, 'maybe something healthy, tuna salad?' she'll refuse to make it, saying she had one two weeks ago, and how about a nice pork chop. I've never liked pork chops. 'In-N-Out Burger?' she says, 'your favourite . . .'

'Healthy! I said healthy!' I then usually storm back to my room, take two sleeping pills and begin all over again.

Today I am at the 'Ralphs' part of my daily routine.

For the first time since Christmas Eve, I am actually hungry. What with the running and the half bagel I seem to have been subsisting on, I am now officially thin. My bra is half empty/half full, my trousers won't stay on my hips, even my shoes feel too big.

So, I shall find myself a treat in Ralphs – with my

increased muscle to fat ratio, I don't even need to feel guilty about it.

I start at the chocolate milk fridge. I seem to be craving something cold, but there are too many confusing lo-fat, 1% fat and 2% fat variants, and what I actually think I want is a Mars milkshake, but they don't have them. I haven't drunk one for a decade. Maybe they don't even exist any more.

I wander across to the freshly baked section. For some reason it reminds me of a lap-dancing club. All those brazen, larger than life simulacrums of real desire, saying 'you know you want me', but you really don't.

No. I end up in the ice cream aisle. The choice is immense, but for me it's always going to be about Ben and Jerry's. 'It's what's inside that counts' – that's their motto, James Stephens, and they're right, James Stephens, they're right. Ben and Jerry would never lie to Mrs Ben and Mrs Jerry about what flights they were or weren't taking, and ruin their Christmases, and steal one of the last fertile years of their lives, thus ensuring that they will die alone, and won't even get eaten by their cats because you can't keep cats in a fifth-floor flat, can you, James Stephens . . .

The sooner I choose some ice cream and go home for my lie down, the better.

What! What's this?

They seem to have at least 40 variants of Ben and Jerry's, and that's without counting the frozen yoghurt.

Brownie Batter? Mission to Marzipan? Cinnamon Buns?! I didn't even know cinnamons had buns. . . .

Imagine Whirled Peace? Imagine living in a civilised nation: America! Land of the free, home of the brave, where Too Much Choice is an inalienable human right.

After ninety minutes, I have narrowed it down to the following:

Brownie Batter
Crème Brûlée
Dave Matthews Band's Magic Brownies
Neapolitan Dynamite
S'mores
Fairly Nuts
Americone Dream
Turtle Soup
and
Willy Nelson's Country Peach Cobbler.
and
Half Baked.

After a further seventy minutes I have knocked out the following:

Peach Cobbler, as it reminds me of Willy Nelson, which reminds me of James.

Turtle Soup – even though it has cashews, my favourite nut – however, the name has unfortunate connotations.

Fairly Nuts – too close for comfort.

Dave Matthews Band's Magic Brownies, because I'm choosing solely on the name, and actually I don't even know any Dave Matthews Band records.

I line up the remaining six options in a row in the freezer and consider. I could buy all six and leave the leftovers for Mum and Lenny, but I always feel bad buying them unhealthy foods as they do such a great job of suicidal eating all by themselves.

Hmm. Give me a minute here.

★

'Where have you been, we've been worried sick! I thought you'd been killed. You could at least have come back with a black eye.' My mother always makes grossly inappropriate jokes when she's anxious.

'What time is it?'

'Nearly 7pm.' That's like midnight round these parts, where people eat early bird blue-plate dinners at 4pm.

I seem to have spent more than three hours staring at the freezer section in the supermarket.

'What's in there?' she says, eyeing up the Ralphs bag under my arm.

'*National Enquirer*?' I say.

'What else?' She snatches it off me before I can lie, not that I ever can lie to her.

'Oh, Sophie! No!'

'What? I'm only going to smoke what's in that bag and I'll stop immediately after.'

'If you are going to smoke those filthy things then at least buy them at the airport.'

Aha! I intend to buy another two hundred at the airport. I'll pack this carton in my case, get more in Duty Free and I'm sorted. And I will give up once I've smoked all of that lot because I haven't had a fag in seven years, and I am not a smoker.

My mother drops me off at the airport for my 6pm flight. After telling me for the nth time that I'll be too cold when I land (she forgets: I do live in England, I am thirty-four, I do know how to dress myself) we settle into a slightly frosty silence. I stare out the window at the cars weaving in and out on the freeway, all in such a rush to get home.

I consider never going home, staying out here, getting a job as a sassy waitress with one of those cool burgundy retro coffee shop aprons, meeting some surfer type, having a life of sunshine and flip flops and air-conned malls. Then I picture the reality: living with my mother and Lenny, getting shouted at for using her special crossword pencil to write a shopping list, watching her drip-feed Lenny to death.

As we're turning off the I-405 towards El Segundo, just a few miles from LAX, she turns to glance at me. I can feel her gaze and I want to turn my head even further away but I can't get past 90 degrees.

She sighs. 'I am your mother, Sophie. I wish you'd tell me what's wrong. I'm not an ogre.'

I face forward and stare at my lap.

'Sophie. What's wrong, darling? Maybe I can help. You never talk to me. Is it that man?'

'Mum, I really don't want to talk about this.'

'I thought so. Lenny noticed it too, he says you're looking so terribly thin.' She reaches out an arm to stroke my shoulder.

'Mum, put both hands on the wheel. Look, Century Boulevard, get in the right lane.'

She takes her hand back. 'I just want you to be happy,' she says, 'I worry about you.'

'I'll be fine,' I say, as I feel one big, fat salty tear drop off the side of my chin on to my seatbelt.

My mother nods. As she turns into the airport's security check zone, I hear her sniff quietly. When we hug goodbye, I feel her face, wet as mine.

I've already checked in online, and while I wait in the bag drop queue I force myself to think about what I'm flying back to. I've left my mobile at home – the temptation to call James would have been too great, and I know that from now on, whatever happens, it has to come from him.

I can't imagine how we can possibly get back together

unless he begs for my forgiveness and commits to having therapy. But if I give him a third chance and he does it again – and why the hell wouldn't he – I'll probably lose my mind.

He wants to 'reflect'. He says he's 'confused'. Yawn.

I wonder if he'll be at the airport waiting for me? Maybe he's emailed Laura to get my flight details and he'll be there when I walk through the gate. That's what I'd do if I were a man. Maybe he'll have written me a letter – it's not really his style, but it would show some thought. Thank God he didn't get round to buying the ring, and I won't have to explain all this shit to anyone at work.

On the board, my flight says 'Delayed'. Typical, a tiny bit of snow in London and everything grinds to a halt. I wonder what James is doing right now. His car's not cut out for snow. He's probably in bed, it's midnight at home, I hope he's okay . . . God, I need to smoke, but I've packed the Ralphs carton in my case, and I don't want to go through to Duty Free airside if the flight's delayed.

I head outside to the smoking area and spot two young guys standing nodding, sucking fags between thumb and forefinger and laughing.

I ask them for a fag, and they find it hilarious that I call a cigarette a fag, and within minutes we are all laughing and joking, and they're lifting up their t-shirts to show me their tattoos.

I'd forgotten men ever fancied me. God, flirting with

hot guys is fun. The hotter of the two is Billy, a 29-year-old from Seattle. He is hilariously inappropriate – a total stoner, sells metal sheeting for a living, snowboards half the year, loves Kung Fu movies and has a giant tattoo on his stomach of a skull wearing a Viking helmet, with a missile where the eye should be.

Together, we are hilariously inappropriate – we head to the airport bar with his buddy, Eli, and Billy's telling me I have a smile that lights up a runway, let alone a room, and how could any fool, let alone an old one, tell me my body's not good, when I'm 'slamming', and how he'd happily impregnate me right now in the car park or the women's toilets – the choice is mine.

Eli has even more ridiculous tattoos than Billy. We drink vodka and tonics, and Eli invites me to come and live with them in Seattle, and I say 'you guys, come to London with me.'

'I haven't got a passport,' says Eli.

'Are you gentlemen on the run from the law?' I say.

'I've done my time,' says Eli, and he and Billy look at each other and laugh because it's true.

'What for?' I say.

'Oh you'd be shocked,' says Eli.

'Was it anything you did to a woman?' I say.

'Hell, no.'

'So fine, tell me!'

'Let's just say someone got set on fire and shot.'

256

'And that someone wasn't you . . .'

'Correct.'

'Is he dead?'

'No, but he wishes he was.'

'What did he do to you?'

'Stole from me,' he says, matter of factly. 'Told you you'd be shocked.'

I'm glad I fancy the other one.

I look up at the departures board and see that my flight is now delayed till 10.30pm.

'Bollocks!' I say.

'What is it, baby?' says Billy, tucking my hair behind my ear. I point to the board. 'That's a silver lining, doll. See my flight – AA137 – two above.' Delayed till 11pm. 'We got time to do it in the car park and the bathroom!'

'Very romantic to tell the grandkids,' I say. 'I first screwed your grandpa up against a toilet door . . .'

'Girl, I love your dirty mouth,' says Billy.

'Give me ten minutes and it'll be dirtier,' I say.

I do not know what's got in to me. Such lewdness, normally not my style. But I've been cooped up with Mum and Lenny, and have barely spoken to another human for five days, let alone hot male ones. I feel like a dog that's just been let out of a car.

'Eli, I fucking love this girl, I'm going to make her my wife,' says Billy, kissing me on the neck. 'Heck, why don't we just drive to Vegas right now and get married.'

257

I reckon this proposal is no less sincere than the one I had a month ago. Who knows, we might make it work. He's been more complimentary about me in forty-five minutes than James was in a year. Besides, he's gorgeous: twinkly blue eyes, messy brown hair, perfect teeth, a dimple on the right. He's young, he has a cool criminal sidekick, he'd never make me listen to Dido on his car stereo. I could get a matching Viking skull tattoo . . .

'I've got a better idea,' I say. 'Eli, do you mind if I borrow him for a while?'

'I'm not gonna stand in the way of my buddy getting laid,' says Eli.

I grab Billy's hand and head towards the Avis car park.

'Left. That's it . . . oooh, now right . . .' I say.

'You sure about this?' says Billy.

'Positive. Can't you go any faster?'

'Patience, darlin', there are limits.'

'God, I am drunk,' I say. 'There, yes . . . In and out . . . I can see it,' I say.

'Oh yeah, baby. In an' fucking out, come on!' screams Billy.

'Shove it there,' I say pointing.

'You're kidding, it'll never fit,' he says.

'You could get a yellow school bus in there, it's huge.'

He looks at me nervously. 'I don't want to scratch it.'

'It's not even yours!'

'Yeah, but they've got my credit card.'

'Oh, stop driving like a girl and just park the bloody thing – I need food.'

He turns the engine off and we stumble into the In-N-Out Burger. I'm much more drunk than he is – I haven't really eaten for a week – and I order two cheeseburgers and fries. He orders the same, and we sit on the bench outside, eating fries and talking about the universe.

Back in the car we start making out, and it is the sweet, raunchy kissing of two people who fancy each other rotten and know they're never going to see a sunrise together. It is so uncomplicated and wonderful.

At the airport gate, Billy puts his hands on my cheeks. 'I think you're amazing.'

'I'm so not,' I say. 'I'm too fat.'

'Girl, you have no idea what you're talking about. Your appetite is so fucking sexy. You're gorgeous. Maybe I'll get on that plane and come home with you.'

I wrap my arms around him. 'Thank you, Billy,' I say. 'For saving me.'

On the plane on the way home things clarify in my mind. I think: Wow, James is just a dick. It's really simple. He's an idiot. And Billy is lovely, and the world may be full of Billys, and all you have to do is talk to a stranger, ask them for a cigarette, and your world can change.

I doze on the plane and wake up an hour from Heathrow feeling like a piece of crap – bloated, hung-over, confused and miserable.

There is no James at the gate. There is no train on the Heathrow Express line (snow). There is no cash in the cash-point near my flat to pay for my £70 cab, no 'Please forgive me' letter on my doormat, and I've run out of fucking tea bags.

I'm sick with nerves when I turn my phone on to see what James has said. Fifteen texts from friends saying 'Happy New Year', four from Laura checking I'm okay, two from Pete, one from Jack saying 'let's have a drink in the New Year' and one from James: I miss you.

January's always shit for everyone, I think. Suck it up.

Laura says: If you want to call him, don't. Write him an e-mail. Don't send it.

So I write him an email every day, and because Devron is in the Maldives, I spend the entire day staring at my

screen, crafting the email, changing the font, deleting, snipping, shaping, adding. I send none of them.

To: j.stephens@jsa-socks.co.uk
From: sophie.klein@fletchers-foods.co.uk

Jan 11th
Dear James,

Thanks for your message.

I miss you too.

I wish I didn't.

I'm sorry I can't see you at the moment but I
need some time to think about things – I know if I
say something now it will be from a position of
hurt and I might regret it, and you might get
angry, so it's best if I say nothing.

S

X

Jan 12th
Dear James,

The more I think about it, the more I cannot
understand what happened between us. I honestly
think that if you could just have some therapy and
understand yourself a bit better, we could work
through this.

P.S. We are putting Philadelphia Cream Cheese

on a 2-for-1 promotion this month. Just thought you might like to know.

Jan 13th

Dear James,

I can't stop crying. When I wake up at three in the morning, I turn over and I expect to see you next to me, sleeping, gently snoring. Sometimes it feels like you actually are there, in my sleep, but the bed's half empty. It hurts. I miss you.

Jan 14th

Dear James,

Last night Laura came round with a take-away from Curry Paradise. It reminded me so much of our second date – that blue shirt you wore, the waiter so desperate to go home because we wouldn't stop nattering – that I couldn't eat a mouthful. I remember kissing in the street. I remember the hope in my heart as I climbed into my bed alone that night. I want this to work. Can this work?

Jan 15th

Dear James,

Do you think about me as much as I think about you? You are the first thing I think about every morning, and the last thing I think about at night, and most of the time in between.

I could lose weight, if that's what this really is about. But I don't think it is. I think you are scared and confused, but we can do this together, James, we can.

Jan 16th
Dear James,

I have been running loads and I can't believe the difference it has made to my body. People keep telling me they don't recognise me!

Jan 17th
Dear James,

I wonder what you're doing. It is so strange to me that you go to bed less than three miles from my flat, under the same moon, and yet it's like we never even met. It does my head in.

Are you not even curious what I am up to? I wish I could just get on with things the way you seem to be able to, but I can't wake up one morning and not have the feelings I have for you.

Jan 18th
Dear James,

I was speaking to Laura about you last night, and

she thinks you are irredeemable. She says that once a man is past forty, he's not going to change — or if he is, he has to really want to do it. Admit his worldview is screwed up, seek help, work at it. I think anyone can change. I know you are a good person. I just think you're scared of committing. Maybe you feel a bit guilty too, but you don't need to. We all make mistakes.

Jan 19th
Dear James,

Thank you for helping me see things about myself that I need to change. I am too defensive; I need to believe in myself more. I forgive you for behaviour that was unkind and weak — I don't think you realised how much it would hurt me.

Jan 20th
Dear James,

I miss you more than I missed you yesterday. I'm going in the wrong direction. I know couples break up every day. I know that's just life. But I'm thinking about it and thinking about it and thinking about it, and it still doesn't add up. I need some closure. I have questions. I need answers. I need to speak to you.

★

I have not spoken to him for nearly a month, since Christmas Day. No texts, no calls, no nothing.

Every day feels like I'm trying to wean myself off a grim Class A drug. Not calling him has become an action I force myself to 'do' each morning when I wake up, each night before I sleep, and all the glorious bits in between.

Most of my self-restraint is actually Laura's. She has listened to me witter in a loop daily since I've been back from LA. I feel like the shittest toy in the glass cage fairground game. Against all odds, Laura's metal arms have picked me up, stabbed into my sides, clutched me tight and rescued me. I don't like it at all, it hurts, but this is apparently what 'winning' in this situation feels like.

I smoke so much that I run out of Duty Free after twelve days. In the seven years since I last bought a packet of fags, the price of fags has become an unfunny joke.

I feel consumed. I feel physically wretched. But I have done it. I never thought I could, but I have. I am very proud of myself.

He must realise that I don't really miss him at all.

I've shown him how strong I am, how I don't 'need' him.

So, I decide it's now okay to call.

To be fair, I do try calling the three 'interceptors' first – friends who've said 'if you ever feel like calling him, day or night, call me instead.' Laura is in a voice-over. Maggie goes straight to voicemail. Pete doesn't pick up. I leave messages with all three, and four minutes later, when no one has called me back, I dial James.

Like Pete, James doesn't pick up either. But while with Pete I assume it's because he's in a meeting or on the loo or away from his phone, with James I know it's because he's avoiding me.

Jesus, why didn't I block my number when I called. I don't want to leave a message, but he'll know I've called now so I should . . . aargh, the beep has gone and I pause for three seconds, panic and hang up. Worst of all worlds.

He leaves it twenty-four hours before calling me back.

'Why haven't you called me?' he says.

'Why didn't you call me?'

'You didn't reply to my text. I figured you'd be in touch when you were ready to talk. I thought you'd have called by now. I was worried.'

'Then you should've called me,' I say.

'But I just explained, I thought you didn't want me to . . .'

When have you ever put what I want before what you want?

'I need to see you,' I say. 'I just want to talk things through, it'd be really helpful for me.'

'Of course, Soph. Whatever happens with us, I'll always be there for you, even if you only want me as a friend.'

Have I missed something here? How has this become my

266

decision to finish our relationship? He's the one who said he didn't love me enough. And now he's pinning it on me.

When I tell Laura that I've called him and that we are meeting, she practically cries. 'Do not do this. It will do you no good. And if you insist on doing this, do not make the situation any worse by doing something stupid. Remember I am your friend and I will always be here for you, whatever you do. But I don't want you to do this.' Seeing that she's more or less okayed it, I can start planning my outfit.

I wear my tightest jeans, which are now loose, high ankle boots, a purple top he likes. For twenty-four hours, I am almost doubled over with stomach cramps, I can't remember being this anxious in my whole life.

I won't let him pick me up. I need to be on neutral territory – can't have him putting a curse on another one of my favourite places – so I suggest a pub in Queen's Park which is very average but where I know we'll be able to get a seat.

When I see his car parked outside my heart starts racing. Laura was right, this was a bad idea. I'm not going to be able to keep my cool. I'm either going to get very angry with him, or fancy him – and neither of these is what I want. I want to be aloof, calm, mature and gracious, but hard as nails.

Look away now.

'You look well,' he says, trying to kiss me as I turn a cheek towards him.

I look like I've had a virus, more like. I take off my coat and scarf and head straight for the loo – partly because I need to check my face isn't too red with nerves, and partly so he can see my new, thinner self in motion.

I start out alright. I ask him about the Cayman Islands. I tell him scant details about LA, other than that I hung out with some good people, and that I had fun. I know I'm meant to keep it brief, be in and out within half an hour, but I just want to chat to him, be near him, kiss him, stroke his hair.

I have to be rock hard. I have four specific questions I want answers to.

'Why did you ask me to marry you?'

'I thought it was what you wanted. I didn't want to lose you.'

But you do now.

'If it was up to you, James, and at this stage believe me, it is not up to you, would you carry on with this relationship?'

'Yes.'

'Why?'

'I think it could still go either way.'

'But you say you don't want me enough and then you say you do want me. It's all in your head James, it's not even about me.'

'I'm confused . . .'

268

I am not willing to be a cause of confusion.

'You know that thing Winston Churchill said?' I say.

'We shall fight them on the beaches . . .?'

'No! That woman called him drunk, and he said "In the morning I'll be sober but you'll still be ugly",' I say.

'I don't think you're ugly.'

Thank you.

'I don't understand what you're saying,' he says.

'I could become a slave to the Stairmaster, but you'll still wake up a shallow, shallow man . . .'

'I am not shallow.'

'You do realise that weight is mutable don't you, James?'

'What are you talking about?'

'I mean, it's like one of your fucking investment funds. It can go down as well as up. I could get thinner, it's not beyond the realms of possibility. And if I have kids, I'll get fatter. Everyone does James, even fucking leg models.'

'Sophie.'

'But you know what can't go down as well as up, James?

'Don't tell me . . . a broken umbrella . . .'

'Your age.'

'Soph, I know you're pissed off, but there's no need for that.'

Pissed off? I'm pissed off if I forget my Oyster card.

'I'm more than pissed off,' I say.

'Disappointed . . .'

269

Again: no. Topshop don't have that cool black vest in a size 8? Disappointed.

'I am angry, James.'

'I don't understand why you're so angry, I haven't done anything wrong. I wish it could be different too, but it is what it is.'

'That's exactly it – nothing *is what it is* with you! You and your emotional sleight of hand, ooh, yes, Soph, Las Vegas is very mild Soph – and all the while your fingers are crossed behind your back.'

'Why are you so bitter?'

Bitter? I AM NOT BITTER. I am full of rage and pain and fury. That's not the same thing.

Enough. I'm not going to ask question four.

'I'd like to go home now,' I say, standing up. I haven't eaten since yesterday afternoon and this drink has gone straight to my head. I feel hot and emotional and worst of all, in spite of what he has said, I want him as much as I've ever wanted anyone.

I go to the toilet and check my make-up. I still have a tan from California, and my cheekbones are the most prominent they've ever been in my life. It is his loss, I think. And mine.

We drive home in silence and he parks outside my block and turns the engine off.

'Soph.'

'What?'

He stares at me and I can tell, 100%, that he realises he

has made a mistake in breaking up. I see it clearly, though we are almost in darkness.

He leans over to kiss me and I don't move an inch.

'What are you doing?' I say.

'I've never felt so close to anyone, ever,' he says.

'Do you love me, James?' Question four.

He nods. I really should know by now that a nod in James-world in no way signifies a yes.

He moves an inch closer and kisses me very, very gently. I feel like I'm having a heart attack. I do nothing for ten whole seconds. And then I kiss him back.

Within moments we are having ardent sex. Well, one of us is. He pauses briefly at the start to open the passenger door in order that he can fully recline my seat. The car's inside light goes on and in the eight seconds before it turns itself off I look up and right, to the back seat, and notice a tiny clothes hook that must come in handy when you need to hang an infant's tuxedo.

And now James is behind me, my jeans are round my ankles, and the central console is crushing my rib cage, and the handbrake is too far to the left, nudging my stomach. My left knee is pressed so hard against the glove compartment I can feel the 3200GT logo angrily imprinting itself on my skin. I push my palm up against the roof to try and get more comfortable and feel the soft finishing, and wonder if it is suede or just suedette.

It is over within minutes and I realise with shock that

271

James has come inside me, and then I remember that my new pill packet starts tomorrow, and even though a pregnancy would perhaps force a reunion, there's no chance I'll be pregnant from this, and the realisation saddens me.

James has collapsed on top of me, breathing heavily. 'That was amazing,' he says. 'We should do that every day.'

And it's so funny because I was thinking the exact opposite.

Unsnap.

'So what do we do now?' I say.

'About what?' he says.

The Reform of the American Electoral System, you nob-end. 'Us,' I say.

'Well, I think I need some time to reflect . . .'

Oh no, no, no. No.

'How do you actually feel, right now, James?'

'It's a relief,' he says, unguardedly. 'To be talking about it.'

Wow. A relief to tell the truth, finally. As if I was the one stopping you doing that.

'Those times in the last few months when you picked up on it, I knew you'd noticed something was up . . .' he says, like he's now in a rush to get this weight off his chest; he has his window.

I take a minute to process this. 'The times I said something isn't right, like that time after the launch party in the car . . .?'

He nods against my shoulder.

'Don't you think,' I push him off and move myself over to the driver's seat to face him, 'that maybe *those* were the times when you might have said something? I *gave* you all those chances . . .'

'I didn't want to say anything. I knew you felt like you were on death row,' he says, reaching out for my hand.

'Because you put me on death row!' I say, snatching it away. And I let you . . .

'I tried, Soph . . .'

'You tried what?'

'To make this work.'

'*You tried!*' I laugh with as much scorn as my heightened state of nausea will allow. '*You tried!* I'm so sorry it was such an effort to get past my looks, James Stephens. Thank you for trying. Here's a fucking gold medal.'

'You are twisting my words. That's not what I meant, Soph.'

'What *do you* mean?'

He pauses, looks truly pained. I almost feel sorry for him, I want to console him.

'– I can never look at you the way you look at me,' he says.

But you did, James, you did.

I know, because I was there.

It is a fatal blow.

How can you ever come back from that?

You can't erase it.

You can't argue with it.

It is what it is. Or isn't.

'Stay away from him,' says Laura.

'I won't see him again,' I say. (Well, not for a week at least, he's gone to China.) I wonder if she can tell I'm lying over the phone.

'I mean it, he's bad news,' she says. 'You need to remove yourself from this situation, it is doing you no good.'

I don't know, I think. Sure, I have no self-respect, no confidence, I can't stop smoking, and any dignity I ever had went out the window when I had sex in a hairdresser's car outside my block of flats with a fat man who'd just told me I wasn't thin enough for him, but hey, I can now fit into a Zara extra-small.

I've decided to take back the watch James gave me for Christmas.

I have the world's oldest mobile phone. While other people use their phones to watch movies, even make movies, the only thing I really want a phone for is to make calls

274

and tell the time. So I don't need a watch. And I particularly don't need a watch that reminds me of my ex-fiancé, and how I am an 'also-ran', every time I look at my own wrist. No, the watch is going back.

I consider calling James in China and asking where the receipt is, because I know this watch cost quite a lot of cash and I want quite a lot of cash to pay for the therapy I reckon I'm going to need off the back of this break-up.

However, he will think I'm calling just to speak to him, and he will think that me taking the watch back is over-reacting, or designed to attack him, or petty, and while I shouldn't care what he thinks, I really do.

So I have no receipt. When the man in Selfridges on the watch counter asks me for my receipt I inadvertently start crying, and he is so embarrassed, as am I, that we continue our conversation through my tears, and he issues me with a credit note for £795 on the proviso that next time I bring an item back to the watch department, I bring a receipt.

There is nothing I could buy in any shop that would make me feel better – besides, I don't want anything new that will remind me of James. I put the credit note in the back of my wallet and head home.

I read his horoscope in the paper. Capricorn: Don't worry about what you are losing. All your dreams are about to come true.

275

I read mine. Sagittarius: Your world will fall apart but you have your friends, family and health to support you.

I would do things that even Courtney Love, drunk, would draw the line at, if it would mean James and I could swap star signs for a week.

Horoscopes are bullshit.

He is due back from China tomorrow. I text to tell him I'm going to pop round with some milk. He texts back saying not to worry, Rosie, his cleaner, will pick some up for him. I reply saying I need to pick up my Bamix blender anyway. 'No, Soph, Rosie will wonder why you're taking your stuff back. I'll bring it to you at the weekend, if that's what you decide you want.'

I don't care if his cleaner thinks it's weird, and why is he so bothered either? Does it diminish his reputation in the eyes of the woman who has to clean his bathroom? What does she care? And what's this 'if that's what you decide you want' bullshit. As if any of this is my decision. Or does this mean he realises what he's throwing away? If so, a text about his cleaner seems a strange place to finally declare his love.

Well, he can't stop me. I have a set of keys. If I want to take him some milk and get my stuff back, I bloody well will.

I haven't been to the house since Christmas Eve. As I park I feel panic rising. Too many memories.

276

Happy memories – of kissing on the doorstep – painful memories.

Be brave. He's not there. Besides, you're thin now. Everything's going to be okay.

I put my key in the Chubb lock. Strange, it's unlocked. Of course – Rosie. I like Rosie but I'm not in the mood to see her; hopefully she's up doing the bedrooms.

I head straight for the kitchen. 'Our' kitchen.

Get this over with quickly. I dump my bag on the counter and open the fridge to put the milk in.

Very strange.

On the top shelf sits half a freshly cut lemon, a bottle of flaxseed oil and a soy fat-free cherry-cinnamon yoghurt with one spoonful removed.

Rosie is sturdy and Jamaican and not the type to eat soy or fat-free anything.

I shut the door, then open it again.

Magic. This time, I notice in the cheese compartment in the door a large midnight blue pot of face cream, two vials of nail polish and some Organic Soy Dogchewz.

Very, very strange.

I hear Rosie's footsteps on the stairs and turn suddenly. She stops at the top of the stairs. 'Jamie?' she says in a thick Russian accent.

I can just see her from the knee down, like the mother in Tom and Jerry. These calves don't look like Rosie's 58-year-old, grandmother-of-five calves. For a start, they're white.

Secondly, they're practically twice the length of Rosie's calves, and end in long, narrow feet. One foot hovers in view – toes pointed downwards, paused. The nails are painted hot pink. A thin diamond chain is hanging off the ankle.

The Not-Rosie's knees come into view, down one step.

Bony, narrow, defined knees. Down another step.

I grab on to the fridge handle for support as I feel my own knees start to buckle.

'Jamie, is you?' she says, in her Not-Rosie voice.

Another step. I can see the next four inches of her thigh. Long, lean, slim, thin, toned.

Another step. More leg. And now a flop of long chestnut hair swings down sideways, followed by the face. Two too-wide pale blue eyes, two dark brows raised in shock.

I turn back to the fridge. In the brushed steel door everything is blurry. My hands are shaking violently as I open the door again, take the milk out and shut the door.

I think my heart might have stopped.

A voice in my head is screaming for me to move but my feet remain static. I don't want to have to pass her on the stairs but I don't want her coming down here either.

It doesn't matter. She's fled back up the stairs, so light on her feet that I barely hear her, except when she slams one of the bedroom doors shut.

By the time I'm back outside by my car, I am shaking so hard that I can't get the key into the door. The metal

278

taps and scratches around the lock like an animal desperate
to be let in.

After a minute I give up, convinced I am being watched
from the house. I run round the corner and hail a taxi.

'Laura's.'

'You'll have to give me a bit more than that, love,' says
the driver.

'Englefield Road.'

He nods and looks at me in the rear view mirror, trying
to figure out if I'm going to puke in his cab.

★

Laura lets me in and I sit on her hall floor, my back against
the front door. She bends and looks in my eyes with an
optician's gaze, but I'm focussing on the past.

'What happened? He's not back is he?' she says.

'Please can you get my car?'

'Sure, where is it?'

'His. Please. Before 8.30.'

'It's seven o' clock now . . .'

'Tomorrow . . . 8.30'

'Okay. I'm going to stay here with you now, and I'll get
it first thing.'

'8.30. The car. I'll get a ticket.'

'I promise I'll go before 8.30.'

'Or a clamp. A clamp. The car.'

Years ago, when my grandpa had a stroke, my brother and I visited him in the hospital. He recognised us okay but when he started talking he came out with sentences such as 'Tell the nurse one two one two' or 'Your grandmother one two one two and there's nothing in the paperwork one two one two,' – all the while counting out numbers on his fingers. My brother had laughed nervously but I remember bursting into tears as soon as we left the ward, seeing this man's brain reduced to a malfunctioning dashboard. This thought comes to me now as I sit on Laura's wooden floorboards, a draft blowing onto my lower back.

'8.30, a clamp, 8.30,' I say.

'It's okay, Sophie. Do you want me to go right now?'

I nod, calmer.

'I'll be back very soon. Don't move . . .'

I am going nowhere. I lean sideways and Laura squeezes past me out of the door through the narrow gap I've allowed. My head is numb, as if packed to the edges with cladding. I can hear my breathing loudly.

I feel the same as I felt after getting chronic food poisoning from a bowl of old rice in the Fletchers' canteen last year. After violent nausea and projectile vomiting by the bins in the car park, I'd sat against a damp brick wall feeling exactly like this. Not a sense of relief. More a sense of 'Oh! That wasn't fun. Okay. Interesting. I can't move.'

I am still sitting here when Laura tries to re-enter her

flat a while later. I shift sideways to let her in and she comes to sit next to me and takes my hands.

'The car's here, it's safe. I bought us some whisky, some Ben and Jerry's, some fags and some Mint Aero Balls. The Four Guilty Pleasures of the Apocalypse.' She unpacks the treats on the hall floor and goes to fetch glasses, spoons and an ashtray.

I shake my head and keel sideways, lying down on the hall floor and shutting my eyes.

'Soph, let's get you to bed,' she says, stroking my hair.

No. 'Pillow. Here. Please.'

One of Laura's nicknames for me is Dormouse because of my ability to fall asleep anytime, anyplace, anywhere. When we used to go clubbing, at 3am she'd be on a podium doing pills like there was no tomorrow. I'd be curled up asleep in the chill-out room, some terrible art student lava lamp graphics synched to the sounds of the Café del Mar album in the background. Compared to a fag-butt sticky corner of Bagley's, Laura's floor is a Posturepedic mattress.

'Soph, just this once, please – you'll be more comfortable in bed. I promise.'

'Please.' I stay on the floor while she half-heartedly tugs my arm. 'Don't make me move, Laura. I can't move.'

When I wake up five hours later I find myself covered by a duvet, a pillow under my head.

There is a flashing blue light on my phone. Three missed calls and a text message from James that he must have sent

281

from Beijing airport: Sophie – she is a friend. She's just staying at the house while I'm away. I promise you that's the truth.

He calls at 8am from Heathrow.

I ignore it.

I lie down on Laura's bed, chain smoke, and think about Noushka – her name like a low punch followed by a slap. I think about how her legs compare to mine. I think about how young she is. How not very bright. How James looked at her when she was on stage that night.

He calls again at 9, 10.30 and 11am. Wow, guilt makes you work hard, I think.

I pick up on the fifth call.

'It's not what you think, Soph.'

'Just tell me how long this has been going on.'

'Soph. I need to see you.'

'I don't need to see you. Just tell me the truth.'

'She is, was staying at mine 'cause she's doing PR days around the launch. I was out of town . . . I haven't even been in the house at the same time as her.'

'She's still there then.'

Silence.

'So, she's still there. And now you're there.'

'Nothing's happened . . . nothing's happening.' He omits to say 'nothing will happen.' So very, very James.

'I don't believe you,' I say. 'You're a fucking liar.'

'I AM NOT,' he says, defiant till the end. 'Listen, I can see why it might look weird, but it has nothing whatsoever to do with what happened with us.'

'What has nothing to do with what happened with us?'

'What?'

'You said "it has nothing to do with what happened with us".'

'No, I didn't, well, it was just a sentence . . . stop analysing everything, you'll always read stuff into the most innocent things, you're mad.'

I will be soon, I think.

'You went to Moscow three times in December,' I say, thinking back to the way his fingers kept fidgeting strangely when he talked about those trips. *I should have said something then. I should have called him on it.* 'Was she there?'

'Her family's in Moscow.'

'Was she there?'

'She was visiting her family.'

'Did you see her?'

'She's a friend, she's got a boyfriend.'

'Was he in Moscow? I didn't see him at the launch.'

'I don't know where her boyfriend was or is. What is this, twenty fucking questions?'

'What's her boyfriend's name? If you two are friends, she must have mentioned his name.'

283

'SOPHIE. I'm not going to be interrogated like this. If you can't calm down and talk about this like an adult . . .'

I slam the phone down.

My mind flits back to when Laura was going out with Carlos, when we were twenty-one. She suspected he was cheating with a girl named Aimee; he denied it. She stood outside Carlos's front door, looking through his letterbox and saw Aimee walking round naked. She rang Carlos, heard his mobile ring *inside the flat,* and heard him down the phone *and through the door*, saying he was in Manchester till the following day. When she told him she was *outside his front door*, he continued to claim he was in Manchester.

Black is the new black, and James is the new Carlos.

I figure out pretty early on the following morning that bunking off work to lie in bed is a bad idea. While the thought of listening to Devron talk about his soft shelf wobblers fills me with despair, the alternative – sitting on my own in my flat and thinking about James – is beyond hellish.

Besides, I now have something urgent on my to-do list: check I don't have the clap. Always good to keep busy after a break-up, isn't that what they say?

The spectacularly lovely thing about my trip to the VD clinic is that it is only three doors down from where James and I kissed in the street, when that crazy tramp woman came up to us. That was the first night I slept with him. We had sex three times that night. I wonder if he'd already realised I wasn't his normal physical type, I think, as I fill out a form asking me if I have ever put my penis in another man's anus.

'I think I have the wrong form,' I say to the lady behind the desk.

'So you do. Try this,' she says, handing me a new clip-board, as I start the box-ticking over again.

As I have walked out of a Tuesday afternoon status meeting at the exact point Devron stood up to present '10 Inspirational Shopping Trolley Designs from Around The World', I am in no hurry to get back to the office. Nonetheless my colleagues think I have just popped to the loo, so I figure twenty minutes is probably the most I can spend in the clinic without alerting Janelle to my absence. (In the last month Janelle has twice caught me hiding in the fridge with Zoe; she's so entirely on to me.)

'Is it alright if I just do the urine, not the scrape thing?' I say to the receptionist.

'It's better if you do both.'

Hmmm, better for who, I think.

I pee in a jar, post it through a cubbyhole and I'm back at my desk fifteen minutes later.

'Where have you been?' says Janelle.

'Er, having a wee?' I say.

And because I am telling the truth – well, a James sort of truth – I appear to be sincere, and she can't haul me up on the fact that I have missed Devron's weekly death-by-boredom slot.

For the second time in a month Laura says: if you want to call him, don't. Write him an e-mail. Don't send it.

So I write him another email every day, and because
Devron is no longer in the Maldives and I am in the final
stages of my custard project, I spend only half the entire
day staring at my screen, crafting the email, changing the
font, deleting, snipping, shaping, adding.

Feb 4th
Hello again James!

Great news! You are STD free. I highly recommend hanging out at your local council-run genital
health clinic, it's a *terrific* way to spend one's leisure
hours. And they're so twenty-first century, they'll
even text you the results!

Feb 5th

Guess what? It's a year ago to the day since I first
met you. You may not remember, but that night *you*
chatted *me* up. Did I pretend I was a 28-year-old leg
model? Did I ever lie to you about what I look like?
You asked *me* to tango, remember? Oh, the bloody
irony.

Feb 6th

All the money in the world can't paper over the
cracks in your soul. You don't want to admit you
cheated because that makes you the bad guy. The
fact that you let Noushka put a soy cherry yoghurt

– which isn't even food – in my bloody fridge, tells
me that you are at best a fool, and at worst,
well . . . the Devil has all the best tunes, so
CLEARLY you are not the devil . . .

Feb 7th

You can tell your new girlfriend next time she's
interviewed and asked to describe her personality,
she might want to include Predator, Fiancé-stealer
and Moron in her list of nouns (and yes, I know
they should be ADJECTIVES, not NOUNS, but
then 'I like jewellery' isn't a personality trait now
is it . . .)

Feb 8th
You are a gold-plated cliché.
Here's what I bet:
You'll end up marrying Noushka or some identikit
hard-bodied, hard as nails gold-digger who is years
younger than you, who you think is feisty but is
actually just spoilt.
The minute you have kids, you will realise that
having kids is not like having toys, and you will
feel your age plus ten years immediately.
Your previously perfect shiny wife will be
knackered and hormonal, like every new mum is,
and will fail to continue making your penis the

centre of her universe. At this point you will begin to wonder what has gone wrong.

Even with the best marriage counselling in the world, you will be resentful and bored after seven years, but by that time your erectile dysfunction will have kicked in, and she'll be shagging Gareth, her personal trainer, who overdoes the free sunbeds at work and wears Lycra t-shirts with deep v necks. And you won't be able to divorce her because then she'll take you for half your cash.

So, to that end I wish you both good luck, Good Luck, GOOD LUCK.

Feb 9th

I have been reading about sociopaths. There are seven signs that identify a sociopath, and you check eight of them. You are irresponsible, selfish, charming, self-interested, impulsive, ruthless and cruel and I rue the day I ever met you. When you told me your grandfather made his fortune by torturing helpless little minks, I should have paid closer attention.

Feb 10th

You are a shallow, emotionally immature, half-baked, fully fledged idiot. You said on our first date that you never lied, yet you are the most dishonest human I've ever met. Your self-justification reflex is so strong, you probably don't even see how cowardly you've been. That wouldn't fit with your view of yourself – Saint James, King James, Mr Wonderful. I've got news for you Mr Wonderful – when you realise what a giant mistake you've made, I won't be sitting around waiting for you. Well, maybe I will, if you realise in the next month or so . . .

Feb 11th

How dare you call my friend Debbie fat! Oh, and by the way, I had my BMI measured yesterday and my body fat is 18.2%, which actually makes me officially 'underweight' according to government statistics.

And another thing! That night you met Pete and you said I should keep losing weight, Pete thought you were an arse.

Feb 12th

In future if you want someone to project manage your kitchen, HIRE A KITCHEN PROJECT MANAGER. (Try Google or the Yellow Pages.) Pay them a 15% fee. This will work out considerably less emotionally damaging for them than a proposal of marriage, which is subsequently retracted.

I would say ask Noushka to help next time, but

no doubt she is brainstorming her next toenail
polish business plan (toes/fingers – they're the same
bloody thing, James!)

Feb 13th
   I am truly myself with you/I want you to be my
wife/I can never look at you the way you look at
me. Spot the odd one out.

Again I send none of them.
Until 11.58pm on Valentine's Day, when I drink a bottle
of red wine, then type:
   'I am hopelessly in love with you.
   I fucking hate you.
   God, I miss you.'

And press send.

I wake up the following morning and enjoy a full seven seconds of peace of mind before I remember what I've done.

Please let this be a Bobby Ewing dream, please . . .

This is not a Bobby Ewing dream.

I feel mortification burning through me. I phone Laura, even though I know Dave has taken her somewhere in Sussex with giant plasma screens in the bathroom for a wanton long weekend, and she could really do without the interruption.

'I've done something stupid but maybe it's not that bad . . .'

Laura is always kind but unfortunately she's always honest, and never just tells me what I want to hear. Sometimes I wish she wasn't my best friend.

Apparently what I've done is 'not cool.'

'I'll send an email this morning saying my e-mail account's been hijacked?'

Apparently this idea is 'not cool' either.

'We could pretend that actually *you* wrote it when you were at my house, drunk, for a dare, and then you sent it to him because . . . er . . .'

Apparently this idea is 'not in any way believable and also not cool.'

I am too scared to go into my email account for the next twenty-four hours, and eventually I make Laura log in from a computer in her hotel.

'Yup,' she says. 'He's read your email.'

I am lying on my bathroom floor at this point. I have been lying here for maybe five hours, wrapped in my granny's pink fluffy robe, with a pillow behind my head, staring at the ceiling. My upstairs neighbour must have had an overflow; there are seventeen hairline cracks in my ceiling, that, like the stars above London, make themselves more apparent the longer you look at them.

I know Laura would offer to read me the email if she thought it was appropriate. She is not offering.

'Oh God, is he angry? Does he think I'm an idiot?' I say.

'Soph. It doesn't matter what he thinks. What matters is how you feel. The only thing he put in his email that I think is worth repeating, because for once I agree with him, is that it might be better if you don't press send when you're drunk.'

'Please delete it, and delete it from the deleted messages bin too.'

'Done,' she says.

I hang up and turn to face the towel rack.

I am sinking. Please help me.

I have cried every day for two weeks. I thought crying was meant to be a release but it only seems to feed itself. I'm not talking about whole-body keening, shaking, wailing. Just a steady flow of tears, out of the eyes, down the face, like a broken tap that's not bad enough to call in the plumber for.

It's weird, it's become like breathing. Actually the breathing, in between the crying phases, is more of a problem than anything. I basically sometimes forget to breathe in: sounds ridiculous, I know. But I can take a breath: in, out. And then at some unconscious level, my brain can't be bothered to issue the command to breathe in again. I have to jump start my lungs about five times a day.

Anyway, the crying: it is absolutely brilliant what you can do quite easily while tears are pouring down your face. Activities include:

- walking down Oxford Street in rush hour without feeling embarrassed

- dancing to 'Come On Eileen' at an 80s party your best friend has dragged you to
- having your hair done at a posh salon off Hanover Square to cheer yourself up – this one is particularly excellent: when a hairdresser sees you crying, they assume it's because you hate what they're doing to your hair, so they give you free cappuccinos and do a superb job on the blow dry
- sitting in the freezer with Zoe, hoping the cold will turn your tears into salty little full stops

There is a shiny silver lining to these clouds: you can't chew and cry at the same time. Just as well; I'm eating like a mountaineer, in the gaps between the tears.

But then there's always another cloud: Devron.

We're due to meet to talk about a 'Change of Direction'.

He asks 'Alright?' in a very matter of fact way, and I start crying, as I always do when anyone talks to me or touches me. I'm like a malfunctioning Tiny Tears doll. At least I'm not spontaneously wetting myself. Not yet, anyway.

'Ah, your grandma,' he says.

'What?'

'She died recently . . .'

'Oh. No, not that recently. This isn't about that.'

'Oh.'

'If it was, I'd say you can take a half day, a day's compassionate leave, if you need it.'

The fact that this is not about my grandma, but about a man, makes me weep with self-disgust.

'You must have been close to her,' Devron says.

'It's not that,' I say. 'I . . . I split with my . . . boyfriend.' I didn't have long enough to think of him as a fiancé.

'New boyfriend?'

'It was just coming up to a year.'

'Oh, so not that serious . . .'

'Actually,' I straighten up in my chair, 'we were engaged.'

'Christ, he didn't stand you up at the altar, did he?'

'No.'

'Because if that'd happened, I could understand you'd be well pissed off. God, the embarrassment, all that cash on a wedding . . .'

'Anyway,' I say, 'I guess I've just taken it pretty hard.'

'But it's not like you were married or had kids or anything.'

Oh. You're right. Silly me! I was getting confused. I thought we'd been married for fourteen years and had two kids and a dog. Now you've pointed out that this wasn't the case, I'm so entirely at peace with the situation. In fact I feel amazing.

'I'm going to do something about it,' I say, blowing my nose. 'I won't let it get in the way of my work.'

'Good. It's not very professional, if you know what I mean.'

Not professional – like picking your nose and sticking your fingers in a pie not professional? Or not professional like shagging Mands from behind on the executive boardroom table? – We've all seen the CCTV, Devron . . .

I walk back to my desk and make two calls: an emergency appointment later today at my GP, and a visit tomorrow to a psychotherapist.

*

My GP appointment is at 3pm, and at 2.58 I show up at the surgery. I have to be back at the office for a final product meeting with Will at 4.30pm and they always make you wait an age here. The receptionist, who I know only as Cerberus, for her un-bedsidely manner, is in discussion with a man who wants to join the practice because his girlfriend's flat is round the corner. She is explaining in an increasingly smug tone, that this is *not* how the NHS works. He thinks he can bulldoze her into giving him the forms by increasing the aggression in his voice. Not a chance.

Sure enough at 3.08 he gives up, calls her an officious cow, and a small victory cheer pips through her smile.

Still in front of me is a paunchy old perma-tanned man. He wants to have a row with Cerberus for being made to wait an hour last week, which meant his brand new Porscha – yes, apparently you pronounce the e as an a – got clamped. Good luck winning that argument, mate.

At 3.17 he too gives up and takes his seat in the waiting room.

'Sophie Klein, I have an appointment with Dr Salter,' I say.

She squints at her screen. 'Your appointment was at 3pm.'

'I've been standing here since 2.58.'

'If you're late again, we won't be able to see you. Do you know how many no-shows this surgery has each week?' she says.

Today is not the day to take the bitch on.

I take my seat, take a deep breath and try to calm myself. I stare at the white wall but all I can think of is a snowy night back in November when James and I stole onto the roof of my block of flats, and with one iPod speaker in each ear, danced round the roof to Dean Martin. We looked out across the silenced city and then James pointed down to the street: 'We've got company.'

I thought Ben the caretaker might have busted us, but when I follow James's finger, I see his car, dusted in snow, and on the roof of it a fox, moving its paws along to the melody.

Memory's a bastard, I think.

I glance over at perma-paunch who is talking to a thin woman of around sixty, dressed in tight white jeans and a white Ralph Lauren shirt.

'I recognise you,' he says, 'I'm Stefan, I own Zarimkadeh, the jeweller's in the high street.' He leans forward, hairy hands on knees spread wide.

'Oh yes!' she says, 'I was in at Christmas, you had those divine yellow diamonds!'

'Next time you come in, I'll do you a deal,' he says. 'You're looking very well, very very good.'

'Thank you,' she says, stroking her collarbone with an elegant, bangled arm.

'You keep yourself well maintained, I can see you take care of yourself,' he says.

She nods energetically.

'A lot of women let themselves go. . . get fat. . . horrible.'

I stare at his shiny, pointed cowboy boots, then up past a huge gut hugged by a hot pink Lacoste t-shirt, spilling over an Hermès belt, then up to his Versace shades that sit on a bonnet of thickly sprayed hair.

'My wife, she does an hour on the treadmill every morning and an hour in the pool every night. She has the body she had when she was sixteen, terrific.'

Long marriage! She must be tolerant to put up with such a creep.

'How old is your wife?' asks the woman.

'Twenty-five,' says Stefan. I chuckle, but from the look he flashes it appears he isn't joking at all.

My name is called and as I walk past him I consider saying various things:

'Your shop is less than one mile away. If you walked to the surgery rather than drove your Porsch-ah, you wouldn't be such a fat douchebag, and you wouldn't get parking tickets.'

'It is OKAY not to be thin when you're sixty, or even when you're sixteen. How dare you talk about how "horrible" it is for an older woman to "get fat" when *you are fat*.'

'You do realise there's no point wasting £600 on an Hermès belt when your tummy's just going to cover it up, don't you?'

'And another thing! I haven't seen boots that try-hard, worn by someone who couldn't look less like a cowboy, since I last went down the Kings Road in 1988.'

Instead when I walk past, I mutter 'arsehole' just loud enough so that he can hear.

Watch me. Any day now my passive-aggression is going to morph into aggressive-aggression.

I hope Devron's around when it does.

'Sadie Klein, date of birth 1953?' says Dr Salter.

'No, we're no relation. Sophie Klein, 1976,' I say.

She looks at me with a touch of suspicion.

'How can I help?' she asks.

I start crying uncontrollably. BORING! I think, as I rapidly grab one tissue after another from the box on her desk, like a depressed magician.

I tell her the one-minute version of the story. I now have multiple formats: a five minute cut-down for strangers on the bus, the twenty-minute version for friends I haven't seen since the break-up and the screenplay, in case Harvey Weinstein comes calling.

Dr Salter chews the end of her pen. 'You don't actually believe any of the things this man said to you, do you?'

I snivel and nod.

'Clearly his behaviour says far more about him than you, there's nothing wrong with your body. And this man must have plenty of his own issues that he's projecting outwards. Was he very body-conscious himself?'

'Only about women . . .'

'Do you ever think about harming yourself?' she asks, looking at a shopping list on her computer screen.

'No, I would never do that, my mother would kill me,' I say, and she laughs, although I'm now the one not joking.

'Okay, well, anti-depressants are not a long-term solution.'

'I don't want to be on them, but I'm worried about losing my job.'

I hate the thought of anti-depressants. I don't like the fact that as a 34-year-old woman I should need them to help get me through a break-up, and I don't want to be anaesthetised against life's ups and downs. Actually, I do want to be anaesthetised against the downs, that's the whole point.

'There are plenty more fish in the sea,' she says, leaning her chin on her hands and her elbows on her knees: two parallel bars blocking my path to the narcs. 'Have you got many friends?' she asks.

'Yes, I'm lucky. I have lots of people who care about me and who I can talk to.'

'Well, if I were you I'd go to a gallery or a museum. Distract yourself, get on with your life. It sounds like you're better off without this man.'

The tears are on a roll, but I am now irritated.

'I can't actually move at the weekends,' I say. 'I tried to see a film the other day and I had to leave the cinema because I was crying so loudly.'

'What was the film?' she asks.

What? 'A French film, about a guy in prison.'

'Try something more upbeat. I hear *Avatar*'s excellent.'

Dr Barry fucking Norman.

'Come on, stiff upper lip,' she says. This is not my approach at all. 'Go and splash some cold water on your face, no one likes to see panda eyes.'

I am rigid with indignation. I'd heard the NHS doled out anti-depressants like sweeties. Now that I can't have them, there's nothing I want more.

'Will you ask me the question on your screen again, please?' I say.

'Sorry?'

'I wasn't concentrating the first time. Ask me again, please.'

'*Do you ever think about harming yourself?*'

'Yes. Sometimes.'

'*Do you? Really?*'

I nod, James-style.

She takes a deep breath. 'Okay. We'll start you on 20mg of Citalopram and let's see how you get on. They take at least a month to kick in . . .'

On my way back to work, my winning green prescription clasped tight, I realise the bottom line: I can't change what James said, what he did, what he thinks, who he's chosen or who he is.

And I find these facts unbearable.

I return to my desk and an email from Devron.

'Sophie.

Tried to find you after our chat but you'd disappeared. So: big 'Change of Direction' from the Board re: your custard project. New objective for next financial year: budget slashing.

Tell suppliers to pull plug on work-in-progress. Updates next week.'

I phone Maggie.

'Help! Devron's just asked me to cancel my whole new range.'

'How far are you from launch?'

'Two weeks.'

'His reason?'

'The Board. Budget cutting?'

'Not a chance, if it's the Board and it's money, he won't fight for you.'

'Appletree have been working on it for a year! Will's

due here any minute to go through the final product specs . . .'

'Shareholders, Sophie. You're not going to win. I'm sorry.'

Will is totally gracious about it even though it's one of the worst things we could do to a supplier.

'I'm so sorry,' I say. 'I think Devron's got another angle in mind, hopefully I'll rebrief next week . . .'

'Don't worry Soph, these things happen. It'll all work out.'

'– Do you want to grab a cup of tea in the canteen?'

He looks at his watch. 'How about that Shake Away?'

I shouldn't really. I need to email all the ops guys to tell them the new range is cancelled . . .

'It's Islington – only twenty minutes in a cab,' says Will.

Besides, I'm weeks behind on purchase orders.

'Hundreds of different milkshakes . . .' he says.

And I really should collect my pills from the chemist.

'You shook on it, remember?' he says.

Or I could escape my life for one hour.

'I'll grab my coat.'

*

'This place is dangerous,' I say, surveying the menu.

'You could have a different milkshake every day for a year and still have some left to try,' says Will, with a look on his face suggesting he's done just that.

304

'What do you recommend?'

'I'm having a Hot Norah – chocolate muffin, dime bar and bits of Malteser.'

'That's a drink?'

'Not for the faint hearted,' he says, a hint of pride creeping into his smile.

'I'll go Chunky Kit Kat if I can try this Norah thing.'

'Verdict?' says Will. 'You think it's too full on?'

'Not full on enough!' I say, taking another sip. Who needs anti-depressants when you've got hot milkshakes with muffins and chocolate bars for croutons?

'What do you reckon? Anything we could do with it from a development point of view?'

I consider for a minute. Yes. You could definitely take the concept and look at it in another format – translate it into a cake or a biscuit. 'Potentially. I'll give it some thought.'

'Great,' he says, smiling broadly. 'You finish the rest – I've got to catch my train.'

'Take this with you,' I say, shoving the drink back in his hand. 'This slope's too slippery for me.'

'What do you mean?' he says.

'Too fattening.'

'What are you talking about?'

'I mean it's full of sugar and fat.'

'No, I know what's in it, I mean why are you saying that? You've got nothing to worry about.'

305

'I've been eating too much.'

'Are you fishing for a compliment?' He smiles at me. 'You're not serious?' he says, his smile faltering.

'Let's start walking to the tube, you'll miss your train,' I say. The sky has turned slate and the wind has picked up. 'I'm freezing.'

'Here. Why don't you borrow this?' He takes off his scarf and places it round my neck.

'Won't you be cold?' I say, blushing as I feel the warmth from his skin on mine.

'I'm fine. You look like you need it – your cheeks have gone all pink . . .'

'Just cold, that's all,' I say, turning in embarrassment and heading towards the station.

He rushes to catch up. 'Did I say something wrong before? I didn't mean to make you feel awkward,' he says, looking perplexed.

'No, ignore me, it's nothing. Anyway, what are you up to this weekend, anything fun?'

'Absolutely! My mum's broken her wrist so I'm driving her to Homebase to help her choose grouting.'

'Rock and roll . . .'

He laughs. 'It gets better. Then I'm going round to my ex-wife's to help her pack up her flat . . .'

His ex-wife who cheated on him? 'You two are still friends?'

'No, not really. But she's moving to Glasgow and she asked me to help.'

'Will, you're a saint!'

'Oh, don't get me wrong, if you'd spoken to me a few years back I wasn't her number one fan . . . but . . . well, time heals and all that.'

'So they say. How long were you married for?'

'Just under three years. But we'd been together for eight before that.'

'You must have got together young,' I say, trying to do the maths – Will's about my age, maybe a year older.

'Youngish. Twenty-two. I think that was part of the problem. I don't know if either of us knew ourselves properly, let alone each other. Anyway, she did what she did and that was quite hard to get my head around.'

'It must have been awful,' I say, remembering with a deep ache in my chest that first sight of Noushka's legs coming down the kitchen stairs.

He shakes his head. 'The weird thing was,' he says, looking momentarily confused, 'I almost felt like it was *my* fault, if that makes any sense?'

I nod.

'But it wasn't my fault. Fault isn't even a helpful way of looking at it, anyway.'

'You make it sound so logical . . .'

He laughs gently. 'It took me a year and a half to get to logical. The way I see it now, she did me a massive favour. We could have had kids and that would have been far messier. Anyway, I don't know why I'm boring you

307

with my life story – all a bit heavy for a Tuesday afternoon!' he says, looking suddenly self-conscious as we enter the dull yellow light of the tube station. 'So . . . I guess this is me. I'll see you soon, Soph,' he says, giving me a peck on the cheek. 'Glad you liked the shake.'

As he heads through the barrier I feel a compulsion to follow him down the long escalator, to keep talking to him. I want to discover his secrets. How can he be so gracious? I want to be like that. Magnanimous. Calm. Storm-free.

Instead, I turn and walk slowly back out to Upper Street.

The minute I reach the bus stop I realise I still have his scarf.

On the way home I wrap it tightly around me. It smells of clean laundry and limes: two of my favourite things.

This road to recovery's a bit bumpy for my liking. The following evening, Pete brings round a curry. I'm already in pyjamas at 7pm, and after I've scraped the last of the chicken dhansak out of the carton I ask him to go round to Tesco's and buy me some bread and hummus.

'You can't still be hungry, Soph,' he says. 'Just give it five minutes and you'll feel full.'

'And some Ben and Jerry's too . . . Phish Food,' I say, giving him a twenty pound note.

While he's gone I make a half-hearted attempt to tidy up. Mail lies unopened on my doormat. My clothes form mole hills throughout the flat. For some reason the Marmite is in the fridge, along with my driving licence.

Pete comes back with a small baguette, hummus and a small tub of Phish Food. We exchange glances.

'Thank you,' I say. 'I meant a big baguette.'

'I'm looking out for you, Soph.'

'I can look out for myself,' I say, ripping into the bread. 'How's it going with that girl then, Carla, was it? That's been a while, must be getting serious.'

'She's fun, but . . . you know, she's not the one.'

'Does she know that?'

'What?'

'That you're wasting her time?'

'I'm not going to propose to her.'

'But if you know it's not right, why carry on?'

'We've just booked a holiday in June, I'll finish it after that probably.'

'But if you feel that way before the holiday, why lead her on? Why don't you just finish it now? That'd be kinder to her.'

'Stop comparing me to James.'

'No, seriously, are you just waiting for someone better to come along, so you don't have to be on your own?'

'Soph. I'm your friend.'

I start to weep. 'Then please say something that will help me move on. I can't seem to shake this sadness.'

'You just need to get some perspective,' he says, giving me a hug.

I just need to get some more bread.

Get some perspective. Your self-pity isn't helping – move on.

Of course I KNOW THIS. But it might as well be written in Webdings:

310

♥⚊🚗✕ ?📱✈🚌 🚍①🐌⊖ ①?●°🐌 🚗📱✈🚍①●◼

💣 !⚊🚊📱 ⚊●◼

But my brain still tries to find the meaning in Webdings. I see a love heart, unanswered questions, big black voids, a man in the distance next to a yacht and a bus – two forms of escape . . .

Zapf Dingbats is more like it:

✹❑◆❑ ▲✳●✳ ❑✳❚❙ ✳▲■☆▼ ✳✳●❑✳■✳ ✤ ○❑✣✳ ❑❒

★

I should be on *Top Gear*. I can now distinguish the purr of a Maserati from any other performance car with my eyes closed. If I hear one, let alone see one, panic grips my guts.

Suddenly London is aswarm with midnight blue Maseratis. Whenever I spot one, I automatically squint to see if James is driving it. It's amazing how many middle-aged men with a slight chin drive midnight blue Maseratis.

God forbid I ever have to cross at a light in front of one. I can't help but stare: these men all have the same expression. It reminds me of an old Garfield poster I had on my wall as a kid, with Garfield saying: 'It's hard to be humble when you're as great as I am!' They often have a sullen twenty-something girlfriend next to them. That's such a simple equation, even Amber could do it:

$$40 < \male < 55 + \pounds\pounds = \Psi + \female < 30$$

311

And all these men race off before the light's turned green, flooring their accelerators, as if you could ever get anywhere in London fast.

That is the best thing about a long distance relationship: breaking up is not so hard to do. But according to Google maps, James lives only 2.5 miles from my door by car, 2.1 by foot.

I walk the streets in fear of seeing him, or worse – him seeing me. I start wearing noise reduction speakers on my iPod, and taking the bus at all times.

It is now March. Spring has yet to sprung and the London sky is relentlessly grey. A year ago, I was sitting opposite James in the Dean Street Townhouse, eating the Queen of Puddings and falling in love. Today I'm sitting opposite Devron in Boardroom 4B, watching him demolish a Benjy's egg and sausage sandwich without chewing it.

Ton of Fun Tom, Julie from packaging and I are here, waiting for Devron to wipe the egg dribble from his chin and then brief us on the 'Change of Direction' he so sweetly shit-bombed last week.

Zoe has already told me what the 'Change of Fucking Direction' is: the Fletchers deep freezer is the retail equivalent of the Deepthroat car park.

Our Research Unit has tapped into twenty-first century lifestyle trends and identified a new female audience ripe for exploitation: SLOTs, Single Long Terms. They're 'cash rich', 'lonely', and 'dissatisfied'. They want single-serve portions of their favourite comfort foods without the temptation of eating a family pack.

'Right, Soph, I don't want you getting all creative with your bin liner biscuits. What we need is three low-cal treats to appeal to these women – 30 to 45, ABC1s. Research says that custard is a big win – reminds them of happy childhoods.'

'Hang on. I've just done a year's work with Appletree on custard, I've got twelve products that are launch-ready, can I use some of those?' Will deserves this brief after all the work he's done on it.

'If you can get them down to less than 3% fat and crush them on costs – 30% cheaper – yes. If not, go from scratch. – I was thinking perhaps we could invent a biscuit that has custard in the middle. Hit these women in their tea break.' I'll hit you in your tea break, dickhead.

'Do you mean a custard cream?' I say. I'd like to have invented the custard cream – quite audacious in its day. Not so innovative now . . .

'Shit. Okay, just whatever, something for tea breaks. And something that's good for commuting, and something in a small bucket for those long nights in front of *Sex and the City* reruns.

'Can we brainstorm together, pleeease?' says Ton of Fun Tom.

Tom is as irritating as a raspberry seed in your molar and equally hard to get rid of.

314

'Yeah, make sure Tom's included in everything. The brand is key. On that note, I've had some ideas for naming the range,' he says, opening his file. 'Okay. One is Fun.'

'Delia's got a book called that,' I say. Besides, one is not fun.

'Julie, write it down,' says Devron. 'Then there's Serves One, or Suit Yourself.'

'Serves One sounds depressing,' says Julie.

'Suit Yourself sounds cool,' says Ton of Fun. 'Empowering. Feminist.'

'The "Suit" thing doesn't work,' I say. 'If it was "Suite Yourself" – but then that's too clever-clever, doesn't really make sense either.'

Devron rolls his eyes. 'Or something more jokey. You know that ice cream brand, Skinny Cow?'

'. . . Yes,' I say.

'So, I'm thinking "Fat Cow," or "Fat Bird," with a cute pink cartoon cow or bird on the packaging. Julie?'

Julie is shaking her head violently.

'The research says women love the concept of Skinny Cow,' says Devron.

'Skinny Cow and Fat Cow are not the same thing,' I say.

'The research also says these women enjoy "badminton, Radio 4 and laughing." They've got a sense of humour.'

'Yes, but does the research say these women enjoy being called fat?'

'They're okay being called cow, what's the difference?' says Devron.

'Big fat difference,' I say.

'Fine, Bird then. We'll put an exclamation mark after Bird!, show it's tongue in cheek. Mands thinks it's brilliant,' says Devron. 'Speak to suppliers, press play on Fat Bird! And remember – what does success look like?!'

I call Will.

'Sophie! I was just thinking about you,' he says.

'Oh, I know I still have your scarf, sorry.'

'My scarf? Oh, I'd forgotten about that.'

'Listen – you're not going to believe Devron's latest genius idea.'

'Go on . . .'

'Low-cal treats for single career women . . .'

'That sounds doable. What's the problem?'

'The name of the range,' I say, shaking my head with embarrassment.

'Go on . . .'

'It's dreadful, I can't say it . . .'

'Give me a clue,'

'It's totally insensitive.'

'You'll have to narrow it down a bit.'

'Okay. Two words, first rhymes with rat, second with word, highly inappropriate for a dessert.'

'. . . Cat Turd . . .?'

'No, but he's probably trademarked that for his value sausage rolls. Okay, think about two words a woman would not want to be called . . .'

'. . . Fat Nerd?'

'Almost! Swap the N for a B.'

There is a pause on the other end of the line, followed by a small snicker.

'Oi! Stop laughing! It's not funny,' I say.

'No, it's deathly serious, Sophie.'

'It is!' I say, knowing full well he can hear my smile down the phone.

'Okay, when are you up to see us?'

'I'll come with a proper brief on Monday?' I say.

'Can't wait. Meet you at the station.'

I've been going to see a Cognitive Behavioural Therapist twice a week for the last fortnight. I saw a shrink a few times after my dad died and I hated it. If I'm going to spend £60 on something, I want it to be wearable, edible, preferably both. But, I have no time to be depressed. The pills haven't kicked in yet; intensive therapy is the way forward.

I like my shrink, I really do. She is smart and kind and has a normal-sized body.

She says that I should treat the relationship as a gift, a 'learning experience'. My idea of a gift is a Marimekko teacup, or if you're feeling flush, a pale blue cashmere blanket. I don't recall putting 'learning experience' on my Christmas list. I'd like to take the following back to Selfridges, please: 1 x clinical depression (size, medium); 1 x dignity removal kit (heavily used). Do you really need a receipt? Just look at my face.

I tell her I feel guilty that I'm not grieving my grandma

more. My shrink thinks this must be why the James situation has hit me so hard – my closest relative in London, my dead father's mother, a double bereavement. But my grandma was ninety-seven, she was bored to buggery. Death was entirely what she wanted.

My shrink also thinks I never dealt with the sadness at the end of my relationship with Nick, and that's compounding everything. But when Nick and I split up, I felt intact, not in pieces. He'd done nothing to take me apart.

She says she doesn't think it was ever about my weight, and that James just attacked where he knew I was vulnerable. 'If it hadn't been your weight, he'd have pinned it on something else.'

'Would that be deliberate or subconscious?' I ask.

She shrugs. 'Might be unconscious. I don't know this man.'

For some reason in the following session, I become obsessed with quantifying exactly what level of badness has taken place. Is James an utter fuckface, or a sadist, a bit of a shit or just a coward, immature or just weak, maybe just human or all of the above? Was there an overlap between me and Noushka? If so, how many days, how many hours? Was she in the Cayman Islands with him over New Year's? This blame game I blame (yes) on my mother. If my mother in California stubs her toe on the sun lounger, it is somehow my fault back in London. When she mislaid her square Japanese omelette pan, she

319

spent a year blaming the builders. I explained to her in many languages (including Japanese) that if the builders were going to steal any of her kitchenware, they wouldn't take the novelty egg pan, they'd go straight for the Le Creuset. She is having none of it. When she eventually finds the pan she convinces herself that the builders have broken into the house to replace it. She wonders if she should call the police. My mother is nuts. I am officially my mother's daughter.

'Can't you just see it as he couldn't meet your needs?' says the shrink. Where's the fun in that, I ask.

In the fourth session we talk about anger. She feels that I took the body blows during the relationship and am now having a very delayed response to them. The truth is I am furious: furious that I took him back, furious that I didn't pick him up on all the comments about my weight, furious that I didn't assert myself more, furious that I shagged him in the car when he was almost definitely seeing Noushka, furious that I put his value above mine, furious that I believed his version of me.

'You should be angry at James, not at yourself,' says the shrink. But I'm too scared to show him my anger, in the same way that when we went to France I was too scared to walk around naked all the time. Like cellulite, I've been conditioned to think of anger as ugly, ugly, ugly.

So, I put all the anger where it is least helpful – into the heart of me.

After four sessions, my counsellor says she's not sure what she can do to help me. I'm not her 'normal type'.

I ask her to please not use that phrase ever, ever again.

She apologises and goes on to say that she thinks I'll resist CBT and argue with its principles.

I argue that I wouldn't be paying for help if I didn't want help.

She smiles gently, and says that she believes I am holding on to the thought of James in my head because I don't want the relationship to be over.

Yes! Of course! And I need her to wave a wand and fix me; or better still, help me get him back. I'll pay her double for that.

'You can show up here every week but ultimately I'm afraid you're going to have to do the work yourself,' she says.

She is *so* fired.

*

On the bus home from my ex-shrink, I decide it would be a marvellous idea to call my ex-fiancé and meet for a coffee, share some of the enlightening things I've learned in therapy. They'd be helpful for him too. Then he can fix himself and everything will be better and I'll be free from this pain.

I know everyone says don't call, but honestly, I feel fine at this precise millisecond and so I dial, feeling an aching sickness as I press the green button on my phone.

It rings and rings. I'm about to hang up when he picks up, sounding surprised.

'Soph?'

The manically cheery tone I was going to use doesn't make it out of my mouth.

'. . . I need to see you,' I say.

'It's not a good time.'

'Just for half an hour, for a coffee. It won't take long.'

'Not today, next week?'

'It's important.'

'I can't now.'

'Okay, later?' Stop talking, Sophie.

'Today's not good.'

'Tomorrow?' Stop it now, Sophie.

'My cab's just pulling up at Heathrow . . .'

'Where are you going?'

'On business.'

'Where?'

There is silence on the line.

'James? Where are you going?'

'Moscow . . .'

I smile. That's fine, of course.

'Soph, I can see you next week . . .'

'No. It's better if you don't.'

★

I remember when I was five, playing in the ocean a few metres further out than my parents had said was safe. I saw the next wave coming and realised too late that it was big. Bigger than me.

I knew that whether I turned sideways, turned my back, crouched down or stood and faced that wave, I was going to go under.

It feels as if that wave is in my head.

On Monday morning I take the train up to Sheffield to brief Appletree on the new spinster custards.

Will is waiting for me at the station with a millefeuille. Of all the desserts in all the world . . . I politely refuse.

'You're quiet today, Soph,' he says, as I stare out of the window.

'Thinking,' I mumble.

'Never a good idea!'

In his office, we talk through the new brief in more detail.

'So – single portions, under 200 calories, custard based, and cheap . . .' I say. 'Do you think there's anything you can do with all the work you've done already?'

'We'll try our best, Soph . . .'

'I'm most worried about the low-cal part,' I say. 'I've never had a low-cal product that tasted as good as the real thing.'

'It's tricky,' says Will. 'You lose the fat, you lose the texture and flavour. We'll look at skimmed milk, soy, and whey . . .'

I shake my head. 'I don't want to make desserts like that . . . it's like eating in black and white . . .'

'I know what you mean,' he says. 'Let's have a stab at it, and if it doesn't work . . . Come on, let's go to the canteen and I'll buy us some lunch.'

We scrub up, put our uniforms on and head through the factory.

In the fruit room I notice a large puddle of scarlet-black cherry juice that looks like a pool of blood.

'Depositor's malfunctioning. Oh, but I've got a brand new robot I think you'll like,' he says, as we walk into the vanilla sugar air of the cake room.

We head over to the Madeira line and as the cakes roll past on the conveyor belt a robot arm suddenly punches one of the cakes off the line onto a smaller belt running parallel. Another robot arm slams a large red 'REJECT' sticker down on to the cake, which then falls through a trap door into a large plastic bin.

'Isn't that great?' he says. 'The scales on the line automatically detect if the cake weighs too much. Anything too heavy goes straight to the dump.'

'Harsh,' I say.

We walk through the wedding cake room, past huge stacks of folded peachy-pink sugar icing. The vast sheets look like flesh, the aftermath of a giant's tummy-tuck.

'Will, I'm really sorry but I think I'm going to take an earlier train. I don't feel good.'

325

'I thought you didn't seem like your normal bubbly self. Is everything okay?' he says, resting his hand on my shoulder.

I nod, scared that if I try to speak, I'll cry.

'Let me take you to the station.'

'I'll call for a cab.'

'I insist.'

'Thank you for the lift.'

'I'll wait with you,' says Will, pulling into a space in the car park.

'The train will be here at twenty past. I'm fine . . .'

'I know you are. To be honest, I could do with a break from the office,' he says, smiling gently.

We walk slowly to the station and find a bench. We sit side by side in silence.

It should feel awkward, this sitting so close saying nothing. To passers-by it must look weird, like we've had a fight. With anyone else I didn't know very well, I'd feel self-conscious.

But for these fifteen minutes until my train arrives, sitting here next to Will, I feel entirely at peace.

★

Later that night Laura drags me to the pub.

If it weren't for Laura, I'd still be with James now. I'd

have taken him back, or worse, begged for him back. I owe her my remaining sanity, but a part of me blames her for cutting me off from my chance of happiness. It's alright for her – she's been with Dave for ten years. She's forgotten how tough it is out there. For some reason, men in London think they're buyers in a buyers' market, and a 34-year-old single woman is like an overpriced studio flat in Zone 5. An overpriced studio flat that's desperate for sperm.

'You need to move on,' she says.

'I just want to understand it. There are only ever two people who know what really happened in any relationship, but I don't feel like one of them,' I say.

'Stop wasting your energy on him. Put it into yourself,' she says.

She might as well have asked me to reconstruct the Hadron Collider in my front room out of Iced Gems.

'You only remember the highs, Soph, but you need to remember what a weasel he was too. And this whole Noushka fixation is crazy. Me and Dave googled her – she's got a bigger chin than Jimmy Hill! What did Dave say . . . she's a total prawn – ignore the head, it's all about the body.'

I smile weakly.

'Look, every time you think about James, just picture a big fat weasel in mid-life crisis jeans and a too-tight shirt, driving a Maserati down Bond Street with a giant prawn sitting next to him dressed in suspenders and stockings.'

'Fishnet?'

'Naturally,' she says, clinking my glass.

'Is the prawn wearing suspenders on all her legs?' I ask.

'No, just four. On the others she's wearing Hellmans . . .'

I laugh, and Laura gives me a long hug.

'You know what you need?' she says.

'A photoshop picture of a weasel and a prawn as my screensaver?'

'Forget him. You need to get out there and meet a decent man. There must be someone knocking around.'

I think immediately of Will, and how comfortable I felt with him earlier. He's so sweet, so kind. But he's just too nice. Plus, he has the baggage of a divorce, he lives in another city, and I work with him.

I guess there's Jack, my granny's neighbour. He texted a month ago asking me out and I never replied.

'Anyone?' she says.

'This guy Jack, maybe . . .'

And before I can stop her she's grabbed my phone and typed: 'Fancy a drink next week?'

'Don't, Laura. DON'T.'

But she's already pressed send.

The following day I'm in a one-to-one with Devron. I've been up since 5am – I don't sleep well at the moment – and I am super-fucking-irritable.

'Special one-off "Value" project for you. Go and spend

£100 at M&S on puddings, do hot and cold, and work out how we can make 'em all cheaper,' he says. He can barely make eye contact with me these days; just as well, as I'm usually pink-eyed, puffy-eyed or panda-eyed.

I will not, I think. That's just wrong.

'Can't be done, Devron, M&S are all about quality. They don't cheapskate on ingredients.'

At the word 'cheapskate', Devron shudders.

'Sophie – this fiscal's all about budget slashing. Maintain quality but make efficiencies where possible – that's the route to the loot.'

A cackle slips out of me. 'Did you just say route to the loot?'

'JFDI,' he says and walks away.

'Eddie, what does JFDI mean?'

'Let's just say he didn't learn it at Ashridge . . .'

I walk over to M&S on Oxford Street and take the escalator down to the food hall. I take a basket, then put it back and grab a trolley and head towards the pudding aisle. I buy 25 different desserts, from Kentish Apple Crumbles to New York Cheesecake Slices to Belgian Chocolate Soufflés, plus double cream and custard for good measure.

I have more bags than I can carry so I put them through car service, then pop upstairs to call Janelle and tell her I'm working from home on a 'Special Project' for the rest of the day. Devron is now off for a week, 'visiting our European competitors,' i.e. taking Mands on a trip to Paris and Venice and billing it to Fletchers. If Janelle wants to snitch on me, let her. I am taking no prisoners.

I hail a taxi, picking up my six bags of puddings en route. The cabbie helps me up to my flat and asks, 'When's the party?'

'All week,' I say. I tip him well and give him a two pack of Berry Cheesecake slices for his troubles. 'Try these, they're delicious.'

'You sure you'll have enough for your guests?'

'I'll make them stretch,' I say, waving him off.

I put the chain on my front door, the puddings in my fridge, and myself into bed.

★

On Wednesday, I set my alarm for 8am. Five puddings to try each day, minus the cabbie's one: one every two hours, eminently doable.

If I eat one portion of each dessert, and the mean, or is it the median, of a portion is 400 calories, I'll be consuming around 2000 calories a day. If I do a small amount of exercise, and don't eat or drink anything else, I'll be fine from a weight gain point of view, and so what if I feel crappy, it's only five days of my long, long life.

I then file all the desserts by their 'Use By' date in my fridge, ones to eat first at the top. I'm feeling supremely on edge so I decide to go and lie down on my sofa, but it's far too bright in my living room, so I go and lie down on my bed.

I wake up when my phone rings: Jack.

'You sound like you're asleep!' he says.

'Of course I'm not . . . what time is it?' I say.

'4.30pm.'

Shit.

'Listen, do you fancy that drink sometime this week?' he says.

'I'm busy . . .'

'Next week better?'

'Okay . . .'

'Great! Tuesday? Do you know the Lansdowne in Primrose Hill?'

James's local. 'How about The Old White Bear in Hampstead?' Maggie says their brownies are almost perfect.

'Eight o'clock next Tuesday. It's a date.'

I haul myself out of bed. I'm now behind schedule and I was meant to walk for an hour, or run for ten minutes, but now it's raining so going outside is technically impossible. I put the kettle on, figuring I can offset the calories in the milk in my tea by having a bite less of the first pudding. Or not.

Have you even tried the Bakewell Cream Slice from M&S? Shortbread base, raspberry compôte, fresh cream, roasted flaked almonds. A classic with a twist; inspired design. Very Maggie, I think, as I work my way through half of the six slices. After slice three I am full and feel sick.

If I am going to marathon eat, my body might need a little help.

I put my granny's pink furry dressing gown on over my nightie and head out.

Amber opens her door dressed in metallic purple leggings and a fur jacket. I think she looks more ridiculous than me. 'Hey babe, not working?' she says.

'Special Project,' I say. 'Listen, you know that £100 I lent you for coke about a year ago?'

'Oh babe, today's a really bad day for me, I've got to pick Annalex up from the vet, poor baby's got terrible worms, and then I'm off to Bikram . . .'

'Fine, on your way back do me a favour. Get me £50 worth of whatever weed your dealer has on him and we'll call it quits. Or I'll have £100 tonight if you prefer . . .'

'I was going to go straight to the spa after . . .'

'Just post it through my letterbox by 5pm, then we're quits. Okay?'

She pouts, but I can tell she'll do it because she looks a tiny bit scared of the new me.

I climb back into bed and when I get up a few hours later, what do you know? There on my doormat sits a beautiful little baggy of sweet smelling skunk.

SHIT! I have no fags, no skins, and it's still pissing down with rain.

This dressing gown is so cosy and my flat is so cold, I can't possibly take it off. Fuck it, it's dark already anyway.

I put on my trainers, put a coat over the dressing gown and a hat against the rain and dash round to the newsagent. For some perverse reason this trip reminds me of dancing naked round the fountain in France, and I let out a small howl of pain.

Good thing I really don't care what I look like these days. I find this fantastically liberating, having spent most of the last year trying to look pretty and slim, rather than furious and insane.

Right. Home. Climb the stairs. Lock the door. Skin up. Smoke weed. Strong weed. I am stoned. Soooo stoned. Eat big bites of all the cold puddings, they all taste amayyyyyyzing. Berry and Cherry Jelly, Belly and Jenny Cherry, Benny and Jerry Chelly, Belly and Jelly and Shelliii . . .

I can't be arsed to write any notes and now I really am soooo stoned and very, very sleepy and it's already 8.30pm and so I climb into bed.

*

Day two, I wake up, get stoned in bed, then drag myself into the kitchen and heat the Belgian Chocolate Marble pudding for four. I sit staring through the oven door, watching as it cooks, but halfway through, my mind flits to a memory of watching James naked through the glass in the swimming pool and I take the half-cooked pudding out and start to eat.

I pour double cream on to dilute the richness; because the pudding's undercooked, the sponge is too dense and hasn't risen properly. I start to feel sick in my throat, but soldier on like the true professional that I am. I make it to the end and halfway through an all butter shortcrust cherry lattice pie before I am slightly sick in my kitchen sink.

Day three – the only way I am going to get through this is if I portion out single servings of each remaining pudding, and give or throw away the rest.

I divide up the food, then summon Ben the caretaker and beg him to take away as much as he can carry. 'And for God's sake take the Millionaire's Shortbread,' I say.

I try to offload on Amber too, but of course she's wheat *and* gluten *and* dairy intolerant this week.

I throw away the extras, guilt-ridden about the waste, and go back to bed exhausted, then remember that I haven't eaten anything yet today. I'm craving something green, or some fruit, but when I bite into an apple it tastes so . . . uncreamy, so I chuck it on top of the pile of puddings in my bin.

A new hit in the hall of shame. I only get through three individual portions of dessert before I burrow through my bin to retrieve seconds of the Salted Caramel Pecan Torte.

Day four and now I can see the weight gain in my face, around my chin. In the bath I can feel my muffin tops rising again. The realisation disturbs me so much that I rush to the kitchen, dismember the chocolate cheesecake, and eat only the crunchy bourbon-biscuit base.

It is only when I go to bed at 6pm that I realise that today is Saturday and I shouldn't have been working at all, and wonder if I can bill Fletchers for a day's overtime and spend the cash on more drugs . . .

Day five – some of my shelf lives are imminent so I decide to keep on working. My flat now stinks of weed, so I decide to smoke only in the bath, and after washing I change into a new selection of clothes that are currently decorating my floor.

I only have two desserts left in the fridge and to this day I have no recollection or understanding of how that can be, as I thought I had at least seven more to go. Regardless, I take the top one out of the fridge and set about eating it as intelligently as I can. It occurs to me that I have written no notes, nor given the slightest bit of thought to the job in hand, i.e. Devron asking me to think about how we could copy any of this lot on the cheap.

It's a Key Lime Pie Tray Bake and for a microsecond I think, well, you could substitute the double cream they've used for a cheaper cream and starch powder, and leave off the zest, try a different base that doesn't use as much butter. Of course, it wouldn't be anywhere near as nice, but Devron doesn't care about nice, Devron cares about cheap.

And then I go to the fridge to fetch the final pudding and recoil in horror when I see what it is. How did I put that in my basket without realising it? I must have scooped it up by accident because there's no way I'd have that in my house willingly.

It is a Tarte Aux Abricots and the very sight of it (or maybe the entire Key Lime Pie I've polished off) makes me violently sick.

I spend the rest of the day in bed staring at the ceiling and sleeping and wishing I was not such a giant loser, and could just shag a barman, ten barmen, and get over this.

And then the following morning, five pounds heavier and six days after I last showed my face, I re-enter the work place.

'Where have you been?' says Janelle. 'Did you not get my messages?'

'My phone broke. I told you . . . Special Project, working from home,' I say.

'That was on Tuesday afternoon.'

'So?'

'Last week.'

'. . . And?'

'. . . What about all the rest of last week? Where were you?'

'I just told you.'

'But you need to tell me in advance if you're working from home.'

'No, I don't, I need to tell Devron. I texted him and then my phone broke.'

'Shall I mark you down as sick?'

'I WAS WORKING!' I say. 'On Wednesday I researched cheesecakes and steamed puddings, Thursday – mousses, soufflés and frozen, Friday – tarts, trifles and pies. I've only just finished my notes. I'll talk Devron through them in due course.'

She pulls the 'you're in a world of shit and I'm glad' face that I've come to know and love and goes back to her desk.

I settle back at mine and click on an email from the Pantry Team inviting anyone with a spare ten minutes to come to the twelfth floor to beat the Monday blues and sample their new 'Super Biscuits' range. With my expert palette and in-depth knowledge of the Treat Market, it's basically my duty to help.

Heartbreak is like the Lynx effect in reverse. Walk around a room with a biscuit in each hand, staring pink-eyes, unbrushed hair and a bottom lip slightly wobbling and I guarantee you won't find yourself having to fend off Raymond Cowell-Trousers from Accounts.

'Take some back to your desk if you like,' says the Product Developer, noticing I've been in the room for the best part of an hour.

How kind! I believe I shall. I build a foundation of two Chocolate Mega-Bics. On top I layer two Fig Newton knock-offs, two shortbread squares, a cherry flapjack and three vanilla bourbons, topped off with a mini Wagon Whirl.

As I'm walking down the stairs trying to balance eleven biscuits on a napkin, the Wagon Whirl topples and falls down the central stairwell. I hear a small yelp. I think about dropping a penny off the Empire State Building. I could really do without killing a colleague today. I hope it's not one of the grannies from the canteen.

When I get down to the fourth floor I see a slim woman in a short skirt looking seriously pissed off, and I think, 'serves you right for walking up these stairs, you could have taken the lift. You're lucky it wasn't a Chocolate Finger, that could have done some serious damage'.

*

I'm due at Maggie's for dinner at 8pm, but before then I need to relax.

I need more weed.

'I'm all out,' says Amber. 'How's Jason?'

'James? Over,' I say.

'Oh, sorry, babe. You know I heard the best advice the other day . . .'

Here we go.

'If a guy dumps you, all you have to say to yourself is "He's just not that into me". Like in that Scarlett Johansson film. It's really amazing, it makes the whole dating thing so simple.'

Fuck off, fuck off, fuck off. 'Yeah, Amber, it was a little more complicated than that, but thanks for the advice.'

'No, really, babe, that's all you have to do. I used to walk Annalex on Primrose Hill, and there was this boy dog Gillespie, and they fell totally in love.'

Don't tell me . . . the owner was some hunky Abercrombie model type, and he dumped you after two dates, and you said 'he's just not that into me' . . . blah blah blah.

'And when Gillespie's owner moved to Brighton, Annalex just cried and cried for like a month . . . It was so sad.'

I'm going to commit an act of violence on Amber, I am. A jury would find me not guilty on the grounds of sufficient provocation.

'How did Annalex pick up the pieces and move on?' I say.

'It just took time and lots of dog biscuits,' says Amber.

'I can't talk to you ever again, Amber.'

★

It's my turn to have Maggie round but I can't let her see the state of my flat, plus I haven't felt like cooking for months. Since the Noushka night, I've subsisted on cakes, takeaways, marijuana and fags. I have not eaten a single piece of fruit that wasn't part of a pudding since January 31st and today is April 11th.

Maggie's cooked my favourite, Armenian Lamb with rice, pine nuts and sour raisins – that's old sour grapes, I think, as I help myself to a third portion. Maggie is looking at me with concern.

'How are you, Soph?' I would have made it through without crying if she hadn't asked. But now she has, and now I'm forced to stop eating for five whole minutes while I try to explain that I can't explain why I'm crying.

'Oh my poor love,' she says, hugging me.

'I'm fine, honestly, I know I'll get over it, I know I will, but I just need that to happen now.'

She heads off to the kitchen and comes back with a ginger tea.

'My ex-husband, Howard, used to tell me I was too opinionated, my hair was too short, and that I didn't wear skirts enough,' she says.

'I didn't know you were ever married,' I say.

'Even though I left him, it still took me five years to get over it. I cried every day for the first year.'

I take a tissue from the box she's holding. 'I can't believe a woman like you would cry over a man – a man who said something as dumb as that.'

'I could say the same to you. But you learn from your mistakes, if you're smart. My marriage changed me, and I'm grateful for it.'

'Er, Maggie, do you have any pudding?' I say, conscious that I am now officially the world's rudest dinner guest.

While she is in the kitchen I look at the teabag in my cup. It's from some cute Californian company that print mantras on their teabag tags. Mine reads 'You can climb a mountain through your strength alone'. Great. I'm seeking spiritual guidance from a cocking tea bag. Is that better or worse than a horoscope?

She returns with two molten middle caramel puddings and a carton of double cream.

'The thing is, Maggie, I can look at my relationship and see a hundred different versions of what happened.'

'Stop looking at it.'

'But if I hadn't let him knock my confidence, I think I could have made it work.'

'What sort of man chips away at a woman's confidence in the first place? Relationships are meant to nurture you, lovers are meant to support you.'

'But he would have, maybe, if I'd just been a little bit more toned.'

'Sophie, you want a tree to be a fish.'

'And he's been shagging Noushka since the minute we broke up, probably since way before that, and he won't have felt a moment of sadness.'

'Men always screw things into their subconscious. They repress their feelings, it's very unhealthy.'

'I can't bear the fact that he's so happy.'

'I bet he's not happy, and he's not going to be happy, because he's incapable of real intimacy, of being vulnerable.'

'Who wants to be vulnerable, Maggie? He's got a Sub-Zero fridge and a Russian model for a girlfriend. Why wouldn't he be happy?

'Sub-Zero fridges are a bloody waste of money. And

who says being a Russian model is better than being a pudding developer?'

'Of course it is, in his world.'

'Fine, let him live in his world. That's not the real world. Besides, it's not about whether *he's* happy. It's about whether *you're* happy.'

'*I know I'm not happy*. By the way, are you going to eat the rest of your pudding?'

The following morning I am on the bus to work. I've forgotten to charge my iPod and I'm staring out of the window when I see Noushka on a poster for L'Esteeme, wearing high heels, tights and nothing else. I feel instantly queasy.

I turn my head and look the other way. There are road-works and the driver has just let in a bendy bus that is now blocking the junction.

In front of me, two 12-year-old boys notice the poster.

'Ah man, check out that arse,' says the first squirt. 'Well fit.'

'I'd tap that from behind,' says the second.

'Bet she'd suck me off better than your sister,' says the first one.

'Your mum,' says the second, and they laugh.

'We could tag team her,' says the first.

'As long as I can have a go on that arse first, I ain't having your sloppy seconds. I bet your dick still smells like Mrs Herbert's minge.'

'More like your nan's mouth.'

Ah, kids, hey?

I consider giving them a lecture about objectifying and disrespecting women. Then I think, if I had a McDonalds milkshake, would I flick them with it? Then I consider knocking their heads together, only lightly, mind. Then I think I should probably get off the bus, now.

I think this is going to be a bad day.

★

And it is. A very bad day.

Noushka's been in Moscow, no doubt with James.

Thank you, internet, thank you, for making it so easy for the lazy, desk-bound stalker: you don't need to invest in binoculars, buy a false moustache from Escapade, sit outside your ex-fiancé's house . . .

I've signed up to Noushka's Twitter account and have been receiving RSS updates on her every bowel movement:

'Noushka is in Moscow for a long weekend, Privyet everyone x.'

'Noushka likes living in London town.'

'Noushka is in love with her new Lara Bohinc necklace.'

'Noushka adores Dior!'

I think about James's money. If he didn't have £12 million, he would not attract a girl like Noushka. But the money is as much a part of James as his nose or the scar in his right eyebrow. It is his nature to compete, to conquer and to win.

343

'Noushka is up all night at the Sanderson ☺.'

'Noushka loves breakfast in bed at the George V ☺ ☺ x x '

It's like a plate of rancid oysters, each more toxic than the last.

Two weeks ago, I read one that said 'Noushka is very very happy.' I then had to cross-reference to her blog and fansite to check she hadn't got engaged. Relief! She'd just landed a contract with a distributor for the toenail polish.

Today I read 'Noushka is sad, boo hoo ☹,' and my heart leaps.

No. They haven't split up. Mona-Coco has hurt her paw in Geneva. Here's a photo of Mona-Coco in a little velvet sling, with Swarovski crystals on it.

Geneva. That's where James's dad lives . . .

I have a new party trick.

I can make myself sick just by thinking about James kissing Noushka. No, honestly – I can sit at my desk, looking at Twitter, and within sixty seconds I can be locked away in the toilet cubicle, vomiting. Time me.

See? I'm back. The light on my phone is flashing. A message, saying my 2% fat custard sample is downstairs.

'Devron, there's a first kitchen sample from Appletree, do you want to taste it?'

'Please.'

I go down to despatch. The boys in despatch cannot locate my custard. 'Check on reception, Soph.'

Reception look blankly in my direction. Back to despatch. Nothing. I go back to Devron's desk. 'I'm really sorry, I can't find it.' He shakes his head. 'Devron, I'll find it.'

Janelle takes me to one side. 'You should never have let that happen. You're really pissing Devron off.'

Christ almighty, it's a pot of custard. 'Okay.'

An hour later, the slightly brain damaged guy who works in the mailroom puts the custard on my desk. I smile weakly and send Devron an email telling him his custard has arrived. He ignores it.

Three hours later, Janelle invites me for 'a friendly catch-up with Devron'.

'Janelle, is this about the custard?'

She shrugs. Of course she knows. Devron is about as discreet as a weeping cold sore. The minute your back is turned in this place the knives come out, and not the butter knives either.

'Because that guy in despatch had it. In his trolley.' She shrugs again.

Devron takes me to a quiet corner of the canteen.

He puts on 'Sympathetic Face 2A' and tilts his head to one side. He needs to trim his nose hair. 'How are you getting on?'

'Okay, thanks. A lot better. The counselling really helped, and I'm taking some medication, too.' I feel my throat start to constrict but take a deep breath and dig my nails hard into my palm to keep the tears in check.

'The thing is, if this isn't what you need in your life right now, you don't need to come in.'

'Oh God, I wouldn't dream of not coming in. I mean, it's good to have a purpose, stuff to do every day. It's great to tick things off a list.'

'Okay. But you won't be letting us down if you don't want to be here.'

'No, thank you, that's very thoughtful of you but I totally want to be here.'

'The thing is – I've had some 360 feedback about you.'

360 feedback, aka gossip, aka 'a slagging'.

'Apparently, you're not fully contributing in meetings.'

I shake my head.

'I have personally seen you staring out of the window when I'm talking.'

Yeah, do you actually remember that meeting we had a few weeks ago where I revealed to you that I had been ditched by my fiancé and was possibly on the verge of a nervous breakdown? Do you remember, Devron, I shamed myself by crying in front of you, and you offered me a fluff-covered Murray Mint as consolation for my ruined

346

life? Do you think maybe, Devron, just maybe, that might have something to do with it?

'And you don't look happy in marketing forums.'

Devron, petal, two things: firstly, you should see how happy I look in my own time, lying on my bathroom floor in foetal position, howling like a dog. If the floors in Fletchers' loos weren't so filthy I'd be doing that here, so count your blessings. Secondly, I have never in my career looked happy in a marketing meeting. 'Oh.'

'Look, I know how you feel. When I split up with my wife, I felt properly down.' Yes, well, you abandoned her and your two kids for a 17-year-old with a tongue ring, so as much as I am moved by our parallel plights, I'll spare the tears.

'But I threw myself into my job 110%, I didn't mope around and wallow, I worked my arse off. I see you leave on the dot of 6pm.'

You have no idea how hard it is for me to get out of bed in the mornings, Devron.

'And it's affecting your colleagues; you just disappeared last week and they didn't know where you were. They're not sure whether to invite you to their meetings.'

Oh, I am *terribly sorry*, colleagues, i.e. Ton of Fun Tom. Here's an idea: why don't you *not* invite me to your meetings. I'll send you a photo of a raspberry, with a big sticker on it saying 'RASPBERRY', and then you won't need my input anyway now, will you? Everyone's a winner.

'Another thing, Sophie.'

I cross my arms and then uncross them and try to play nice.

'I've heard that if something is not desk specific, you'll assume you can eat it.'

'Is this about that Chocolate and Pear Crumble? I didn't realise it was the only sample that existed . . .'

He holds his hand up in a stop sign.

'You don't seem to be engaged.' Nice choice of words, Devron. Very sensitive. 'And you really need to get engaged quickly, do you understand?'

If he says that word once more, I'm going to smash his face in.

'110% engaged or we'll need to meet with HR more formally next time.'

I bite my bottom lip so hard I can taste the blood, and stand up to leave.

'Are we good?' he says.

'No, Devron, we are definitely, absolutely, 110% not good,' I say, and I walk out of the room and out of the office and possibly out of my job.

To be fair, I do sympathise with the man. I wouldn't want a loon working for me either. It's not helpful when you're en route to the loot.

★

Possibly not the best timing for a first date with a sexy architect, when you're clinically depressed, full of rage, self-loathing and a week's worth of cake and have just stomped out of the day job.

Still, no point cancelling now – tonight could be the start of something new and exciting!

Or not.

Even though I'm home from work prematurely, I have to lie down, calm down. I set my alarm but then hit snooze too many times, and finally roll out of bed twenty minutes before I'm meant to meet Jack.

I then spend thirty minutes staring into my full wardrobe wondering why I have nothing to wear.

Nothing fits, NOTHING FITS.

I don't feel like dressing sexily, but I force myself into a pretty, stripy dress, clean my teeth, put mascara on for the first time in a week and rush out the door. In the mirror in the entrance hall I see that I've only put mascara on one eye and my face has no colour, so I haul myself back upstairs, put on more mascara and too much blusher. The blusher brush makes me sneeze and the mascara prints a perfect join-the-dots smile under my eye.

By the time I've remade my face, found a cab and gone via a cashpoint, I'm forty minutes late. Jack is sitting at a table reading the paper and the minute I see him, I realise I shouldn't have agreed to meet. His nose is smaller than James's. He's shorter than James. He is not James.

'So sorry I'm late, let me get you a drink,' I say, hovering over him. 'Wine?'

He moves to stand and greet me but I head to the bar before he's halfway out of his chair.

Now I may be out of a job, but for some reason this feels like a cause to celebrate, plus I feel shitty about turning up so late, so I decide to treat us to a stupidly extravagant bottle. I study the wine list for a good five minutes, during which time I try to work through my normal first date exit strategies: emergency phone call from a friend. Big meeting in the morning. Headache. I can't use any of these, Jack was friends with my granny. I'm going to have to stay for at least two hours.

I pick a £50 bottle of sparkling wine, the second priciest, purely on the basis that the menu describes it as 'biscuity'. I realise just as the barman opens it, that this bottle, the most expensive I have ever bought, is from that world famous wine-growing region: Sussex.

'I'm really sorry, but can I change my mind about the wine, I didn't realise it was English.'

'It says it clearly on the menu,' says the barman.

'Yes, but it's called Nyetimber, that's not an English word.'

'It says Sussex, England just after it says Nyetimber . . .'

'I didn't see that.'

'Well, I've just popped the cork. So, no. We can't change it. Anyway, it's very good,' he says. 'It does say English on the list.'

'You shouldn't trick people like that.'

'What, luv?'

'Calling it a foreign name like that . . . it's lying.'

'Pin number,' he says.

I stab in my pin and stare at the bar top. Jack looks over my shoulder at the barman as I walk back to the table.

'Are you okay?' he says.

'Uh-huh.'

'What was all that about?'

'Nothing. That barman's a dick.' I pour two glasses.

'What are we celebrating?'

'The death of hope,' I say, clinking his glass and taking a sip.

'Sorry?'

'I think I quit my job,' I say, remembering that this poor man is a human being and that I am an utter idiot.

'You quit today?'

'Don't know. Maybe.'

Over a drink I tell him a highly abbreviated version of my ongoing feud with Devron.

'. . . And it was only a bloody custard sample I lost, not the Turin Shroud . . . And, he thinks we don't know, but we've all seen the footage, that he's been shagging in the office, plus – one: he cheats his expenses, and b: he's fucking lazy, and four: he has this dreadful high-pitched shrill laugh like a goat . . . and basically I don't want to work for a moronic, misogynistic little twat . . . has that wine gone already . . .?'

351

'Looks that way,' Jack says, raising his eyebrows.

'Shall we get another bottle?'

'I'm fine, I'm driving,' he says, awkwardly.

'You're over the limit, aren't you? You've just drunk half a bottle.'

'Er. No. I've only had the one,' he says, pointing at his glass which still has quite a bit left in the bottom.

'Look at your glass! Weirdo. Why aren't you drinking?'

'Actually, I've got a slight migraine.'

'Can you get us another bottle, I can't go up there again . . . thanks . . . not the same stuff.'

He hurries to the bar.

'Not English!' I shout after him. 'READ THE MENU! They'll trick you!'

While he's at the bar it occurs to me that it might be sensible to eat some food, so I summon the waitress and order two of the brownies Maggie was raving about.

Jack returns with another bottle and a large glass of tap water. 'There you go, Sophie.'

'What do I want water for? Water's for babies. Anyway, yeah, so my boss is a douchus, dufus, douchebag dickwad,' I say, swallowing a burp.

Jack laughs nervously.

'So, what are you up to tomorrow?' I say.

'I've got a big meeting first thing down at the Southbank with a developer . . .'

'Where's my brownie . . . I ordered you a brownie, I

352

need a brownie . . . Ah, here we are, my two brownies, like my two dads but with brownies instead of Charlie Sheen and who's that other guy . . .?'

The waitress puts the brownies down on the table and Jack asks her for two forks.

'Forks are for babies!' I say, as I pick off a corner of warm brownie with my fingers. God, it's a proper squidgy brownie, more like a mousse inside. 'Try some, delish,' I say, pushing his plate towards him.

'I think I'll wait for the fork, thanks,' he says.

'Suit yourself,' I say. 'But by the time that fork gets here, I might have eaten both of these . . .'

'You couldn't eat two of them, you'd be sick.'

'Are you calling me a pig?'

'Sorry?'

'Are you saying I'm fat?'

'No! Not at all!' he says, turning scarlet.

'You are though, aren't you. You think I'm fat.'

'Not at all, you've got a great body.'

'Ooh, a great body! A good woman! You say that now and then a year down the line you'll turn around and say you can't love me because I'm fat and white and you only like skinny black girls. That's why you're single at forty! No one's good enough for you!'

'What are you talking about?'

'Like as if I pretended I was taller . . . or thinner . . . or black or whatever . . .'

353

'Will you excuse me for a minute,' he says, standing up and heading off to the loo.

While he's gone I check my phone: Laura, asking how it's going. 'Better than I thought. He's cute x,' I reply, realising now he's left the table that I do actually quite fancy him.

Jack's taking his time. I decide to make good on my promise and finish off both the brownies. The forks have still not materialised; my right hand is now smothered in brownie innards.

The pub has thinned out and we seem to be the only table left in here. The evil barman is standing polishing glasses, staring at me with a smirk on his face.

Where is Jack? I could really do with popping to the loo to wash these brownies off my hand.

My phone beeps again.

Jack!

Jack?

'Am sorry Sophie, my friend called with a flat tyre – I had to go and help her. Take care.'

I think it's been three days since I walked out on Devron, and Jack walked out on me, so it's probably a Friday? I am trying to scan a red pepper in Fletchers at the self-service till. I hate these tills — they never work, but the regular queues are mammoth and I need to get home to start thinking about when I'm going to think about my future. I hate red peppers too, but I've read somewhere that eating vitamin B will cure my insanity, so I'm upping my intake. I also have a pineapple under my arm — apparently tryptophan will restore my harmony and well-being if the red pepper doesn't quite cut it.

The built-in scales are broken. I have a bag of cleaning products already scanned — soon I'll start cleaning my flat again, I'm sure of it. The machine says 'ask the Help-friend'. The Help-friend is wearing his invisible cloak. I press a few buttons, hoping I can outsmart the machine. I consider stealing my shopping. I imagine at that point the Help-friend would make himself visible, at which

355

point I imagine smashing the Help-Friend in the jaw with the Toilet Duck.

I am dressed in a tracksuit, sparkly ballet pumps, a Soul II Soul hoodie from 1988 and a sweetie necklace that Laura gave me. Plus the pineapple wedged in my armpit. I look like a crackhead prostitute clown. If I'm going to get busted for shoplifting from my soon-to-be ex-employer, I cannot allow this to be the outfit I'm immortalised in on my mugshot. This is not what success looks like.

I wait. I press a few more buttons. I say 'fuck' twice, quite loudly. I slap the checkout machine screen. I shove my staff discount card in the slot and this sets off an alarm, and I whisper the word 'cunt'.

I have another flashback to my third date with James and the crazy woman in Soho who he gave £20 to, to demonstrate the 'KIND', 'GENEROUS' and 'COMPASSIONATE' facets of his character. I think about how this situation could be any worse – oh yes, if James and Noushka suddenly appeared behind me in the queue. Luckily Noushka doesn't eat anything apart from cotton wool balls soaked in cold pressed flaxseed oil which she buys from Harrods Food Hall, so that is one disgrace I am spared.

I abandon the shopping, dump the pineapple on the help desk and head back to the car park. In my car I let out one long, loud primal scream. No one is around to witness this latest shame and madness. Nonetheless, I feel like I am my own witness, standing looking into my car at a stranger losing her mind.

Ladies and gentlemen, boys and girls, welcome to the fight of the century, inside Sophie Klein's very own head! On tonight's billing, we have a selection of brutal and pointless bouts:

You had to give him a second chance
vs
You should never have taken him back

He manipulated your insecurities
vs
You LET him do all of it

It's not about your weight, he's just pinning it on that
vs
Wow, you're fat!

It was a car crash waiting to happen
vs
If you'd played this differently, you could have won

THERE IS NO DOUBT: I HAVE GONE BATSHIT CRAZY.

Today I got out of bed for the first time in nine days and thought about changing my sheets. I wish sheets were like hair and cleaned themselves after two weeks.

Today I actually got as far as stripping my sheets and dumping them in the washing machine.

Today I turned the machine on and washed the sheets. Tomorrow I'll dry them.

I forgot that changing your sheets is a complex, multi-stage process and involves putting the sheets back on the bed. At the height of my relationship with James, I changed these sheets daily and made up the bed like a boutique hotel. It has taken me three weeks of planning and four days of doing to wash these sheets.

Today, I moved the clean sheets back into my room and into a pile on the floor.

How did I ever put a double duvet cover back on by myself?

★

The first two hours of every day are the worst. Whether my day starts at 3am, 5am or 11am, my first thought is of James and Noushka having rigorous, vigorous sex on my 94% quartz kitchen counter. Heated, animal, insatiable, mind-blowing, desperately hot hot hot sex that is better sex than anyone in the universe has ever had.

My second thought is usually that it is all my fault a) for not being as thin as Noushka, and b) for encouraging him to go that party with her.

All subsequent thoughts involve me pondering how happy, fulfilled and over-sexed he is, and how I will never find a human being on this planet who can accept me as a size 10. I can feel my mind poisoning me.

If I can just sit upright, then 4 times out of 10, I can actually get out of bed. If I can get fully vertical, I can make most of the thoughts fall down, out of my brain, like a handful of earth in a fine sieve. A few little rocks always stick, no matter how much I try to tamp them down: I don't love you enough. I'm not going to marry just anyone. I can never look at you the way you look at me.

★

I lie in my bed and think:

By the age of fifteen, you've sussed your place in the beauty pecking order. At school, you can see that Juliet Parker has boys stuck to her like Velcro, and why ever not.

She has long lean legs, ice white hair, deep blue eyes. If you can't be her, you want to be her best friend.

You see Amanda Leicester reading in the library: acned, heavy-jawed, dumpy, nicknamed 'Lezzer' by the local boys' school.

And you can place yourself on the spectrum between these two, preferably nearer the Juliet end, and know that with your face, that is pretty enough for everyday use, you'll be fine.

And so you learn to appreciate how you are blessed with other abilities: you cook well, you're interested in other people, and they in you. You understand that for most of us in the middle of that spectrum, your value is not based on just looks, but on character, spirit, kindness, a sense of adventure, what you do for the world.

And you see Juliet Parker marry Max Allford, the best looking bloke at the boys' school, when she is twenty-three, buy a four-storey house in West Hampstead, and have two beautiful blond children, who you occasionally see lying on the floor of your local Pizza Express, screaming for more ice cream.

And one day, Juliet Allford opens her husband's laptop and sees, on his Facebook account, a string of obscene emails between him and a girl whose name rings a vague bell from some Credit Suisse conference Max attended a year ago in Prague, that time he missed his flight home 'because of the traffic'. And her beautiful Boden life comes apart at the seams.

And you see 'Lezzer' get a double first from Cambridge, lose a shitload of weight with the help of amphetamines, and still she has a rather heavy jaw, but – can you believe it – in spite of her jaw she has managed to become an anthropologist? And now she's on BBC4 once a week with her own TV show, and you know what, that jaw looks quite beautiful on camera.

One of the things I hate about being on Citalopram – aside from the fact that I see it as proof of my own backboneless, pathetic inability to cope with something akin to a broken fingernail in the greater scheme of things – is the way the pill packet is labelled.

My birth control pills used to go round in a circle, clockwise. You always knew were you stood with them. But these little white dots, with an indent in the middle that looks like an open mouth, almost a smile – why, they go left to right, left to right. And because I am used to taking pills that go round in a circle, I take them in a circle, and it is not until Thursday of the second week in bed that I think: did I take my pill yet today? Is it Thursday or Wednesday? I don't know what day it is. Then it occurs to me that I can't even be sure of what month it is. I have to look on my mobile phone and this strikes me as a bad sign.

I think the pills might finally be kicking in.

They feel weird – like they're Botoxing my emotions and I now have Liz Hurley's forehead for a psyche. They don't stop the loop of thoughts: he never loved you, you're unloveable, it's all your fault. But they do mostly stop me from crying, even though I want to cry. It's as if my tear ducts are constipated.

The only good thing is that I now seem to be a more socially functioning human being. I still find getting out of bed brutal: so brutal that I have, six years after buying it, finally mastered how the auto-timer on my oven works.

Forget alarm clocks. Forget alarm clocks in another room. Forget Laura phoning to cajole me. Forget writing motivational coloured post-it notes that flap like hyper-coloured moths on my bedside table saying 'you are great', 'life is short', 'get over it'.

I've found that the only foolproof method of making sure I get up is to put a pain au chocolat in my oven the night before, timed to be cooked exactly two minutes after my snooze has gone off three times the following morning.

The first time I tried this I messed up the oven programming and cried with frustration onto the yellowed pages of the oven manual.

The second time was worse. I'd figured out the programming but I thought I could get away with another ten minutes of snooze time. If a Nokia phone alarm won't get you out of bed, your smoke alarm sure as shit will.

But since day three, I've been up and out of bed eating perfectly cooked pain au chocolats by 10am every morning.

So, I can now get myself out of bed in the morning. This feels like a rather impressive achievement.

I can also now read again. I realise that since the day I found Noushka in James's house, I have not read a single book, newspaper or recipe. I haven't watched TV, listened to the radio – the one time I went to the cinema turns out I picked the wrong film . . .

I read in one of my books that I have dysphoria and dysmorphia; maybe they're the same thing and I actually have dyslexia. I'd like to read *Anna Karenina* or *Catch 22* or some Lorrie Moore – something funny or brilliant or profound, to distract me. But what I've been reading is a library of self-help books that Laura sent me while I was bed-bound during the dark days.

The pills are one thing, but I need to sort my life out. I've been off work for three weeks now. I sent Devron a text a week ago saying sorry and that I'll be in touch and that I'm not feeling well. He sent one back saying 'Speak to Janelle about any forms you need to fill in. Let me know what your half-year profit forecast is.'

For two weeks, I read. A lot.

I have learnt about Freud and Jung and David Lynch's views on Transcendental Meditation; CBT, NLP, EST, EFT. Yoga, Yoga, Yoga. The power of the breath, the power of positive thinking, the power of 'no', The Power of Now. Black Dogs, White Knights. Skilful vs. Unskilful. Change curves, grief cycles, Kubler-Ross, Transference, Projection, Object Relations. Seratonin, Dopamine, Good breast, Bad breast. Love Addicts, Love Avoidants, Sadists, Masochists, Commitment-phobes, Triangles of abuse, Circles of valid-ation. Women Who Love Too Much, Men Who Love Too Little, Introverts, Extroverts, Perverts and Hair Shirts.

Look who's a clever girl, James. Not me.

Here's what I figure it all boils down to:

The greatest love of all. Start with yourself. (Darn it! Whitney Houston was right all along . . .)

You are on your own out there. Not in a 'we all die alone' way, merely this: you are responsible for building your own life. Depression can be a useful hiding place.

You are in charge of creating your own happiness and for your own reactions to the world.

That is what being a grown-up is.

That sounds hard.

I am a 34-year-old woman and I do not want to go to a museum or a gallery or join a book club or take up knitting or mountain climbing or go on an Exodus holiday or a Skyros or make new friends or do online dating or help those less fortunate in my community. I want to sit in my flat all day and eat myself into borderline obesity.

But instead, I call Devron, and tell him I'll be back in on Monday morning, and not to worry about paying my wages while I've been away; I'll take the time as unpaid leave.

On Sunday night, as I'm trying to restore order to the dumping ground that my flat has become, I'm side-tracked by a box of photos.

Here's one from last August, of my grandma with Evie holding up my laptop, and my brother and niece on the computer screen. The look of amazement and joy on my grandmother's face is beautiful.

Here's one my brother must have taken, of me with my parents – I must be about four – sitting on my father's lap in Marine Ices in Camden Town. I am dwarfed by a huge bowl of ice cream. My face is covered in chocolate sauce, under which I am clearly beaming. My dad's arm is tucked tightly round my mother. She must be the same age as I am now. Her hair is still long, and she's pinned it up behind one ear with a clip that looks like a butterfly. She's turning sideways to look up at my dad and is smiling softly.

And another, of Nick – holding up a bowl of spaghetti with tomato sauce and meatballs, with a candle in it – as a surprise breakfast on my thirtieth birthday. He'd taken my grandma out for tea four times before she'd shared the secret of her outstanding tomato sauce with him: butter, butter and more butter – my grandma's answer to everything. The butter tempers any acidity from the tomato.

Such a sweetness, that boy. Nick made me feel safe. He was on my side.

God, I miss him.

I miss being loved.

In one of my self-help books, there's a long list of Dos and Don'ts. Turns out I've already done all the Don'ts with James: Don't call him. Don't see him. Don't self-destruct. Don't compound your problems by messing up at work. Don't date on the rebound. Don't park outside his house (okay, I made Pete do that one, but that's probably even

366

worse). Don't lie in bed for two weeks with dirty hair on dirty sheets. Don't eat puddings out of the bin.

I think often of that day James and I went to the Tate. I live in that day. Not because of the sex, not because of the cake James bought me. But because of the way I felt en route to meet him – my best self, full of joy, full of hope.

I go to my wardrobe and look at the white cotton sundress I wore. It wouldn't fit me now, I'm sure. I take it out and hold it up to the light. There are still tiny sparkles of silver glitter caught up in the hem. I take a Fletchers plastic bag from my kitchen and shove the dress into the bag, along with the purple dress I wore on our first date, the red sundress I wore the day James drove to Sheffield to win me back, and the jeans I wore the last night I saw James and shagged him in his car. Oxfam can have the lot, as long as they promise not to put any of it on display in the window.

Within a week of being back at work, I figure it's time to find new employment for two reasons.

Firstly, I need a job where eating multiple free meals a day is not an option. The weight has been creeping up ever since I picked myself up from Laura's hall floor. My trousers tell me I've put on a dress size. I tell my trousers to stop talking to me.

I am now a massive size 12. Two years ago, I'd have been happy being a 12. But six months ago, I was an 8. Size 12 means James was right and I can't let him be right. I need to do something drastic, and soon.

Yesterday I gatecrashed two Phase 4 meetings before noon: Halloween Potato Snacking and Moultry Newness. (Moultry – Devron's joint venture between our meat and poultry departments.) In the Moultry Newness, I almost spat in the cup for the first time in my career after eating a mouthful of chicken stuffed with pork belly and brie. Trust me, those textures in combo do not a happy three-way make.

Secondly, I need a new job because I have way too much time to fill. I am not exactly employee of the month and Devron has avoided handing me back any real responsibility. I have large chunks of the day where I sit at my desk, taking handfuls of wasabi peas from a large jar: Russian roulette for the nose, little balls of self-harm, the masochist's best friend. I sit, I eat, and I continue to cyberstalk Noushka's every move. Unwise.

Today I'm suffering from a particularly virulent attack of the Googles. Noushka's been twittering like a songbird in the last few weeks. 'In Sardinia,' 'In the penthouse at The Mercer,' 'In the presidential suite at the Burj Al Arab'. James swore he'd never go to Dubai.

Any day now I'm going to have to stop stalking her.

I decide to google something more constructive. I type various loser combinations that my IT department will no doubt have a field day over: 'instantly thin + fat-farms + spanx'; 'when will it ever end + lunch-break liposuction'; and finally 'get sane in 24 hours'.

Up pops 'Dr Dannika's Guide to Getting Your Life Back'. Sounds promising; well, more so than a teabag.

'I'm Dr Donna Dannika and I believe in TOUGH LOVE. In the twenty-three years I've been helping clients, many of them truly damaged along life's highways, the one thing I have seen, time and time again, is that women will put up with a whole WORLD of bullcrap, just for the sake of a relationship.'

Even though her name sounds like a drunken Irish jig, I like her already.

'Let me tell you: no man in the WORLD is worth losing your self-respect over. Heck, no man in the world is worth losing a night's sleep over.

I love and respect men. But that's because I LOVE AND RESPECT ME MORE.

My husband Kevan has brought me breakfast in bed every morning for the last twenty-one years. Am I the most beautiful woman in the world? To Kevan, yes. Because true beauty comes from SELF-BELIEF. Every day, while Kevan is flipping my pancakes, I say to myself Donna – YOU ARE AWESOME. I LOVE you, Donna. I VALUE you, Donna. You are UNIQUE.

Say it loud now. Say it: I am AWESOME.'

Eddie's at lunch. I look over the top of my screen to check if Lisa has her headphones on. Yes. I should try it. And I get as far as saying 'I am . . .' when a message pops up on screen.

From Noushka's Twitter-alert.

The worst three words in the English language: Noushka is engaged!

The thing I fear most has happened. He's committed: just not to me. She won. She's better than me. I hate her. Please let me stop hating her. She has come to represent everything that isn't good enough about me in human form.

Except that when I cross-reference to her blog I see the man in the pictures is not tall and dark, with a big nose and a beautiful smile. He is short and dark and middle-Eastern, and the two of them look very happy together.

And for the first time in a long time I feel almost okay.

Not because James is now free.

But because I am.

Time for a celebration.

I ask Lisa if she has a spare cigarette.

'I thought you'd given up,' she says.

'Uh-huh, just the one.'

'I'll join you.'

It's hot outside, the middle of May. How did that happen?

'So, where have you been for a month?' says Lisa, lighting my fag.

'Having a mini nervous breakdown and waiting for my anti-depressants to kick in,' I say, smiling nervously.

'Cool,' she says. 'Which ones?'

'Citalopram.'

'20mg?'

'Bingo.'

She high-fives me.

'How long have you been on them?' I say.

'Two and a half years.' She takes a deep drag on her cigarette. 'So, is this all about that guy you were involved with?' she says.

I nod. I explain the three-second version: girl meets boy, girl loses boy, girl loses mind.

'What did you do when you found the Russian in his house?' she says.

'Lay on the bathroom floor. Binge ate. Cried.'

'But what did you do to him?'

I never really thought about revenge; revenge for what? Yes, he lied to me. I lied to myself – I pretended that everything was okay, when part of me knew it wasn't. He didn't love me enough. Along the way, I feel like he pulled my legs off one by one, like a fly under glass. But I flew under that glass, and I stayed under it. I could have gotten out with a few legs left. Instead I waited until I was just a dot.

'Didn't you stick his CD collection on eBay?'

Not a huge market for heavily played Dido . . .

'I gave all Greg's favourite clothes to Oxfam,' she says.

'I gave all *my* favourite clothes to Oxfam . . .'

That's the thing. I don't think James meant to hurt me. In fact, I've hurt me more than he ever did.

'And, I had sex with Greg's best friend. And I emailed all Greg's staff, telling them how I'd once found him wanking off to a picture of Margaret Thatcher.'

'Did it help?' I say.

'For twelve minutes. The only thing that helps is time.'

'How much time?'

'I'll let you know,' she says.

★

They say the best revenge is living well.

I suspect that doesn't encompass sitting in a meeting with Devron and Tom, arguing about the packaging of Fat Bird! custard.

'Right, we need some fresh, original ideas,' says Devron.

'I was reading in Marketing Week about Gü's new range, packaging's wicked,' says Tom.

'Great, get that in and see if we can do a me-too.'

'Sorry, Devron, I thought you said original?' I say.

'And aren't you going to Paris with Appletree for your inspiration trip?' says Devron.

'. . .Yeah, in a few weeks. Why?'

'With Will Slater?'

'And . . .?'

'Right – you can nick some ideas from the French. And pick Will's brains too, he's smart, for a supplier.'

'I thought you wanted something fresh?' Not stolen.

'Julie's working on illustrations for the labels, of three cute little fat birds. I told her to do a redhead, a blond and a brunette, Mandy's idea actually . . .'

'Devron, you aren't seriously still thinking of calling it Fat Bird?'

'Here we go, Germaine Greer . . .' he says, rolling his eyes at Tom.

'The research says Fat Bird! has huge recall,' says Tom.

'So would Shithead Custard, Tom, it's an awful name.'

'Sophie!' says Devron.

373

'Sorry. But I think Fat Bird is offensive. And derivative and stupid and unappealing.'

'Your opinion goes against the research,' says Devron.

'You, your girlfriend and Tom? That's research, is it?' I say.

'JFDI,' says Tom.

I know I've only been back a week from my extended trip to La La Land, but I really think I need another holiday.

I return to my desk, click back on Google and take my credit card out of my wallet.

★

That night James calls.

How funny that he should call on the same day Noushka announces her engagement. No such thing as a coincidence, isn't that what Freud says? Maybe he's following me following her on Twitter and knows that I know.

Lord no. Men don't sink to the depths that women do; not men like James.

When I see his number come up, my heart leaps to my collarbone. God, how I wish my body would obey Laura's mind. Stay cool. Turn my back.

I pick up on the fourth ring.

'We should meet,' he says. There is a thin but definite layer of sadness to his voice, like the crispy edge on a chocolate mini egg.

'Why should we meet?'

'I think we have some unfinished business,' he says, ever the romantic.

'Do we?'

'Soph. I know you think there was something going on between me and her . . .' He can't even bring himself to say her name. She must have wounded him.

'She's irrelevant,' I say. She always was; she was a symptom, not the cause.

'Yes. Well, anyway, I'd like to make dinner for you next week.'

'Bad timing,' I say. 'I've just booked flights an hour ago, I'm off this Sunday.'

'Where to?'

'Italy.' Sounds a tad cooler than 'a fat farm in Italy for women with eroded self-esteem'.

'When are you back?'

'Next weekend.'

'Okay, the following Monday.'

'Busy.'

'Tuesday.'

'No.'

'Wednesday.'

'In Paris with a supplier on Wednesday.'

'Thursday.'

This is why James is so good at making money. If he senses the slightest opportunity, he'll pounce.

If this goes to Round Three, he thinks he's going to win. But I've finally figured out the way he plays. And I know exactly how I can win.

'A week on Thursday,' I say. 'But I'm not coming to your house. I'll text you where on the day.'

Icing

1. *noun* – a sugar preparation, the finishing touch to a cake or biscuit
2. *noun* – an unexpected bonus

I have a mountain to climb: literal not metaphorical. Or 'una montagna,' as the locals call it. The old lady who runs this farmhouse claims it's merely a large hill: 'una alta collina'. Trust me, it is *not* una alta collina. But either way, we're not climbing it till day five, and it's only day one.

It feels like I've been here a very long time already.

Boot camp.

So not my idea of fun. And that's exactly why I'm doing it: push myself out of the comfort zone. Get fit, get strong and get over it.

To clarify: this isn't soft bathrobes, massages, five light meals a day. No, this is sweat. And right here's where you start paying. In cash. Lots of cash, for 12-hours-a-day cardio, taught by two ex-SAS tough nuts: Big Tony and Grant. No fluff, no frills. Oh, and no food.

When we arrived around lunchtime we were weighed. Ten minutes later we were fed two oatcakes and half a beaker of vegetable stock: a 'halfway stage' in getting our stomachs used to smaller portions. Halfway? No way.

You want *more* masochism? Okay! Did I mention we're in Italy? Home of cannoli *and* cannelloni, focaccia, mozzarella, gelato, mascarpone. Where tomatoes actually taste like tomatoes. Not that we're allowed tomatoes. Too much sugar, apparently. Tomatoes are 'bad'.

Also 'bad': carbs (not true), caffeine (fuck right off) dairy (☹), booze.

Our daily treat: a 1-inch square of dark chocolate.

Our time is cut up into neat little squares too. One hour PT. Twenty minutes press-ups. Two minutes to fill water bottles. They never tell you what's coming up till the end of the ordeal you're currently on. That's intended to keep you focussed on your abs or your lats. Stay in the now! Just as well – if I knew what was going to be forced upon me with more than a minute's notice, I'd think of forty-three different excuses why I couldn't do it.

My fellow inmates: Jojo (Go-Go) – already a tri-athlete, feels she must tri-harder; Sephonie – Fulham's very own Paris Hilton; Mary – overweight, kind, 48; Hildegunn – likes the outdoors.

★

I'm lying in bed at the end of day one. I'm sharing a room with Mary; we were the last two to book. (Along with

Ton of Fun Tom telling me to 'Just Fucking Do It', my tipping point was when my size 12 black cords started slicing into the top of my hips.) When I told Laura I was going to boot camp, she pointed out that I'd spent all of last year being bullied by a man about my weight, now I'm paying to have two men do the same?

After lunch, and I mean five minutes after, we were made to hike up a very steep hill, twice. It was extremely warm, and although we were barked at to 'hydrate', I don't think Mary drank enough water. She's looking peaky now.

After the hike we had twenty minutes of Swim Sprint. Hideous.

'Count your lengths today, then we'll do swim test on the last day and you all have to beat your scores,' says Big Tony.

Go-Go claps with delight.

Then we had 'dinner' (two bites of chicken stew, seven green beans), and I had my first tantrum. I asked Big Tony for more vegetables. He explained the 'regime' was strictly calorie controlled. I explained that I knew more about nutrition than he did, as it's what I do for a living, and that it was extremely bad for a body to eat so few calories while expending so many. He told me to stop arguing and drink a glass of water, and that if I really wanted, I could have a slice of lemon in it.

I'm glad he didn't give us more food: five minutes after putting down our forks we were made to sprint up and down the netball court for an hour.

So now Mary and I are in our twin beds. I'm feeling angry that this place costs £200 a night. Mary is feeling sick.

Mary is now being sick. Mary is projectile vomiting, and I am running around like a lunatic, trying to find a bin for her to yak in, and eventually I find one but she has unfortunately puked all over my bed, her bed, our floor, her hair and my trainers.

'How could you puke up so much food? We only ate three mouthfuls,' I say after I've put her in the shower and helped her clean herself up.

'I'm so so sorry,' she says.

'Don't apologise. They should moderate the course based on people's fitness.'

I call Big Tony and ask him to arrange for our bedroom to be cleaned, but of course the maid only comes in the morning, so Mary and I sleep in the lounge on two lumpy old sofas. 'You pushed her too hard,' I say to Big Tony.

'It's the body's natural reaction to a jump start, she'll be fine in the morning.'

Day 2. Boot camp. Fall In.

Mary has been taken to the local hospital, suffering from severe dehydration. According to Big Tony, Mary's 'incident' has nothing whatsoever to do with the exercise she did, nor the food she did or did not eat – she was just a bit hot in the sun. If she's gone, can I have her chocolate rations, please?

382

'Girls, dehydration is a very serious problem,' says Big Tony. 'Make sure you keep your water bottles filled. Signs of dehydration include dry lips, headache, dark urine, the inability to produce tears.'

Inability to produce tears: I want me some of that.

*

And then there were four. Four makes 'falling in' easier. Before each session, Big Tony screams 'Fall in', and we have to race to stand in front of him in two rows of two, like trained dogs at the world's most boring dog show.

We were meant to fall in at 6.30am today, but Sephonie shows up late in her D&G tracksuit, and Big Tony makes us all do twenty press-ups to underline the importance of punctuality. We're a team. If one person fucks up, we all pay.

Then we do an hour of cardio, then we climb another bloody big hill, and now it's netball!

I was never sporty at school. In games class, Gaby Adler and I tried to out-gross each other in our excuses to Mr Harcourt, gym teacher, and later convicted paedo. We moved through 'lady problems' to 'irritating itches' to 'severe seepage'. After Gaby claimed a full-on fistula, he hung his head in defeat and told us not to bother showing up again. Instead we spent Wednesday afternoons tarring our 14-year-old lungs with Silk Cut in McDonalds. Happy days.

But within a few minutes of playing netball I get in to it.

Team games are fun! You have to use your brain a bit, you almost forget you're doing exercise! I'm paired with Hildegunn and we're doing pretty well until Go-Go throws Sephonie the ball, I leap to intercept, and Sephonie pushes me over, hard.

I pick myself up from the gravel and laugh it off. But my left knee is throbbing and swollen, and my right knee is grazed quite deeply.

'Sit this one out,' says Grant, but I think: this is £50 of my money, so unless you're offering me a cash refund, I'm still playing.

After netball we have a lecture on 'Nutrition'. Diane, a 19-year-old with a qualification from the inside of a sugar-coated cereal packet tips up to educate us.

'Who here knows how many calories are in 100 grams of chicken?' says Diane.

'Skin on, roast – 171 per 100g, skin off, grilled – 116,' says Go-Go.

Go home now, Diane, you are out of your league.

'Ladies! You know your calories pretty well! That's great,' says Diane.

Is it great, Diane? Or is it tragic, that a room full of supposedly bright women with decent jobs are so brainwashed that they focus so much attention on this crap? I think back to my first boss, fifty-two and a size 8, who was married to a controlling partner at Deutsche Bank. Beautiful five-storey house in Notting Hill, off-street parking and everything. She treated herself to one chocolate digestive biscuit every Friday at 4pm; I never saw her laugh once.

'I'm not at all hungry,' says Go-Go, as we sit down to 'lunch': two oatcakes, one small pot of guacamole.

'My appetite's already shrunk,' says Sephonie.

'I can't even finish mine,' says Hildegunn.

You are all mad, I think. I haven't stopped obsessing about food since we arrived.

I take Hildegunn up on her kind donation of half an oatcake.

*

In the afternoon we head off on a four-hour hike. I love this part of boot camp. I get to see the countryside and not have to listen to inane witterings about broccoli being bad for you. I fall behind the group and think about one of the things my shrink said: a trauma such as a break-up can bring to the surface other unresolved issues that can snowball into a depression. I think about my day job. Fletchers was a decent enough place in which to have a complete meltdown, but Fletchers under Devron's rule is not a world I want to live in. I've forgotten that I'm good at my job; there are other, better companies I could work for.

We are at the summit and it's time for our inch of chocolate. I take the silver-foiled square out of my rucksack, and nibble away like I have milk teeth. I make one tiny square last twenty minutes – Charlie Bucket, eat your heart out. But this is not self-control. Self-control involves having a choice. If I had the whole bar in front of me, would I be able to stop myself eating it? Fat chance.

On the way back down we pass a river and Big Tony says, 'Right girls, jump in.'

'I haven't got my swimsuit,' I say.

'Do it in what you're wearing,' he says.

'It's freezing in there, and then I'll be freezing on the walk home,' I say.

Hildegunn is already splashing about in the water in just her knickers, and shouting 'it's vunderful!'

Go-Go never needs to be asked twice, and she's in too.

'This is Stella McCartney for Adidas, dry clean only,' says Sephonie.

I take my shorts and t-shirt off and wade in. It is freezing, but after a minute you sort of get used to it, and the icy water on my swollen knee feels kind of vunderful.

This is so not me, and I feel a tiny bit proud of myself.

We head to dinner, exhausted.

'Something smells good,' says Hildegunn.

'Something smells small,' I say – and it is: two bites of lamb casserole, 14 borlotti beans, one floret of broccoli.

After dinner – a treat! Half an orange. One thing I will

386

say about this place: you learn very quickly to be grateful for the small things in life; this half orange tastes like the sweetest thing on earth. It practically makes me cry with delight.

My bedroom still smells so I sleep on the sofa again and dream of eating a simple sandwich – cheap white bread, butter, ham, a tiny bit of mustard.

Day 3. Boot camp. Fall in.

Sephonie tips up late again, iPod on, sporting fuschia Juicy Couture.

'Twenty minutes late,' says Big Tony. 'Everyone, 40 push-ups.'

Go-Go couldn't be happier, and I count her doing 45. Hildegunn and I exchange a look, and I say to Sephonie, 'Do you want to borrow my alarm clock?'

'I've got an alarm on my iPhone. I just like to do my own thing.'

'So you've been sitting in your room fannying about?'

She shrugs. That shrug reminds me of James.

*

We've been warned that on Day 3, we might feel 'a bit emotional'. Welcome to my year.

Breakfast is porridge made with watered-down water, and even though I find it unpalatable, the tininess of the portion enrages me.

Meanwhile my knee is throbbing and swollen. Grant tells me to put an ice pack on and rest. This means missing dodgeball – my chance to get Sephonie back – but Grant insists.

I sit on the terrace listening to the grunts from the netball court. If I have to live for the rest of my life never eating a baguette after a curry, then that's what I'll do. I don't want to ever come to a place like this again. It's not worth it, it's too boring, it's too hard. Balance is the key. The middle ground. Learn to live in it.

My ice pack has started to melt so I go into the kitchen to fetch another from the freezer. We are not allowed in the kitchen, for obvious reasons. It even has a lock on the door. But this is a medical emergency, and Grant has left me the key.

I open the lock and it makes a pleasing click.

Mo-ther-fuck-ers! It is piled high with crisps, Kit Kats, fresh crusty bread, tomatoes! I open the fridge and see a giant pot of chicken stew, cheese, butter, cream, Parma ham, parmesan, cold beers.

I could do it. I could eat something and they'd never know. Even if they did find out, what are they going to do? Sit on me and make me have my stomach pumped? I could make myself that ham sandwich, have a beautiful cold beer . . . That is what I want. That is what I want.

Instead, I go to the freezer and get another ice pack, Velcro it round my knee and head back out.

★

388

After lunch – and truly, I can't even now bear to recall day three's pitiful offering – it is 'Ultra-ultra circuits'. Did I mention I'm not the sporty type? Did I say I hate gyms? I hate hate hate circuits. Hard, boring, repetitive.

But you're either in it or you're not, as I once said to James, so I push myself and push myself round the 20 different stations till I'm sweating and exhausted and my muscles are burning.

'How many side crunchies did you do?' says Go-Go.

'Wasn't counting,' I say.

'Grant, how many side crunchies did I do?' says Go-Go.

'48, good performance,' says Grant.

'Ladies, no time for sitting down, let's do it all again,' says Big Tony.

And around we go. I can barely walk, and yet here I am, bench-pressing, doing half push-ups, planks and tricep kick-backs. Big Tony is shouting 'That's it girls, smash it out,' and I'm thinking only two more 'stations' to go and I'm done. And the penultimate 'station' is an exercise called a 'Russian Lying Dumb-bell Twist', and I think, ah, the story of my life.

★

We finish the circuit and we are all broken. We lie on the grass, bodies trembling, and Go-Go asks how many crunchies she did this time round, and Grant says, '49', and Go-Go hisses 'Yes!' and makes a little fist.

'And those were the best tricep kickbacks I've ever seen a girl do, Sophie,' says Grant. I blush with pride. I think that's the nicest thing anyone's ever said to me! Go-Go glares at me out of the corner of her eye.

As we stand up, Hildegunn points to my leg – 'What have you done?'

My knee is bleeding quite heavily. I must have knocked yesterday's scab off when I was on my knees doing the half push-ups, and now it'll be bleeding for a while.

'Let's get you tidied up,' says Grant. He sits me down on a chair with my leg up and applies clear liquid to my knee that stings like hell, but smells divine.

'Is that alcohol?' I say, bringing my nose toward my knee and inhaling deeply.

He laughs.

'Can I lick my own knee?' I say. 'You won't tell Big Tony, will you?'

*

Tonight I cried for the first time in weeks. Not because I miss James, not even because I miss my friends or family, but because I miss bread. I called Laura and sobbed down the phone to her, and she told me it would all soon be over, and that we'd go for a medium-sized curry the night I come home. I love you, Laura, I do.

*

Day 4. Boot camp. Fall out.

Today we climb another, even bigger hill. I really overdid it yesterday, I can barely bend my arms or legs. The knee swelling means that every downward step feels like a gremlin's fist is punching the front of my knee from inside. First James rejected my body. Then I rejected my body. Now my body's rejecting me.

We break for our square of chocolate, but I have already snuffled mine when no one was looking, as today's act of minor and pointless rebellion. I sit on a rock and I think: one day the words 'James Stephens' will move from being a mantra to being just a string of letters. They'll have no power to make my heart hurt. One day, when I've untangled this knot of pain, he'll recede in my mind to just being a guy I was in love with, and then just a guy I went out with, and then just a guy in a bar looking for a woman, and then just some guy. One day I'll feel as good as I felt the day before I met him. I finally believe this is true. Thank God.

Lunch is a joke without laughs and then it's lecture time. Today's sermon is called 'Live to Eat vs. Eat to Live'. I know exactly what Big Tony is going to say, and I'm already annoyed.

Big Tony is standing at the front with his charts, and the other three are sitting on stability balls, bouncing on his every word.

'Who in this room weighs themselves?' says Big Tony.

We all put our hands up.

'How often?' says Big Tony.

'Twice a day,' says Go-Go; 'Every day,' say the other two; 'Not often, I look at how my clothes fit,' I say.

'Right,' says Big Tony. 'Here's what I eat every day. Breakfast – porridge with water, berries. Lunch – wholemeal bread, chicken, veg. Dinner – steak or chicken, a medium-sized potato, loads of veg. Snacks – yoghurt in the morning, a cube of cheese at 4pm. I have two beers on a Saturday night, and a curry once a week. That's what I do, week in, week out. I never have to think about food.'

But I like thinking about food.

I put my hand up.

'What?' says Big Tony.

'Do you like cooking?' I say.

'Once in a while,' he says. 'You have to understand, the body needs calories like a car needs petrol.'

I put my hand up again.

'Can't it wait?' says Big Tony.

'Do you actually like eating?' I say.

'Listen. Some people live to eat, but that's just wrong. You only need to put in the tank what you use every day. Food is just fuel.'

The others are nodding, but I feel my old self rise up again and I can't put a lid on it.

'That's bollocks,' I say. 'Food is not just fuel. Food is life. Food is family, and sociability and pleasure, showing

someone you care. Waitrose sell 19 types of mushroom –
that's not fuel. It's part of the fabric of our lives.'

Big Tony's hands are on his hips. The others are staring
at me.

'I understand exercise is important, being healthy, taking
care of yourself. But whether it's our boyfriends, Heat
magazine, or whatever other forces conspiring to make us
feel crap about our bodies – we have to understand – it
is okay not to be perfect! We have to reject a culture that
says "Britney's too fat", or "Lindsay's too skinny".'

I think back to how I made Noushka the focus of all
my rage and self-loathing. I blamed her and ignored all the
things that were already wrong in my relationship.

'The beauty industry trades on our low self-esteem. We
have to learn to love and accept our own bodies. Food is
not the enemy! We need to teach our daughters the value
of kindness and strength!'

I'm expecting this to be my Spartacus moment. Together
the four of us will rise up, storm the kitchen, get our hands
on those Kit Kats.

But no. The others look at me like I've just announced
I'm having a coprophilia pool party, animals and kids
welcome.

So now I'm the black sheep. Even Sephonie comes up to
me at the end and accuses me of 'ruining it for other people'.

★

This evening we do boxing. I'm partnered with Sephonie who keeps on taking off and putting on her Zadig et Voltaire cashmere hoody – she's too hot, too cold, too hot.

I've been holding up the pads, straddling her, while she does sit-ups with a follow-through punch. Hard at the best of times, let alone four days in, with precious little 'fuel' in 'the tank'.

'Punch THROUGH the pain,' screams Big Tony

Even though it looks easy, holding the pads is almost as hard as punching, and it takes all my strength to keep them up so the bitch doesn't punch me in the face.

Then it's change-over time, and I'm lying on my back on the mat with Sephonie straddling me, holding the pads up in front of her face in lacklustre fashion. I have no strength left in me, but I visualise Devron's face on the black dot at the centre of the pads, and, along with the pleasing thwack of the gloves on the pads, it gives me enough oomph to keep going.

'COME ON GIRLS, PUSH IT OUT.'

Just three more jabs to go, and I force my stomach muscles to haul me up and my bicep to punch, but on the last one I can barely do it, and then I think 'JUST ONE MORE,' and throw my right arm straight at where the pad was, but where Sephonie's jaw now is – she's dropped her pad at the last minute from exhaustion.

It really was an accident. Honest.

★

Day 5. Boot camp.

And then there were three.

'Sephonie's fine, but she's still got a headache. She doesn't feel like doing the mountain today,' says Big Tony, giving me a stern look as we fall in. Oh for goodness' sake, having 32 teeth is so last season.

I have become chief lag at this facility. As we pack our bags for our day-long hike, I sidle up to Go-Go and Hildegunn, and they trade me their chocolate squares for the fruit I have not eaten for the last two days. They are more focussed on the weigh-in than I will ever be, and this barter system suits us all. We load up our rucksacks with oatcakes and a pack of power-seeds for a 'treat'.

We spend the whole day walking and finally come to the summit of a very small montagna. The view is breathtaking, and makes me think: this is special and beautiful, and I am very lucky.

I shake the power-seeds into my palm and look at the tiny black and brown dots, like dashes, commas and full stops. I rejoice that tomorrow I can have a treat of my choice: a nectarine, a piece of toast with butter and Marmite, a glass of orange juice!

On the way back down I realise that I lost myself when I found James. I thought he was the prize. He wasn't.

But one day, when I have truly stopped caring about my weight, and found peace with myself and this one gift of a body that lets me dance and climb mountains and see the world in all its glory, I will look back at those golden days James and I had, and I'll be truly glad of the joy that he gave me, that I gave him, that we created together.

Because for those days I felt all the potential and the beauty and the hope that this world has to offer.

I felt alive and I felt love.

I didn't imagine it – it was there, and some people never even get to feel that.

I will realise how lucky we were.

And maybe he will realise that too.

When we return to basecamp, Big Tony says 'Pool! Swim Sprint! Time to beat your day one scores.'

Go-Go jumps from side to side with excitement. Hildegunn nods stoically, and I shake my head. I have just climbed a bloody mountain; I am tired. I don't need to prove anything else to myself or to any man, and while part of me thinks it's a cop-out, the larger part of me thinks: from now on, I will do what I want. If it doesn't hurt anyone else, then I shall please myself.

And I say to Big Tony that I have 'women's problems', and fortunately he is just as embarrassed as Mr Harcourt always was, and I am let off games. I sit by the pool and watch Go-Go power through the water, and Hildegunn take a more leisurely approach, and I think: I'm okay. I'm very okay.

★

396

Before the final weigh-in, Big Tony asks the three of us still standing what were our highlights and lowlights of boot camp.

'High – when I bench-pressed 50kg,' says Go-Go. 'And low – when I couldn't do that fourteenth chin-press,' she says.

'High – jumping in the river,' says Hildegunn. 'Low – feeling tired all the time.'

I think long and hard. Highs: punching Sephonie. Figuring out a way to get more chocolate. Doing great tricep-kickbacks. Lows: the hunger. The rationing. The joylessness of extreme cardio.

'High – getting my mind and my body back,' I say. 'That was worth all the lows.'

As we wait for the final weigh-in, Go-Go keeps rushing to the loo to emit any last mass that might show up on the scales.

I'm eating another piece of chocolate and drinking a cup of tea, because I like chocolate and I like tea.

'I can't believe you're eating before the weigh-in!' says Go-Go.

'I'm having a curry when I get home,' I say, knowing how much this will appal her.

'But what about keeping up the good work?' says Hildegunn.

'I'll do more exercise,' I say. 'Moderation in all things.'

I step on the scales and Grant smiles. 'Terrific, Sophie, you lost 8 lbs. You worked really hard, you should be proud of yourself.'

I am, Grant. I am.

There is a phone call I need to make and it can't wait.

We're taxiing on the runway back into Gatwick and before I can talk myself out of it, I dial.

'It's me. I know you're probably busy but I need to see you, tonight – it can't wait,' I say. 'I've been doing a lot of thinking. Can I come round?'

And Maggie says, 'Of course.'

'You're looking fantastic,' says Eddie as I walk in on Monday morning, my size 12 cords now gently hugging my hips. 'How was it?'

'A cross between prison and hell with better scenery,' I say.

'Did they feed you much?'

'Don't!' I'm still mildly traumatised by how it felt to be utterly at the mercy of someone else being in charge of what I could eat.

'Sophie, I know you've just got back in, but we've got a 9.15 with Devron on Fat Bird!' says Ton of Fun Tom, 'are you coming?'

'I've never been readier,' I say.

*

Devron's staring at a pile of papers on his desk when Tom and I walk in.

'Right, let's get on with it,' he says. 'I've been reading

your Phase 2 update, Sophie – what's this about you and Appletree not thinking you can quality benchmark on the low-cal custards?'

'Will and I have talked extensively about how to reduce the fat content on the existing products. We've trialled versions with skimmed milk powder, soy, whey, and maize starch, and they all taste bad. We've researched them with panel-groups; housewives also think they taste bad.

'Yeah, I can see the quotes: "tastes like misery" . . . "lacks any sense of indulgence" . . . "I'd rather be fat than have to eat this" . . .' Did you write these yourself, Sophie?

'Er, no.'

'Well, I don't give a rat's arse what a few chunky northern housewives think. Forget the existing products, what about a blank page approach?'

'We've tried. We've tried biscuits with custard, frozen custards, tarts and trifles. Bottom line is that anything with lower than 3% fat has a weird, gloopy texture and needs so much sugar we go off the scale on the RDAs. If we use aspartame, it tastes totally synthetic.'

'Is this Will Slater being difficult because of the reduced margins?'

'No, it's Will Slater being honest about an unrealistic brief,' I say.

'Don't let your friendship with a supplier get in the way of your judgement,' he says.

'Devron. If you're on a diet and you want a treat, you're better off eating a square of dark chocolate; at least it's full of phenols. If you fuck with all the raw materials in custard and substitute them with synthetic crap, you upset the stability, tolerance, life and taste of the product. Diet custard is an oxymoron. That's like moron, only more so.'

'Sophie, a word?' says Devron at the end of the meeting.

Of course, I knew I wouldn't get away with quite that level of insolence in front of a wider audience. Let Devron say whatever he needs to say to re-masculate himself. I have climbed a mountain, jumped in a river in my pants. I am not scared of Devron.

'I'd like your thoughts on this,' he says, handing me a sheet of A4. I expect it to be an outline of some dumb new scheme he's cooked up – combining Poultry and Fish as Pish or Foultry. Or making us all devise a menu for Mandy's 21st Roller Disco Birthday Dinner.

But no. It is a list, in Janelle's handwriting, of all the Phase 4 tastings I have attended in an unofficial capacity in the last three months. That Croissant session, ooh la la! And I'd forgotten all about the Chinese Ready Meal Breakfast buffet. Sixteen meetings in total.

I shrug. I learnt to shrug from the best.

'Sophie, do you work for Marie in Bakery?' he says.

'No, Devron.'

'And do you work for Jason in Ethnic?'

'No.'

'Do you work for Ingrid in Moultry?'

'Er, nope.'

'And do you work for Clive in biscuits?'

'No.' My, this one could run and run.

'Do you actually work for me? Devron?'

'No.'

'Pardon?'

'No, thank you?'

★

I am in such an insanely good mood after quitting that my first instinct is to call James and tell him, let's not wait till Thursday, let's go out tonight! Such a bummer that after everything that's happened he's still one of the first people I want to share my good news with.

But first there's a message on my voicemail from Will to call him straight back. I realise that I'm not going to be able to go to Paris with him on Wednesday anymore, and I feel a bit gutted.

'Will, I'm so sorry, but I've got good news and bad.'

'Are you okay?'

'Yes, I'm pretty great actually. I just handed in my notice.'

'Congratulations! So, what's the bad news?'

'I won't be able to come to Paris for research with you.'

'Why not?'

'Well, I guess you'll want to wait and take my replacement, won't you? I mean, I'm leaving the business . . .'

'Don't worry about that! Consider it your leaving lunch. Actually, that was why I was calling – have you ever been to Hotel Costes?'

'I've always wanted to go.'

'Great. I'll book it. I'll meet you at St Pancras at 6.30am. – It's a real shame you're leaving, Soph. You're one of the best developers I've worked with.'

'I bet you say that to all your clients . . .'

'No, truly. You're dedicated and passionate and you're always really honest with us. I've never worked with someone who's so considerate of their suppliers.'

'Stop it, Will! You're making me blush.'

'Bet you're counting the days already. No more Devron picking his nose in tastings . . .'

'Oh, my God! Don't ever tell him I told you that.'

'Sophie Klein, what sort of a man do you think I am?'

I don't know. I never gave it enough thought. Until now.

As I put the phone down a smile creeps up on me, and at the back of my mind I know there's something I was about to do before I called Will, but I can't quite remember what, and I head off to the kitchen to make Eddie and Lisa some tea.

★

That evening I call Maggie again.

'Your voice sounds lighter already!' she says.

'I'm working another month, and then . . .'

'Yup, the future. I'm proud of you, Sophie.'

'I need the name of your brioche guy in Paris, please – I'm there on Wednesday with Appletree.'

'Ah, lovely Will. Send him my regards. I always had a soft spot for Will . . .'

'Really?'

'Absolutely. I always thought you two would make a nice couple . . .'

'Me and Will? No, he's a bit too nice. And you know he was married?'

'Stop right there. I'm not having this.'

'What?'

'You have three choices, young lady. You can either keep that arsehole James on a pedestal and keep any decent guy at arms' length, because of some stupid nonsense reason . . .'

'Maggie . . .'

'So he's divorced! So what? At least he's capable of a commitment! I mean, that's a ridiculous reason, one of the silliest I've ever heard . . .'

'Maggie . . .'

'Or you can find another selfish, immature manchild just like James, who's equally emotionally unavailable and callous. Believe me, there are plenty of them out there, and I know what I'm talking about . . .'

'Maggie . . .'

'Or you can realise your own worth – you are a talented, smart, gorgeous, real woman – and find someone who is actually interested in making you happy.'

'Bloody hell, Maggie, I only called to get the name of the brioche guy.'

'Yes, well . . . I don't know his name, but he's the third stall in at the Canal St Martin market. Get there by 3pm, or he'll be sold out. And tell him La Madame Anglaise et Difficile says hello . . .'

The rain is relentless on Wednesday morning and for some reason I feel weirdly down again. Maybe it's the anti-climax after the excitement of quitting. Maybe it's just the weather. Or maybe I realise that secretly I'm wishing I was going to Paris with James. Will is lovely but he's just a bit too straight for me.

I can't decide what to wear. The simple navy cap-sleeved dress from Topshop with the tie waist that I can loosen after lunch, or the slightly sexier black jersey one from Whistles . . . Why am I even thinking of this as a date, I wonder, as I choose the comfortable option. This is not a date, because the last time I went on a date, I drunkenly disgraced myself and was abandoned mid-date, therefore I am not yet ready to date. More to the point, this is a work date, with a colleague. Just because this colleague is polite and thoughtful and doesn't point out your physical inadequacies does not mean he fancies you.

I grab my umbrella, head for the tube, and when I pop

up the other end at St Pancras, I see Will sitting reading *Private Eye*, waiting for me.

'Breakfast,' he says, handing me a paper bag with a toasted ham and cheese croissant in. 'And I got you a coffee, I'm pretty sure you're white, no sugar.'

'Thank you – let me give you some cash . . .'

'Don't be ridiculous. Today's on Appletree.'

On the train I doze off, and wake up when Will taps me gently on the shoulder.

'We'll be there in a minute.'

'Already?'

'You just conked out the minute you'd finished breakfast,' he says.

'Sorry, how rude.'

'No, it was sweet. You were like a dormouse, curled up over there.'

'These seats are pretty comfy . . . I'm not used to business class. Fletcher's won't pay for it unless you're part of the Toolkit.'

'The what?'

'That's what they've rebranded the board. The "essential tools to make our strategic engine run" . . .'

'. . . So, Devron must be a power-tool?' says Will, with a straight face.

'The biggest,' I say, trying not to laugh.

★

'So what's the plan?' I ask, grabbing my bag and umbrella as we head out to the taxi queue.

'It's 11am now, table's at 12.30pm, so I thought we could head down to St Germain, go to Gilles Fevier, then potter back up past the Pyramid and the Louvre on our way to lunch.'

'Gilles Fevier?'

'I thought you'd know him? He's this trendy artisan chocolate maker.'

'And what's his packaging like?'

'Why? Do you want to do some research?'

'Not particularly. But I feel bad if Appletree are paying . . .'

'Soph. Here's an idea,' he says, opening the cab door for me. 'Why don't you just have a good time and not feel guilty about it. You've earned this trip – enjoy it.'

As we drive down the wide boulevards towards the Seine and the city opens up in all its beauty, I decide I'm going to do just that.

★

The chocolate shop is hilarious. There is a giant photo of Gilles Fevier on each wall, arms folded, long black hair flowing, with the caption, 'Je suis Artist du Chocolat!'

'Chocolate artist!' says Will. 'That's a Yorkshire euphemism for something else . . .'

The chocolates are amazing, mini architectural forms with names such as 'Destiny's Dark Satin', and 'Paraguayan Orchid'.

'Can I help?' says the assistant, after we've been pointing and giggling for a few minutes.

'I'm looking for something a little more pretentious . . .' says Will.

'Pardon?'

'Do you have any Dairy Milk?' says Will.

'Milk? We 'ave The Ecuadorean – a goat's milk and hibiscus truffle, enrobed in 80% Ecuadorean chocolat with air-dried goat's milk shavings on top.'

'Sounds rank, shall we get some?' Will whispers to me.

'How much are they?' says Will.

'It is done by weight.'

'Fine, we'll take two,' says Will.

Eight euros lighter, we exit the chocolate artist's studio.

'I feel sick already,' I say. 'Four euros each?

'When in Rome . . .' says Will, popping one in his mouth. 'Urgh . . .'

'Not good?'

'So not good,' he shakes his head and hands me the other truffle.

'I'll save mine for later,' I say, putting it in my handbag.

★

Will's booked us a table at Hotel Costes overlooking a beautiful courtyard. It's raining now, and we sit in plush velvet chairs breathing in the generic smell of luxury boutique hotel: tuberose single note perfume, cedar and sandalwood candles. All around us the Eurotrash air-kiss, and push the calories across their plates.

'I thought you'd like it here,' says Will. 'The people watching's great and the food's terrific.'

Two bottles of wine, two steaks and a tureen of super-smooth mash later, we're trying to work out if the old man in tight leather trousers who's walked past our table four times in the last hour is a) en route to the loo to feed his cocaine habit, b) Peter Stringfellow's French doppelganger, c) incontinent, d) all of the above.

'I'm going to find out once and for all,' says Will, following him to the men's room. 'Back in a sec, work out what we're having for dessert . . .'

While he's gone I study the pudding menu. I suddenly realise that I'm having proper fun, and this thought strikes me with shock and a bit of panic, like the thought that I might have left my hair straighteners plugged in.

'Right, what are we having?' says Will, sitting back down and smiling.

'I'm not sure there's any pudding that'll beat that mash. You decide – excuse me . . .'

I stagger off to the loo and by the time I return he's ordered.

'So,' he says, 'that guy who picked you up that time, is he your other half?'

The memory of that day instantly makes my heart hurt, and my reflex is to reach for my wine glass which is empty. 'Is it ok if we have some more wine?'

'Sure . . . are you okay?'

'Yes, fine. No. No, he's not my other half. Why?'

'Just curious. He seemed very pleased with himself, that's all . . .'

'He was . . . he was a guy I used to know.'

The waiter approaches our table carrying another tureen of mash.

'Not for us,' I say.

'. . . It is,' says Will, looking sheepish.

'Seriously? Good work, William,' I say, giving him a high five. He smiles with relief and I'm sure it's the wine working its boozy magic, but honestly his teeth are just unbelievably perfect.

★

'It's 4pm already,' says Will, helping me on with my coat. 'We've got an hour before we have to be at the station, what do you fancy doing?'

'There's the brioche guy Maggie loves, but she said be there by 3pm . . . Why don't we go to Colette? It's a few blocks this way I think.'

'What's Colette?'

'It's funny.'

We enter the shop and the bulky doorman immediately points to my umbrella and demands I hand it over.

'Do I have to?' I say. 'I'll forget it, I know I will.'

'You won't,' says Will. 'It's pissing down out there. Wow, this place is something.'

The store is full of Japanese people and rich kids and fashionistas desperate to buy something, anything, that will make them feel ahead of the curve. A small teddy made out of wood – 1,000 euros. That'll show anyone who ever bullied me at school that I AM NOW A WINNER.

'Look at this scarf,' says Will, 'I thought the motif was a crest . . .' The repeat pattern is actually two naked busty women humping a snow leopard. '845 euros! Bargain. Actually, Sophie, you've still got my scarf, so I guess you owe me a scarf, don't you?'

'Sure, I'll get my purse. We could get matching his and hers, do you think they'll do us a BOGOF?'

He laughs. 'Seriously, Sophie. Who would actually buy something like this? I'm not being all "we just ate coal for breakfast up North when I was a kid", but really . . .'

'Now that's more like it,' I say, spying an electric blue fake fur coat with diamante buttons. I pause to stroke it – it's softer than the real thing.

'Try it on,' says Will.

We have to get security to unhook the coat, which

costs 2,000 Ecuadorean truffles. I slip it on, petrified that in my slightly drunken state I'll rip it and be forced to re-mortgage my flat.

'Very glamorous,' says Will, taking a step back and gesturing for me to do a twirl.

'Cookie Monster does Vegas, don't you think?'

'Diamonds are a bit much, but that shape suits you perfectly. You look great.'

I stop and look at him. I'm sure again it's just the booze talking but his eyes are the most unusually beautiful slate grey-blue. We're standing a few centimetres closer than friends. I know I should stop staring but there's something behind his gaze that makes me unable to break off. What am I doing? Will's someone I work with, worked with. He's divorced. He's a bit short. He lives in another city. For all I know, he has a girlfriend. This is not a date. The booze halo will wear off in an hour, and I'll feel really silly for even considering there's any mutual spark here.

'We'd better get a move on,' I say, turning round and putting the coat back on its hanger. The assistant swoops and rebolts like the chief jailer.

As we head out I ask the doorman for my umbrella, but he shrugs and says there is no navy umbrella.

'I left it here twenty minutes ago,' I say, trying not to sound rude or bratty, but conscious that the rain outside will maximise my hair frizz, and all of a sudden I care very much about looking pretty and shiny haired in front of Will.

'No, nothing,' says the doorman.

'Don't worry,' says Will, 'we'll get straight in a cab.'

'Your hair's gone all curly!' says Will, as we take our seats on the Eurostar.

'I hate it,' I say, pulling it back into a ponytail. 'Out of control, crazy, makes me look like Goldilocks . . .'

'That's why I like it,' says Will. 'I feel like I'm seeing the real you. You're normally so straight at work.'

'Me? You're the straight one!'

'You're the one doing research on your leaving lunch. Hold on . . .'

A middle-aged lady is hovering by the seats opposite us, struggling with two large bags from Bon Marché and a suitcase.

'Here, let me,' says Will leaping up.

'Thank you! If you could put the food bags on top.'

'That shop is amazing, isn't it?' I say.

'My husband's going to kill me! I spent 200 euros on cheese, I nearly had a heart attack at the till! Would you mind awfully keeping an eye on that lot while I pop to the ladies'?' she says.

On her way, she crosses paths with a guy in his thirties coming towards our seats. He wears white linen over-pocketed trousers, a Billionaire Boys Club t-shirt, and a

414

scarf that looks like he's spent many effortful minutes in front of a mirror honing the knot.

He's carrying two large Colette bags, a laptop bag and a sopping wet umbrella. With his phone cradled between shoulder and ear he starts piling the bags in the storage area.

'YEAH, I SAID TO THE GUYS AT RED BULL, IF WE CAN DO A DEAL WITH DUBAI, IT'S ALL GRAVY. WE ARE GOING TO RAPE THE MARKET, ZAK, RAPE IT,' he says, placing his Colette bags above, and slinging his wet umbrella casually on top of the lady's food shopping.

Will leaps up to move her bags out of the way and the guy looks at us as if to say 'Why the fuck is your shopping above my seat when you're sitting over there?'

'YEAH, SO TELL THAT PR NUMPTY AT FREUDS TO PULL HIS FINGER OUT OF HIS BOYFRIEND'S ASS AND DO A TIE-UP WITH ONE OF THE MAJORS, AND WE'LL GO BALLS OUT FOR SPRING. GOTTA GO DAWG, THE HATERS BE HATING ON ME . . .'

Will's sat back down, and the guy stands up again, sniffs at the shopping, and with an exaggerated gesture pushes the Bon Marché bags of cheese further away from his Colette shopping. Will sticks a finger up at the guy's back at the same time as I flash the tosser sign.

'You're very mature,' I say, laughing.

'Ditto,' says Will.

415

The guy sits back down, puts on his iPod and starts reading a copy of *GQ*.

Will suddenly kicks me lightly under the table and points at the guy's neck.

'What?'

He beckons me closer and whispers 'check out Bozo's scarf,' and sure enough, buddy next to us *is* the guy who buys the 845 euro scarf printed with naked women shagging a large cat.

'What a wanker,' I say, staring up at his shopping.

'Yup.'

'No, I mean total and utter wanker. I'm sure that's my umbrella!' I say, noticing two of the spokes are broken.

'Do you want me to say something?' says Will.

'I'll do it,' I say. 'Excuse me,' I tap him on the arm.

'Huh?' he says.

'I'm sorry, but I think you might have picked up my umbrella in Colette . . . it's just I noticed the one up there has two broken spokes, like mine.'

'Oh, small world,' he says. 'That's really funny.'

'Right . . .'

'D'you want it *back*?' he asks, as if I'm being gratuitously vulgar.

'Yes! If that's okay!' I say.

'Law of umbrellas, isn't it? Some you win, some you lose . . .'

'Not really, when it's pissing down with rain!' I say.

He blows out sharply. 'Whatever. Take it,' he says, 'it's like a £2, broken umbrella.'

Yeah, I'm sorry it isn't limited edition, Japanese and covered with naked lesbians, I'll try harder to be fashionable next time you want to steal something from me.

The guy just shakes his head as if I'm out of line, gets up and heads towards the bar.

'Did I just imagine that conversation or is he the world's biggest cock?' I say to Will, who is shaking his head in disgust.

A moment later Will says '. . . have you still got that truffle from earlier?'

'You're going to pin him down and stuff it in him?'

'Almost. Can you keep a straight face?'

'What are you up to?'

'Karma police . . .'

Will heads off to the bar and returns carrying two gin and tonics and quietly chuckling to himself. He is followed a short while later by the world's biggest cock, carrying a can of Guinness.

'What?' I mouth at Will.

'Good things come to those who wait . . .' he says, handing me a glass and relaxing back into his seat with a secret smile.

'Ah, good gin and tonic, lots of lime,' I say, taking a large sip.

'I love lime,' says Will.

'Me too! But only with booze or savouries. I can't be

dealing with it in desserts, although I will make an exception for a decent Key Lime Pie.'

'Did you know Key Lime is also known as Mexican Lime?' says Will.

'Is it?' I say, taking another sip. 'Mexican Lime Pie . . . I'd actually like a pie made entirely of limes and avocados, not cooked of course. Nothing worse than a hot avocado.'

'Hot avocado's almost as bad as chicken sushi.'

'What?'

'Raw chicken. They eat it in Japan.'

'No! Not possible,' I say.

'It's true, I've seen it on a menu. Anyway, tell me more about your exciting new pie. So far it seems to consist of some avocados . . . and some lime,' he says, a small smile forming at the corners of his mouth.

'Okay. So, maybe the pie bit is made out of puff pastry. No, that won't work, texture's too soft with the avocado. Aha! Tortilla chips?'

'An avocado. And some tortilla chips?' says Will, raising an eyebrow at me.

'Yes,' I nod.

'I think TGI Friday's already sell that and call it guacamole, don't they?'

'No. Yes. Well, it would be so much more than just guacamole. You could have . . . like . . . a guacamole and crisp ensemble but in a circle, or a triangle. Yes! A triangle . . . to reflect the shape of a tortilla chip, but much bigger

. . . a giant tortilla chip base with crisps coming up the side like fangs but not scary fangs, friendly fangs . . . Stop looking at me like I'm drunk, Will, this is a terrific idea! Is this a double measure?'

'Might be,' he says, laughing. 'I didn't realise you were going to neck it so quickly. I'll get you another,' he says, standing up.

'No, no, my round,' I say, wobbling a little as I head towards the bar, thinking that I do hope Will stays in touch after I leave. Otherwise I think I might miss him.

Will is giggling to himself when I return with the drinks.

'What's so funny?' I say.

'Nothing, just – ah, nothing. So, what's next after Fletchers?'

'Actually, I do have a plan . . .'

'Tell me more,' he says.

'Oh, it's highly top secret, I'm not sure I can tell you on a train. You never know who's listening . . .'

'Well, why don't you whisper it then?' he says, looking at me with a smile.

'Maybe I will.' I lean across the table and he moves to meet me halfway.

My lips are an inch from his earlobe. Our faces are almost touching.

If he turned his face slightly we'd be kissing.

I think I want us to be kissing.

I'm distracted by a movement to my left. Scarf Boy has chosen this exact moment to stand up noisily and head to the bar, and he is impossible to ignore.

I can't quite believe what I'm seeing. I look at Will who is trying hard to keep from smiling, and simply nods his head once: yes. It's true. And yes – I did it.

As Scarf Boy walks through the carriage I see a row of heads doing double takes at the sight of a grown man in white linen trousers, sauntering along, entirely unaware that a dark brown Ecuadorean hibiscus mess is squishing out of his bottom.

I'm amazed Will is capable of such a silly yet audacious manoeuvre. I didn't think he was the type. 'Why did you do that?' I say.

'Because he deserved it,' he says. 'He was rude and arrogant, and he stole your umbrella.'

'You were defending my honour?'

'That, and I didn't want the chocolate to go to waste. Four euros is four euros – we are in a recession, you know.'

'What if he realises and comes back out and decks you?'

'I'll take my chances, Soph. If he challenges me to a duel, you'll back me up, won't you?'

'We'll go out in a blaze of glory . . .'

★

As our train pulls into St Pancras, I feel a twinge of sadness. I don't want today to be over. I don't even know if I'm going to see Will again. If he lived in London I'm sure I would. But he doesn't – so now what?

'I'm sorry, but I have to sprint over the other side to make my train,' he says, grabbing his coat from the rack and handing me my umbrella. 'You take very good care of this now!'

'Thank you for today,' I say. 'I had so much fun.' More than I've had all year.

'Me too,' he says, smiling. 'Do you think we might do it again sometime?'

I try to ignore the little wave of hope that swells up in me. I've only just moved from crushed to bruised.

Love's a risk, but I'm not sure I'm ready to take it just yet.

★

That night, for the first time since I kissed James Stephens nearly a year and a half ago, I go to bed not thinking about him.

But when I wake up, he's the first thought on my mind.

Today's the day. I text James to meet me at 7pm at 181 Picadilly. It's round the corner from his office and I imagine him in the pub off Jermyn Street, downing a gin and tonic and working out exactly how he's going to play this.

I leave work early, head home and put on my favourite

421

ever vintage dress. The only time I ever felt annoyed that I'd shrunk to a size 8 was when I tried on this dress and it failed to cling to me.

This dress is made of black taffeta and was made in Los Angeles in the 50s. It has a square low neck, perfect elbow length sleeves, a tiny waist, and a full skirt and is pure Betty Draper all the way. This dress makes me feel strong and like a woman, and tonight it is a perfect fit.

James is at the counter staring at the door when I walk in.

His face lights up and it's so very fucking annoying because the minute I see him, I realise I still entirely, chemically, utterly fancy him, and that as long as he and I are in the same room this will always be the case.

'Great dress!' he says, standing up to kiss me. When his body is next to mine, I have to stop my arms from wrapping themselves around him.

'What are you going to order?' he says, handing me the menu.

'Don't need the menu,' I say. 'Knickerbocker Glory with a cherry on top. You?'

'A bottle of red! So. Why did you choose this place?' he says, looking at me carefully and then smiling.

'Just felt like it. My granny used to bring me here when I was little.'

'Good holiday?'

'Yes. Have you been keeping well?'

He nods. 'Keeping busy. Oh . . . I've got you something . . .'

He motions to the waiter who reaches under the counter and brings out a small box.

'Rob was in New York at the weekend, I told him to bring this back . . .'

I open the lid and can't help but smile: an original Compost Cookie.

'Thank you. Thank you, Rob,' I say.

He looks at me and smiles. He puts his hand on my knee and I don't brush it off.

'I haven't told you, him and Lena are having a baby! He's been putting in the extra hours drinking, 'cause she'll have him padlocked indoors any day now . . .'

'I'm sure he'll figure out the combination in no time.'

'He's freaking out about it all, thinks it's the end of his freedom . . .'

'Well, it's the end of him being the child in that relationship . . .'

'Do you think our kids would be better looking than Rob and Lena's?'

'Apparently firstborns look like their dads, so it depends on who the father of my kids is . . .'

'What? No, I meant our kids, imagine our kids . . .'

What I can imagine is being heavily pregnant and you going out with Rob to the pub every night because you can't bear to look at my swollen ankles.

'I think Genghis and Jasmine would definitely be better looking,' says James.

'I don't care if they're better looking. I'd just want them to be healthy and kind and smart, if possible.'

'Yeah, of course. But it'd be better if they were good-looking, too.'

I take the cherry off my ice cream sundae, its bottom covered in whipped cream, and I squidge it on James's nose, then eat the cherry. 'You're still a total idiot,' I say, smiling. 'Now why did you want to meet me?'

'Because I wanted some feisty girl in a sexy black dress to cover my nose in whipped cream in the middle of Fortnum and Mason's, and the birds from the escort service said they don't do that kinky stuff . . .'

'Why else?'

'I needed to give you the cookie.'

'You've given me the cookie.'

He pauses, looks at me and takes a breath.

'And because I think, maybe, I messed up with us.'

I wonder if he's going to say it. The one word I want to hear. No, not 'love' – I learnt to live without that from him, grudgingly, like I'm now learning to live without too much white bread. No, the one word he's never said and he'd never even think to say: sorry.

But does he need to? I've forgiven him. I've forgiven myself.

He takes another breath. 'I miss talking to you,' he says.

'I miss talking to you too.'

424

'I miss singing in the car with you, and going for walks, and all the fun we always had together.'

'So do I.' Every day.

'I miss the way you think about the world. I miss your cooking!' he says.

I miss cooking for you. But I don't miss you telling me to eat fewer peanuts.

'I miss lying in bed with you and babbling about random, silly stuff.'

Me too. Me too. But I don't miss feeling strung out from insecurity because this Tuesday you do want to shag me, but last Wednesday you didn't.

I know what my life would be like with James. If I stayed slim and well maintained and aloof and played a constant game and kept him on his toes all the time, he'd eat out of my hand, for a while. If I never had a bad day, never showed weakness, never put on weight, never needed reassurance, never got old, I'd be just fine.

'What are you thinking?' he says.

I love you, but.

Love is a risk.

And actually, I am prepared to take it again.

Just not with you.

'Soph, tell me what you want.'

I want to live with a man in a home that we share, that is filled with books and silly postcards we've found in weird and random places across the world.

I want to spend weekends eating nothing but very strong cheddar cheese on fresh bread, with loads of unsalted butter, and not have someone call me fat on a Sunday night.

I want to grow old gracefully, and never feel like sticking a needleful of Botox in my forehead because my husband's started to eye up younger women.

I want a relationship like my grandparents, where my grandpa made my grandma a cup of tea every morning for fifty-five years and told her she was the most beautiful woman in the world, even though she could be crotchety, difficult and wouldn't win the swimsuit round in Miss World.

I don't want a man who has to 'try to get past' my weight. I don't want a man who my friends think is an idiot. I don't want a 45-year-old who acts like a 25-year-old – that's the worst of all worlds.

Turns out I don't really want you, James Stephens. I want a better man.

'I wish you were built differently,' I say.

'I wish I was too, Soph . . .'

'No, you don't. You wish I was.'

'What?'

'You wish my hips were narrower, my bottom was smaller, my legs were better.'

'I don't know why you think that,' he says.

'Because you've said it. To my face. Twice. And you say it every time you tell me not to eat so many bar snacks.'

426

'Soph, you are totally over-reacting.'

'No, I'm not. I've been under-reacting for so long, you just got used to it.'

'Listen, this place is about to close. Let's go and get some supper and talk about this. We could see if we can get into that nice Italian round the corner . . .'

'James. I'm going to stay here and eat this ice cream sundae. I'm going to enjoy every single mouthful of it. And you can sit there and watch me if you like. Or you can get in to your Maserati and tell yourself "all women are mad". That's your choice. But when I've finished, I'm going outside to get the bus back home. On my own. And that is my choice.'

And while I want him to fight for me, and tell me he's realised he's making a mistake, and that he wants me, fat, thin or in the middle, the truth is, he really isn't built that way.

And for the first time I actually start to feel sorry for him.

It's the Sunday after my final day at Fletchers, and I've invited Laura and Dave, Pete, and Zoe and her new girl-friend Cheryl round for tea. Will's driving down from Sheffield especially. He's been down a couple of times since we went to Paris. I like being around Will. A lot.

The flat is tidy. I've been all the way over to Columbia Road this morning and bought five bunches of orange tulips. I popped in to St John for a perfect bacon sarnie and a couple of loaves of fresh crusty bread. Then I drove into town and spent the Selfridges gift voucher from the watch James gave me, on some cases of great wine. I'll give one to each of the guys later, and one to Maggie when I see her.

Sandwiches are made, as is a pitcher of frozen margarita. I made it with my new ice-crushing machine that I asked for as a leaving gift from work. Zoe did a great job on my collection – I also got £300 of John Lewis vouchers. It won't stretch to a Sub-Zero fridge, but no one actually needs a Sub-Zero.

The cannolis are lined up in rows on my countertop: vanilla, chocolate, custard, and strawberries and cream.

The only thing left to do is take the final set of biscuits out of the oven and let them cool down. I've made six different batches. I reckon Laura will love the ones with Mint Aero pieces. And I've put chunks of Lion bar in a batch especially for Pete. If you can't use your friends as guinea pigs, what can you use them for?

The oven timer goes and I put on my new extra long oven gloves (no more burns!) and take the tray out and rest it on the side.

Twenty minutes till the biscuits are ready for lift off, and the doorbell goes. My guests have arrived.

Today I woke up at 6.30am to a blue sky, went for a twenty minute run, then came home, showered and put on jeans and my favourite t-shirt. I walked to work and arrived at the office half an hour early. Maggie's given me my own set of keys, and I let myself in, made a pot of tea in her gorgeous red Liberty teapot, and sat at my new desk!

It's going to be a busy day. I need to finalise which versions of my new biscuits I put out to market first. I have 18 recipes that are all working well, and I want to launch with no more than a dozen.

Will's been amazing. He knows so much about so many things. He's been helping me out on packaging, distribution, and how to extend the softness of the biscuits without compromising taste or texture. My biscuits will have a good life – at least four days – and I think they'll do well as gifts if I can get the branding and the name right. So far I've been through Bliss-cuits, Biscuits Deluxe, Choco-maniacs and The Little Venice Biscuit Boutique; I don't like any of those enough. I'm toying with naming them after my grandma and putting an illustration of her hand holding a wooden spoon on the packaging. I think she'd approve.

On the cannolis, I need to find a way of making the strawberries and cream version 20% cheaper, and fast. If I can launch with such a classic British flavour while it's still summer, I know I can get great PR. Plus, I really want to try layering dark chocolate on the inside of the custard cannoli, but that'll have to wait till tomorrow.

Maggie can only afford to pay me half of what I was on at Fletchers, but I'll take home 80% of the profit on all my products and if things go well, she'll make me a partner in a year or two. Who knows, in five years maybe I'll be able to buy my own Maserati.

You know what? I'd much rather walk.

Epilogue

Turns out time's a decent healer. One year on, and it gets easier every day. James is now just a series of small scars: stretch marks. They'll fade but they'll never disappear. I'm learning to like them. They're a part of me – a reminder that I've grown.

I thank the universe for giving me such patient, generous friends who have stood by me through thick and thin. That's what Pete used to call James and me in the dark days, 'thick and thin'.

I love my new job.

I've been off the happy pills for three months. I've gone from rock bottom to rock steady in the last year. It hurt like hell. I never thought it would pass, but it has.

I run for twenty minutes, three mornings a week. If I do this, I can eat whatever I like within reason (just not apricots). I never look at calories, I never weigh myself. I never want to go for that run, but I'm always glad afterwards – not for what it does for my thighs, but for what it does for my head.

If Will's down at mine for the weekend, he'll tell me to have a lie-in, not be so ridiculous, and that I'm perfect just the way I am.

If I'm at his place in Sheffield, I'll sit up in bed and pretend I'm about to put on my trainers. Me, go running in a city built on seven hills? Never.

Nonetheless, he'll race to the kitchen and start frying some bacon: works every time. Will's a clever man.

And he's a grown-up. And he's funny and sexy and hard-working and generous. Above all, he is kind.

And that is what I want.

I saw James tonight in Soho. He didn't see me. I was with Pete on my way to get a burrito and as we walked past The Crown, there he was with Rob, standing outside, drinking a pint, chatting up a couple of girls. The girls were giggling at something Rob had said, and I could sense Rob was about to swoop in for the kill.

James was wearing the blue shirt he wore on our second date, and he was smiling his beautiful smile.

I remembered how happy I used to feel, waking up to that smile.

And for the longest moment my heart paused.

But my legs kept on moving.

Food in the book

If you like cooking, you might like to try some of the recipes for food mentioned in Pear-Shaped.

Compost Cookies

The most exciting to make, in that they are different every time, are Compost Cookies. The recipe can be found in *Momofuku Milkbar* by Christina Tosi, which is available on Amazon USA and is worth the wait/extra cost for postage. On my blog, stellanewmansblog.blogspot.com, you'll find a few tips on how to minimise the chances of messing up the recipe (I've made these cookies four times with varying results: always delicious but sometimes too flat.) In the book you'll also find the recipe for Crack Pie, which is only slightly better for you than Crack Without The Pie, but more socially acceptable.

Orange and Almond Cake

Claudia Roden is a brilliant, inspiring and influential writer and *The Book of Jewish Food* is one of my top ten cookbooks of all time. You will never be bored with a chicken if you own this book. Her Orange and Almond cake recipe (Sophie cooks it for Maggie Bainbridge in her original job interview) can be found here, and also in her *Book of Middle Eastern Food*.

Ottolenghi's Chargrilled Broccoli with Chilli and Garlic; and Apple and Sultana Cake

Both these recipes can be found in *Ottolenghi*, the first of his books, which will have you dribbling over the pages.

The broccoli, as the book rightly points out, is a 'destination' dish – people go there especially to eat it. I've made it at home and it is labour intensive but entirely satisfying and worth the effort.

The cake is called Apple and Olive Oil Cake with Maple Icing in the book – and to tell you the truth I've never made it, as I'm lazy and just buy it from his shop.

Custard

I have not referenced a recipe for custard, largely due to the existence of M&S Thick and Creamy Custard – my custard of choice.★ Made with creamy Channel Island milk and Madagascan bourbon vanilla, it is entirely thick, pale,

★ I am also not averse to a small pot of Ambrosia custard, not least because it keeps for ages and ages and is handily small-portioned for when your self-control is weak.

luscious and vanilla-y, and scattered with little black dots of vanilla, like stars. I do think life's too short to make your own custard when custard like this exists. I usually eat it cold, straight from the pot, or cold with a hot crumble.

In the event of an apocalypse, my greatest 'DOH!' moment wouldn't be that I'd neglected to learn how to start a fire, divine water, or build a basic shelter. I'd regret never having become self-sufficient in the art of replicating this custard.

Toast and cream cheese

I have no idea what avocado on cream cheese on toast tastes like. All I can vouch for is that if you like 1980s-style fruit cheesecakes, you will probably like jam on cream cheese on toast. My personal favourites are raspberry, then strawberry, then apricot jam, spread on toast that already has full fat Philadelphia on it. (Not all three jams at once, that is merely my order of preference.)

I do not believe in lesser fat versions of Philadelphia. I have, in my time, been content enough with Philadelphia Light, but when you return to the mother ship of full fat, you will realise they are ultimately incomparable, and if you're going to eat cream cheese, you might as well eat real cream cheese.

A *word on brownies* . . .

Much like Sophie, I believe that an average brownie is worse than none at all.

I'm not convinced by any of the commercial British brownie brands–and trust me, I've done some research . . . The best brownie I've eaten in the UK is in a pub in London called The Old White Bear in Hampstead (unlike Sophie I did not eat it with my fists.) It is intensely squidgy, dark and rich – neither cakey nor floury, with no distractions. It is entirely to the point, and is served warm with something good on the side – crème fraiche or ice cream.

Ottolenghi's are good, in that they're insanely rich – BUT – they contain nuts, and I am one of those people who considers finding a nut in a brownie almost akin to finding a tooth in a brownie: in the words of Ned Flanders, wrong-diddly-ong.

In New York, there is a fabulous brownie brand called 'Fat Witch' – which has a very cute illustration of, yes, a fat witch, on the label. I love this brand, partly because I have been called a witch on several occasions in my life – mostly not as a compliment – but I took it as such regardless. And also because it is a brave and brilliant move to use the word 'fat' on a brownie, rather than, say, 'skinny'. Fat Witch – I salute you.

Fat Witch do lots of varieties of brownie. I like the classic, but also the Caramel Witch too. Americans generally tend to like things pretty sweet, but Fat Witch doesn't over-sugar.

But the best brownies are, I think, home-made. On my blog you will see some postings about my experiments in brownie-making. I favour Nigella and Nigel Slater's approach, but there are so many opposing schools of thought on what a brownie 'should' be, it's worse than some religions.

I dream of running a brownie business one day. Writing is a solitary and often lonely endeavour. I imagine that making and selling brownies, while equally labour-intensive, would suit me quite well. Do me a favour: google 'Stella Newman' and 'brownies' about once a year, for the next five years. If I ever do manage to build my brownie empire – a) then you will know about it, and b) if you still have a copy of this book, you will be entitled to a free deluxe brownie of your choice!

A *few of my favourite things* . . .

The following is an overview of some places I like to eat in my two favourite cities, London and New York. I've listed specific dishes but it doesn't mean I don't like other things on the menu – it just means I'm a creature of habit/ on a limited word count.

LONDON

The London food scene seems to be getting better and better all the time. From farmer's markets to Michelin superstars, Londoners have more choice than ever of gastronomic delights.

At heart I am all about the cheap eat. While I'd never say no to a meal at Le Gavroche (set lunch = excellent value considering the quality of the food, plus it includes half a bottle of beautiful wine) – I am never happier than when I'm eating something delicious that costs a tenner or less. Simple things done well – *that* is a t-shirt I'd wear, along with Team Aniston, and one with a picture of Alec

Baldwin's face on it. I love Alec Baldwin so bad it hurts, but more of that in my second novel.

So, in no particular order:

Fitou, 1–3 Dalgarno Gardens, W10 (near Wormwood Scrubs prison. Glamourama . . .)

This is probably my favourite restaurant in London. It is totally cheap and cheerful, hard to spend more than about £15 a head even if you're being a total pig (it's BYO) – but most importantly the food is outstanding. I once saw the Prime Minister here, but don't hold that against the place if you're not a fan.

Starters: Fish Cakes, Papaya Salad – super super spicy, not for the faint hearted.

Mains: Gaeng Penang chicken – a really thick, hot red coconutty curry with lime leaves and fresh chillies, again super spicy and addictive.

Pad See Ew: stir fried broad rice noodles with eggs and green vegetables in a thick soy sauce. A perfect combination of soft, crunch, salt, almost sweet and above all tasty.

Coconut rice – sets off the spicy chicken curry perfectly.

St John – Smithfields, Spitalfields, and others

Most people love St John because of the whole nose to tail eating thing. They rave about the trotters, or whisper sweet nothings about chewing on a pig's ear. Well I'll admit it.

I'm scared of offal. I like liver, but anything more adventurous and I fold.

There are two reasons why I like St John so much, and neither of them have anything to do with soft tissue:

1. The Custard Donut of the Gods. They serve these at the Spitalfields branch during a brief window, only on a Sunday morning and now at their Bermondsey bakery, only on a Saturday morning. When I first ate one of these donuts I became obsessed. Thick, dense, Madagascan vanilla custard, injected into the crispest, lightest donut casing. If I ever become really rich and move to the South of France, I will, like Elvis with his peanut butter, bacon and banana sandwiches at the Colorado Mine Company, fly back to Bermondsey on my private jet just for a taste of one of these.

2. Welsh Rarebit. The opposite of adventurous I know. But really really great Welsh Rarebit. Goes back to A Simple Thing Done Well. It helps that St John make some of the finest bread in London. On top of their white sandwich loaf they put a combination of Neal's Yard Montgomery cheddar, Guinness, Lea & Perrins, Coleman's mustard and a touch of cayenne. Savoury, salty, tangy, melting perfection.

Ottolenghi, Upper Street N1 and various

Every thing I've ever eaten here has been perfectly executed
and I've eaten almost everything. Come for breakfast, lunch
or a cake – dinner if it's payday. Ottolenghi uses herbs and
spices so brilliantly that he elevates an ingredient as prosaic
as broccoli into something stellar. The food looks magnificent
and bounteous and tastes better than it looks.

My Ottolenghi rules of engagement:

If you go to the Upper Street branch at the weekend,
go EARLY or expect to queue forever.

Do not take a boyfriend whom there is any danger of
you splitting up with at a subsequent date. You do not want
to scar Ottolenghi with the sadness of happy memories.

But do go there with at least one other person, so you
can try all their salads, and their cake (and, I suppose, vice
versa . . .)

If you order bread, make sure you get cornbread in the
selection – spicy, crumbly and slightly sweet – utterly
delicious.

The broccoli is better than any broccoli you've ever
had anywhere. Ditto the butternut squash, ditto anything
with green beans, ditto the granola, home-made nutella
and jams. Their banana jam made me un-hate bananas,
temporarily.

Take a cake home for someone you love – including

yourself. I can think of no greater expression of appreciation and affection than something sweet in a white paper bag from Ottolenghi.

C&R café, Rupert Court, W1

This is the sort of place I'd walk straight past if I didn't know not to. It's garishly lit, in a crappy alley in Soho, and shows no indication of its greatness – other than an occasional queue. A word of warning – do not let them seat you in the basement if you have a sensitive nose and don't like the smell of toilets.

C&R's strengths are soups and noodle dishes – every time I've strayed from these I've regretted it. (Except for the roti canai side dish – a light, buttery Malaysian bread served with a searingly hot spicy dipping sauce – an essential starter, whatever you're ordering for your main.)

The greatest dish on the menu is the Singapore Laksa – by far the best of its kind I've had in London. A spicy coconut milk broth, with chunks of chicken, prawn, tofu, noodles and other floating wonders – it is a truly satisfying one-bowl soup meal. Some folk struggle to finish the generous portion but not for want of trying.

NEW YORK

I love New York for its energy, for its buildings, for its people, but most of all for its food. Everything changes so quickly in New York that it's impossible to keep up with what's hot and what's not. Regardless, I tend to eschew fashionable restaurants anyway as they're often more about the scene than what's coming out of the kitchen. (Incidentally isn't eschew an odd word? So strange.)

Corner Bistro, 331 West 4th Street

While there's always at least a handful of new contenders every year for the position of Number 1 burger in town, my favourite will always be the cheeseburger at Corner Bistro. It's no frills, you'll have to queue, and there's nothing innovative or modern about it – and that's why I love it. Beef that tastes of beef, the perfect thickness of patty, the perfect-dimensioned bun, the golden ratio of bun to beef to cheese. It satisfies one's deepest caveman longings for beef, and doesn't embarrass itself by trying to introduce foolishness such as 'boiled egg' or 'beetroot' into the equation, like some other burgers I could mention . . .

Num Pang, 21 East 12th Street

A tiny Cambodian sandwich bar close to Union Square, with a succinct menu of delicious food. The absolute all-star winning sandwich is the hoisin meatball with basil, stewed tomatoes and Num Pang's signature chili mayo. Like all their sandwiches, it comes served with cucumber, pickled carrots, coriander and chili mayo, on fresh white bread from Parisi Bakery down in Little Italy. It is the best sandwich I've ever eaten – spicy, sweet, crunchy, soft, piquant and fresh.

Rocco's, 243 Bleeker Street

Avoid the tourist queues at Magnolia's – I never understand what all the fuss about cupcakes is anyway – and head further down Bleeker Street to Rocco's for a cannoli. Perfect crunchy crispy cigars, stuffed with thick ricotta cream and chocolate chips – again, there's something very perfect about the dimensions and proportions of Rocco's cannolis, which might explain why it's been a West Village favourite for decades.

Momofuku Milk Bar, 251 East 13th Street

David Chang's cookie shop in the East Village is always on my to-do list whenever I visit New York. Try and go on the final day you're in town, so that you can take back cookies for friends and family alike – they last at least 4 days – that is if you don't eat them all on the plane / the Heathrow Express / walking up the stairs to your front door . . .

Obviously the Compost Cookie is a must, but the chocolate-chocolate cookie is so salty, fudgy and dark you almost feel like you're in the middle of it. And make room for a slice of Crack Pie, as above. Be warned – it's named Crack Pie for a reason, folks . . .

City Bakery, 3 West 18th Street

If it's cold out, go to City Bakery for their legendary hot chocolate. Not for the faint hearted, or those who like their hot chocolate to resemble something you could buy from a vending machine. It's more like a very thick, extremely velvety chocolate soup – but if that's how you like your hot chocolate (and that is how I like mine) – make the pilgrimage.

Further reading

Heartburn, Nora Ephron

The book that most inspired me when writing *Pear Shaped* was Nora Ephron's *Heartburn* (subsequently made into a film with Jack Nicholson and Meryl Streep). While I like the film, and love the actors, the book is superior.

It is an excellent blend of comedy and sadness, interwoven with recipes. Ephron's writing is always sharp, wise, funny and honest and that is all I ever want in fiction.

Take Care of Yourself, Sophie Calle

Sophie Calle is a French conceptual artist and writer. Her book *Take Care of Yourself* was inspired by an e-mail her ex-boyfriend sent her, finishing their relationship. Calle had the e-mail analysed by 107 different women from different professions and in doing so, turned her heartbreak into a fascinating, original, creative and intriguing work of art. Plus the book has a gorgeous shiny pink cover and cool DVDs within.

The Beauty Myth, Naomi Wolf

It seems unlikely that the beauty, diet and anti-ageing industries will do anything other than grow in the future. There's an awful lot of money to be made in manipulating female insecurity. An important and disturbing book.

The Sociopath Next Door, Martha Stout

This best-selling popular psychology book came out in 2005, and is subtitled *The Ruthless versus The Rest of Us*. It posits that 1 in 20 of us 'normal' folk is in fact sociopathic, i.e. capable of acting without a conscience, and thus potentially extremely dangerous to be involved with. It is quite scary, when you look at the checklist in the book, to realise that you probably work with, or are friends with, at least one bona fide sociopath. Fascinating and useful.

Poems

I'm not terribly good with poetry. Usually it makes me feel a bit thick, because I don't ever understand all the layers of meaning the poet intended. However I mentioned two poems in *Pear Shaped* that I do like, and that I think I understand.

Nora Criona, by James Stephens

James Stephens was an Irish novelist and poet. I don't know much about him but according to Wikipedia he was mates with James Joyce, and from his photo it looks like he wore hats a little too small for his head. As far as I'm aware he did not drive a Maserati. The poem Sophie mentions on the first page of the book is called 'Nora Criona', and is about the perils of being too attentive to a man.

Bluebird, by Charles Bukowski

The second poem is Sophie's and her ex Nick's favourite poem, 'Bluebird', by the American writer Charles Bukowski. Bukowski wrote an awful lot of poems, including an excellent one about becoming a writer, and 'Bluebird', about love. I think it's rather wonderful.

Acknowledgements

To the many people who have encouraged, supported and helped me while I was writing this book, most notably:

Kowski – for being brilliant and being better.

My dear friends Bobby, Baz, Dalia and Nicole. For enduring my first drafts and for being there always with patience, honesty and wisdom.

Lisa B – for pushing me up the mountain of Kong and tobogganing down the other side, roll ups in hand.

Ed McD for some perspective. What *would* Madonna do?

Mavis – for the material and the immaterial. There's no one I'd rather eat apricots with.

Matt – for hitting me in the Harwood with a packet of granola and making me cry, and for 15 years of Saab driver wisdom.

To Sophie and Sean, for the extreme generosity in lending us the best house in the world. I promise Dave didn't lay a finger on Barbie. Maybe in her . . .

451

Kathryn F – for being the perfect mother-in-law, and giving me the kindest feedback always.

Anna H & Simon D – for bringing me chocolate seashells when I couldn't see the shore.

Debbi A – two numbers for you dude. Seven. Eleven. The most fun ever. xx

Kate Long, Jeremy Sheldon, and everyone on my Arvon course – for advice, hope, and laughing at my jokes.

Jenny B, Queen of Puddings, for your fabulous knowledge of desserts and letting me tag along to the cake factory. Best. Job. Ever.

Nat F – for your time, your immense talent and for being a 24-hour go-to emergency service. We tried, my darling, at least we tried.

Anna T and Joy for being my surrogate Buddhas and having the patience of many saints.

Ben & Gabi, and Russell & Keren – Dyer to play Devron?

Oliver 'Paul' Newman – for the kiss of life.

The beautiful Flanders and Liv – house-stealers extraordinaire.

My oldest BF, BFK – for the weasel.

Margarita, Jane, Anand, Allan and Melanie – for taking care of my mind, body and soul.

Ellie 'Business Critical' G, Anna 'Big Balls' P, Lauren 'Legs' S, and Hazel 'clever clogs and heels' W, for the sympathetic eyes.

Susie A – for being deadpan, sassy, wise, and the best hitman/wingman a girl could ask for. Sorry this isn't in yellow . . .

Lou – for being the opposite of Devron and for believing in me.

Antonello – Segize dice grazie per le lezioni di Italiano.

Fern 'CEO' V, for the cover stories.

Simon K – for dropping everything at a moment's notice to simulate sex with me in your high performance Italian sports car – still laughing.

Dominic – for pointing out the difference between being in gear and neutral, teaching me how to spell betterer, and for the funniest grammar joke ever.

Andrew, a great, generous and loyal friend, for actually buying a Sub-Zero.

Sanj – for always being Mr Saturday Night and in my hour of need Mr Wednesday Night. And for letting me drive the DB9. Such a footballer's car . . .

My beloved Gerry. Hyrum was right about us bad kids in the back row.

Nate – for showing me your tattoos.

The fabulous Slater boys – for being almost as funny as each other. And not quite as funny as the gorgeous Alvin.

Daniel S – idea generator, triangle giver and taker, ice-cream connoisseur. What're the odds that we haven't played badminton by the time you finally get round to reading this book?

Jenny K – the fag what needs no lighter. I could not

have done this without you. For the c-punch, the e-mail, the g-force. You next please.

Claire B. Thank you. Thank you.

Charlotte – for perpetual grace and good cheer.

Cathryn and Becki – for all your hard work and support.

All of the Avon ladies – for immense patience, hard work and energy on my behalf.

C – for the joy, and for the learning experience.

Mr and Mrs Jones – for generosity beyond compare.

My dear sister – for being a tough crowd all the way. Now will you take this to your book group?

Tabby and Cesca – the icing on my cake.

My first husband, paint-drinker, lamb-wrangler, horse-stealer of the highest order R Genn – the biggest brain, the biggest heart – to whom I owe a debt of more than 55 million x

And finally to Mum and Dad – for giving me strong legs.